THE ALTAR STEPS

Copyright © 2007 BiblioBazaar
All rights reserved
ISBN: 978-1-4346-2499-4

Original copyright: 1922,
NEW YORK

Compton MacKenzie
Author of "Carnival," "Youth's Encounter," "Poor Relations," etc.

THE ALTAR STEPS

BIBLIOBAZAAR

THE ALTAR STEPS

THIS BOOK, THE PRELUDE TO
The Parson's Progress

I INSCRIBE
WITH DEEPEST AFFECTION
TO MY MOTHER

S. Valentine's Day, 1922.

"Perhaps my Guardian Angel was beside me all the time, because, look! here's a feather."

He eyed his mother, hoping against hope that she would pretend to accept his suggestion; but alas, she was severely unimaginative.

"Now, darling, don't talk foolishly. You know perfectly that is only a feather which has worked its way out of your pillow."

"Why?"

The monosyllable had served Mark well in its time; but even as he fell back upon this stale resource he knew it had failed at last.

"I can't stay to explain 'why' now; but if you try to think you'll understand why."

"Mother, if I don't have any gas at all, will you sit with me in the dark for a little while, a tiny little while, and stroke my forehead where I bumped it on the knob of the bed? I really did bump it quite hard—I forgot to tell you that. I forgot to tell you because when it was you I was so excited that I forgot."

"Now listen, Mark. Mother wants you to be a very good boy and turn over and go to sleep. Father is very worried and very tired, and the Bishop is coming tomorrow."

"Will he wear a hat like the Bishop who came last Easter? Why is he coming?"

"No darling, he's not that kind of bishop. I can't explain to you why he's coming, because you wouldn't understand; but we're all very anxious, and you must be good and brave and unselfish. Now kiss me and turn over."

Mark flung his arms round his mother's neck, and thrilled by a sudden desire to sacrifice himself murmured that he would go to sleep in the dark.

"In the quite dark," he offered, dipping down under the clothes so as to be safe by the time the protecting candle-light wavered out along the passage and the soft closing of his mother's door assured him that come what might there was only a wall between him and her.

"And perhaps she won't go to sleep before I go to sleep," he hoped.

At first Mark meditated upon bishops. The perversity of night thoughts would not allow him to meditate upon the pictures of some child-loving bishop like St. Nicolas, but must needs fix his contemplation upon a certain Bishop of Bingen who was eaten by rats. Mark could not remember why he was eaten by rats, but he could with dreadful distinctness remember that the prelate escaped to a castle on an island in the middle of the Rhine, and that the rats swam after him and swarmed in by every window until his castle was—ugh!—Mark tried to banish from his mind the picture of the wicked Bishop Hatto and the rats, millions of them, just going to eat him up. Suppose a lot of rats came swarming up Notting Hill and unanimously turned to the right into Notting Dale and ate him? An earthquake would be better than that. Mark began to feel thoroughly frightened again; he wondered if he dared call out to his mother and put forward the theory that there actually was a rat in his room. But he had promised her to be brave and unselfish, and . . . there was always the evening hymn to fall back upon.

Now the day is over,
Night is drawing nigh,
Shadows of the evening
Steal across the sky.

Mark thought of a beautiful evening in the country as beheld in a Summer Number, more of an afternoon really than an evening, with trees making shadows right across a golden field, and spotted cows in the foreground. It was a blissful and completely soothing picture while it lasted; but it soon died away, and he was back in the midway of a London night with icy stretches of sheet to right and left of him instead of golden fields.

Now the darkness gathers,
Stars begin to peep,
Birds and beasts and flowers
Soon will be asleep.

But rats did not sleep; they were at their worst and wakefullest in the night time.

Jesu, give the weary
Calm and sweet repose,

*With thy tenderest blessing
May mine eyelids close.*

Mark waited a full five seconds in the hope that he need not finish the hymn; but when he found that he was not asleep after five seconds he resumed:

*Grant to little children
Visions bright of Thee;
Guard the sailors tossing
On the deep blue sea.*
Mark envied the sailors.
*Comfort every sufferer
Watching late in pain.*

This was a most encouraging couplet. Mark did not suppose that in the event of a great emergency—he thanked Mrs. Ewing for that long and descriptive word—the sufferers would be able to do much for him; but the consciousness that all round him in the great city they were lying awake at this moment was most helpful. At this point he once more waited five seconds for sleep to arrive. The next couplet was less encouraging, and he would have been glad to miss it out.

*Those who plan some evil
From their sin restrain.*

Yes, but prayers were not always answered immediately. For instance he was still awake. He hurried on to murmur aloud in fervour:

*Through the long night watches
May Thine Angels spread
Their white wings above me,
Watching round my bed.*

A delicious idea, and even more delicious was the picture contained in the next verse.

*When the morning wakens,
Then may I arise
Pure, and fresh, and sinless
In Thy Holy Eyes.*

*Glory to the Father,
Glory to the Son,
And to thee, blest Spirit,
Whilst all ages run. Amen.*

Mark murmured the last verse with special reverence in the hope that by doing so he should obtain a speedy granting of the various requests in the earlier part of the hymn.

In the morning his mother put out Sunday clothes for him.

"The Bishop is coming today," she explained.

"But it isn't going to be like Sunday?" Mark inquired anxiously. An extra Sunday on top of such a night would have been hard to bear.

"No, but I want you to look nice."

"I can play with my soldiers?"

"Oh, yes, you can play with your soldiers."

"I won't bang, I'll only have them marching."

"No, dearest, don't bang. And when the Bishop comes to lunch I want you not to ask questions. Will you promise me that?"

"Don't bishops like to be asked questions?"

"No, darling. They don't."

Mark registered this episcopal distaste in his memory beside other facts such as that cats object to having their tails pulled.

CHAPTER II

THE LIMA STREET MISSION

In the year 1875, when the strife of ecclesiastical parties was bitter and continuous, the Reverend James Lidderdale came as curate to the large parish of St. Simon's, Notting Hill, which at that period was looked upon as one of the chief expositions of what Disraeli called "man-millinery." Inasmuch as the coiner of the phrase was a Jew, the priests and people of St. Simon's paid no attention to it, and were proud to consider themselves an outpost of the Catholic Movement in the Church of England. James Lidderdale was given the charge of the Lima Street Mission, a tabernacle of corrugated iron dedicated to St. Wilfred; and Thurston, the Vicar of St. Simon's, who was a wise, generous and single-hearted priest, was quick to recognize that his missioner was capable of being left to convert the Notting Dale slum in his own way.

"If St. Simon's is an outpost of the Movement, Lidderdale must be one of the vedettes," he used to declare with a grin.

The Missioner was a tall hatchet-faced hollow-eyed ascetic, harsh and bigoted in the company of his equals whether clerical or lay, but with his flock tender and comprehending and patient. The only indulgence he accorded to his senses was in the forms and ceremonies of his ritual, the vestments and furniture of his church. His vicar was able to give him a free hand in the obscure squalor of Lima Street; the ecclesiastical battles he himself had to fight with bishops who were pained or with retired military men who were disgusted by his own conduct of the services at St. Simon's were not waged within the hearing of Lima Street. There, year in, year out for six years, James Lidderdale denied himself nothing in religion, in life everything. He used to preach in the parish church during the penitential seasons, and with such effect upon the pockets of his congregation that the Lima Street Mission was rich for a long while afterward. Yet few of the worshippers in the parish church visited the object of their charity, and those that did venture seldom came twice. Lidderdale did not consider that it was part of the Lima Street religion to be polite to well-dressed explorers of the slum; in fact he rather encouraged Lima Street to suppose the contrary.

"I don't like these dressed up women in my church," he used to tell his vicar. "They distract my people's attention from the altar."

"Oh, I quite see your point," Thurston would agree.

"And I don't like these churchy young fools who come simpering down in top-hats, with rosaries hanging out of their pockets. Lima Street doesn't like them either. Lima Street is provoked to obscene comment, and that just before Mass. It's no good, Vicar. My people are savages, and I like them to remain savages so long as they go to their duties, which Almighty God be thanked they do."

On one occasion the Archdeacon, who had been paying an official visit to St. Simon's, expressed a desire to see the Lima Street Mission.

"Of which I have heard great things, great things, Mr. Thurston," he boomed condescendingly.

The Vicar was doubtful of the impression that the Archdeacon's gaiters would make on Lima Street, and he was also doubtful of the impression that the images and prickets of St. Wilfred's would make on the Archdeacon. The Vicar need not have worried. Long before Lima Street was reached, indeed, halfway down Strugwell Terrace, which was the main road out of respectable Notting Hill into the Mission area, the comments upon the Archdeacon's appearance became so embarrassing that the dignitary looked at his watch and remarked that after all he feared he should not be able to spare the time that afternoon.

"But I am surprised," he observed when his guide had brought him safely back into Notting Hill. "I am surprised that the people are still so uncouth. I had always understood that a great work of purification had been effected, that in fact—er—they were quite—er—cleaned up."

"In body or soul?" Thurston inquired.

"The whole district," said the Archdeacon vaguely. "I was referring to the general tone, Mr. Thurston. One might be pardoned for supposing that they had never seen a clergyman before. Of course one is loath—very loath indeed—to criticize sincere effort of any kind, but I think that perhaps almost the chief value of the missions we have established in these poverty-stricken areas lies in their capacity for civilizing the poor people who inhabit them. One is so anxious to bring into their drab lives a little light, a little air. I am a great believer in education. Oh, yes, Mr. Thurston, I have great hopes of popular education. However, as I say, I should not dream of criticizing your work at St. Wilfred's."

"It is not my work. It is the work of one of my curates. And," said the Vicar to Lidderdale, when he was giving him an account of the projected visitation, "I believe the pompous ass thought I was ashamed of it."

Thurston died soon after this, and, his death occurring at a moment when party strife in the Church was fiercer than ever, it was considered expedient by the Lord Chancellor, in whose gift the living was, to appoint a more moderate man than the late vicar. Majendie, the new man, when he was sure of his audience, claimed to be just as advanced as Thurston; but he was ambitious of preferment, or as he himself put it, he felt that, when a member of the Catholic party had with the exercise of prudence and tact an opportunity of enhancing the prestige of his party in a higher ecclesiastical sphere, he should be wrong to neglect it. Majendie's aim therefore was to avoid controversy with his ecclesiastical superiors, and at a time when, as he told Lidderdale, he was stepping back in order to jump farther, he was anxious that his missioner should step back with him.

"I'm not suggesting, my dear fellow, that you should bring St. Wilfred's actually into line with the parish church. But the Asperges, you know. I can't countenance that. And the Adoration of the Cross on Good Friday. I really think that kind of thing creates unnecessary friction."

Lidderdale's impulse was to resign at once, for he was a man who found restraint galling where so much passion went to his belief in the truth of his teaching. When, however, he pondered how little he had done and how much he had vowed to do, he gave way and agreed to step back with his vicar. He was never convinced that he had taken the right course at this crisis, and he spent hours in praying for an answer by God to a question already answered by himself. The added strain of these hours of prayer, which were not robbed from his work in the Mission, but from the already short enough time he allowed himself for sleep, told upon his health, and he was ordered by the doctor to take a holiday to avoid a complete breakdown of health. He stayed for two months in Cornwall, and came back with a wife, the daughter of a Cornish parson called Trehawke. Lidderdale had been a fierce upholder of celibacy, and the news of his marriage astonished all who knew him.

Grace Lidderdale with her slanting sombre eyes and full upcurving lips made the pink and white Madonnas of the little mission church look insipid, and her husband was horrified when he found himself criticizing the images whose ability to lure the people of Lima Street to worship in the way he believed to be best for their souls he had never doubted. Yet, for all her air of having *trafficked for strange webs with Eastern merchants*, Mrs. Lidderdale was only outwardly Phoenician or Iberian or whatever other dimly imagined race is chosen for the strange types that in Cornwall more than elsewhere so often occur. Actually she was a simple and devout soul, loving husband and child and the poor people with whom they lived. Doubtless she had looked more appropriate to her surroundings in the tangled garden of her father's vicarage than in the bleak Mission House of Lima Street; but inasmuch as she never thought about her appearance it would have been a waste of time for anybody to try to romanticize her. The civilizing effect of her presence in the slum was quickly felt; and though Lidderdale continued to scoff at the advantages of civilization, he finally learnt to give a grudging welcome to her various schemes for making the bodies of the flock as comfortable as her husband tried to make their souls.

When Mark was born, his father became once more the prey of gloomy doubt. The guardianship of a soul which he was responsible for bringing into the world was a ceaseless care, and in his anxiety to dedicate his son to God he became a harsh and unsympathetic parent. Out of that desire to justify himself for having been so inconsistent as to take a wife and beget a son Lidderdale redoubled his efforts to put the Lima Street Mission on a permanent basis. The civilization of the slum, which was attributed by pious visitors to regular attendance at Mass rather than to Mrs. Lidderdale's gentleness and charm, made it much easier for outsiders to explore St. Simon's parish as far as Lima Street. Money for the great church he designed to build on a site adjoining the old tabernacle began to flow in; and five years after his marriage Lidderdale had enough money subscribed to begin to build. The rubbish-strewn wasteground overlooked by the back-windows of the Mission House was thronged with workmen; day by day the walls of the new St. Wilfred's rose higher. Fifteen years after Lidderdale took charge of the Lima Street Mission, it was decided to ask for St. Wilfred's, Notting Dale, to be created a separate parish. The Reverend Aylmer Majendie had become a canon residentiary of Chichester and had been succeeded as vicar by the Reverend L. M. Astill, a man more of the type of Thurston and only too anxious to help his senior curate to become a vicar, and what is more cut £200 a year off his own net income in doing so.

But when the question arose of consecrating the new St. Wilfred's in order to the creation of a new parish, the Bishop asked many questions that were never asked about the Lima Street Mission. There were Stations of the Cross reported to be of an unusually idolatrous nature. There was a second chapel apparently for the express purpose of worshipping the Virgin Mary.

"He writes to me as if he suspected me of trying to carry on an intrigue with the Mother of God," cried Lidderdale passionately to his vicar.

"Steady, steady, dear man," said Astill. "You'll ruin your case by such ill-considered exaggeration."

"But, Vicar, these cursed bishops of the Establishment who would rather a whole parish went to Hell than give up one jot or one tittle of their prejudice!" Lidderdale ejaculated in wrath.

Furthermore, the Bishop wanted to know if the report that on Good Friday was held a Roman Catholic Service called the Mass of the Pre-Sanctified followed by the ceremony of Creeping to the Cross was true. When Majendie departed, the Lima Street Missioner jumped a long way forward in one leap. There were many other practices which he (the Bishop) could only characterize as highly objectionable and quite contrary to the spirit of the Church of England, and would Mr. Lidderdale pay him a visit at Fulham Palace as soon as possible. Lidderdale went, and he argued with the Bishop until the Chaplain thought his Lordship had heard enough, after which the argument was resumed by letter. Then Lidderdale was invited to lunch at Fulham Palace and to argue the whole question over again in person. In the end the Bishop was sufficiently impressed by the Missioner's sincerity and zeal to agree to withhold his decision until the Lord Bishop Suffragan of Devizes had paid a visit to the proposed new parish. This was the visit that was expected on the day after Mark Lidderdale woke from a nightmare and dreamed that London was being swallowed up by an earthquake.

CHAPTER III

RELIGIOUS EDUCATION

When Mark was grown up and looked back at his early childhood—he was seven years old in the year in which his father was able to see the new St. Wilfred's an edifice complete except for consecration—it seemed to him that his education had centered in the prevention of his acquiring a Cockney accent. This was his mother's dread and for this reason he was not allowed to play more than Christian equality demanded with the boys of Lima Street. Had his mother had her way, he would never have been allowed to play with them at all; but his father would sometimes break out into fierce tirades against snobbery and hustle him out of the house to amuse himself with half-a-dozen little girls looking after a dozen babies in dilapidated perambulators, and countless smaller boys and girls ragged and grubby and mischievous.

"You leave that kebbidge-stalk be, Elfie!"

"Ethel! Jew hear your ma calling you, you naughty girl?"

"Stanlee! will you give over fishing in that puddle, this sminute. I'll give you such a slepping, you see if I don't."

"Come here, Maybel, and let me blow your nose. Daisy Hawkins, lend us your henkerchif, there's a love! Our Maybel wants to blow her nose. Oo, she is a sight! Come here, Maybel, do, and leave off sucking that orange peel. There's the Father's little boy looking at you. Hold your head up, do."

Mark would stand gravely to attention while Mabel Williams' toilet was adjusted, and as gravely follow the shrill raucous procession to watch pavement games like Hop Scotch or to help in gathering together enough sickly greenery from the site of the new church to make the summer grotto, which in Lima Street was a labour of love, since few of the passers by in that neighbourhood could afford to remember St. James' grotto with a careless penny.

The fact that all the other little boys and girls called the Missioner Father made it hard for Mark to understand his own more particular relationship to him, and Lidderdale was so much afraid of showing any more affection to one child of his flock than to another that he was less genial with his own son than with any of the other children. It was natural that in these circumstances Mark should be even more dependent than most solitary children upon his mother, and no doubt it was through his passion to gratify her that he managed to avoid that Cockney accent. His father wanted his first religious instruction to be of the communal kind that he provided in the Sunday School. One might have thought that he distrusted his wife's orthodoxy, so strongly did he disapprove of her teaching Mark by himself in the nursery.

"It's the curse of the day," he used to assert, "this pampering of children with an individual religion. They get into the habit of thinking God is their special property and when they get older and find he isn't, as often as not they give up religion altogether, because it doesn't happen to fit in with the spoilt notions they got hold of as infants."

Mark's bringing up was the only thing in which Mrs. Lidderdale did not give way to her husband. She was determined that he should not have a Cockney accent, and without irritating her husband any more than was inevitable she was determined that he should not gobble down his religion as a solid indigestible whole. On this point she even went so far as directly to contradict the boy's father and argue that an intelligent boy like Mark was likely to vomit up such an indigestible whole later on, although she did not make use of such a coarse expression.

"All mothers think their sons are the cleverest in the world."

"But, James, he *is* an exceptionally clever little boy. Most observant, with a splendid memory and plenty of imagination."

"Too much imagination. His nights are one long circus."

"But, James, you yourself have insisted so often on the personal Devil; you can't expect a little boy of Mark's sensitiveness not to be impressed by your picture."

"He has nothing to fear from the Devil, if he behaves himself. Haven't I made that clear?"

Mrs. Lidderdale sighed.

"But, James dear, a child's mind is so literal, and though I know you insist just as much on the reality of the Saints and Angels, a child's mind is always most impressed by the things that have power to frighten it."

"I want him to be frightened by Evil," declared James. "But go your own way. Soften down everything in our Holy Religion that is ugly and difficult. Sentimentalize the whole business. That's our modern method in everything."

This was one of many arguments between husband and wife about the religious education of their son.

Luckily for Mark his father had too many children, real children and grown up children, in the Mission to be able to spend much time with his son; and the teaching of Sunday morning, the clear-cut uncompromising statement of hard religious facts in which the Missioner delighted, was considerably toned down by his wife's gentle commentary.

Mark's mother taught him that the desire of a bad boy to be a good boy is a better thing than the goodness of a Jack Horner. She taught him that God was not merely a crotchety old gentleman reclining in a blue dressing-gown on a mattress of cumulus, but that He was an Eye, an all-seeing Eye, an Eye capable indeed of flashing with rage, yet so rarely that whenever her little boy should imagine that Eye he might behold it wet with tears.

"But can God cry?" asked Mark incredulously.

"Oh, darling. God can do everything."

"But fancy crying! If I could do everything I shouldn't cry."

Mrs. Lidderdale perceived that her picture of the wise and compassionate Eye would require elaboration.

"But do you only cry, Mark dear, when you can't do what you want? Those are not nice tears. Don't you ever cry because you're sorry you've been disobedient?"

"I don't think so, Mother," Mark decided after a pause. "No, I don't think I cry because I'm sorry except when you're sorry, and that sometimes makes me cry. Not always, though. Sometimes I'm glad you're sorry. I feel so angry that I like to see you sad."

"But you don't often feel like that?"

"No, not often," he admitted.

"But suppose you saw somebody being ill-treated, some poor dog or cat being teased, wouldn't you feel inclined to cry?"

"Oh, no," Mark declared. "I get quite red inside of me, and I want to kick the people who is doing it."

"Well, now you can understand why God sometimes gets angry. But even if He gets angry," Mrs. Lidderdale went on, for she was rather afraid of her son's capacity for logic, "God never lets His anger get the better of Him. He is not only sorry for the poor dog, but He is also sorry for the poor person who is ill-treating the dog. He knows that the poor person has perhaps never been taught better, and then the Eye fills with tears again."

"I think I like Jesus better than God," said Mark, going off at a tangent. He felt that there were too many points of resemblance between his own father and God to make it prudent to persevere with the discussion. On the subject of his father he always found his mother strangely uncomprehending, and the only times she was really angry with him was when he refused out of his basic honesty to admit that he loved his father.

"But Our Lord *is* God," Mrs. Lidderdale protested.

Mark wrinkled his face in an effort to confront once more this eternal puzzle.

"Don't you remember, darling, three Persons and one God?"

Mark sighed.

"You haven't forgotten that clover-leaf we picked one day in Kensington Gardens?"

"When we fed the ducks on the Round Pond?"

"Yes, darling, but don't think about ducks just now. I want you to think about the Holy Trinity."

"But I can't understand the Holy Trinity, Mother," he protested.

"Nobody can understand the Holy Trinity. It is a great mystery."

"Mystery," echoed Mark, taking pleasure in the word. It always thrilled him, that word, ever since he first heard it used by Dora the servant when she could not find her rolling-pin.

"Well, where that rolling-pin's got to is a mystery," she had declared.

Then he had seen the word in print. The Coram Street Mystery. All about a dead body. He had pronounced it "micetery" at first, until he had been corrected and was able to identify the word as the one used by Dora about her rolling-pin. History stood for the hard dull fact, and mystery stood for all that history was not. There were no dates in "mystery:" Mark even at seven years, such was the fate of intelligent precocity, had already had to grapple with a few conspicuous dates in the immense tale of humanity. He knew for instance that William the Conqueror landed in 1066, and that St. Augustine landed in 596, and that Julius Cæsar landed, but he could never remember exactly when. The last time he was asked that date, he had countered with a request to know when Noah had landed.

"The Holy Trinity is a mystery."

It belonged to the category of vanished rolling-pins and dead bodies huddled up in dustbins: it had no date.

But what Mark liked better than speculations upon the nature of God were the tales that were told like fairy tales without its seeming to matter whether you remembered them or not, and which just because it did not matter you were able to remember so much more easily. He could have listened for ever to the story of the lupinseeds that rattled in their pods when the donkey was trotting with the boy Christ and His mother and St. Joseph far away from cruel Herod into Egypt and how the noise of the rattling seeds nearly betrayed their flight and how the plant was cursed for evermore and made as hungry as a wolf. And the story of how the robin tried to loosen one of the cruel nails so that the blood from the poor Saviour drenched his breast and stained it red for evermore, and of that other bird, the crossbill, who pecked at the nails until his beak became crossed. He could listen for ever to the tale of St. Cuthbert who was fed by ravens, of St. Martin who cut off his cloak and gave it to a beggar, of St. Anthony who preached to the fishes, of St. Raymond who put up his cowl and floated from Spain to Africa like a nautilus, of St. Nicolas who raised three boys from the dead after they had been killed and cut up and salted in a tub by a cruel man that wanted to eat them, and of that strange insect called a Praying Mantis which alighted upon St. Francis' sleeve and sang the *Nunc Dimittis* before it flew away.

These were all stories that made bedtime sweet, stories to remember and brood upon gratefully in the darkness of the night when he lay awake and when, alas, other stories less pleasant to recall would obtrude themselves.

Mark was not brought up luxuriously in the Lima Street Mission House, and the scarcity of toys stimulated his imagination. All his toys were old and broken, because he was only allowed to have the toys left over at the annual Christmas Tree in the Mission Hall; and since even the best of toys on that tree were the castoffs of rich little children whose parents performed a vicarious act of charity in presenting them to the poor, it may be understood that Mark's share of these was not calculated to spoil him. His most conspicuous toy was a box of mutilated grenadiers, whose stands had been melted by their former owner in the first rapture of discovering that lead melts in fire and who in consequence were only able to stand up uncertainly when stuck into sliced corks.

Luckily Mark had better armies of his own in the coloured lines that crossed the blankets of his bed. There marched the crimson army of St. George, the blue army of St. Andrew, the green army of St. Patrick, the yellow army of St. David, the rich sunset-hued army of St. Denis, the striped armies of St. Anthony and St. James. When he lay awake in the golden light of the morning, as golden in Lima Street as anywhere else, he felt ineffably protected by the Seven Champions of Christendom; and sometimes even at night he was able to think that with their bright battalions they were still marching past. He used to lie awake, listening to the sparrows and wondering what the country was like and most of all the sea. His father would not let him go into the country until he was considered old enough to go with one of the annual school treats. His mother told him that the country in Cornwall was infinitely more beautiful than Kensington Gardens, and that compared with the sea the Serpentine was nothing at all. The sea! He had heard it once in a prickly shell, and it had sounded beautiful. As for the country he had read a story by Mrs. Ewing called *Our Field*, and if the country was the tiniest part as wonderful as that, well . . . meanwhile Dora brought him back from the greengrocer's a pot of musk, which Mark used to sniff so enthusiastically that Dora said he would sniff it right away if he wasn't careful. Later on when Lima Street was fetid in the August sun he gave this pot of musk to a little girl with a broken leg, and when she died in September her mother put it on her grave.

CHAPTER IV

HUSBAND AND WIFE

Mark was impressed by the appearance of the Bishop of Devizes; a portly courtly man, he brought to the dingy little Mission House in Lima Street that very sense of richness and grandeur which Mark had anticipated. The Bishop's pink plump hands of which he made such use contrasted with the lean, scratched, and grimy hands of his father; the Bishop's hair white and glossy made his father's bristly, badly cut hair look more bristly and worse cut than ever, and the Bishop's voice ripe and unctuous grew more and more mellow as his father's became harsher and more assertive. Mark found himself thinking of some lines in *The Jackdaw of Rheims* about a cake of soap worthy of washing the hands of the Pope. The Pope would have hands like the Bishop's, and Mark who had heard a great deal about the Pope looked at the Bishop of Devizes with added interest.

"While we are at lunch, Mr. Lidderdale, you will I am sure pardon me for referring again to our conversation of this morning from another point of view—the point of view, if I may use so crude an expression, the point of view of—er—expediency. Is it wise?"

"I'm not a wise man, my lord."

"Pardon me, my dear Mr. Lidderdale, but I have not completed my question. Is it right? Is it right when you have an opportunity to consolidate your great work . . . I use the adjective advisedly and with no intention to flatter you, for when I had the privilege this morning of accompanying you round the beautiful edifice that has been by your efforts, by your self-sacrifice, by your eloquence, and by your devotion erected to the glory of God . . . I repeat, Mr.

Lidderdale, is it right to fling all this away for the sake of a few—you will not misunderstand me—if I call them a few excrescences?"

The Bishop helped himself to the cauliflower and paused to give his rhetoric time to work.

"What you regard, my lord, as excrescences I regard as fundamentals of our Holy Religion."

"Come, come, Mr. Lidderdale," the Bishop protested. "I do not think that you expect to convince me that a ceremony like the—er—Asperges is a fundamental of Christianity."

"I have taught my people that it is," said the Missioner. "In these days when Bishops are found who will explain away the Incarnation, the Atonement, the Resurrection of the Body, I hope you'll forgive a humble parish priest who will explain away nothing and who would rather resign, as I told you this morning, than surrender a single one of these excrescences."

"I do not admit your indictment, your almost wholesale indictment of the Anglican episcopate; but even were I to admit at lunch that some of my brethren have been in their anxiety to keep the Man in the Street from straying too far from the Church, have been as I was saying a little too ready to tolerate a certain latitude of belief, even as I said just now were that so, I do not think that you have any cause to suspect me of what I should repudiate as gross infidelity. It was precisely because the Bishop of London supposed that I should be more sympathetic with your ideals that he asked me to represent him in this perfectly informal—er—"

"Inquest," the Missioner supplied with a fierce smile.

The Bishop encouraged by the first sign of humour he had observed in the bigoted priest hastened to smile back.

"Well, let us call it an inquest, but not, I hope, I sincerely and devoutly hope, Mr. Lidderdale, not an inquest upon a dead body." Then hurriedly he went on. "I may smile with the lips, but believe me, my dear fellow labourer in the vineyard of Our Lord Jesus Christ, believe me that my heart is sore at the prospect of your resignation. And the Bishop of London, if I have to go back to him with such news, will be pained, bitterly grievously pained. He admires your work, Mr. Lidderdale, as much as I do, and I have no doubt that if it were not for the unhappy controversies that are tearing asunder our National Church, I say I do not doubt that he would give you a free hand. But how can he give you a free hand when his own hands are tied by the necessities of the situation? May I venture to observe that some of you working priests are too ready to criticize men like myself who from no desire of our own have been called by God to occupy a loftier seat in the eyes of the world than many men infinitely more worthy. But to return to the question immediately before us, let me, my dear Mr. Lidderdale, do let me make to you a personal appeal for moderation. If you will only consent to abandon one or two—I will not say excrescences since you object to the word—but if you will only abandon one or two purely ceremonial additions that cannot possibly be defended by any rubric in the Book of Common Prayer, if you will only consent to do this the Bishop of London will, I can guarantee, permit you a discretionary latitude that he would scarcely be prepared to allow to any other priest in his diocese. When I was called to be Bishop Suffragan of Devizes, Mr. Lidderdale, do you suppose that I did not give up something? Do you suppose that I was anxious to abandon some of the riches to which by my reading of the Ornaments Rubric we are entitled? But I felt that I could do something to help the position of my fellow priests struggling against the prejudice of ignorance and the prey of political moves. In twenty years from now, Mr. Lidderdale, you will be glad you took my advice. Ceremonies that today are the privilege of the few will then be the privilege of the many. Do not forget that by what I might almost describe as the exorbitance of your demands you have gained more freedom than any other priest in England. Be moderate. Do not resign. You will be inhibited in every diocese; you will have the millstone of an unpaid debt round your neck; you are a married man."

"That has nothing . . ." Lidderdale interrupted angrily.

"Pray let me finish. You are a married man, and if you should seek consolation, where several of your fellow priests have lately sought it, in the Church of Rome, you will have to seek it as a layman. I do not pretend to know your private affairs, and I should consider it impertinent if I tried to pry into them at such a moment. But I do know your worth as a priest, and I have no hesitation in begging you once more with a heart almost too full for words to pause, Mr. Lidderdale, to pause and reflect before you take the irreparable step that you are contemplating. I have already talked too much, and I see that your good wife is looking anxiously at my plate. No more cauliflower, thank you, Mrs. Lidderdale, no more of anything, thank you. Ah, there is a pudding on the way? Dear me, that sounds very tempting, I'm afraid."

The Bishop now turned his attention entirely to Mrs. Lidderdale at the other end of the table; the Missioner sat biting his nails; and Mark wondered what all this conversation was about.

While the Bishop was waiting for his cab, which, he explained to his hosts, was not so much a luxury as a necessity owing to his having to address at three o'clock precisely a committee of ladies who were meeting in Portman Square to discuss the dreadful condition of the London streets, he laid a fatherly arm on the Missioner's threadbare cassock.

"Take two or three days to decide, my dear Mr. Lidderdale. The Bishop of London, who is always consideration personified, insisted that you were to take two or three days to decide. Once more, for I hear my cab-wheels, once more let me beg you to yield on the following points. Let me just refer to my notes to be sure that I have not omitted anything of importance. Oh, yes, the following points: no Asperges, no unusual Good Friday services, except of course the Three Hours. *Is* not that enough?"

"The Three Hours I *would* give up. It's a modern invention of the Jesuits. The Adoration of the Cross goes back . . ."

"Please, please, Mr. Lidderdale, my cab is at the door. We must not embark on controversy. No celebrations without communicants. No direct invocation of the Blessed Virgin Mary or the Saints. Oh, yes, and on this the Bishop is particularly firm: no juggling with the *Gloria in Excelsis*. Goodbye, Mr. Lidderdale, goodbye, Mrs. Lidderdale. Many thanks for your delicious luncheon. Goodbye, young man. I had a little boy like you once, but he is grown up now, and I am glad to say a soldier."

The Bishop waved his umbrella, which looked much like a pastoral staff, and lightly mounted the step of his cab.

"Was the Bishop cross with Father?" Mark inquired afterward; he could find no other theory that would explain so much talking to his father, so little talking by his father.

"Dearest, I'd rather you didn't ask questions about the Bishop," his mother replied, and discerning that she was on the verge of one of those headaches that while they lasted obliterated the world for Mark, he was silent. Later in the afternoon Mr. Astill, the Vicar, came round to see the Missioner and they had a long talk together, the murmur of which now softer now louder was audible in Mark's nursery where he was playing by himself with the cork-bottomed grenadiers. His instinct was to play a quiet game, partly on account of his mother's onrushing headache, which had already driven her to her room, partly because he knew that when his father was closeted like this it was essential not to make the least noise. So he tiptoed about the room and disposed the cork-bottomed grenadiers as sentinels before the coal-scuttle, the washstand, and other similar strongholds. Then he took his gun, the barrel of which, broken before it was given to him, had been replaced by a thin bamboo curtain-rod, and his finger on the trigger (a wooden match) he waited for an invader. After ten minutes of statuesque silence Mark began to think that this was a dull game, and he wished that his mother had not gone to her room with a headache, because if she had been with him she could have undoubtedly invented, so clever was she, a method of invading the nursery without either the attackers or the defenders making any noise about it. In her gentle voice she would have whispered of the hordes that were stealthily creeping up the mountain side until Mark and his vigilant cork-bottomed grenadiers would have been in a state of suppressed exultation ready to die in defence of the nursery, to die stolidly and silently at their posts with nobody else in the house aware of their heroism.

"Rorke's Drift," said Mark to himself, trying to fancy that he heard in the distance a Zulu *impi* and whispering to his cork-bottomed grenadiers to keep a good look-out. One of them who was guarding the play-cupboard fell over on his face, and in the stillness the noise sounded so loud that Mark did not dare cross the room to put him up again, but had to assume that he had been shot where he stood. It was no use. The game was a failure; Mark decided to look at *Battles of the British Army*. He knew the pictures in every detail, and he could have recited without a mistake the few lines of explanation at the bottom of each page; but the book still possessed a capacity to thrill, and he turned over the pages not pausing over Crecy or Poitiers or Blenheim or Dettingen; but enjoying the storming of Badajoz with soldiers impaled on *chevaux de frise* and lingering over the rich uniforms and plumed helmets in the picture of Joseph Bonaparte's flight at Vittoria. There was too a grim picture of the Guards at Inkerman fighting in their greatcoats with clubbed muskets against thousands of sinister dark green Russians looming in the snow; and there was an attractive picture of a regiment crossing the Alma and eating the grapes as they clambered up the banks where they grew. Finally there was the Redan, a mysterious wall, apparently of wickerwork, with bombs bursting and broken scaling-ladders and dead English soldiers in the open space before it.

Mark did not feel that he wanted to look through the book again, and he put it away, wondering how long that murmur of voices rising and falling from his father's study below would continue. He wondered whether Dora would be annoyed if he went down to the kitchen. She had been discouraging on the last two or three occasions he had visited her, but that had been because he could not keep his fingers out of the currants. Fancy having a large red jar crammed full of currants on the floor of the larder and never wanting to eat one! The thought of those currants produced in Mark's mouth a craving for something sweet, and as quietly as possible he stole off downstairs to quench this craving somehow or other if it were only with a lump of sugar. But when he reached the kitchen he found Dora in earnest talk with two women in bonnets, who were nodding away and clicking their tongues with pleasure.

"Now whatever do you want down here?" Dora demanded ungraciously.

"I wanted," Mark paused. He longed to say "some currants," but he had failed before, and he substituted "a lump of sugar." The two women in bonnets looked at him and nodded their heads and clicked their tongues.

"Did you ever?" said one.

"Fancy! A lump of sugar! Goodness gracious!"

"What a sweet tooth!" commented the first.

The sugar happened to be close to Dora's hand on the kitchen-table, and she gave him two lumps with the command to "sugar off back upstairs as fast as you like." The craving for sweetness was allayed; but when Mark had crunched up the two lumps on the dark kitchen-stairs, he was as lonely as he had been before he left the nursery. He wished now that he had not eaten up the sugar so fast, that he had taken it back with him to the nursery and eked it out to wile away this endless afternoon. The prospect of going back to the nursery depressed him; and he turned aside to linger in the dining-room whence there was a view of Lima Street, down which a dirty frayed man was wheeling a barrow and shouting for housewives to bring out their old rags and bottles and bones. Mark felt the thrill of trade and traffick, and he longed to be big enough to open the window and call out that he had several rags and bottles and bones to sell; but instead he had to be content with watching two self-important little girls chaffer on behalf of their mothers, and go off counting their pennies. The voice of the rag-and-bone man, grew fainter and fainter round corners out of sight; Lima Street became as empty and uninteresting as the nursery. Mark wished that a knife-grinder would come along and that he would stop under the dining-room window so that he could watch the sparks flying from the grindstone. Or that a gipsy would sit down on the steps and begin to mend the seat of a chair. Whenever he had seen those gipsy chair-menders at work, he had been out of doors and afraid to linger watching them in case he should be stolen and his face stained with walnut juice and all his clothes taken away from him. But from the security of the dining-room of the Mission House he should enjoy watching them. However, no gipsy came, nor anybody else except women with men's caps pinned to their skimpy hair and little girls with wrinkled stockings carrying jugs to and from the public houses that stood at every corner.

Mark turned away from the window and tried to think of some game that could be played in the dining-room. But it was not a room that fostered the imagination. The carpet was so much worn that the pattern was now scarcely visible and, looked one at it never so long and intently, it was impossible to give it an inner life of its own that gradually revealed itself to the fanciful observer. The sideboard had nothing on it except a dirty cloth, a bottle of harvest burgundy, and half a dozen forks and spoons. The cupboards on either side contained nothing edible except salt, pepper, mustard, vinegar, and oil. There was a plain deal table without a drawer and without any interesting screws and levers to make it grow smaller or larger at the will of the creature who sat beneath it. The eight chairs were just chairs; the wallpaper was like the inside of the bath, but alas, without the water; of the two pictures, the one over the mantelpiece was a steel-engraving of the Good Shepherd and the one over the sideboard was an oleograph of the Sacred Heart. Mark knew every fly speck on their glasses, every discoloration of their margins. While he was sighing over the sterility of the room, he heard the door of his father's study open, and his father and Mr. Astill do down the passage, both of them still talking unceasingly. Presently the front door slammed, and Mark watched them walk away in the direction of the new church. Here was an opportunity to go into his father's study and look at some of the books. Mark never went in when his father was there, because once his mother had said to his father:

"Why don't you have Mark to sit with you?"

And his father had answered doubtfully:

"Mark? Oh yes, he can come. But I hope he'll keep quiet, because I shall be rather busy."

Mark had felt a kind of hostility in his father's manner which had chilled him; and after that, whenever his mother used to suggest his going to sit quietly in the study, he had always made some excuse not to go. But if his father was out he used to like going in, because there were always books lying about that were interesting to look at, and the smell of tobacco smoke and leather bindings was grateful to the senses. The room smelt even more strongly than usual of tobacco smoke this afternoon, and Mark inhaled the air with relish while he debated which of the many volumes he should pore over. There was a large Bible with pictures of palm-trees and camels and long-bearded patriarchs surrounded by flocks of sheep, pictures of women with handkerchiefs over their mouths drawing water from wells, of Daniel in the den of lions and of Shadrach, Meshach and Abednego in the fiery furnace. The frontispiece was a coloured picture of Adam and Eve in the Garden of Eden surrounded by amiable lions, benevolent tigers, ingratiating bears and leopards and wolves. But more interesting than the pictures were some pages at the beginning on which, in oval spaces framed in leaves and flowers, were written the names of his grandfather and grandmother, of his father and of his father's brother and sister, with the dates on which they were born and baptized and confirmed. What a long time ago his father was born! 1840. He asked his mother once about this Uncle Henry and Aunt Helen; but she told him they had quarrelled with his father, and she had said nothing more about them. Mark had been struck by the notion that grown-up people could quarrel: he had supposed quarrelling to be peculiar to childhood. Further, he noticed that Henry Lidderdale had married somebody called Ada Prewbody who had died the same year; but nothing was said in the oval that enshrined his father about his having married anyone. He asked his mother the reason of this, and she explained to him that the Bible had belonged to his grandfather who had kept the entries up to date until he died, when the Bible came to his eldest son who was Mark's father.

"Does it worry you, darling, that I'm not entered?" his mother had asked with a smile.

"Well, it does rather," Mark had replied, and then to his great delight she took a pen and wrote that James Lidderdale had married Grace Alethea Trehawke on June 28th, 1880, at St. Tugdual's Church, Nancepean, Cornwall, and to his even greater delight that on April 25th, 1881, Mark Lidderdale had been born at 142 Lima Street, Notting Dale, London, W., and baptized on May 21st, 1881, at St. Wilfred's Mission Church, Lima Street.

"Happy now?" she had asked.

Mark had nodded, and from that moment, if he went into his father's study, he always opened the Family Bible and examined solemnly his own short history wreathed in forget-me-nots and lilies of the valley.

This afternoon, after looking as usual at the entry of his birth and baptism written in his mother's pretty pointed handwriting, he searched for Dante's *Inferno* illustrated by Gustave Doré, a large copy of which had recently been presented to his father by the Servers and Choir of St. Wilfred's. The last time he had been looking at this volume he had caught a glimpse of a lot of people buried in the ground with only their heads sticking out, a most attractive picture which he had only just discovered when he had heard his father's footsteps and had closed the book in a hurry.

Mark tried to find this picture, but the volume was large and the pictures on the way of such fascination that it was long before he found it. When he did, he thought it even more satisfying at a second glance, although he wished he knew what they were all doing buried in the ground like that. Mark was not satisfied with horrors even after he had gone right through the Dante; in fact, his appetite was only whetted, and he turned with relish to a large folio of Chinese tortures, in the coloured prints of which a feature was made of blood profusely outpoured and richly tinted. One picture of a Chinaman apparently impervious to the pain of being slowly sawn in two held him entranced for five minutes. It was growing dusk by now, and as it needed the light of the window to bring out the full quality of the blood, Mark carried over the big volume, propped it up in a chair behind the curtains, and knelt down to gloat over these remote oriental barbarities without pausing to remember that his father might come back at any moment, and that although he had never actually been forbidden to look at this book, the thrill of something unlawful always brooded over it. Suddenly the door of the study opened and Mark sat transfixed by terror as completely as the Chinaman on the page before him was transfixed by a sharpened bamboo; then he heard his mother's voice, and before he could discover himself a conversation between her and his father had begun of which Mark understood enough to know that both of them would be equally angry if they knew that he was listening. Mark was not old enough to escape tactfully from such a difficult situation, and the only thing he could think of doing was to stay absolutely still in the hope that they would presently go out of the room and never know that he had been behind the curtain while they were talking.

"I didn't mean you to dress yourself and come downstairs," his father was saying ungraciously.

"My dear, I should have come down to tea in any case, and I was anxious to hear the result of your conversation with Mr. Astill."

"You can guess, can't you?" said the husband.

Mark had heard his father speak angrily before; but he had never heard his voice sound like a growl. He shrank farther back in affright behind the curtains.

"You're going to give way to the Bishop?" the wife asked gently.

"Ah, you've guessed, have you? You've guessed by my manner? You've realized, I hope, what this resolution has cost me and what it's going to cost me in the future. I'm a coward. I'm a traitor. *Before the cock crow twice, thou shalt deny me thrice.* A coward and a traitor."

"Neither, James—at any rate to me."

"To you," the husband scoffed. "I should hope not to you, considering that it is on your account I am surrendering. Do you suppose that if I were free, as to serve God I ought to be free, do you suppose then that I should give up my principles like this? Never! But because I'm a married priest, because I've a wife and family to support, my hands are tied. Oh, yes, Astill was very tactful. He kept insisting on my duty to the parish; but did he once fail to rub in the position in which I should find myself if I did resign? No bishop would license me; I should be inhibited in every diocese—in other words I should starve. The beliefs I hold most dear, the beliefs I've fought for all these years surrendered for bread and butter! *Woman, what have I to do with thee?* Our Blessed Lord could speak thus even to His Blessed Mother. But I! *He that loveth son or daughter more than me is not worthy of me. And he that taketh not his cross, and followeth after me, is not worthy of me.*"

The Missioner threw himself into his worn armchair and stared into the unlighted grate. His wife came behind him and laid a white hand upon his forehead; but her touch seemed to madden him, and he sprang away from her.

"No more of that," he cried. "If I was weak when I married you I will never be weak again. You have your child. Let that be enough for your tenderness. I want none of it myself. Do you hear? I wish to devote myself henceforth to my parish. My parish! The parish of a coward and a traitor."

Mark heard his mother now speaking in a voice that was strange to him, in a voice that did not belong to her, but that seemed to come from far away, as if she were lost in a snowstorm and calling for help.

"James, if you feel this hatred for me and for poor little Mark, it is better that we leave you. We can go to my father in Cornwall, and you will not feel hampered by the responsibility of having to provide for us. After what you have said to me, after the way you have looked at me, I could never live with you as your wife again."

"That sounds a splendid scheme," said the Missioner bitterly. "But do you think I have so little logic that I should be able to escape from my responsibilities by planting them on the shoulders of another? No, I sinned when I married you. I did not believe and

I do not believe that a priest ought to marry; but having done so I must face the situation and do my duty to my family, so that I may also do my duty to God."

"Do you think that God will accept duty offered in that spirit? If he does, he is not the God in Whom I believe. He is a devil that can be propitiated with burnt offerings," exclaimed the woman passionately.

"Do not blaspheme," the priest commanded.

"Blaspheme!" she echoed. "It is you, James, who have blasphemed nature this afternoon. You have committed the sin against the Holy Ghost, and may you be forgiven by your God. I can never forgive you."

"You're becoming hysterical."

"How dare you say that? How dare you? I have loved you, James, with all the love that I could give you. I have suffered in silence when I saw how you regarded family life, how unkind you were to Mark, how utterly wrapped up in the outward forms of religion. You are a Pharisee, James, you should have lived before Our Lord came down to earth. But I will not suffer any longer. You need not worry about the evasion of your responsibilities. You cannot make me stay with you. You will not dare keep Mark. Save your own soul in your own way; but Mark's soul is as much mine as yours to save."

During this storm of words Mark had been thinking how wicked it was of his father to upset his mother like that when she had a headache. He had thought also how terrible it was that he should apparently be the cause of this frightening quarrel. Often in Lima Street he had heard tales of wives who were beaten by their husbands and now he supposed that his own mother was going to be beaten. Suddenly he heard her crying. This was too much for him; he sprang from his hiding place and ran to put his arms round her in protection.

"Mother, mother, don't cry. You are bad, you are bad," he told his father. "You are wicked and bad to make her cry."

"Have you been in the room all this time?" his father asked.

Mark did not even bother to nod his head, so intent was he upon consoling his mother. She checked her emotion when her son put his arms round her neck, and whispered to him not to speak. It was almost dark in the study now, and what little light was still filtering in at the window from the grey nightfall was obscured by the figure of the Missioner gazing out at the lantern spire of his new church. There was a tap at the door, and Mrs. Lidderdale snatched up the volume that Mark had let fall upon the floor when he emerged from the curtains, so that when Dora came in to light the gas and say that tea was ready, nothing of the stress of the last few minutes was visible. The Missioner was looking out of the window at his new church; his wife and son were contemplating the picture of an impervious Chinaman suspended in a cage where he could neither stand nor sit nor lie.

CHAPTER V

PALM SUNDAY

Mark's dream from which he woke to wonder if the end of the world was at hand had been a shadow cast by coming events. So far as the world of Lima Street was concerned, it was the end of it. The night after that scene in his father's study, which made a deeper impression on him than anything before that date in his short life, his mother came to sleep in the nursery with him, to keep him company so that he should not be frightened any more, she offered as the explanation of her arrival. But Mark, although of course he never said so to her, was sure that she had come to him to be protected against his father.

Mark did not overhear any more discussions between his parents, and he was taken by surprise when one day a week after his mother had come to sleep in his room, she asked him how he should like to go and live in the country. To Mark the country was as remote as Paradise, and at first he was inclined to regard the question as rhetorical to which a conventional reply was expected. If anybody had asked him how he should like to go to Heaven, he would have answered that he should like to go to Heaven very much. Cows, sheep, saints, angels, they were all equally unreal outside a picture book.

"I would like to go to the country very much," he said. "And I would like to go to the Zoological Gardens very much. Perhaps we can go there soon, can we, mother?"

"We can't go there if we're in the country."

Mark stared at her.

"But really go in the country?"

"Yes, darling, really go."

"Oh, mother," and immediately he checked his enthusiasm with a sceptical "when?"

"Next Monday."

"And shall I see cows?"

"Yes."

"And donkeys? And horses? And pigs? And goats?"

To every question she nodded.

"Oh, mother, I will be good," he promised of his own accord. "And can I take my grenadiers?"

"You can take everything you have, darling."

"Will Dora come?" He did not inquire about his father.

"No."

"Just you and me?"

She nodded, and Mark flung his arms round her neck to press upon her lips a long fragrant kiss, such a kiss as only a child can give.

On Sunday morning, the last Sunday morning he would worship in the little tin mission church, the last Sunday morning indeed that any of the children of Lima Street would worship there, Mark sat close beside his mother at the children's Mass. His father looking as he always looked, took off his chasuble, and in his alb walked up and down the aisle preaching his short sermon interspersed with questions.

"What is this Sunday called?"

There was a silence until a well-informed little girl breathed through her nose that it was called Passion Sunday.

"Quite right. And next Sunday?"

"Palm Sunday," all the children shouted with alacrity, for they looked forward to it almost more than to any Sunday in the year.

"Next Sunday, dear children, I had hoped to give you the blessed palms in our beautiful new church, but God has willed otherwise, and another priest will come in my place. I hope you will listen to him as attentively as you have listened to me, and I hope you will try to encourage him by your behaviour both in and out of the church, by your punctuality and regular attendance at Mass, and by your example to other children who have not had the advantage of learning all about our glorious Catholic faith. I shall think about you all when I am gone and I shall never cease to ask our Blessed Lord Jesus Christ to guard you and keep you safe for Him. And I want you to pray to Our Blessed Lady and to our great patron Saint Wilfred that they will intercede for you and me. Will you all do this?"

There was a unanimous and sibilant "Yes, father," from the assembled children, and then one little girl after being prodded by her companions on either side of her spoke up and asked the Missioner why he was going.

"Ah, that is a very difficult question to answer; but I will try to explain it to you by a parable. What is a parable?"

"Something that isn't true," sang out a too ready boy from the back of the church.

"No, no, Arthur Williams. Surely some other boy or girl can correct Arthur Williams? How many times have we had that word explained to us! A parable is a story with a hidden meaning. Now please, every boy and girl, repeat that answer after me. A parable is a story with a hidden meaning."

And all the children baa'd in unison:

"A parable is a story with a hidden meaning."

"That's better," said the Missioner. "And now I will tell you my parable. Once upon a time there was a little boy or a little girl, it doesn't matter which, whose father put him in charge of a baby. He was told not to let anybody take it away from him and he was told to look after it and wheel it about in the perambulator, which was a very old one, and not only very old but very small for the baby, who was growing bigger and bigger every day. Well, a lot of kind people clubbed together and bought a new perambulator, bigger than the other and more comfortable. They told him to take this perambulator home to his father and show him what a beautiful present they had made. Well, the boy wheeled it home and his father was very pleased with it. But when the boy took the baby out again, the nursemaid told him that the baby had too many clothes on and said that he must either take some of the clothes off or else she must take away the new perambulator. Well, the little boy had promised his father, who had gone far away on a journey, that nobody should touch the baby, and so he said he would not take off any of the clothes. And when the nurse took away the perambulator the little boy wrote to his father to ask what he should do and his father wrote to him that he would put one of his brothers in charge who would know how to do what the nurse wanted." The Missioner paused to see the effect of his story. "Now, children, let us see if you can understand my parable. Who is the little boy?"

A concordance of opinion cried "God."

"No. Now think. The father surely was God. And now once more, who was the little boy?"

Several children said "Jesus Christ," and one little boy who evidently thought that any connexion between babies and religion must have something to do with the Holy Innocents confidently called out "Herod."

"No, no, no," said the Missioner. "Surely the little boy is myself. And what is the baby?"

Without hesitation the boys and girls all together shouted "Jesus Christ."

"No, no. The baby is our Holy Catholic Faith. For which we are ready if necessary to—?"

There was no answer.

"To do what?"

"To be baptized," one boy hazarded.

"To die," said the Missioner reproachfully.

"To die," the class complacently echoed.

"And now what is the perambulator?"

This was a puzzle, but at last somebody tried:

"The Body and Blood of Our Lord, Jesus Christ."

"No, no. The perambulator is our Mission here in Lima Street. The old perambulator is the Church where we are sitting at Mass and the new perambulator is—"

"The new church," two children answered simultaneously.

"Quite right. And now, who is the nursemaid? The nursemaid is the Bishop of London. You remember that last Sunday we talked about bishops. What is a bishop?"

"A high-priest."

"Well, that is not a bad answer, but don't you remember we said that bishop meant 'overseer,' and you all know what an overseer is. Any of your fathers who go out to work will tell you that. So the Bishop like the nursemaid in my parable thought he knew better what clothes the baby ought to wear in the new perambulator, that is to say what services we ought to have in the new St. Wilfred's. And as God is far away and we can only speak to Him by prayer, I have asked Him what I ought to do, and He has told me that I ought to go away and that He will put a brother in charge of the baby in the new perambulator. Who then is the brother?"

"Jesus Christ," said the class, convinced that this time it must be He.

"No, no. The brother is the priest who will come to take charge of the new St. Wilfred's. He will be called the Vicar, and St. Wilfred's, instead of being called the Lima Street Mission, will become a parish. And now, dear children, there is no time to say any more words to you. My heart is sore at leaving you, but in my sorrow I shall be comforted if I can have the certainty that you are growing up to be good and loyal Catholics, loving Our Blessed Lord and His dear Mother, honouring the Holy Saints and Martyrs, hating the Evil One and all his Spirits and obeying God with whose voice the Church speaks. Now, for the last time children, let me hear you sing *We are but little children weak.*"

They all sang more loudly than usual to express a vague and troubled sympathy:

There's not a child so small and weak
But has his little cross to take,
His little work of love and praise
That he may do for Jesus' sake.

And they bleated a most canorous *Amen.*

Mark noticed that his mother clutched his hand tightly while his father was speaking, and when once he looked up at her to show how loudly he too was singing, he saw that her eyes were full of tears.

The next morning was Monday.

"Goodbye, Mark, be a good boy and obedient to your mother," said his father on the platform at Paddington.

"Who is that man?" Mark whispered when the guard locked them in.

His mother explained, and Mark looked at him with as much awe as if he were St. Peter with the keys of Heaven at his girdle. He waved his handkerchief from the window while the train rushed on through tunnels and between gloomy banks until suddenly the world became green, and there was the sun in a great blue and white sky. Mark looked at his mother and saw that again there were tears in her eyes, but that they sparkled like diamonds.

CHAPTER VI

NANCEPEAN

The Rhos or, as it is popularly written and pronounced, the Rose is a tract of land in the south-west of the Duchy of Cornwall, ten miles long and six at its greatest breadth, which on account of its remoteness from the railway, its unusual geological formation, and its peninsular shape possesses both in the character of its inhabitants and in the peculiar aspects of the natural scene all the limitations and advantages of an island. The main road running south to Rose Head from Rosemarket cuts the peninsula into two unequal portions, the eastern and by far the larger of which consists of a flat tableland two or three hundred feet above the sea covered with a bushy heath, which flourishes in the magnesian soil and which when in bloom is of such a clear rosy pink, with nothing to break the level monochrome except scattered drifts of cotton grass, pools of silver water and a few stunted pines, that ignorant observers have often supposed that the colour gave its name to the whole peninsula. The ancient town of Rosemarket, which serves as the only channel of communication with the rest of Cornwall, lies in the extreme north-west of the peninsula between a wide creek of the Roseford river and the Rose Pool, an irregular heart-shaped water about four miles in circumference which on the west is only separated from the Atlantic by a bar of fine shingle fifty yards across.

The parish of Nancepean, of which Mark's grandfather the Reverend Charles Elphinstone Trehawke had been vicar for nearly thirty years, ran southward from the Rose Pool between the main road and the sea for three miles. It was a country of green valleys unfolding to the ocean, and of small farms fertile enough when they were sheltered from the prevailing wind; but on the southern confines of the parish the soil became shallow and stony, the arable fields degenerated into a rough open pasturage full of gorse and foxgloves and gradually widening patches of heather, until finally the level monochrome of the Rhos absorbed the last vestiges of cultivation, and the parish came to an end.

The actual village of Nancepean, set in a hollow about a quarter of a mile from the sea, consisted of a smithy, a grocer's shop, a parish hall and some two dozen white cottages with steep thatched roofs lying in their own gardens on either side of the unfrequented road that branched from the main road to follow the line of the coast. Where this road made the turn south a track strewn with grey shingle ran down between the cliffs, at this point not much more than grassy hummocks, to Nancepean beach which extended northward in a wide curve until it disappeared two miles away in the wooded heights above the Rose Pool. The metalled coast road continued past the Hanover Inn, an isolated house standing at the head of a small cove, to make the long ascent of Pendhu Cliff three hundred and fifty feet high, from the brow of which it descended between banks of fern past St. Tugdual's Church to the sands of Church Cove, whence it emerged to climb in a steep zigzag the next headland, beyond which it turned inland again to Lanyon and rejoined the main road to Rose Head. The church itself had no architectural distinction; but the solitary position, the churchyard walls sometimes washed by high spring tides, the squat tower built into the rounded grassy cliff that protected it from the direct attack of the sea, and its impressive antiquity combined to give it more than the finest architecture could give. Nowhere in the surrounding landscape was there a sign of human habitation, neither on the road down from Pendhu nor on the road up toward Lanyon, not on the bare towans sweeping from the beach to the sky in undulating waves of sandy grass, nor in the valley between the towans and Pendhu, a wide green valley watered by a small stream that flowed into the cove, where it formed a miniature estuary, the configuration of whose effluence changed with every tide.

The Vicarage was not so far from the church as the church was from the village, but it was some way from both. It was reached from Nancepean by a road or rather by a gated cart-track down one of the numerous valleys of the parish, and it was reached from the church by another cart-track along the valley between Pendhu and the towans. Probably it was an ancient farmhouse, and it must have been a desolate and austere place until, as at the date when Mark first came there, it was graced by the perfume and gold of acacias, by wistaria and jasmine and honeysuckle, by the ivory goblets of magnolias, by crimson fuchsias, and where formerly its grey walls grew mossy north and east by pink and white camelias and the waxen bells of lapagerias. The garden was a wilderness of scarlet rhododendrons from the thickets of which innumerable blackbirds and thrushes preyed upon the peas. The lawns were like meadows; the lily ponds were marbled with weeds; the stables were hardly to be reached on account of the tangle of roses and briers that filled the abandoned yard. The front drive was bordered by evergreen oaks, underneath the shade of which blue hydrangeas flowered sparsely with a profusion of pale-green foliage and lanky stems.

Mark when he looked out of his window on the morning after his arrival thought that he was in fairyland. He looked at the rhododendrons; he looked at the raindrops of the night sparkling in the morning sun; he looked at the birds, and the blue sky, and across the valley to a hillside yellow with gorse. He hardly knew how to restrain himself from waking his mother with news of the wonderful sights and sounds of this first vision of the country; but when he saw a clump of daffodils nodding in the grass below, it was no longer possible to be considerate. Creeping to his mother's door, he gently opened it and listened. He meant only to whisper "Mother," but in his excitement he shouted, and she suddenly roused from sleep by his voice sat up in alarm.

"Mother, there are seven daffodils growing wild under my window."

"My darling, you frightened me so. I thought you'd hurt yourself."

"I don't know how my voice came big like that," said Mark apologetically. "I only meant it to be a whisper. But you weren't dreadfully frightened? Or were you?"

His mother smiled.

"No, not dreadfully frightened."

"Well, do you think I might dress myself and go in the garden?"

"You mustn't disturb grandfather."

49

"Oh, mother, of course not."

"All right, darling. But it's only six o'clock. Very early. And you must remember that grandfather may be tired. He had to wait an hour for us at Rosemarket last night."

"He's very nice, isn't he?"

Mark did not ask this tentatively; he really did think that his grandfather was very nice, although he had been puzzled and not a little frightened by his bushy black eyebrows slanting up to a profusion of white hair. Mark had never seen such eyebrows, and he wondered whatever grandfather's moustache would be like if it were allowed to grow.

"He's a dear," said Mrs. Lidderdale fervidly. "And now, sweetheart, if you really intend to dress yourself run along, because Mother wants to sleep a little longer if she can."

The only difficulty Mark had was with his flannel front, because one of the tapes vanished like a worm into its hole, and nothing in his armoury was at once long enough and pointed enough to hook it out again. Finally he decided that at such an early hour of the morning it would not matter if he went out exposing his vest, and soon he was wandering in that enchanted shrubbery of rhododendrons, alternating between imagining it to be the cave of Aladdin or the beach where Sinbad found all the pebbles to be precious stones. He wandered down hill through the thicket, listening with a sense of satisfaction to the increasing squelchiness of the peaty soil and feeling when the blackbirds fled at his approach with shrill quack and flapping wings much more like a hunter than he ever felt in the nursery at Lima Street. He resolved to bring his gun with him next time. This was just the place to find a hippopotamus, or even a crocodile. Mark had reached the bottom of the slope and discovered a dark sluggish stream full of decayed vegetable matter which was slowly oozing on its course. Or even a crocodile, he thought again; and he looked carefully at a half-submerged log. Or even a crocodile . . . yes, but people had often thought before that logs were not crocodiles and had not discovered their mistake until they were half way down the crocodile's throat. It had been amusing to fancy the existence of crocodiles when he was still close to the Vicarage, but suppose after all that there really were crocodiles living down here? Feeling a little ashamed of his cowardice, but glossing it over with an assumption of filial piety,

Mark turned to go back through the rhododendrons so as not to be late for breakfast. He would find out if any crocodiles had been seen about here lately, and if they had not, he would bring out his gun and . . . suddenly Mark was turned inside out by terror, for not twenty yards away there was without any possibility of self-deception a wild beast something between an ant-eater and a laughing hyena that with nose to the ground was evidently pursuing him, and what was worse was between him and home. There flashed through Mark's mind the memories of what other hunters had done in such situations, what ruses they had adopted if unarmed, what method of defence if armed; but in the very instant of the panoramic flash Mark did what countless uncelebrated hunters must have done, he ran in the opposition direction from his enemy. In this case it meant jumping over the stream, crocodile or not, and tearing his away through snowberries and brambles until he emerged on the moors at the bottom of the valley.

It was not until he had put half a dozen small streams between himself and the unknown beast that Mark paused to look round. Behind him the valley was lost in a green curve; before him another curve shut out the ultimate view. On his left the slope of the valley rose to the sky in tiers of blazing yellow gorse; to his right he could see the thickets through which he had emerged upon this verdant solitude. But beyond the thickets there was no sign of the Vicarage. There was not a living thing in sight; there was nothing except the song of larks high up and imperceptible against the steady morning sun that shed a benign warmth upon the world, and particularly upon the back of Mark's neck when he decided that his safest course was to walk in the direction of the valley's gradual widening and to put as many more streams as he could between him and the beast. Having once wetted himself to the knees, he began to take a pleasure in splashing through the vivid wet greenery. He wondered what he should behold at the next curve of the valley; without knowing it he began to walk more slowly, for the beauty of the day was drowsing his fears; the spell of earth was upon him. He walked more slowly, because he was passing through a bed of forget-me-nots, and he could not bear to blind one of those myriad blue eyes. He chose most carefully the destination of each step, and walking thus he did not notice that the valley would curve no more, but was opening at last. He looked up in a sudden consciousness of added space, and there serene as the sky above was spread the sea. Yesterday from the train Mark had had what was actually his first view of the sea; but the rain had taken all the colour out of it, and he had been thrilled rather by the word than by the fact. Now the word was nothing, the fact was everything. There it was within reach of him, blue as the pictures always made it. The streams of the valley had gathered into one, and Mark caring no more what happened to the forget-me-nots ran along the bank. This morning when the stream reached the shore it broke into twenty limpid rivulets, each one of which ploughed a separate silver furrow across the glistening sand until all were merged in ocean, mighty father of streams and men. Mark ran with the rivulets until he stood by the waves' edge. All was here of which he had read, shells and seaweed, rocks and cliffs and sand; he felt like Robinson Crusoe when he looked round him and saw nothing to break the solitude. Every point of the compass invited exploration and promised adventure. That white road running northward and rising with the cliffs, whither did it lead, what view was outspread where it dipped over the brow of the high table-land and disappeared into the naked sky beyond? The billowy towans sweeping up from the beach appeared to him like an illimitable prairie on which buffaloes and bison might roam. Whither led the sandy track, the summit of whose long diagonal was lost in the brightness of the morning sky? And surely that huddled grey building against an isolated green cliff must be grandfather's church of which his mother had often told him. Mark walked round the stone walls that held up the little churchyard and, entering by a gate on the farther side, he looked at the headstones and admired the feathery tamarisks that waved over the tombs. He was reading an inscription more legible than most on a headstone of highly polished granite, when he heard a voice behind him say:

"You mind what you're doing with that grave. That's my granfa's grave, that is, and if you touch it, I'll knock 'ee down."

Mark looked round and beheld a boy of about his own age and size in a pair of worn corduroy knickerbockers and a guernsey, who was regarding him from fierce blue eyes under a shock of curly yellow hair.

"I'm not touching it," Mark explained. Then something warned him that he must assert himself, if he wished to hold his own with this boy, and he added:

"But if I want to touch it, I will."

"Will 'ee? I say you won't do no such a thing then."

Mark seized the top of the headstone as firmly as his small hands would allow him and invited the boy to look what he was doing.

"Lev go," the boy commanded.

"I won't," said Mark.

"I'll make 'ee lev go."

"All right, make me."

The boy punched Mark's shoulder, and Mark punched blindly back, hitting his antagonist such a little way above the belt as to lay himself under the imputation of a foul blow. The boy responded by smacking Mark's face with his open palm; a moment later they were locked in a close struggle, heaving and panting and pushing until both of them tripped on the low railing of a grave and rolled over into a carefully tended bed of primroses, whence they were suddenly jerked to their feet, separated, and held at arm's length by an old man with a grey beard and a small round hole in the left temple.

"I'll learn you to scat up my tombs," said the old man shaking them violently. "'Tisn't the first time I've spoken to you, Cass Dale, and who's this? Who's this boy?"

"Oh, my gosh, look behind 'ee, Mr. Timbury. The bullocks is coming into the churchyard."

Mr. Timbury loosed his hold on the two boys as he turned, and Cass Dale catching hold of Mark's hand shouted:

"Come on, run, or he'll have us again."

They were too quick for the old man's wooden leg, and scrambling over the wall by the south porch of the church they were soon out of danger on the beach below.

"My gosh, I never heard him coming. If I hadn't have thought to sing out about the bullocks coming, he'd have laid that stick round us sure enough. He don't care where he hits anybody, old man Timbury don't. I belong to hear him tap-tapping along with his old wooden stump, but darn 'ee I never heard 'un coming this time."

The old man was leaning over the churchyard wall, shaking his stick and abusing them with violent words.

53

"That's fine language for a sexton," commented Cass Dale. "I'd be ashamed to swear like that, I would. You wouldn't hear my father swear like that. My father's a local preacher."

"So's mine," said Mark.

"Is he? Where to?"

"London."

"A minister, is he?"

"No, he's a priest."

"Does he kiss the Pope's toe? My gosh, if the Pope asked me to kiss his toe, I'd soon tell him to kiss something else, I would."

"My father doesn't kiss the Pope's toe," said Mark.

"I reckon he does then," Cass replied. "Passon Trehawke don't though. Passon Trehawke's some fine old chap. My father said he'd lev me go church of a morning sometimes if I'd a mind. My father belongs to come himself to the Harvest Home, but my granfa never came to church at all so long as he was alive. 'Time enough when I'm dead for that' he used to say. He was a big man down to the Chapel, my granfa was. Mostly when he did preach the maids would start screeching, so I've heard tell. But he were too old for preaching when I knawed 'un."

"My grandfather is the priest here," said Mark.

"There isn't no priest to Nancepean. Only Passon Trehawke."

"My grandfather's name is Trehawke."

"Is it, by gosh? Well, why for do 'ee call him a priest? He isn't a priest."

"Yes, he is."

"I say he isn't then. A parson isn't a priest. When I'm grown up I'm going to be a minister. What are you going to be?"

Mark had for some time past intended to be a keeper at the Zoological Gardens, but after his adventure with the wild beast in the thicket and this encounter with the self-confident Cass Dale he decided that he would not be a keeper but a parson. He informed Cass of his intention.

"Well, if you're a parson and I'm a minister," said Cass, "I'll bet everyone comes to listen to me preaching and none of 'em don't go to hear you."

"I wouldn't care if they didn't," Mark affirmed.

"You wouldn't care if you had to preach to a parcel of empty chairs and benches?" exclaimed Cass.

"St. Francis preached to the trees," said Mark. "And St. Anthony preached to the fishes."

"They must have been a couple of loonies."

"They were saints," Mark insisted.

"Saints, were they? Well, my father doesn't think much of saints. My father says he reckons saints is the same as other people, only a bit worse if anything. Are you saved?"

"What from?" Mark asked.

"Why, from Hell of course. What else would you be saved from?"

"You might be saved from a wild beast," Mark pointed out. "I saw a wild beast this morning. A wild beast with a long nose and a sort of grey colour."

"That wasn't a wild beast. That was an old badger."

"Well, isn't a badger a wild beast?"

Cass Dale laughed scornfully.

"My gosh, if that isn't a good one! I suppose you'd say a fox was a wild beast?"

"No, I shouldn't," said Mark, repressing an inclination to cry, so much mortified was he by Cass Dale's contemptuous tone.

"All the same," Cass went on. "It don't do to play around with badgers. There was a chap over to Lanbaddern who was chased right across the Rose one evening by seven badgers. He was in a muck of sweat when he got home. But one old badger isn't nothing."

Mark had been counting on his adventure with the wild beast to justify his long absence should he be reproached by his mother on his return to the Vicarage. The way it had been disposed of by Cass Dale as an old badger made him wonder if after all it would be accepted as such a good excuse.

"I ought to be going home," he said. "But I don't think I remember the way."

"To Passon Trehawke's?"

Mark nodded.

"I'll show 'ee," Cass volunteered, and he led the way past the mouth of the stream to the track half way up the slope of the valley.

"Ever eat furze flowers?" asked Cass, offering Mark some that he had pulled off in passing. "Kind of nutty taste they've got, I reckon. I belong to eat them most days."

Mark acquired the habit and agreed with Cass that the blossoms were delicious.

"Only you don't want to go eating everything you see," Cass warned him. "I reckon you'd better always ask me before you eat anything. But furze flowers is all right. I've eaten thousands. Next Friday's Good Friday."

"I know," said Mark reverently.

"We belong to get limpets every Good Friday. Are you coming with me?"

"Won't I be in church?" Mark inquired with memories of Good Friday in Lima Street.

"Yes, I suppose they'll have some sort of a meeting down Church," said Cass. "But you can come afterward. I'll wait for 'ee in Dollar Cove. That's the next cove to Church Cove on the other side of the Castle Cliff, and there's some handsome cave there. Years ago my granfa knawed a chap who saw a mermaid combing out her hair in Dollar Cove. But there's no mermaids been seen lately round these parts. My father says he reckons since they scat up the apple orchards and give over drinking cider they won't see no more mermaids to Nancepean. Have you signed the pledge?"

"What's that?" Mark asked.

"My gosh, don't you know what the pledge is? Why, that's when you put a blue ribbon in your buttonhole and swear you won't drink nothing all your days."

"But you'd die," Mark objected. "People must drink."

"Water, yes, but there's no call for any one to drink anything only water. My father says he reckons more folk have gone to hell from drink than anything. You ought to hear him preach about drink. Why, when it gets known in the village that Sam Dale's going to preach on drink there isn't a seat down Chapel. Well, I tell 'ee he frightened me last time I sat under him. That's why old man Timbury has it in for me whenever he gets the chance."

Mark looked puzzled.

"Old man Timbury keeps the Hanover Inn. And he reckons my pa's preaching spoils his trade for a week. That's why he's sexton to the church. 'Tis the only way he can get even with the chapel folk. He used to be in the Navy, and he lost his leg and got that hole in his head in a war with the Rooshians. You'll hear him talking big about the Rooshians sometimes. My father says anybody listening to old Steve Timbury would think he'd fought with the Devil, instead of a lot of poor leary Rooshians."

Mark was so much impressed by the older boy's confident chatter that when he arrived back at the Vicarage and found his mother at breakfast he tried the effect of an imitation of it upon her.

"Darling boy, you mustn't excite yourself too much," she warned him. "Do try to eat a little more and talk a little less."

"But I can go out again with Cass Dale, can't I, mother, as soon as I've finished my breakfast? He said he'd wait for me and he's going to show me where we might find some silver dollars. He says they're five times as big as a shilling and he's going to show me where there's a fox's hole on the cliffs and he's . . ."

"But, Mark dear, don't forget," interrupted his mother who was feeling faintly jealous of this absorbing new friend, "don't forget that I can show you lots of the interesting things to see round here. I was a little girl here myself and used to play with Cass Dale's father when he was a little boy no bigger than Cass."

Just then grandfather came into the room and Mark was instantly dumb; he had never been encouraged to talk much at breakfast in Lima Street. He did, however, eye his grandfather from over the top of his cup, and he found him less alarming in the morning than he had supposed him to be last night. Parson Trehawke kept reaching across the table for the various things he wanted until his daughter jumped up and putting her arms round his neck said:

"Dearest father, why don't you ask Mark or me to pass you what you want?"

"So long alone. So long alone," murmured Parson Trehawke with an embarrassed smile and Mark observed with a thrill that when he smiled he looked exactly like his mother, and had Mark but known it exactly like himself.

"And it's so wonderful to be back here," went on Mrs. Lidderdale, "with everything looking just the same. As for Mark, he's so happy that—Mark, do tell grandfather how much you're enjoying yourself."

Mark gulped several times, and finally managed to mutter a confirmation of his mother's statement.

"And he's already made friends with Cass Dale."

"He's intelligent but like his father he thinks he knows more than he does," commented Parson Trehawke. "However, he'll make quite a good companion for this young gentleman."

As soon as breakfast was over Mark rushed out to join Cass Dale, who sitting crosslegged under an ilex-tree was peeling a pithy twig for a whistle.

CHAPTER VII

LIFE AT NANCEPEAN

For six years Mark lived with his mother and his grandfather at Nancepean, hearing nothing of his father except that he had gone out as a missionary to the diocese of some place in Africa he could never remember, so little interested was he in his father. His education was shared between his two guardians, or rather his academic education; the real education came either from what he read for himself in his grandfather's ancient library of from what he learnt of Cass Dale, who was much more than merely informative in the manner of a sixpenny encyclopædia. The Vicar, who made himself responsible for the Latin and later on for the Greek, began with Horace, his own favourite author, from the rapid translation aloud of whose Odes and Epodes one after another he derived great pleasure, though it is doubtful if his grandson would have learnt much Latin if Mrs. Lidderdale had not supplemented Horace with the Primer and Henry's Exercises. However, if Mark did not acquire a vocabulary, he greatly enjoyed listening to his grandfather's melodious voice chanting forth that sonorous topography of Horace, while the green windows of the study winked every other minute from the flight past of birds in the garden. His grandfather would stop and ask what bird it was, because he loved birds even better than he loved Horace. And if Mark was tired of Latin he used to say that he wasn't sure, but that he thought it was a lesser-spotted woodpecker or a shrike or any one of the birds that experience taught him would always distract his grandfather's attention from anything that he was doing in order that he might confirm or contradict the rumour. People who are much interested in birds are less sociable than other naturalists.

Their hobby demands a silent and solitary pursuit of knowledge, and the presence of human beings is prejudicial to their success. Parson Trehawke found that Mark's company was not so much of a handicap as he would have supposed; on the contrary he began to find it an advantage, because his grandson's eyes were sharp and his observation if he chose accurate: Parson Trehawke, who was growing old, began to rely upon his help. It was only when Mark was tired of listening to the translation of Horace that he called thrushes shrikes: when he was wandering over the cliffs or tramping beside his grandfather across the Rhos, he was severely sceptical of any rarity and used to make short work of the old gentleman's Dartford warblers and fire-crested wrens.

It was usually over birds if ever Parson Trehawke quarrelled with his parishioners. Few of them attended his services, but they spoke well of him personally, and they reckoned that he was a fine old boy was Parson. They would not however abandon their beastly habit of snaring wildfowl in winter with fish-hooks, and many a time had Mark seen his grandfather stand on the top of Pendhu Cliff, a favourite place to bait the hooks, cursing the scattered white houses of the village below as if it were one of the cities of the plain.

Although the people of Nancepean except for a very few never attended the services in their church they liked to be baptized and married within its walls, and not for anything would they have been buried outside the little churchyard by the sea. About three years after Mark's arrival his grandfather had a great fight over a burial. The blacksmith, a certain William Day, died, and although he had never been inside St. Tugdual's Church since he was married, his relations set great store by his being buried there and by Parson Trehawke's celebrating the last rites.

"Never," vowed the Parson. "Never while I live will I lay that blackguard in my churchyard."

The elders of the village remonstrated with him, pointing out that although the late Mr. Day was a pillar of the Chapel it had ever been the custom in Nancepean to let the bones of the most obstinate Wesleyan rest beside his forefathers.

"Wesleyan!" shouted the Parson. "Who cares if he was a Jew? I won't have my churchyard defiled by that blackguard's corpse. Only a week before he died, I saw him with my own eyes fling two or three pieces of white-hot metal to some ducks that were looking for worms in the ditch outside his smithy, and the wretched birds gobbled them down and died in agony. I cursed him where he stood, and the judgment of God has struck him low, and never shall he rest in holy ground if I can keep him out of it."

The elders of the village expressed their astonishment at Mr. Trehawke's unreasonableness. William Day had been a God-fearing and upright man all his life with no scandal upon his reputation unless it were the rumour that he had got with child a half lunatic servant in his house, and that was never proved. Was a man to be refused Christian burial because he had once played a joke on some ducks? And what would Parson Trehawke have said to Jesus Christ about the joke he played on the Gadarene swine?

There is nothing that irritates a Kelt so much as the least consideration for any animal, and there was not a man in the whole of the Rhos peninsula who did not sympathize with the corpse of William Day. In the end the dispute was settled by a neighbouring parson's coming over and reading the burial service over the blacksmith's grave. Mark apprehended that his grandfather resented bitterly the compromise as his fellow parson called it, the surrender as he himself called it. This was the second time that Mark had witnessed the defeat of a superior being whom he had been taught to regard as invincible, and it slightly clouded that perfect serenity of being grown up to which, like most children, he looked forward as the end of life's difficulties. He argued the justification of his grandfather's action with Cass Dale, and he found himself confronted by the workings of a mind naturally nonconformist with its rebellion against authority, its contempt of tradition, its blend of self-respect and self-importance. When Mark found himself in danger of being beaten in argument, he took to his fists, at which method of settling a dispute Cass Dale proved equally his match; and the end of it was that Mark found himself upside down in a furze bush with nothing to console him but an unalterable conviction that he was right and, although tears of pain and mortification were streaming down his cheeks, a fixed resolve to renew the argument as soon as he was the right way up again, and if necessary the struggle as well.

Luckily for the friendship between Mark and Cass, a friendship that was awarded a mystical significance by their two surnames,

Lidderdale and Dale, Parson Trehawke, soon after the burial episode, came forward as the champion of the Nancepean Fishing Company in a quarrel with those pirates from Lanyon, the next village down the coast. Inasmuch as a pilchard catch worth £800 was in dispute, feeling ran high between the Nancepean Daws and the Lanyon Gulls. All the inhabitants of the Rhos parishes were called after various birds or animals that were supposed to indicate their character; and when Parson Trehawke's championship of his own won the day, his parishioners came to church in a body on the following Sunday and put one pound five shillings and tenpence halfpenny in the plate. The reconciliation between the two boys took place with solemn preliminary handshakes followed by linking of arms as of old after Cass reckoned audibly to Mark who was standing close by that Parson Trehawke was a grand old chap, the grandest old chap from Rosemarket to Rose Head. That afternoon Mark went back to tea with Cass Dale, and over honey with Cornish cream they were brothers again. Samuel Dale, the father of Cass, was a typical farmer of that part of the country with his fifty or sixty acres of land, the capital to work which had come from fish in the fat pilchard years. Cass was his only son, and he had an ambition to turn him into a full-fledged minister. He had lost his wife when Cass was a baby, and it pleased him to think that in planning such a position for the boy he was carrying out the wishes of the mother whom outwardly he so much resembled. For housekeeper Samuel Dale had an unmarried sister whom her neighbours accused of putting on too much gentility before her nephew's advancement warranted such airs. Mark liked Aunt Keran and accepted her hospitality as a tribute to himself rather than to his position as the grandson of the Vicar. Miss Dale had been a schoolmistress before she came to keep house for her brother, and she worked hard to supplement what learning Cass could get from the village school before, some three years after Mark came to Nancepean, he was sent to Rosemarket Grammar School.

Mark was anxious to attend the Grammar School with Cass; but Mrs. Lidderdale's dread nowadays was that her son would acquire a West country burr, and it was considered more prudent, economically and otherwise, to let him go on learning with his grandfather and herself. Mark missed Cass when he went to school in Rosemarket, because there was no such thing as playing truant there, and it was so far away that Cass did not come home for the midday meal. But in summertime, Mark used to wait for him outside the town, where a lane branched from the main road into the unfrequented country behind the Rose Pool and took them the longest way home along the banks on the Nancepean side, which were low and rushy unlike those on the Rosemarket side, which were steep and densely wooded. The great water, though usually described as heart-shaped, was really more like a pair of Gothic arches, the green cusp between which was crowned by a lonely farmhouse, El Dorado of Mark and his friend, and the base of which was the bar of shingle that kept out the sea. There was much to beguile the boys on the way home, whether it was the sight of strange wildfowl among the reeds, or the exploration of a ruined cottage set in an ancient cherry-orchard, or the sailing of paper boats, or even the mere delight of lying on the grass and listening above the murmur of insects to the water nagging at the sedge. So much indeed was there to beguile them that, if after sunset the Pool had not been a haunted place, they would have lingered there till nightfall. Sometimes indeed they did miscalculate the distance they had come and finding themselves likely to be caught by twilight they would hurry with eyes averted from the grey water lest the kelpie should rise out of the depths and drown them. There were men and women now alive in Nancepean who could tell of this happening to belated wayfarers, and it was Mark who discovered that such a beast was called a kelpie. Moreover, the bar where earlier in the evening it was pleasant to lie and pluck the yellow sea-poppies, listening to tales of wrecks and buried treasure and bygone smuggling, was no place at all in the chill of twilight; moreover, when the bar had been left behind and before the coastguards' cottages came into sight there was a two-mile stretch of lonely cliff that was a famous haunt of ghosts. Drowned light dragoons whose bodies were tossed ashore here a hundred years ago, wreckers revisiting the scene of their crimes, murdered excisemen . . . it was not surprising that the boys hurried along the narrow path, whistling to keep up their spirits and almost ready to cry for help if nothing more dangerous than a moth fanned their pale cheeks in passing. And after this Mark had to undo alone the nine gates between the Vicarage and Nancepean, though Cass would go with him as far along his road as the last light of the village could be seen, and what was more stay there whistling for as long as Mark could hear the heartening sound.

But if these adventures demanded the companionship of Cass, the inspiration of them was Mark's mother. Just as in the nursery games of Lima Street it had always been she who had made it worth while to play with his grenadiers, which by the way had perished in a troopship like their predecessors the light dragoons a century before, sinking one by one and leaving nothing behind except their cork-stands bobbing on the waves.

Mrs. Lidderdale knew every legend of the coast, so that it was thrilling to sit beside her and turn over the musty pages of the church registers, following from equinox to equinox in the entries of the burials the wrecks since the year 1702:

> The bodies of fifteen seamen from the brigantine *Ann Pink* wrecked in Church Cove, on the afternoon of Dec. 19, 1757.
> The body of a child washed into Pendhu Cove from the high seas during the night of Jan. 24, 1760.
> The body of an unknown sailor, the breast tattooed with a heart and the initials M. V. found in Hanover Cove on the morning of March 3, 1801.

Such were the inscriptions below the wintry dates of two hundred years, and for each one Mark's mother had a moving legend of fortune's malice. She had tales too of treasure, from the golden doubloons of a Spanish galleon wrecked on the Rose Bar in the sixteenth century to the silver dollars of Portugal, a million of them, lost in the narrow cove on the other side of the Castle Cliff in the lee of which was built St. Tugdual's Church. At low spring tides it was possible to climb down and sift the wet sand through one's fingers on the chance of finding a dollar, and when the tide began to rise it was jolly to climb back to the top of the cliff and listen to tales of mermaids while a gentle wind blew the perfume of the sea-campion along the grassy slopes. It was here that Mark first heard the story of the two princesses who were wrecked in what was now called Church Cove and of how they were washed up on the cliff and vowed to build a church in gratitude to God and St. Tugdual on the very spot where they escaped from the sea, of how they quarrelled about the site because each sister wished to commemorate the exact spot where she was saved, and of how finally one built the tower on her spot and the other built the church on hers, which was the reason why the church and the tower were not joined to this day. When Mark went home that afternoon, he searched among his grandfather's books until he found the story of St. Tugdual who, it seemed, was a holy man in Brittany, so holy that he was summoned to be Pope of Rome. When he had been Pope for a few months, an angel appeared to him and said that he must come back at once to Brittany, because since he went to Rome all the women were become barren.

"But how am I to go back all the way from Rome to Brittany?" St. Tugdual asked.

"I have a white horse waiting for you," the angel replied.

And sure enough there was a beautiful white horse with wings, which carried St. Tugdual back to Brittany in a few minutes.

"What does it mean when a woman becomes barren?" Mark inquired of his mother.

"It means when she does not have any more children, darling," said Mrs. Lidderdale, who did not believe in telling lies about anything.

And because she answered her son simply, her son did not perplex himself with shameful speculations, but was glad that St. Tugdual went back home so that the women of Brittany were able to have children again.

Everything was simple at Nancepean except the parishioners; but Mark was still too young and too simple himself to apprehend their complicacy. The simplest thing of all was the Vicar's religion, and at an age when for most children religion means being dressed up to go into the drawing-room and say how d'you do to God, Mark was allowed to go to church in his ordinary clothes and after church to play at whatever he wanted to play, so that he learned to regard the assemblage of human beings to worship God as nothing more remarkable than the song of birds. He was too young to have experienced yet a personal need of religion; but he had already been touched by that grace of fellowship which is conferred upon a small congregation, the individual members of which are in church to please themselves rather than to impress others. This was always the case in the church of Nancepean, which had to contend not merely with the popularity of methodism, but also with the situation of the Chapel in the middle of the village. On the dark December evenings there would be perhaps not more than half a dozen worshippers, each one of whom would have brought his own candle and stuck it on the shelf of the pew. The organist would have two candles for the harmonium; the choir of three little boys and one little girl would have two between them; the altar would have two; the Vicar would have two. But when all the candle-light was put together, it left most of the church in shadow; indeed, it scarcely even illuminated the space between the worshippers, so that each one seemed wrapped in a golden aura of prayer, most of all when at Evensong the people knelt in silence for a minute while the sound of the sea without rose and fell and the noise of the wind scuttling through the ivy on the walls was audible. When the congregation had gone out and the Vicar was standing at the churchyard gate saying "good night," Mark used to think that they must all be feeling happy to go home together up the long hill to Pendhu and down into twinkling Nancepean. And it did not matter whether it was a night of clear or clouded moonshine or a night of windy stars or a night of darkness; for when it was dark he could always look back from the valley road and see a company of lanthorns moving homeward; and that more than anything shed upon his young spirit the grace of human fellowship and the love of mankind.

CHAPTER VIII

THE WRECK

One wild night in late October of the year before he would be thirteen, Mark was lying awake hoping, as on such nights he always hoped, to hear somebody shout "A wreck! A wreck!" A different Mark from that one who used to lie trembling in Lima Street lest he should hear a shout of "Fire! or Thieves!"

And then it happened! It happened as a hundred times he had imagined its happening, so exactly that he could hardly believe for a moment he was not dreaming. There was the flash of a lanthorn on the ceiling, a thunderous, knocking on the Vicarage door. Mark leapt out of bed; flinging open his window through which the wind rushed in like a flight of angry birds, he heard voices below in the garden shouting "Parson! Parson! Parson Trehawke! There's a brig driving in fast toward Church Cove." He did not wait to hear more, but dashed along the passage to rouse first his grandfather, then his mother, and then Emma, the Vicar's old cook.

"And you must get soup ready," he cried, standing over the old woman in his flannel pyjamas and waving his arms excitedly, while downstairs the cuckoo popped in and out of his door in the clock twelve times. Emma blinked at him in terror, and Mark pulled off all the bedclothes to convince the old woman that he was not playing a practical joke. Then he rushed back to his own room and began to dress for dear life.

"Mother," he shouted, while he was dressing, "the Captain can sleep in my bed, if he isn't drowned, can't he?"

"Darling, do you really want to go down to the sea on such a night?"

"Oh, mother," he gasped, "I'm practically dressed. And you will see that Emma has lots of hot soup ready, won't you? Because it'll be much better to bring all the crew back here. I don't think they'd want to walk all that way over Pendhu to Nancepean after they'd been wrecked, do you?"

"Well, you must ask grandfather first before you make arrangements for his house."

"Grandfather's simply tearing into his clothes; Ernie Hockin and Joe Dunstan have both got lanthorns, and I'll carry ours, so if one blows out we shall be all right. Oh, mother, the wind's simply shrieking through the trees. Can you hear it?"

"Yes, dearest, I certainly can. I think you'd better shut your windows. It's blowing everything about in your room most uncomfortably."

Mark's soul expanded in gratitude to God when he found himself neither in a dream nor in a story, but actually, and without any possibility of self-deception hurrying down the drive toward the sea beside Ernie and Joe, who had come from the village to warn the Vicar of the wreck and were wearing oilskins and sou'westers, thus striking the keynote as it were of the night's adventure. At first in the shelter of the holm-oaks the storm seemed far away overhead; but when they turned the corner and took the road along the valley, the wind caught them full in the face and Mark was blown back violently against the swinging gate of the drive. The light of the lanthorns shining on a rut in the road showed a field-mouse hurrying inland before the rushing gale. Mark bent double to force himself to keep up with the others, lest somebody should think, by his inability to maintain an equal pace that he ought to follow the field-mouse back home. After they had struggled on for a while a bend of the valley gave them a few minutes of easy progress and Mark listened while Ernie Hockin explained to the Vicar what had happened:

"Just before dark Eddowes the coastguard said he reckoned there was a brig making very heavy weather of it and he shouldn't be surprised if she come ashore tonight. Couldn't seem to beat out of the bay noways, he said. And afterwards about nine o'clock when me and Joe here and some of the chaps were in the bar to the Hanover, Eddowes come in again and said she was in a bad way by the looks of her last thing he saw, and he telephoned along to

Lanyon to ask if they'd seen her down to the lifeboat house. They reckoned she was all right to the lifeboat, and old man Timbury who do always go against anything Eddowes do say shouted that of course she was all right because he'd taken a look at her through his glass before it grew dark. Of course she was all right. 'She's on a lee shore,' said Eddowes. 'It don't take a coastguard to tell that,' said old man Timbury. And then they got to talking one against the other the same as they belong, and they'd soon got back to the same old talk whether Jackie Fisher was the finest admiral who ever lived or no use at all. 'What's the good in your talking to me?' old man Timbury was saying. 'Why afore you was born I've seen' . . . and we all started in to shout 'ships o' the line, frigates, and cavattes,' because we belong to mock him like that, when somebody called 'Hark, listen, wasn't that a rocket?' That fetched us all outside into the road where we stood listening. The wind was blowing harder than ever, and there was a parcel of sea rising. You could hear it against Shag Rock over the wind. Eddowes, he were a bit upset to think he should have been talking and not a-heard the rocket. But there wasn't a light in the sky, and when we went home along about half past nine we saw Eddowes again and he said he'd been so far as Church Cove and should walk up along to the Bar. No mistake, Mr. Trehawke, he's a handy chap is Eddowes for the coastguard job. And then about eleven o'clock he saw two rockets close in to Church Cove and he come running back and telephoned to Lanyon, but they said no one couldn't launch a boat tonight, and Eddowes he come banging on the doors and windows shouting 'A Wreck' and some of us took ropes along with Eddowes, and me and Joe here come and fetched you along. Eddowes said he's afeard she'll strike in Dollar Cove unless she's lucky and come ashore in Church Cove."

"How's the tide?" asked the Vicar.

"About an hour of the ebb," said Ernie Hockin. "And the moon's been up this hour and more."

Just then the road turned the corner, and the world became a waste of wind and spindrift driving inland. The noise of the gale made it impossible for anybody to talk, and Mark was left wondering whether the ship had actually struck or not. The wind drummed in his ears, the flying grit and gravel and spray stung his face; but he struggled on hoping that this midnight walk would not come to an abrupt end by his grandfather's declining to go any farther. Above the drumming of the wind the roar of the sea became more audible every moment; the spume was thicker; the end of the valley, ordinarily the meeting-place of sand and grass and small streams with their yellow flags and forget-me-nots, was a desolation of white foam beyond which against the cliffs showing black in the nebulous moonlight the breakers leapt high with frothy tongues. Mark thought that they resembled immense ghosts clawing up to reach the summit of the cliff. It was incredible that this hell-broth was Church Cove.

"Hullo!" yelled Ernie Hockin. "Here's the bridge."

It was true. One wave at the moment of high tide had swept snarling over the stream and carried the bridge into the meadow beyond.

"We'll have to get round by the road," shouted the Vicar.

They turned to the right across a ploughed field and after scrambling through the hedge emerged in the comparative shelter of the road down from Pendhu.

"I hope the churchyard wall is all right," said the Vicar. "I never remember such a night since I came to Nancepean."

"Sure 'nough, 'tis blowing very fierce," Joe Dunstan agreed. "But don't you worry about the wall, Mr. Trehawke. The worst of the water is broken by the Castle and only comes in sideways, as you might say."

When they drew near the gate of the churchyard, the rain of sand and small pebbles was agonizing, as it swept across up the low sandstone cliffs on that side of the Castle. Two or three excited figures shouted for them to hurry because she was going to strike in Dollar Cove, and everybody began to scramble up the grassy slope, clutching at the tuffets of thrift to aid their progress. It was calm here in the lee; and Mark panting up the face thought of those two princesses who were wrecked here ages ago, and he understood now why one of them had insisted on planting the tower deep in the foundation of this green fortress against the wind and weather. While he was thinking this, his head came above the sky line, his breath left him at the assault of the wind, and he had to crawl on all fours toward the sea. He reached the edge of the cliff just as something like the wings of a gigantic bat flapped across the dim wet moonlight, and before he realized that this was the brig he heard

70

the crashing of her spars. The watchers stood up against the wind, battling with it to fling lines in the vain hope of saving some sailor who was being churned to death in that dreadful creaming of the sea below. Yes, and there were forms of men visible on board; two had climbed the mainmast, which crashed before they could clutch at the ropes that were being flung to them from land, crashed and carried them down shrieking into the surge. Mark found it hard to believe that last summer he had spent many sunlit hours dabbling in the sand for silver dollars of Portugal lost perhaps on such a night as this a hundred years ago, exactly where these two poor mariners were lost. A few minutes after the mainmast the hull went also; but in the nebulous moonlight nothing could be seen of any bodies alive or dead, nothing except wreckage tossing upon the surge. The watchers on the cliff turned away from the wind to gather new breath and give their cheeks a rest from the stinging fragments of rock and earth. Away up over the towans they could see the bobbing lanthorns of men hurrying down from Chypie where news of the wreck had reached; and on the road from Lanyon they could see lanthorns on the other side of Church Cove waiting until the tide had ebbed far enough to let them cross the beach.

Suddenly the Vicar shouted:

"I can see a poor fellow hanging on to a ledge of rock. Bring a rope! Bring a rope!"

Eddowes the coastguard took charge of the operation, and Mark with beating pulses watched the end of the rope touch the huddled form below. But either from exhaustion or because he feared to let go of the slippery ledge for one moment the sailor made no attempt to grasp the rope. The men above shouted to him, begged him to make an effort; but he remained there inert.

"Somebody must go down with the rope and get a slip knot under his arms," the Vicar shouted.

Nobody seemed to pay attention to this proposal, and Mark wondered if he was the only one who had heard it. However, when the Vicar repeated his suggestion, Eddowes came forward, knelt down by the edge of the cliff, shook himself like a bather who is going to plunge into what he knows will be very cold water, and then vanished down the rope. Everybody crawled on hand and knees to see what would happen. Mark prayed that Eddowes, who was a great friend of his, would not come to any harm, but that he would rescue the sailor and be given the Albert medal for saving life. It was Eddowes who had made him medal wise. The coastguard struggled to slip the loop under the man's shoulders along his legs; but it must have been impossible, for presently he made a signal to be raised.

"I can't do it alone," he shouted. "He's got a hold like a limpet."

Nobody seemed anxious to suppose that the addition of another rescuer would be any more successful.

"If there was two of us," Eddowes went on, "we might do something."

The people on the cliff shook their heads doubtfully.

"Isn't anybody coming down along with me to have a try?" the coastguard demanded at the top of his voice.

Mark did not hear his grandfather's reply; he only saw him go over the cliff's edge at the end of one rope while Eddowes went down on another. A minute later the slipknot came untied (or that was how the accident was explained) and the Vicar went to join the drowned mariners, dislodging as he fell the man whom he had tried to save, so that of the crew of the brig *Happy Return* not one ever came to port.

It would be difficult to exaggerate the effect upon Mark Lidderdale of that night. He was twelve years old at the time; but the years in Cornwall had retarded that precocious development to which he seemed destined by the surroundings of his early childhood in Lima Street, and in many ways he was hardly any older than he was when he left London. In after years he looked back with gratitude upon the shock he received from what was as it were an experience of the material impact of death, because it made him think about death, not morbidly as so many children and young people will, but with the apprehension of something that really does come in a moment and for which it is necessary for every human being to prepare his soul. The platitudes of age may often be for youth divine revelations, and there is nothing so stimulating as the unaided apprehension of a great commonplace of existence. The awe with which Mark was filled that night was too vast to evaporate in sentiment, and when two days after this there came news from Africa that his father had died of black-water fever that awe was crystallized indeed. Mark looking round at his small world perceived that nobody was safe. Tomorrow his mother might die; tomorrow he might die himself. In any case the death of his grandfather would have meant a profound change in the future of his mother's life and his own; the living of Nancepean would fall to some other priest and with it the house in which they lived. Parson Trehawke had left nothing of any value except Gould's *Birds of Great Britain* and a few other works of ornithology. The furniture of the Vicarage was rich neither in quality nor in quantity. Three or four hundred pounds was the most his daughter could inherit. She had spoken to Mark of their poverty, because in her dismay for the future of her son she had no heart to pretend that the dead man's money was of little importance.

"I must write and ask your father what we ought to do." . . . She stopped in painful awareness of the possessive pronoun. Mark was unresponsive, until there came the news from Africa, which made him throw his arms about his mother's neck while she was still alive. Mrs. Lidderdale, whatever bitterness she may once have felt for the ruin of her married life, shed fresh tears of sorrow for her husband, and supposing that Mark's embrace was the expression of his sympathy wept more, as people will when others are sorry for them, and then still more because the future for Mark seemed hopeless. How was she to educate him? How clothe him? How feed him even? At her age where and how could she earn money? She reproached herself with having been too ready out of sensitiveness to sacrifice Mark to her own pride. She had had no right to leave her husband and live in the country like this. She should have repressed her own emotion and thought only of the family life, to the maintenance of which by her marriage she had committed herself. At first it had seemed the best thing for Mark; but she should have remembered that her father could not live for ever and that one day she would have to face the problem of life without his help and his hospitality. She began to imagine that the disaster of that stormy night had been contrived by God to punish her, and she prayed to Him that her chastisement should not be increased, that at least her son might be spared to her.

Mrs. Lidderdale was able to stay on at the Vicarage for several weeks, because the new Vicar of Nancepean was not able to take over his charge immediately. This delay gave her time to hold a sale of her father's furniture, at which the desire of the neighbours to be generous fought with their native avarice, so that in the end the furniture fetched neither more nor less than had been expected, which was little enough. She kept back enough to establish herself and Mark in rooms, should she be successful in finding some unfurnished rooms sufficiently cheap to allow her to take them, although how she was going to live for more than two years on what she had was a riddle of which after a month of sleepless nights she had not found the solution.

In the end, and as Mrs. Lidderdale supposed in answer to her prayers, the solution was provided unexpectedly in the following letter:

> Haverton House,
> Elmhurst Road,
> Slowbridge.
> November 29th.
>
> Dear Grace,
>
> I have just received a letter from James written when he was at the point of death in Africa. It appears that in his zeal to convert the heathen to Popery he omitted to make any provision for his wife and child, so that in the event of his death, unless either your relatives or his relatives came forward to support you I was given to understand that you would be destitute. I recently read in the daily paper an account of the way in which your father Mr. Trehawke lost his life, and I caused inquiries to be made in Rosemarket about your prospects. These my informant tells me are not any too bright. You will, I am sure, pardon my having made these inquiries without reference to you, but I did not feel justified in offering you and my nephew a home with my sister Helen and myself unless I had first assured myself that some such offer was necessary. You are probably aware that for many years my brother James and myself have not been on the best of terms. I on my side found his religious teaching so eccentric as to repel me; he on his side was so bigoted that he could not tolerate my tacit disapproval. Not being a Ritualist but an Evangelical, I can perhaps bring myself more easily to forgive my brother's faults and at the

same time indulge my theories of duty, as opposed to forms and ceremonies, theories that if carried out by everybody would soon transform our modern Christianity. You are no doubt a Ritualist, and your son has no doubt been educated in the same school. Let me hasten to give you my word that I shall not make the least attempt to interfere either with your religious practices or with his. The quarrel between myself and James was due almost entirely to James' inability to let me and my opinions alone.

I am far from being a rich man, in fact I may say at once that I am scarcely even "comfortably off" as the phrase goes. It would therefore be outside my capacity to undertake the expense of any elaborate education for your son; but my own school, which while it does not pretend to compete with some of the fashionable establishments of the time is I venture to assert a first class school and well able to send your son into the world at the age of sixteen as well equipped, and better equipped than he would be if he went to one of the famous public schools. I possess some influence with a firm of solicitors, and I have no doubt that when my nephew, who is I believe now twelve years old, has had the necessary schooling I shall be able to secure him a position as an articled clerk, from which if he is honest and industrious he may be able to rise to the position of a junior partner. If you have saved anything from the sale of your father's effects I should advise you to invest the sum. However small it is, you will find the extra money useful, for as I remarked before I shall not be able to afford to do more than lodge and feed you both, educate your son, find him in clothes, and start him in a career on the lines I have already indicated. My local informant tells me that you have kept back a certain amount of your father's furniture in order to take lodgings elsewhere. As this will now be unnecessary I hope that you will sell the rest. Haverton House is sufficiently furnished, and we should not be able to find room for any more furniture. I suggest your coming to us next Friday. It will be easiest for you to take the fast train up to Paddington when you will be able to catch the 6.45 to Slowbridge arriving at 7.15. We usually dine at 7.30, but on Friday dinner will be at 8 p.m. in order to give you plenty of time. Helen sends her love. She would have written also, but I assured her that one letter was enough, and that a very long one.

> Your affectionate brother-in-law,
>
> Henry Lidderdale.

Mrs. Lidderdale would no doubt have criticized this letter more sharply if she had not regarded it as inspired, almost actually written by the hand of God. Whatever in it was displeasing to her she accepted as the Divine decree, and if anybody had pointed out the inconsistency of some of the opinions therein expressed with its Divine authorship, she would have dismissed the objection as made by somebody who was incapable of comprehending the mysterious action of God.

"Mark," she called to her son. "What do you think has happened? Your Uncle Henry has offered us a home. I want you to write to him like a dear boy and thank him for his kindness." She explained in detail what Uncle Henry intended to do for them; but Mark would not be enthusiastic. He on his side had been praying to God to put it into the mind of Samuel Dale to offer him a job on his farm; Slowbridge was a poor substitute for that.

"Where is Slowbridge?" he asked in a gloomy voice.

"It's a fairly large place near London," his mother told him. "It's near Eton and Windsor and Stoke Poges where Gray wrote his Elegy, which we learned last summer. You remember, don't you?" she asked anxiously, for she wanted Mark to cut a figure with his uncle.

"Wolfe liked it," said Mark. "And I like it too," he added ungraciously. He wished that he could have said he hated it; but Mark always found it difficult to tell a lie about his personal feelings, or about any facts that involved him in a false position.

"And now before you go down to tea with Cass Dale, you will write to your uncle, won't you, and show me the letter?"

Mark groaned.

"It's so difficult to thank people. It makes me feel silly."

"Well, darling, mother wants you to. So sit down like a dear boy and get it done."

"I think my nib is crossed."

"Is it? You'll find another in my desk."

"But, mother, yours are so thick."

"Please, Mark, don't make any more excuses. Don't you want to do everything you can to help me just now?"

"Yes, of course," said Mark penitently, and sitting down in the window he stared out at the yellow November sky, and at the magpies flying busily from one side of the valley to the other.

> The Vicarage,
> Nancepean,
> South Cornwall.
>
> My dear Uncle Henry,
>
> Thank you very much for your kind invitation to come and live with you. We should enjoy it very much. I am going to tea with a friend of mine called Cass Dale who lives in Nancepean, and so I must stop now. With love,
>
> I remain,
> Your loving nephew,
>
> Mark.

And then the pen must needs go and drop a blot like a balloon right over his name, so that the whole letter had to be copied out again before his mother would say that she was satisfied, by which time the yellow sky was dun and the magpies were gone to rest.

Mark left the Dales about half past six, and was accompanied by Cass to the brow of Pendhu. At this point Cass declined to go any farther in spite of Mark's reminder that this would be one of the last walks they would take together, if it were not absolutely the very last.

"No," said Cass. "I wouldn't come up from Church Cove myself not for anything."

"But I'm going down by myself," Mark argued. "If I hadn't thought you'd come all the way with me, I'd have gone home by the fields. What are you afraid of?"

"I'm not afraid of nothing, but I don't want to walk so far by myself. I've come up the hill with 'ee. Now 'tis all down hill for both of us, and that's fair."

"Oh, all right," said Mark, turning away in resentment at his friend's desertion.

Both boys ran off in opposite directions, Cass past the splash of light thrown across the road by the windows of the Hanover Inn, and on toward the scattered lights of Nancepean, Mark into the gloom of the deep lane down to Church Cove. It was a warm and humid evening that brought out the smell of the ferns and earth in the high banks on either side, and presently at the bottom of the hill the smell of the seaweed heaped up in Church Cove by weeks of gales. The moon, about three days from the full, was already up, shedding her aqueous lustre over the towans of Chypie, which slowly penetrated the black gulfs of shadow in the countryside until Mark could perceive the ghost of a familiar landscape. There came over him, whose emotion had already been sprung by the insensibility of Cass, an overwhelming awareness of parting, and he gave to the landscape the expression of sentiment he had yearned to give his friend. His fear of seeing the spirits of the drowned sailors, or as he passed the churchyard gate of perceiving behind that tamarisk the tall spectre of his grandfather, which on the way down from Pendhu had seemed impossible to combat, had died away; and in his despair at losing this beloved scene he wandered on past the church until he stood at the edge of the tide. On this humid autumnal night the oily sea collapsed upon the beach as if it, like everything else in nature, was overcome by the prevailing heaviness. Mark sat down upon some tufts of samphire and watched the Stag Light occulting out across St. Levan's Bay, distant forty miles and more, and while he sat he perceived a glow-worm at his feet creeping along a sprig of samphire that marked the limit of the tide's advance. How did the samphire know that it was safe to grow where it did, and how did the glow-worm know that the samphire was safe?

Mark was suddenly conscious of the protection of God, for might not he expect as much as the glow-worm and the samphire? The ache of separation from Nancepean was assuaged. That dread of the future, with which the impact of death had filled him, was allayed.

"Goodnight, sister glow-worm," he said aloud in imitation of St. Francis. "Goodnight, brother samphire."

A drift of distant fog had obliterated the Stag Light; but of her samphire the glow-worm had made a moonlit forest, so brightly was she shining, yes, a green world of interlacing, lucid boughs.

Let your light so shine before men, that they may see your good works, and glorify your Father which is in heaven.

And Mark, aspiring to thank God Who had made manifest His protection, left Nancepean three days later with the determination to become a lighthouse-keeper, to polish well his lamp and tend it with care, so that men passing by in ships should rejoice at his good works and call him brother lighthouse-keeper, and glorify God their Father when they walked again upon the grass, harking to the pleasant song of birds and the hum of bees.

CHAPTER IX

SLOWBRIDGE

When Mark came to live with Uncle Henry Lidderdale at Slowbridge, he was large for his age, or at any rate he was so loosely jointed as to appear large; a swart complexion, prominent cheek-bones, and straight lank hair gave him a melancholy aspect, the impression of which remained with the observer until he heard the boy laugh in a paroxysm of merriment that left his dark blue eyes dancing long after the outrageous noise had died down. If Mark had occasion to relate some episode that appealed to him, his laughter would accompany the narrative like a pack of hounds in full cry, would as it were pursue the tale to its death, and communicate its zest to the listener, who would think what a sense of humour Mark had, whereas it was more truly the gusto of life.

Uncle Henry found this laughter boisterous and irritating; if his nephew had been a canary in a cage, he would have covered him with a table-cloth. Aunt Helen, if she was caught up in one of Mark's narratives, would twitch until it was finished, when she would rub her forehead with an acorn of menthol and wrap herself more closely in a shawl of soft Shetland wool. The antipathy that formerly existed between Mark and his father was much sharper between Mark and his uncle. It was born in the instant of their first meeting, when Uncle Henry bent over, his trunk at right angles to his legs, so that one could fancy the pelvic bones to be clicking like the wooden joints of a monkey on a stick, and offered his nephew an acrid whisker to be saluted.

"And what is Mark going to be?" Uncle Henry inquired.

"A lighthouse-keeper."

"Ah, we all have suchlike ambitions when we are young. I remember that for nearly a year I intended to be a muffin-man," said Uncle Henry severely.

Mark hated his uncle from that moment, and he fixed upon the throbbing pulse of his scraped-out temples as the feature upon which that dislike should henceforth be concentrated. Uncle Henry's pulse seemed to express all the vitality that was left to him; Mark thought that Our Lord must have felt about the barren fig-tree much as he felt about Uncle Henry.

Aunt Helen annoyed Mark in the way that one is annoyed by a cushion in an easy chair. It is soft and apparently comfortable, but after a minute or two one realizes that it is superfluous, and it is pushed over the arm to the floor. Unfortunately Aunt Helen could not be treated like a cushion; and there she was soft and comfortable in appearance, but forever in Mark's way. Aunt Helen was the incarnation of her own drawing-room. Her face was round and stupid like a clock's; she wore brocaded gowns and carpet slippers; her shawls resembled antimacassars; her hair was like the stuff that is put in grates during the summer; her caps were like lace curtains tied back with velvet ribbons; cameos leant against her bosom as if they were upon a mantelpiece. Mark never overcame his dislike of kissing Aunt Helen, for it gave him a sensation every time that a bit of her might stick to his lips. He lacked that solemn sense of relationship with which most children are imbued, and the compulsory intimacy offended him, particularly when his aunt referred to little boys generically as if they were beetles or mice. Her inability to appreciate that he was Mark outraged his young sense of personality which was further dishonoured by the manner in which she spoke of herself as Aunt Helen, thus seeming to imply that he was only human at all in so far as he was her nephew. She continually shocked his dignity by prescribing medicine for him without regard to the presence of servants or visitors; and nothing gave her more obvious pleasure than to get Mark into the drawing-room on afternoons when dreary mothers of pupils came to call, so that she might bully him under the appearance of teaching good manners, and impress the parents with the advantages of a Haverton House education.

As long as his mother remained alive, Mark tried to make her happy by pretending that he enjoyed living at Haverton House, that he enjoyed his uncle's Preparatory School for the Sons of Gentlemen, that he enjoyed Slowbridge with its fogs and laburnums, its perambulators and tradesmen's carts and noise of whistling trains; but a year after they left Nancepean Mrs. Lidderdale died of pneumonia, and Mark was left alone with his uncle and aunt.

"He doesn't realize what death means," said Aunt Helen, when Mark on the very afternoon of the funeral without even waiting to change out of his best clothes began to play with soldiers instead of occupying himself with the preparation of lessons that must begin again on the morrow.

"I wonder if you will play with soldiers when Aunt Helen dies?" she pressed.

"No," said Mark quickly, "I shall work at my lessons when you die."

His uncle and aunt looked at him suspiciously. They could find no fault with the answer; yet something in the boy's tone, some dreadful suppressed exultation made them feel that they ought to find severe fault with the answer.

"Wouldn't it be kinder to your poor mother's memory," Aunt Helen suggested, "wouldn't it be more becoming now to work harder at your lessons when your mother is watching you from above?"

Mark would not condescend to explain why he was playing with soldiers, nor with what passionate sorrow he was recalling every fleeting expression on his mother's face, every slight intonation of her voice when she was able to share in his game; he hated his uncle and aunt so profoundly that he revelled in their incapacity to understand him, and he would have accounted it a desecration of her memory to share his grief with them.

Haverton House School was a depressing establishment; in after years when Mark looked back at it he used to wonder how it had managed to survive so long, for when he came to live at Slowbridge it had actually been in existence for twenty years, and his uncle was beginning to look forward to the time when Old Havertonians, as he called them, would be bringing their sons to be educated at the old place. There were about fifty pupils, most of them the sons of local tradesmen, who left when they were about fourteen, though a certain number lingered on until they were as much as sixteen in what was called the Modern Class, where they were supposed to receive at least as practical an education as they would have received behind the counter, and certainly a more genteel one. Fine fellows those were in the Modern Class at Haverton House, stalwart heroes who made up the cricket and football teams and strode about the playing fields of Haverton House with as keen a sense of their own importance as Etonians of comparable status in their playing fields not more than two miles away. Mark when everything else in his school life should be obliterated by time would remember their names and prowess . . . Borrow, Tull, Yarde, Corke, Vincent, Macdougal, Skinner, they would keep throughout his life some of that magic which clings to Diomed and Deiphobus, to Hector and Achilles.

Apart from these heroic names the atmosphere of Haverton House was not inspiring. It reduced the world to the size and quality of one of those scratched globes with which Uncle Henry demonstrated geography. Every subject at Haverton House, no matter how interesting it promised to be, was ruined from an educative point of view by its impedimenta of dates, imports, exports, capitals, capes, and Kings of Israel and Judah. Neither Uncle Henry nor his assistants Mr. Spaull and Mr. Palmer believed in departing from the book. Whatever books were chosen for the term's curriculum were regarded as something for which money had been paid and from which the last drop of information must be squeezed to justify in the eyes of parents the expenditure. The teachers considered the notes more important than the text; genealogical tables were exalted above anything on the same page. Some books of history were adorned with illustrations; but no use was made of them by the masters, and for the pupils they merely served as outlines to which, were they the outlines of human beings, inky beards and moustaches had to be affixed, or were they landscapes, flights of birds.

Mr. Spaull was a fat flabby young man with a heavy fair moustache, who was reading for Holy Orders; Mr. Palmer was a stocky bow-legged young man in knickerbockers, who was good at football and used to lament the gentle birth that prevented his becoming a professional. The boys called him Gentleman Joe; but they were careful not to let Mr. Palmer hear them, for he had a punch and did not believe in cuddling the young. He used to jeer openly at his colleague, Mr. Spaull, who never played football, never did anything in the way of exercise except wrestle flirtatiously with the boys, while Mr. Palmer was bellowing up and down the field of play and charging his pupils with additional vigour to counteract the feebleness of Mr. Spaull. Poor Mr. Spaull, he was ordained about three years after Mark came to Slowbridge, and a week later he was run over by a brewer's dray and killed.

CHAPTER X

WHIT-SUNDAY

Mark at the age of fifteen was a bitter, lonely, and unattractive boy. Three years of Haverton House, three years of Uncle Henry's desiccated religion, three years of Mr. Palmer's athletic education and Mr. Spaull's milksop morality, three years of wearing clothes that were too small for him, three years of Haverton House cooking, three years of warts and bad haircutting, of ink and Aunt Helen's confident purging had destroyed that gusto for life which when Mark first came to Slowbridge used to express itself in such loud laughter. Uncle Henry probably supposed that the cure of his nephew's irritating laugh was the foundation stone of that successful career, which it would soon be time to discuss in detail. The few months between now and Mark's sixteenth birthday would soon pass, however dreary the restrictions of Haverton House, and then it would be time to go and talk to Mr. Hitchcock about that articled clerkship toward the fees for which the small sum left by his mother would contribute. Mark was so anxious to be finished with Haverton House that he would have welcomed a prospect even less attractive than Mr. Hitchcock's office in Finsbury Square; it never occurred to him that the money left by his mother could be spent to greater advantage for himself. By now it was over £500, and Uncle Henry on Sunday evenings when he was feeling comfortably replete with the day's devotion would sometimes allude to his having left the interest to accumulate and would urge Mark to be up and doing in order to show his gratitude for all that he and Aunt Helen had conferred upon him. Mark felt no gratitude; in fact at this period he felt nothing except a kind of surly listlessness. He was like somebody who through the carelessness of his nurse or guardian has been crippled in youth, and who is preparing to enter the world with a suppressed resentment against everybody and everything.

"Not still hankering after a lighthouse?" Uncle Henry asked, and one seemed to hear his words snapping like dry twigs beneath the heavy tread of his mind.

"I'm not hankering after anything," Mark replied sullenly.

"But you're looking forward to Mr. Hitchcock's office?" his uncle proceeded.

Mark grunted an assent in order to be left alone, and the entrance of Mr. Palmer who always had supper with his headmaster and employer on Sunday evening, brought the conversation to a close.

At supper Mr. Palmer asked suddenly if the headmaster wanted Mark to go into the Confirmation Class this term.

"No thanks," said Mark.

Uncle Henry raised his eyebrows.

"I fancy that is for me to decide."

"Neither my father nor my mother nor my grandfather would have wanted me to be confirmed against my will," Mark declared. He was angry without knowing his reasons, angry in response to some impulse of the existence of which he had been unaware until he began to speak. He only knew that if he surrendered on this point he should never be able to act for himself again.

"Are you suggesting that you should never be confirmed?" his uncle required.

"I'm not suggesting anything," said Mark. "But I can remember my father's saying once that boys ought to be confirmed before they are thirteen. My mother just before she died wanted me to be confirmed, but it couldn't be arranged, and now I don't intend to be confirmed till I feel I want to be confirmed. I don't want to be prepared for confirmation as if it was a football match. If you force me to go to the confirmation I'll refuse to answer the Bishop's questions. You can't make me answer against my will."

"Mark dear," said Aunt Helen, "I think you'd better take some Eno's Fruit Salts tomorrow morning." In her nephew's present mood she did not dare to prescribe anything stronger.

"I'm not going to take anything tomorrow morning," said Mark angrily.

"Do you want me to thrash you?" Uncle Henry demanded.

Mr. Palmer's eyes glittered with the zeal of muscular Christianity.

"You'll be sorry for it if you do," said Mark. "You can of course, if you get Mr. Palmer to help you, but you'll be sorry if you do."

Mr. Palmer looked at his chief as a terrier looks at his master when a rabbit is hiding in a bush. But the headmaster's vanity would not allow him to summon help to punish his own nephew, and he weakly contented himself with ordering Mark to be silent.

"It strikes me that Spaull is responsible for this sort of thing," said Mr. Palmer. "He always resented my having any hand in the religious teaching."

"That poor worm!" Mark scoffed.

"Mark, he's dead," Aunt Helen gasped. "You mustn't speak of him like that."

"Get out of the room and go to bed," Uncle Henry shouted.

Mark retired with offensive alacrity, and while he was undressing he wondered drearily why he had made himself so conspicuous on this Sunday evening out of so many Sunday evenings. What did it matter whether he were confirmed or not? What did anything matter except to get through the next year and be finished with Haverton House?

He was more sullen than ever during the week, but on Saturday he had the satisfaction of bowling Mr. Palmer in the first innings of a match and in the second innings of hitting him on the jaw with a rising ball.

The next day he rose at five o'clock on a glorious morning in early June and walked rapidly away from Slowbridge. By ten o'clock he had reached a country of rolling beech-woods, and turning aside from the high road he wandered over the bare nutbrown soil that gave the glossy leaves high above a green unparagoned, a green so lambent that the glimpses of the sky beyond seemed opaque as turquoises amongst it. In quick succession Mark saw a squirrel, a woodpecker, and a jay, creatures so perfectly expressive of the place, that they appeared to him more like visions than natural objects; and when they were gone he stood with beating heart in silence as if in a moment the trees should fly like woodpeckers, the sky flash and flutter its blue like a jay's wing, and the very earth leap like a squirrel for his amazement. Presently he came to an open space where the young bracken was springing round a pool. He flung himself down in the frondage, and the spice of it in his nostrils was as if he were feeding upon summer. He was happy until he caught sight of his own reflection in the pool, and then he could not bear to stay any longer in this wood, because unlike the squirrel and the woodpecker and the jay he was an ugly intruder here, a scarecrow in ill-fitting clothes, round the ribbon of whose hat like a chain ran the yellow zigzag of Haverton House. He became afraid of the wood, perceiving nothing round him now except an assemblage of menacing trunks, a slow gathering of angry and forbidding branches. The silence of the day was dreadful in this wood, and Mark fled from it until he emerged upon a brimming clover-ley full of drunken bees, a merry clover-ley dancing in the sun, across which the sound of church bells was being blown upon a honeyed wind. Mark welcomed the prospect of seeing ugly people again after the humiliation inflicted upon him by the wood; and he followed a footpath at the far end of the ley across several stiles, until he stood beneath the limes that overhung the churchyard gate and wondered if he should go inside to the service. The bells were clanging an agitated final appeal to the worshippers; and Mark, unable to resist, allowed himself to flow toward the cool dimness within. There with a thrill he recognized the visible signs of his childhood's religion, and now after so many years he perceived with new eyes an unfamiliar beauty in the crossings and genuflexions, in the pictures and images. The world which had lately seemed so jejune was crowded like a dream, a dream moreover that did not elude the recollection of it in the moment of waking, but that stayed with him for the rest of his life as the evidence of things not seen, which is Faith.

It was during the Gospel that Mark began to realize that what was being said and done at the Altar demanded not merely his attention but also his partaking. All the services he had attended since he came to Slowbridge had demanded nothing from him, and even when he was at Nancepean he had always been outside the sacred mysteries. But now on this Whit-sunday morning he heard in the Gospel:

Hereafter I will not talk much with you: for the prince of this world cometh and hath nothing in me.

And while he listened it seemed that Jesus Christ was departing from him, and that unless he were quick to offer himself he should be left to the prince of this world; so black was Mark's world in those days that the Prince of it meant most unmistakably the Prince of Darkness, and the prophecy made him shiver with affright. With conviction he said the Nicene Creed, and when the celebrating priest, a tall fair man, with a gentle voice and of a mild and benignant aspect, went up into the pulpit and announced that there would be a confirmation in his church on the Feast of the Visitation of the Blessed Virgin Mary Mark felt in this newly found assurance of being commanded by God to follow Him that somehow he must be confirmed in this church and prepared by this kindly priest. The sermon was about the coming of the Holy Ghost and of our bodies which are His temple. Any other Sunday Mark would have sat in a stupor, while his mind would occasionally have taken flights of activity, counting the lines of a prayer-book's page or following the tributaries in the grain of the pew in front; but on this Sunday he sat alert, finding every word of the discourse applicable to himself.

On other Sundays the first sentence of the Offertory would have passed unheeded in the familiarity of its repetition, but this morning it took him back to that night in Church Cove when he saw the glow-worm by the edge of the tide and made up his mind to be a lighthouse-keeper.

Let your light so shine before men, that they may see your good works, and glorify your Father which is in heaven.

"I will be a priest," Mark vowed to himself.

Give grace, O heavenly Father, to all Bishops and Curates that they may both by their life and doctrines set forth thy true and lively word, and rightly and duly administer thy holy Sacraments.

"I will, I will," he vowed.

Hear what comfortable words our Saviour Christ saith unto all that truly turn to him. Come unto me all that travail and are heavy laden, and I will refresh you.

Mark prayed that with such words he might when he was a priest bring consolation.

Through Jesus Christ our Lord; according to whose most true promise, the Holy Ghost came down as at this time from heaven with a sudden great sound, as it had been a mighty wind, in the likeness of fiery tongues, lighting upon the Apostles, to teach them and to lead them to all truth;

The red chasuble of the priest glowed with Pentecostal light.

giving them both the gift of divers languages, and also boldness with fervent zeal constantly to preach the Gospel unto all nations; whereby we have been brought out of darkness and error into the clear light and true knowledge of thee, and of thy Son Jesus Christ.

And when after this proper preface of Whit-sunday, which seemed to Mark to be telling him what was expected of his priesthood by God, the quire sang the Sanctus, *Therefore with Angels and Archangels, and with all the company of heaven, we laud and magnify thy glorious Name; evermore praising thee, and saying, Holy, Holy, Holy, Lord God of Hosts, heaven and earth are full of thy glory: Glory be to thee, O Lord most High. Amen*, that sublime proclamation spoke the fullness of his aspiring heart.

Mark came out of church with the rest of the congregation, and walked down the road toward the roofs of the little village, on the outskirts of which he could not help stopping to admire a small garden full of pinks in front of two thatched cottages that had evidently been made into one house. While he was standing there looking over the trim quickset hedge, an old lady with silvery hair came slowly down the road, paused a moment by the gate before she went in, and then asked Mark if she had not seen him in church. Mark felt embarrassed at being discovered looking over a hedge into somebody's garden; but he managed to murmur an affirmative and turned to go away.

"Stop," said the old lady waving at him her ebony crook, "do not run away, young gentleman. I see that you admire my garden. Pray step inside and look more closely at it."

Mark thought at first by her manner of speech that she was laughing at him; but soon perceiving that she was in earnest he followed her inside, and walked behind her along the narrow winding paths, nodding with an appearance of profound interest when she poked at some starry clump and invited his admiration. As they drew nearer the house, the smell of the pinks was merged in the smell of hot roast beef, and Mark discovered that he was hungry, so hungry indeed that he felt he could not stay any longer to be tantalized by the odours of the Sunday dinner, but must go off and find an inn where he could obtain bread and cheese as quickly as possible. He was preparing an excuse to get away, when the garden wicket clicked, and looking up he saw the fair priest coming down the path toward them accompanied by two ladies, one of whom resembled him so closely that Mark was sure she was his sister. The other, who looked windblown in spite of the serene June weather, had a nervous energy that contrasted with the demeanour of the other two, whose deliberate pace seemed to worry her so that she was continually two yards ahead and turning round as if to urge them to walk more quickly.

The old lady must have guessed Mark's intention, for raising her stick she forbade him to move, and before he had time to mumble an apology and flee she was introducing the newcomers to him.

"This is my daughter Miriam," she said pointing to one who resembled her brother. "And this is my daughter Esther. And this is my son, the Vicar. What is your name?"

Mark told her, and he should have liked to ask what hers was, but he felt too shy.

"You're going to stay and have lunch with us, I hope?" asked the Vicar.

Mark had no idea how to reply. He was much afraid that if he accepted he should be seeming to have hung about by the Vicarage gate in order to be invited. On the other hand he did not know how to refuse. It would be absurd to say that he had to get home, because they would ask him where he lived, and at this hour of the morning he could scarcely pretend that he expected to be back in time for lunch twelve miles and more from where he was.

"Of course he's going to stay," said the old lady.

And of course Mark did stay; a delightful lunch it was too, on chairs covered with blue holland in a green shadowed room that smelt of dryness and ancientry. After lunch Mark sat for a while with the Vicar in his study, which was small and intimate with its two armchairs and bookshelves reaching to the ceiling all round. He had not yet managed to find out his name, and as it was obviously too late to ask as this stage of their acquaintanceship he supposed that he should have to wait until he left the Vicarage and could ask somebody in the village, of which by the way he also did not know the name.

"Lidderdale," the Vicar was saying meditatively, "Lidderdale. I wonder if you were a relative of the famous Lidderdale of St. Wilfred's?"

Mark flushed with a mixture of self-consciousness and pleasure to hear his father spoken of as famous, and when he explained who he was he flushed still more deeply to hear his father's work praised with such enthusiasm.

"And do you hope to be a priest yourself?"

"Why, yes I do rather," said Mark.

"Splendid! Capital!" cried the Vicar, his kindly blue eye beaming with approval of Mark's intention.

Presently Mark was talking to him as though he had known him for years.

"There's no reason why you shouldn't be confirmed here," the Vicar said. "No reason at all. I'll mention it to the Bishop, and if you like I'll write to your uncle. I shall feel justified in interfering on account of your father's opinions. We all look upon him as one of the great pioneers of the Movement. You must come over and lunch with us again next Sunday. My mother will be delighted to see you. She's a dear old thing, isn't she? I'm going to hand you over to her now and my youngest sister. My other sister and I have got Sunday schools to deal with. Have another cigarette? No. Quite right. You oughtn't to smoke too much at your age. Only just fifteen, eh? By Jove, I suppose you oughtn't to have smoked at all. But what rot. You'd only smoke all the more if it was absolutely forbidden. Wisdom! Wisdom! Wisdom with the young! You don't mind being called young? I've known boys who hated the epithet."

Mark was determined to show his new friend that he did not object to being called young, and he could think of no better way to do it than by asking him his name, thus proving that he did not mind if such a question did make him look ridiculous.

"Ogilvie—Stephen Ogilvie. My dear boy, it's we who ought to be ashamed of ourselves for not having had the gumption to enlighten you. How on earth were you to know without asking? Now, look here, I must run. I expect you'll be wanting to get home, or I'd suggest your staying until I get back, but I must lie low after tea and think out my sermon. Look here, come over to lunch on Saturday, haven't you a bicycle? You could get over from

Slowbridge by one o'clock, and after lunch we'll have a good tramp in the woods. Splendid!"

Then chanting the *Dies Irae* in a cheerful tenor the Reverend Stephen Ogilvie hurried off to his Sunday School. Mark said goodbye to Mrs. Ogilvie with an assured politeness that was typical of his new found ease; and when he started on his long walk back to Slowbridge he felt inclined to leap in the air and wake with shouts the slumberous Sabbath afternoon, proclaiming the glory of life, the joy of living.

Mark had not expected his uncle to welcome his friendship with the Vicar of Meade Cantorum; but he had supposed that after a few familiar sneers he should be allowed to go his own way with nothing worse than silent disapproval brooding over his perverse choice. He was surprised by the vehemence of his uncle's opposition, and it must be added that he thoroughly enjoyed it. The experience of that Whit-sunday had been too rich not to be of enduring importance to his development in any case; but the behaviour of Uncle Henry made it more important, because all this criticism helped Mark to put his opinions into shape, consolidated the position he had taken up, sharpened his determination to advance along the path he had discovered for himself, and gave him an immediate target for arrows that might otherwise have been shot into the air until his quiver was empty.

"Mr. Ogilvie knew my father."

"That has nothing to do with the case," said Uncle Henry.

"I think it has."

"Do not be insolent, Mark. I've noticed lately a most unpleasant note in your voice, an objectionably defiant note which I simply will not tolerate."

"But do you really mean that I'm not to go and see Mr. Ogilvie?"

"It would have been more courteous if Mr. Ogilvie had given himself the trouble of writing to me, your guardian, before inviting you out to lunch and I don't know what not besides."

"He said he would write to you."

"I don't want to embark on a correspondence with him," Uncle Henry exclaimed petulantly. "I know the man by reputation. A bigoted Ritualist. A Romanizer of the worst type. He'll only fill your head with a lot of effeminate nonsense, and that at a time

93

when it's particularly necessary for you to concentrate upon your work. Don't forget that this is your last year of school. I advise you to make the most of it."

"I've asked Mr. Ogilvie to prepare me for confirmation," said Mark, who was determined to goad his uncle into losing his temper.

"Then you deserve to be thrashed."

"Look here, Uncle Henry," Mark began; and while he was speaking he was aware that he was stronger than his uncle now and looking across at his aunt he perceived that she was just a ball of badly wound wool lying in a chair. "Look here, Uncle Henry, it's quite useless for you to try to stop my going to Meade Cantorum, because I'm going there whenever I'm asked and I'm going to be confirmed there, because you promised Mother you wouldn't interfere with my religion."

"Your religion!" broke in Mr. Lidderdale, scornful both of the pronoun and the substantive.

"It's no use your losing your temper or arguing with me or doing anything except letting me go my own way, because that's what I intend to do."

Aunt Helen half rose in her chair upon an impulse to protect her brother against Mark's violence.

"And you can't cure me with Gregory Powder," he said. "Nor with Senna nor with Licorice nor even with Cascara."

"Your behaviour, my boy, is revolting," said Mr. Lidderdale. "A young Mohawk would not talk to his guardians as you are talking to me."

"Well, I don't want you to think I'm going to obey you if you forbid me to go to Meade Cantorum," said Mark. "I'm sorry I was rude, Aunt Helen. I oughtn't to have spoken to you like that. And I'm sorry, Uncle Henry, to seem ungrateful after what you've done for me." And then lest his uncle should think that he was surrendering he quickly added: "But I'm going to Meade Cantorum on Saturday." And like most people who know their own minds Mark had his own way.

CHAPTER XI

MEADE CANTORUM

Mark did not suffer from "churchiness" during this period. His interest in religion, although it resembled the familiar conversions of adolescence, was a real resurrection of emotions which had been stifled by these years at Haverton House following upon the paralyzing grief of his mother's death. Had he been in contact during that time with an influence like the Vicar of Meade Cantorum, he would probably have escaped those ashen years, but as Mr. Ogilvie pointed out to him, he would also never have received such evidence of God's loving kindness as was shown to him upon that Whit-sunday morning.

"If in the future, my dear boy, you are ever tempted to doubt the wisdom of Almighty God, remember what was vouchsafed to you at a moment when you seemed to have no reason for any longer existing, so black was your world. Remember how you caught sight of yourself in that pool and shrank away in horror from the vision. I envy you, Mark. I have never been granted such a revelation of myself."

"You were never so ugly," said Mark.

"My dear boy, we are all as ugly as the demons of Hell if we are allowed to see ourselves as we really are. But God only grants that to a few brave spirits whom he consecrates to his service and whom he fortifies afterwards by proving to them that, no matter how great the horror of their self-recognition, the Holy Ghost is within them to comfort them. I don't suppose that many human beings are granted such an experience as yours. I myself tremble at the thought of it, knowing that God considers me too weak a subject for such a test."

"Oh, Mr. Ogilvie," Mark expostulated.

"I'm not talking to you as Mark Lidderdale, but as the recipient of the grace of God, to one who before my own unworthy eyes has been lightened by celestial fire. *Mine eyes have seen thy salvation, O Lord.* As for yourself, my dear boy, I pray always that you may sustain your part, that you will never allow the memory of this Whitsuntide to be obscured by the fogs of this world and that you will always bear in mind that having been given more talents by God a sharper account will be taken of the use you make of them. Don't think I'm doubting your steadfastness, old man, I believe in it. Do you hear? I believe in it absolutely. But Catholic doctrine, which is the sum of humanity's knowledge of God and than which nothing more can be known of God until we see Him face to face, insists upon good works, demanding as it were a practical demonstration to the rest of the world of the grace of God within you. You remember St. Paul? *Faith, Hope, and Love. But the greatest of these is Love.* The greatest because the least individual. Faith will move mountains, but so will Love. That's the trouble with so many godly Protestants. They are inclined to stay satisfied with their own godliness, although the best of them like the Quakers are examples that ought to make most of us Catholics ashamed of ourselves. And one thing more, old man, before we get off this subject, don't forget that your experience is a mercy accorded to you by the death of our Lord Jesus Christ. You owe to His infinite Love your new life. What was granted to you was the visible apprehension of the fact of Holy Baptism, and don't forget St. John the Baptist's words: *I indeed baptize you with water unto repentance, but he that cometh after me is mightier than I. He shall baptise you with the Holy Ghost, and with fire: whose fan is in his hand, and he will thoroughly purge his floor, and gather his wheat into the garner; but he will burn up the chaff with unquenchable fire.* Those are great words for you to think of now, and during this long Trinitytide which is symbolical of what one might call the humdrum of religious life, the day in day out sticking to it, make a resolution never to say mechanically *The grace of our Lord Jesus Christ, and the love of God and the fellowship of the Holy Ghost, be with us all evermore. Amen.* If you always remember to say those wonderful words from the heart and not merely with the lips, you will each time you say them marvel more and more at the great condescension of Almighty God in favouring you, as He has favoured you, by teaching you the meaning of these words Himself in a way that no poor mortal priest, however eloquent, could teach you it. On that night when you watched beside the glow-worm at the sea's edge the grace of our Lord gave you an apprehension, child as you were, of the love of God, and now once more the grace of our Lord gives you the realization of the fellowship of the Holy Ghost. I don't want to spoil your wonderful experience with my parsonic discoursing; but, Mark, don't look back from the plough."

Uncle Henry found it hard to dispose of words like these when he deplored his nephew's collapse into ritualism.

"You really needn't bother about the incense and the vestments," Mark assured him. "I like incense and vestments; but I don't think they're the most important things in religion. You couldn't find anybody more evangelical than Mr. Ogilvie, though he doesn't call himself evangelical, or his party the Evangelical party. It's no use your trying to argue me out of what I believe. I know I'm believing what it's right for me to believe. When I'm older I shall try to make everybody else believe in my way, because I should like everybody else to feel as happy as I do. Your religion doesn't make you feel happy, Uncle Henry!"

"Leave the room," was Mr. Lidderdale's reply. "I won't stand this kind of talk from a boy of your age."

Although Mark had only claimed from his uncle the right to believe what it was right for him to believe, the richness of his belief presently began to seem too much for one. His nature was generous in everything, and he felt that he must share this happiness with somebody else. He regretted the death of poor Mr. Spaull, for he was sure that he could have persuaded poor Mr. Spaull to cut off his yellow moustache and become a Catholic. Mr. Palmer was of course hopeless: Saint Augustine of Hippo, St. Paul himself even, would have found it hard to deal with Mr. Palmer; as for the new master, Mr. Blumey, with his long nose and long chin and long frock coat and long boots, he was obviously absorbed by the problems of mathematics and required nothing more.

Term came to an end, and during the holidays Mark was able to spend most of his time at Meade Cantorum. He had always been a favourite of Mrs. Ogilvie since that Whit-sunday nearly two months ago when she saw him looking at her garden and invited him in, and every time he revisited the Vicarage he had devoted some of his time to helping her weed or prune or do whatever she wanted to do in her garden. He was also on friendly terms with Miriam, the elder of Mr. Ogilvie's two sisters, who was very like her brother in appearance and who gave to the house the decorous loving care he gave to the church. And however enthralling her domestic ministrations, she had always time to attend every service; while, so well ordered was her manner of life, her religious duties never involved the household in discomfort. She never gave the impression that so many religious women give of going to church in a fever of self-gratification, to which everything and everybody around her must be subordinated. The practice of her religion was woven into her life like the strand of wool on which all the others depend, but which itself is no more conspicuous than any of the other strands. With so many women religion is a substitute for something else; with Miriam Ogilvie everything else was made as nearly and as beautifully as it could be made a substitute for religion. Mark was intensely aware of her holiness, but he was equally aware of her capable well-tended hands and of her chatelaine glittering in and out of a lawn apron. One tress of her abundant hair was grey, which stood out against the dark background of the rest and gave her a serene purity, an austere strength, but yet like a nun's coif seemed to make the face beneath more youthful, and like a cavalier's plume more debonair. She could not have been over thirty-five when Mark first knew her, perhaps not so much; but he thought of her as ageless in the way a child thinks of its mother, and if any woman should ever be able to be to him something of what his mother had been, Mark thought that Miss Ogilvie might.

Esther Ogilvie the other sister was twenty-five. She told Mark this when he imitated the villagers by addressing her as Miss Essie and she ordered him to call her Esther. He might have supposed from this that she intended to confer upon him a measure of friendliness, even of sisterly affection; but on the contrary she either ignored him altogether or gave him the impression that she considered his frequent visits to Meade Cantorum a nuisance. Mark was sorry that she felt like that toward him, because she seemed unhappy, and in his desire for everybody to be happy he would have liked to proclaim how suddenly and unexpectedly happiness may come. As a sister of the Vicar of the parish, she went to church regularly, but Mark did not think that she was there except in body. He once looked across at her open prayer book during the *Magnificat*, and noticed that she was reading the Tables of Kindred and Affinity. Now, Mark knew from personal experience that when one is reduced to reading the Tables of Kindred and Affinity it argues a mind untouched by the reality of worship. In his own case, when he sat beside his uncle and aunt in the dreary Slowbridge church of their choice, it had been nothing more than a sign of his own inward dreariness to read the Tables of Kindred and Affinity or speculate upon the Paschal full moons from the year 2200 to the year 2299 inclusive. But St. Margaret's, Meade Cantorum, was a different church from St. Jude's, Slowbridge, and for Esther Ogilvie to ignore the joyfulness of worshipping there in order to ponder idly the complexities of Golden Numbers and Dominical Letters could not be ascribed to inward dreariness. Besides, she wasn't dreary. Once Mark saw her coming down a woodland glade and almost turned aside to avoid meeting her, because she looked so fay with her wild blue eyes and her windblown hair, the colour of last year's bracken after rain. She seemed at once the pursued and the pursuer, and Mark felt that whichever she was he would be in the way.

"Taking a quick walk by myself," she called out to him as they passed.

No, she was certainly not dreary. But what was she?

Mark abandoned the problem of Esther in the pleasure of meeting the Reverend Oliver Dorward, who arrived one afternoon at the Vicarage with a large turbot for Mrs. Ogilvie, and six Flemish candlesticks for the Vicar, announcing that he wanted to stay a week before being inducted to the living of Green Lanes in the County of Southampton, to which he had recently been presented by Lord Chatsea. Mark liked him from the first moment he saw him pacing the Vicarage garden in a soutane, buckled shoes, and beaver hat, and he could not understand why Mr. Ogilvie, who had often laughed about Dorward's eccentricity, should now that he had an opportunity of enjoying it once more be so cross about his friend's arrival and so ready to hand him over to Mark to be entertained.

"Just like Ogilvie," said Dorward confidentially, when he and Mark went for a walk on the afternoon of his arrival. "He wants spiking up. They get very slack and selfish, these country clergy. Time he gave up Meade Cantorum. He's been here nearly ten years.

Too long, nine years too long. Hasn't been to his duties since Easter. Scandalous, you know. I asked him, as soon as I'd explained to the cook about the turbot, when he went last, and he was bored. Nice old pussy cat, the mother. Hullo, is that the *Angelus*? Damn, I knelt on a thistle."

"It isn't the *Angelus*," said Mark quietly. "It's the bell on that cow."

But Mr. Dorward had finished his devotion before he answered.

"I was half way through before you told me. You should have spoken sooner."

"Well, I spoke as soon as I could."

"Very cunning of Satan," said Dorward meditatively. "Induced a cow to simulate the *Angelus*, and planted a thistle just where I was bound to kneel. Cunning. Cunning. Very cunning. I must go back now and confess to Ogilvie. Good example. Wait a minute, I'll confess tomorrow before Morning Prayer. Very good for Ogilvie's congregation. They're stuffy, very stuffy. It'll shake them. It'll shake Ogilvie too. Are you staying here tonight?"

"No, I shall bicycle back to Slowbridge and bicycle over to Mass tomorrow."

"Ridiculous. Stay the night. Didn't Ogilvie invite you?"

Mark shook his head.

"Scandalous lack of hospitality. They're all alike these country clergy. I'm tired of this walk. Let's go back and look after the turbot. Are you a good cook?"

"I can boil eggs and that sort of thing," said Mark.

"What sort of things? An egg is unique. There's nothing like an egg. Will you serve my Mass on Monday? Saying Mass for Napoleon on Monday."

"For whom?" Mark exclaimed.

"Napoleon, with a special intention for the conversion of the present government in France. Last Monday I said a Mass for Shakespeare, with a special intention for an improvement in contemporary verse."

Mark supposed that Mr. Dorward must be joking, and his expression must have told as much to the priest, who murmured:

"Nothing to laugh at. Nothing to laugh at."

"No, of course not," said Mark feeling abashed. "But I'm afraid I shouldn't be able to serve you. I've never had any practice."

"Perfectly easy. Perfectly easy. I'll give you a book when we get back."

Mark bicycled home that afternoon with a tall thin volume called *Ritual Notes*, so tall that when it was in his pocket he could feel it digging him in the ribs every time he was riding up the least slope. That night in his bedroom he practised with the help of the wash-stand and its accessories the technique of serving at Low Mass, and in his enthusiasm he bicycled over to Meade Cantorum in time to attend both the Low Mass at seven said by Mr. Dorward and the Low Mass at eight said by Mr. Ogilvie. He was able to detect mistakes that were made by the village boys who served that Sunday morning, and he vowed to himself that the Monday Mass for the Emperor Napoleon should not be disfigured by such inaccuracy or clumsiness. He declined the usual invitation to stay to supper after Evening Prayer that he might have time to make perfection more perfect in the seclusion of his own room, and when he set out about six o'clock of a sun-drowsed morning in early August, apart from a faint anxiety about the *Lavabo*, he felt secure of his accomplishment. It was only when he reached the church that he remembered he had made no arrangement about borrowing a cassock or a cotta, an omission that in the mood of grand seriousness in which he had undertaken his responsibility seemed nothing less than abominable. He did not like to go to the Vicarage and worry Mr. Ogilvie who could scarcely fail to be amused, even contemptuously amused at such an ineffective beginning. Besides, ever since Mr. Dorward's arrival the Vicar had been slightly irritable.

While Mark was wondering what was the best thing to do, Miss Hatchett, a pious old maid who spent her nights in patience and sleep, her days in worship and weeding, came hurrying down the churchyard path.

"I am not late, am I?" she exclaimed. "I never heard the bell. I was so engrossed in pulling out one of those dreadful sow-thistles that when my maid came running out and said 'Oh, Miss Hatchett, it's gone the five to, you'll be late,' I just ran, and now I've brought my trowel and left my prayer book on the path . . ."

"I'm just going to ring the bell now," said Mark, in whom the horror of another omission had been rapidly succeeded by an almost unnatural composure.

"Oh, what a relief," Miss Hatchett sighed. "Are you sure I shall have time to get my breath, for I know Mr. Ogilvie would dislike to hear me panting in church?"

"Mr. Ogilvie isn't saying Mass this morning."

"Not saying Mass?" repeated the old maid in such a dejected tone of voice that, when a small cloud passed over the face of the sun, it seemed as if the natural scene desired to accord with the chill cast upon her spirit by Mark's announcement.

"Mr. Dorward is saying Mass," he told her, and poor Miss Hatchett must pretend with a forced smile that her blank look had been caused by the prospect of being deprived of Mass when really . . .

But Mark was not paying any more attention to Miss Hatchett. He was standing under the bell, gazing up at the long rope and wondering what manner of sound he should evoke. He took a breath and pulled; the rope quivered with such an effect of life that he recoiled from the new force he had conjured into being, afraid of his handiwork, timid of the clamour that would resound. No louder noise ensued than might have been given forth by a can kicked into the gutter. Mark pulled again more strongly, and the bell began to chime, irregularly at first with alternations of sonorous and feeble note; at last, however, when the rhythm was established with such command and such insistence that the ringer, looking over his shoulder to the south door, half expected to see a stream of perturbed Christians hurrying to obey its summons. But there was only poor Miss Hatchett sitting in the porch and fanning herself with a handkerchief.

Mark went on ringing . . .

Clang—clang—clang! All the holy Virgins were waving their palms. Clang—clang—clang! All the blessed Doctors and Confessors were twanging their harps to the clanging. Clang—clang—clang! All the holy Saints and Martyrs were tossing their haloes in the air as schoolboys toss their caps. Clang—clang—clang! Angels, Archangels, and Principalities with faces that shone like brass and with forms that quivered like flames thronged the noise. Clang—clang—clang! Virtues, Powers, and Dominations bade the morning stars sing to the ringing. Clang—clang—clang! The ringing reached up to the green-winged Thrones who sustain the seat of the Most High. Clang—clang—clang! The azure Cherubs heard the bells within their contemplation: the scarlet Seraphs felt them within their love. Clang—clang—clang! The lidless Eye of God looked down, and Miss Hatchett supposing it to be the sun crossed over to the other side of the porch.

Clang—clang—clang—clang—clang—clang—clang—clang . . .

"Hasn't Dorward come in yet? It's five past eight already. Go on ringing for a little while. I'll go and see how long he'll be."

Mark in the absorption of ringing the bell had not noticed the Vicar's approach, and he was gone again before he remembered that he wanted to borrow a cassock and a cotta. Had he been rude? Would Mr. Ogilvie think it cheek to ring the bell without asking his permission first? But before these unanswered questions had had time to spoil the rhythm of his ringing, the Vicar came back with Mr. Dorward, and the congregation, that is to say Miss Hatchett and Miss Ogilvie, was already kneeling in its place.

Mark in a cassock that was much too long for him and in a cotta that was in the same ratio as much too short preceded Mr. Dorward from the sacristy to the altar. A fear seized him that in spite of all his practice he was kneeling on the wrong side of the priest; he forgot the first responses; he was sure the Sanctus-bell was too far away; he wished that Mr. Dorward would not mutter quite so inaudibly. Gradually, however, the meetness of the gestures prescribed for him by the ancient ritual cured his self-consciousness and included him in its pattern, so that now for the first time he was aware of the significance of the preface to the Sanctus: *It is very meet, right, and our bounden duty, that we should at all times, and in all places, give thanks unto thee, O Lord, Holy Father, Almighty Everlasting God.*

Twenty minutes ago when he was ringing the church bell Mark had experienced the rapture of creative noise, the sense of individual triumph over time and space; and the sound of his ringing came back to him from the vaulted roof of the church with such exultation as the missal thrush may know when he sits high above the fretted boughs of an oak and his music plunges forth upon the January wind. Now when Mark was ringing the Sanctus-bell, it was with a sense of his place in the scheme of worship. If one listens to the twitter of a single linnet in open country or

103

to the buzz of a solitary fly upon a window pane, how incredible it is that myriads of them twittering and buzzing together should be the song of April, the murmur of June. And this Sanctus-bell that tinkled so inadequately, almost so frivolously when sounded by a server in Meade Cantorum church, was yet part of an unimaginable volume of worship that swelled in unison with Angels and Archangels lauding and magnifying the Holy Name. The importance of ceremony was as deeply impressed upon Mark that morning as if he had been formally initiated to great mysteries. His coming confirmation, which had been postponed from July 2nd to September 8th seemed much more momentous now than it seemed yesterday. It was no longer a step to Communion, but was apprehended as a Sacrament itself, and though Mr. Ogilvie was inclined to regret the ritualistic development of his catechumen, Mark derived much strength from what was really the awakening in him of a sense of form, which more than anything makes emotion durable. Perhaps Ogilvie may have been a little jealous of Dorward's influence; he also was really alarmed at the prospect, as he said, of so much fire being wasted upon poker-work. In the end what between Dorward's encouragement of Mark's ritualistic tendencies and the "spiking up" process to which he was himself being subjected, Ogilvie was glad when a fortnight later Dorward took himself off to his own living, and he expressed a hope that Mark would perceive Dorward in his true proportions as a dear good fellow, perfectly sincere, but just a little, well, not exactly mad, but so eccentric as sometimes to do more harm than good to the Movement. Mark was shrewd enough to notice that however much he grumbled about his friend's visit Mr. Ogilvie was sufficiently influenced by that visit to put into practice much of the advice to which he had taken exception. The influence of Dorward upon Mark did not stop with his begetting in him an appreciation of the value of form in worship. When Mark told Mr. Ogilvie that he intended to become a priest, Mr. Ogilvie was impressed by the manifestation of the Divine Grace, but he did not offer many practical suggestions for Mark's immediate future. Dorward on the contrary attached as much importance to the manner in which he was to become a priest.

"Oxford," Mr. Dorward pronounced. "And then Glastonbury."
"Glastonbury?"

"Glastonbury Theological College."

Now to Mark Oxford was a legendary place to which before he met Mr. Dorward he would never have aspired. Oxford at Haverton House was merely an abstraction to which a certain number of people offered an illogical allegiance in order to create an excuse for argument and strife. Sometimes Mark had gazed at Eton and wondered vaguely about existence there; sometimes he had gazed at the towers of Windsor and wondered what the Queen ate for breakfast. Oxford was far more remote than either of these, and yet when Mr. Dorward said that he must go there his heart leapt as if to some recognized ambition long ago buried and now abruptly resuscitated.

"I've always been Oxford," he admitted.

When Mr. Dorward had gone, Mark asked Mr. Ogilvie what he thought about Oxford.

"If you can afford to go there, my dear boy, of course you ought to go."

"Well, I'm pretty sure I can't afford to. I don't think I've got any money at all. My mother left some money, but my uncle says that that will come in useful when I'm articled to this solicitor, Mr. Hitchcock. Oh, but if I become a priest I can't become a solicitor, and perhaps I could have that money. I don't know how much it is . . . I think five hundred pounds. Would that be enough?"

"With care and economy," said Mr. Ogilvie. "And you might win a scholarship."

"But I'm leaving school at the end of this year."

Mr. Ogilvie thought that it would be wiser not to say anything to his uncle until after Mark had been confirmed. He advised him to work hard meanwhile and to keep in mind the possibility of having to win a scholarship.

The confirmation was held on the feast of the Nativity of the Blessed Virgin. Mark made his first Confession on the vigil, his first Communion on the following Sunday.

CHAPTER XII

THE POMEROY AFFAIR

Mark was so much elated to find himself a fully equipped member of the Church Militant that he looked about him again to find somebody whom he could make as happy as himself. He even considered the possibility of converting his uncle, and spent the Sunday evening before term began in framing inexpugnable arguments to be preceded by unanswerable questions; but always when he was on the point of speaking he was deterred by the lifelessness of his uncle. No eloquence could irrigate his arid creed and make that desert blossom now. And yet, Mark thought, he ought to remember that in the eyes of the world he owed his uncle everything. What did he owe him in the sight of God? Gratitude? Gratitude for what? Gratitude for spending a certain amount of money on him. Once more Mark opened his mouth to repay his debt by offering Uncle Henry Eternal Life. But Uncle Henry fancied himself already in possession of Eternal Life. He definitely labelled himself Evangelical. And again Mark prepared one of his unanswerable questions.

"Mark," said Mr. Lidderdale. "If you can't keep from yawning you'd better get off to bed. Don't forget school begins tomorrow, and you must make the most of your last term."

Mark abandoned for ever the task of converting Uncle Henry, and pondered his chance of doing something with Aunt Helen. There instead of exsiccation he was confronted by a dreadful humidity, an infertile ooze that seemed almost less susceptible to cultivation than the other.

"And I really don't owe *her* anything," he thought. "Besides, it isn't that I want to save people from damnation. I want people to be happy. And it isn't quite that even. I want them to understand how happy I am. I want people to feel fond of their pillows when they turn over to go to sleep, because next morning is going to be what? Well, sort of exciting."

Mark suddenly imagined how splendid it would be to give some of his happiness to Esther Ogilvie; but a moment later he decided that it would be rather cheek, and he abandoned the idea of converting Esther Ogilvie. He fell back on wishing again that Mr. Spaull had not died; in him he really would have had an ideal subject.

In the end Mark fixed upon a boy of his own age, one of the many sons of a Papuan missionary called Pomeroy who was glad to have found in Mr. Lidderdale a cheap and evangelical schoolmaster. Cyril Pomeroy was a blushful, girlish youth, clever at the routine of school work, but in other ways so much undeveloped as to give an impression of stupidity. The notion of pointing out to him the beauty and utility of the Catholic religion would probably never have occurred to Mark if the boy himself had not approached him with a direct complaint of the dreariness of home life. Mark had never had any intimate friends at Haverton House; there was something in its atmosphere that was hostile to intimacy. Cyril Pomeroy appealed to that idea of romantic protection which is the common appendage of adolescence, and is the cause of half the extravagant affection at which maturity is wont to laugh. In the company of Cyril, Mark felt ineffably old than which upon the threshold of sixteen there is no sensation more grateful; and while the intercourse flattered his own sense of superiority he did feel that he had much to offer his friend. Mark regarded Cyril's case as curable if the right treatment were followed, and every evening after school during the veiled summer of a fine October he paced the Slowbridge streets with his willing proselyte, debating the gravest issues of religious practice, the subtlest varieties of theological opinion. He also lent Cyril suitable books, and finally he demanded from him as a double tribute to piety and friendship that he should prove his metal by going to Confession. Cyril, who was incapable of refusing whatever Mark demanded, bicycled timorously behind him to Meade Cantorum one Saturday afternoon, where he gulped out the table of his sins to Mr. Ogilvie, whom Mark had fetched from the

Vicarage with the urgency of one who fetches a midwife. Nor was he at all abashed when Mr. Ogilvie was angry for not having been told that Cyril's father would have disapproved of his son's confession. He argued that the priest was applying social standards to religious principles, and in the end he enjoyed the triumph of hearing Mr. Ogilvie admit that perhaps he was right.

"I know I'm right. Come on, Cyril. You'd better get back home now. Oh, and I say, Mr. Ogilvie, can I borrow for Cyril some of the books you lent me?"

The priest was amused that Mark did not ask him to lend the books to his friend, but to himself. However, when he found that the neophyte seemed to flourish under Mark's assiduous priming, and that the fundamental weakness of his character was likely to be strengthened by what, though it was at present nothing more than an interest in religion, might later on develop into a profound conviction of the truths of Christianity, Ogilvie overlooked his scruples about deceiving parents and encouraged the boy as much as he could.

"But I hope your manipulation of the plastic Cyril isn't going to turn *you* into too much of a ritualist," he said to Mark. "It's splendid of course that you should have an opportunity so young of proving your ability to get round people in the right way. But let it be the right way, old man. At the beginning you were full of the happiness, the secret of which you burnt to impart to others. That happiness was the revelation of the Holy Spirit dwelling in you as He dwells in all Christian souls. I am sure that the eloquent exposition I lately overheard of the propriety of fiddle-backed chasubles and the impropriety of Gothic ones doesn't mean that you are in any real danger of supposing chasubles to be anything more important relatively than, say, the uniform of a soldier compared with his valour and obedience and selflessness. Now don't overwhelm me for a minute or two. I haven't finished what I want to say. I wasn't speaking sarcastically when I said that, and I wasn't criticizing you. But you are not Cyril. By God's grace you have been kept from the temptations of the flesh. Yes, I know the subject is distasteful to you. But you are old enough to understand that your fastidiousness, if it isn't to be priggish, must be safeguarded by your humility. I didn't mean to sandwich a sermon to you between my remarks on Cyril, but your disdainful upper lip compelled that testimony. Let us leave you and your virtues alone. Cyril is weak. He's the weak pink type that may fall to women or drink or anything in fact where an opportunity is given him of being influenced by a stronger character than his own. At the moment he's being influenced by you to go to Confession, and say his rosary, and hear Mass, and enjoy all the other treats that our holy religion gives us. In addition to that he's enjoying them like the proverbial stolen fruit. You were very severe with me when I demurred at hearing his confession without authority from his father; but I don't like stolen fruit, and I'm not sure even now if I was right in yielding on that point. I shouldn't have yielded if I hadn't felt that Cyril might be hurt in the future by my scruples. Now look here, Mark, you've got to see that I don't regret my surrender. If that youth doesn't get from religion what I hope and pray he will get . . . but let that point alone. My scruples are my own affair. Your convictions are your own affair. But Cyril is our joint affair. He's your convert, but he's my penitent; and Mark, don't overdecorate your building until you're sure the foundations are well and truly laid."

Mark was never given an opportunity of proving the excellence of his methods by the excellence of Cyril's life, because on the morning after this conversation, which took place one wet Sunday evening in Advent he was sent for by his uncle, who demanded to know the meaning of This. This was a letter from the Reverend Eustace Pomeroy.

The Limes,
38, Cranborne Road,
Slowbridge.
December 9.

Dear Mr. Lidderdale,

My son Cyril will not attend school for the rest of this term. Yesterday evening, being confined to the house by fever, I went up to his bedroom to verify a reference in a book I had recently lent him to assist his divinity studies under you. When I took down the book from the shelf I noticed several books hidden away behind, and my curiosity being aroused I examined them, in case they should be works of an unpleasant nature. To my horror and disgust, I found that they were all works of an extremely Popish character, most of them belonging to a clergyman in this neighbourhood called Ogilvie, whose illegal practices have for several years been a scandal to this diocese. These I am sending to the Bishop that he may see with his own eyes the kind of propaganda that is going on. Two of the books, inscribed Mark Lidderdale, are evidently the property of your nephew to whom I suppose my son is indebted for this wholesale corruption. On questioning my son I found him already so sunk in the mire of the pernicious doctrines he has imbibed that he actually defied his own father. I thrashed him severely in spite of my fever, and he is now under lock and key in his bedroom where he will remain until he sails with me to Sydney next week whither I am summoned to the conference of Australasian missionaries. During the voyage I shall wrestle with the demon that has entered into my son and endeavour to persuade him that Jesus only is necessary for salvation. And when I have done so, I shall leave him in Australia to earn his own living remote from the scene of his corruption. In the circumstances I assume that you will deduct a proportion of his school fees for this term. I know that you will be as much horrified and disgusted as I was by your nephew's conduct, and I trust that you will be able to wrestle with him in the Lord and prove to him that Jesus only is necessary to salvation.

Yours very truly,

Eustace Pomeroy.

P.S. I suggest that instead of £6 6s. 0d. I should pay £5 5s. 0d. for this term, plus, of course, the usual extras.

The pulse in Mr. Lidderdale's temple had never throbbed so remarkably as while Mark was reading this letter.

"A fine thing," he ranted, "if this story gets about in Slowbridge. A fine reward for all my kindness if you ruin my school. As for this man Ogilvie, I'll sue him for damages. Don't look at me with that expression of bestial defiance. Do you hear? What prevents my thrashing you as you deserve? What prevents me, I say?"

But Mark was not paying any attention to his uncle's fury; he was thinking about the unfortunate martyr under lock and key in The Limes, Cranborne Road, Slowbridge. He was wondering what would be the effect of this violent removal to the Antipodes and how that fundamental weakness of character would fare if Cyril were left to himself at his age.

"I think Mr. Pomeroy is a ruffian," said Mark. "Don't you, Uncle Henry? If he writes to the Bishop about Mr. Ogilvie, I shall write to the Bishop about him. I hate Protestants. I hate them."

"There's your father to the life. You'd like to burn them, wouldn't you?"

"Yes, I would," Mark declared.

"You'd like to burn me, I suppose?"

"Not you in particular."

"Will you listen to him, Helen," he shouted to his sister. "Come here and listen to him. Listen to the boy we took in and educated and clothed and fed, listen to him saying he'd like to burn his uncle. Into Mr. Hitchcock's office you go at once. No more education if this is what it leads to. Read that letter, Helen, look at that book, Helen. *Catholic Prayers for Church of England People by the Reverend A.H. Stanton.* Look at this book, Helen. *The Catholic Religion by Vernon Staley.* No wonder you hate Protestants, you ungrateful boy. No wonder you're longing to burn your uncle and aunt. It'll be in the *Slowbridge Herald* tomorrow. Headlines! Ruin! They'll think I'm a Jesuit in disguise. I ought to have got a very handsome sum of money for the good-will. Go back to your class-room, and if you have a spark of affection in your nature, don't brag about this to the other boys."

Mark, pondering all the morning the best thing to do for Cyril, remembered that a boy called Hacking lived at The Laurels, 36, Cranborne Road. He did not like Hacking, but wishing to utilize his back garden for the purpose of communicating with the prisoner he made himself agreeable to him in the interval between first and second school.

"Hullo, Hacking," he began. "I say, do you want a cricket bat? I shan't be here next summer, so you may as well have mine."

Hacking looked at Mark suspicious of some hidden catch that would make him appear a fool.

"No, really I'm not ragging," said Mark. "I'll bring it round to you after dinner. I'll be at your place about a quarter to two. Wait for me, won't you?"

Hacking puzzled his brains to account for this generous whim, and at last decided that Mark must be "gone" on his sister Edith. He supposed that he ought to warn Edith to be about when Mark called; if the bat was not forthcoming he could easily prevent a meeting. The bat however turned out to be much better than he expected, and Hacking was on the point of presenting Cressida to Troilus when Troilus said:

"That's your garden at the back, isn't it?"

Hacking admitted that it was.

"It looks rather decent."

Hacking allowed modestly that it wasn't bad.

"My father's rather dead nuts on gardening. So's my kiddy sister," he added.

"I vote we go out there," Mark suggested.

"Shall I give a yell to my kiddy sister?" asked Pandarus.

"Good lord, no," Mark exclaimed. "Don't the Pomeroys live next door to you? Look here, Hacking, I want to speak to Cyril Pomeroy."

"He was absent this morning."

Mark considered Hacking as a possible adjutant to the enterprise he was plotting. That he finally decided to admit Hacking to his confidence was due less to the favourable result of the scrutiny than to the fact that unless he confided in Hacking he would find it difficult to communicate with Cyril and impossible to manage his escape. Mark aimed as high as this. His first impulse had been to approach the Vicar of Meade Cantorum, but on second thoughts he had rejected him in favour of Mr. Dorward, who was not so likely to suffer from respect for paternal authority.

"Look here, Hacking, will you swear not to say a word about what I'm going to tell you?"

"Of course," said Hacking, who scenting a scandal would have promised much more than this to obtain the details of it.

"What will you swear by?"

"Oh, anything," Hacking offered, without the least hesitation. "I don't mind what it is."

"Well, what do you consider the most sacred thing in the world?"

If Hacking had known himself, he would have said food; not knowing himself, he suggested the Bible.

"I suppose you know that if you swear something on the Bible and break your oath you can be put in prison?" Mark demanded sternly.

"Yes, of course."

The oath was administered, and Hacking waited goggle-eyed for the revelation.

"Is that all?" he asked when Mark stopped.

"Well, it's enough, isn't it? And now you've got to help him to escape."

"But I didn't swear I'd do that," argued Hacking.

"All right then. Don't. I thought you'd enjoy it."

"We should get into a row. There'd be an awful shine."

"Who's to know it's us? I've got a friend in the country. And I shall telegraph to him and ask if he'll hide Pomeroy."

Mark was not sufficiently sure of Hacking's discretion or loyalty to mention Dorward's name. After all this business wasn't just a rag.

"The first thing is for you to go out in the garden and attract Pomeroy's attention. He's locked in his bedroom."

"But I don't know which is his bedroom," Hacking objected.

"Well, you don't suppose the whole family are locked in their bedrooms, do you?" asked Mark scornfully.

"But how do you know his bedroom is on this side of the house?"

"I don't," said Mark. "That's what I want to find out. If it's in the front of the house, I shan't want your help, especially as you're so funky."

Hacking went out into the garden, and presently he came back with the news that Pomeroy was waiting outside to talk to Mark over the wall.

"Waiting outside?" Mark repeated. "What do you mean, waiting outside? How can he be waiting outside when he's locked in his bedroom?"

"But he's not," said Hacking.

Sure enough, when Mark went out he found Cyril astride the party wall between the two gardens waiting for him.

"You can't let your father drag you off to Australia like this," Mark argued. "You'll go all to pieces there. You'll lose your faith, and take to drink, and—you must refuse to go."

Cyril smiled weakly and explained to Mark that when once his father had made up his mind to do something it was impossible to stop him.

Thereupon Mark explained his scheme.

"I'll get an answer from Dorward tonight and you must escape tomorrow afternoon as soon as it's dark. Have you got a rope ladder?"

Cyril smiled more feebly than ever.

"No, I suppose you haven't. Then what you must do is tear up your sheets and let yourself down into the garden. Hacking will whistle three times if all's clear, and then you must climb over into his garden and run as hard as you can to the corner of the road where I'll be waiting for you in a cab. I'll go up to London with you and see you off from Waterloo, which is the station for Green Lanes where Father Dorward lives. You take a ticket to Galton, and I expect he'll meet you, or if he doesn't, it's only a seven mile walk. I don't know the way, but you can ask when you get to Galton. Only if you could find your way without asking it would be better, because if you're pursued and you're seen asking the way you'll be caught more easily. Now I must rush off and borrow some money from Mr. Ogilvie. No, perhaps it would rouse suspicions if I were absent from afternoon school. My uncle would be sure to guess, and—though I don't think he would—he might try to lock me up in my room. But I say," Mark suddenly exclaimed in indignation, "how on earth did you manage to come and talk to me out here?"

Cyril explained that he had only been locked in his bedroom last night when his father was so angry. He had freedom to move about in the house and garden, and, he added to Mark's annoyance, there would be no need for him to use rope ladders or sheets to escape. If Mark would tell him what time to be at the corner of the road and would wait for him a little while in case his father saw him going out and prevented him, he would easily be able to escape.

"Then I needn't have told Hacking," said Mark. "However, now I have told him, he must do something, or else he's sure to let out what he knows. I wish I knew where to get the money for the fare."

"I've got a pound in my money box."

"Have you?" said Mark, a little mortified, but at the same time relieved that he could keep Mr. Ogilvie from being involved. "Well, that ought to be enough. I've got enough to send a telegram to Dorward. As soon as I get his answer I'll send you word by Hacking. Now don't hang about in the garden all the afternoon or your people will begin to think something's up. If you could, it would be a good thing for you to be heard praying and groaning in your room."

Cyril smiled his feeble smile, and Mark felt inclined to abandon him to his fate; but he decided on reflection that the importance of vindicating the claims of the Church to a persecuted son was more important than the foolishness and the feebleness of the son.

"Do you want me to do anything more?" Hacking asked.

Mark suggested that Hacking's name and address should be given for Mr. Dorward's answer, but this Hacking refused.

"If a telegram came to our house, everybody would want to read it. Why can't it be sent to you?"

Mark sighed for his fellow-conspirator's stupidity. To this useless clod he had presented a valuable bat.

"All right," he said impatiently, "you needn't do anything more except tell Pomeroy what time he's to be at the corner of the road tomorrow."

"I'll do that, Lidderdale."

"I should think you jolly well would," Mark exclaimed scornfully.

Mark spent a long time over the telegram to Dorward; in the end he decided that it would be safer to assume that the priest would shelter and hide Cyril rather than take the risk of getting an answer. The final draft was as follows:—

Dorward Green Lanes Medworth Hants

>Am sending persecuted Catholic boy by 7.30 from Waterloo Tuesday please send conveyance Mark Lidderdale.

Mark only had eightpence, and this message would cost tenpence. He took out the *am*, changed *by 7.30 from Waterloo* to *arriving 9.35* and *send conveyance* to *meet*. If he had only borrowed Cyril's sovereign, he could have been more explicit. However, he flattered himself that he was getting full value for his eightpence. He then worked out the cost of Cyril's escape.

	s.	d.
Third Class single to Paddington	1	6
Third Class return to Paddington (for self)	2	6
Third Class single Waterloo to Galton	3	11
Cab from Paddington to Waterloo	3	6?
Cab from Waterloo to Paddington (for self)	3	6?
Sandwiches for Cyril and Self	1	0
Ginger-beer for Cyril and Self	(4 bottles)	8
Total	16	7

The cab of course might cost more, and he must take back the eightpence out of it for himself. But Cyril would have at least one and sixpence in his pocket when he arrived, which he could put in the offertory at the Mass of thanksgiving for his escape that he would attend on the following morning. Cyril would be useful to old Dorward, and he (Mark) would give him some tips on serving if they had an empty compartment from Slowbridge to Paddington. Mark's original intention had been to wait at the corner of Cranborne Road in a closed cab like the proverbial postchaise of elopements, but he discarded this idea for reasons of economy. He hoped that Cyril would not get frightened on the way to the station and turn back. Perhaps after all it would be wiser to order a cab and give up the ginger-beer, or pay for the ginger-beer with the money for the telegram. Once inside a cab Cyril was bound to go on. Hacking might be committed more completely to the enterprise by waiting inside until he arrived with Cyril. It was a pity that Cyril was not locked in his room, and yet when it came to it he would probably have funked letting himself down from the window by knotted sheets. Mark walked home with Hacking after school, to give his final instructions for the following day.

"I'm telling you now," he said, "because we oughtn't to be seen together at all tomorrow, in case of arousing suspicion. You must get hold of Pomeroy and tell him to run to the corner of the road at half-past-five, and jump straight into the fly that'll be waiting there with you inside."

"But where will you be?"

"I shall be waiting outside the ticket barrier with the tickets."

"Supposing he won't?"

"I'll risk seeing him once more. Go and ask if you can speak to him a minute, and tell him to come out in the garden presently. Say you've knocked a ball over or something and will Master Cyril throw it back. I say, we might really put a message inside a ball and throw it over. That was the way the Duc de Beaufort escaped in *Twenty Years After*."

Hacking looked blankly at Mark.

"But it's dark and wet," he objected. "I shouldn't knock a ball over on a wet evening like this."

"Well, the skivvy won't think of that, and Pomeroy will guess that we're trying to communicate with him."

Mark thought how odd it was that Hacking should be so utterly blind to the romance of the enterprise. After a few more objections which were disposed of by Mark, Hacking agreed to go next door and try to get the prisoner into the garden. He succeeded in this, and Mark rated Cyril for not having given him the sovereign yesterday.

"However, bunk in and get it now, because I shan't see you again till tomorrow at the station, and I must have some money to buy the tickets."

He explained the details of the escape and exacted from Cyril a promise not to back out at the last moment.

"You've got nothing to do. It's as simple as A B C. It's too simple, really, to be much of a rag. However, as it isn't a rag, but serious, I suppose we oughtn't to grumble. Now, you are coming, aren't you?"

Cyril promised that nothing but physical force should prevent him.

"If you funk, don't forget that you'll have betrayed your faith and . . ."

At this moment Mark in his enthusiasm slipped off the wall, and after uttering one more solemn injunction against backing out at the last minute he left Cyril to the protection of Angels for the next twenty-four hours.

Although he would never have admitted as much, Mark was rather astonished when Cyril actually did present himself at Slowbridge station in time to catch the 5.47 train up to town. Their compartment was not empty, so that Mark was unable to give Cyril that lesson in serving at the altar which he had intended to give him. Instead, as Cyril seemed in his reaction to the excitement of the escape likely to burst into tears at any moment, he drew for him a vivid picture of the enjoyable life to which the train was taking him.

"Father Dorward says that the country round Green Lanes is ripping. And his church is Norman. I expect he'll make you his ceremonarius. You're an awfully lucky chap, you know. He says that next Corpus Christi, he's going to have Mass on the village green. Nobody will know where you are, and I daresay later on you can become a hermit. You might become a saint. The last English saint to be canonized was St. Thomas Cantilupe of Hereford. But of course Charles the First ought to have been properly canonized. By the time you die I should think we should have got back canonization in the English Church, and if I'm alive then I'll propose your canonization. St. Cyril Pomeroy you'd be."

Such were the bright colours in which Mark painted Cyril's future; when he had watched him wave his farewells from the window of the departing train at Waterloo, he felt as if he were watching the bodily assumption of a saint.

"Where have you been all the evening?" asked Uncle Henry, when Mark came back about nine o'clock.

"In London," said Mark.

"Your insolence is becoming insupportable. Get away to your room."

It never struck Mr. Lidderdale that his nephew was telling the truth.

The hue and cry for Cyril Pomeroy began at once, and though Mark maintained at first that the discovery of Cyril's hiding-place was due to nothing else except the cowardice of Hacking, who when confronted by a detective burst into tears and revealed all he knew, he was bound to admit afterward that, if Mr. Ogilvie had been questioned much more, he would have had to reveal the secret himself. Mark was hurt that his efforts to help a son of Holy Church should not be better appreciated by Mr. Ogilvie; but he forgave his friend in view of the nuisance that it undoubtedly must have been to have Meade Cantorum beleaguered by half a dozen corpulent detectives. The only person in the Vicarage who seemed to approve of what he had done was Esther; she who had always seemed to ignore him, even sometimes in a sensitive mood to despise him, was full of congratulations.

"How did you manage it, Mark?"

"Oh, I took a cab," said Mark modestly. "One from the corner of Cranborne Road to Slowbridge, and another from Paddington to Waterloo. We had some sandwiches, and a good deal of ginger-beer at Paddington because we thought we mightn't be able to get any at Waterloo, but at Waterloo we had some more ginger-beer. I wish I hadn't told Hacking. If I hadn't, we should probably have pulled it off. Old Dorward was up to anything. But Hacking is a hopeless ass."

"What does your uncle say?"

"He's rather sick," Mark admitted. "He refused to let me go to school any more, which as you may imagine doesn't upset me very much, and I'm to go into Hitchcock's office after Christmas. As far as I can make out I shall be a kind of servant."

"Have you talked to Stephen about it?"

"Well, he's a bit annoyed with me about this kidnapping. I'm afraid I have rather let him in for it. He says he doesn't mind so much if it's kept out of the papers."

"Anyway, I think it was a sporting effort by you," said Esther. "I wasn't particularly keen on you until you brought this off. I hate pious boys. I wish you'd told me beforehand. I'd have loved to help."

"Would you? I say, I am sorry. I never thought of you," said Mark much disappointed at the lost opportunity. "You'd have been much better than that ass Hacking. If you and I had been the only people in it, I'll bet the detectives would never have found him."

"And what's going to happen to the youth now?"

"Oh, his father's going to take him to Australia as he arranged. They sail tomorrow. There's one thing," Mark added with a kind of gloomy relish. "He's bound to go to the bad, and perhaps that'll be a lesson to his father."

The hope of the Vicar of Meade Cantorum and equally it may be added the hope of Mr. Lidderdale that the affair would be kept out of the papers was not fulfilled. The day after Mr. Pomeroy and his son sailed from Tilbury the following communication appeared in *The Times*:

> Sir,—The accompanying letter was handed to me by my friend the Reverend Eustace Pomeroy to be used as I thought fit and subject to only one stipulation—that it should not be published until he and his son were out of England. As President of the Society for the Protection of the English Church against Romish Aggression I feel that it is my duty to lay the facts before the country. I need scarcely add that I have been at pains to verify the surprising and alarming accusations made by a clergyman against two other clergymen, and I earnestly request the publicity of your columns for what I venture to believe is positive proof of the dangerous conspiracy existing in our very midst to romanize the Established Church of England. I shall be happy to produce for any of your readers who find Mr. Pomeroy's story incredible at the close of the nineteenth century the signed statements of witnesses and other documentary evidence.
>
> > I am, Sir,
> > Your obedient servant,
> >
> > Danvers.

The Right Honble. the Lord Danvers, P.C.
President of the Society for the Protection of the English Church against Romish Aggression.

My Lord,

I have to bring to your notice as President of the S.P.E. C.R.A. what I venture to assert is one of the most daring plots to subvert home and family life in the interests of priestcraft that has ever been discovered. In taking this step I am fully conscious of its seriousness, and if I ask your lordship to delay taking any measures for publicity until the unhappy principal is upon the high seas in the guardianship of his even more unhappy father, I do so for the sake of the wretched boy whose future has been nearly blasted by the Jesuitical behaviour of two so-called Protestant clergymen.

Four years ago, my lord, I retired from a lifelong career as a missionary in New Guinea to give my children the advantages of English education and English climate, and it is surely hard that I should live to curse the day on which I did so. My third son Cyril was sent to school at Haverton House, Slowbridge, to an educational establishment kept by a Mr. Henry Lidderdale, reputed to be a strong Evangelical and I believe I am justified in saying rightly so reputed. At the same time I regret that Mr. Lidderdale, whose brother was a notorious Romanizer I have since discovered, should not have exercised more care in the supervision of his nephew, a fellow scholar with my own son at Haverton House. It appears that Mr. Lidderdale was so lax as to permit his nephew to frequent the services of the Reverend Stephen Ogilvie at Meade Cantorum, where every excess such as incense, lighted candles, mariolatry and creeping to the cross is openly practised. The Revd. S. Ogilvie I may add is a member of the S.S.C., that notorious secret society whose machinations have been so often exposed and the originators of that filthy book "The Priest in Absolution." He is also a member of the Guild of All Souls which has for its avowed object the restoration of the Romish doctrine of Purgatory with all its attendant horrors, and finally I need scarcely add he is a member of the Confraternity of the "Blessed Sacrament" which seeks openly to popularize the idolatrous and blasphemous cult of the Mass.

Young Lidderdale presumably under the influence of this disloyal Protestant clergyman sought to corrupt my son, and was actually so far successful as to lure him to attend the idolatrous services at Meade Cantorum church, which of course he was only able to do by inventing lies and excuses to his father to account for his absence from the simple worship to which all his life he had been accustomed. Not content with this my unhappy son was actually persuaded to confess his sins to this self-styled "priest"! I wonder if he confessed the sin of deceiving his own father to "Father" Ogilvie who supplied him with numerous Mass books, several of which I enclose for your lordship's inspection. You will be amused if you are not too much horrified by these puerile and degraded works, and in one of them, impudently entitled "Catholic Prayers for Church of England People" you will actually see in cold print a prayer for the "Pope of Rome." This work emanates from that hotbed of sacerdotal disloyalty, St. Alban's, Holborn.

These vile books I discovered by accident carefully hidden away in my son's bedroom. "Facilis descensus Averni!" You will easily imagine the humiliation of a parent who, having devoted his life to bring the Gospel of Jesus Christ to the heathen, finds that his own son has fallen as low as the lowest savage. As soon as I made my discovery, I removed him from Haverton House, and warned the proprietor of the risk he was running by not taking better care of his pupils. Having been summoned to a conference of missionaries in Sydney, N.S.W., I determined to take my son with me in the hope that a long voyage in the company of a loving parent, eager to help him back to the path of Truth and Salvation from which he had strayed, might cure him of his idolatrous fancies, and restore him to Jesus.

What followed is, as I write this, scarcely credible to myself; but however incredible, it is true. Young Lidderdale, acting no doubt at the instigation of "Father" Ogilvie (as my son actually called him to my face, not realizing the blasphemy of according to a mortal clergyman the title that belongs to God alone), entered into a conspiracy with another Romanizing clergyman, the Reverend Oliver Dorward, Vicar of Green Lanes, Hants, to abduct my son from his own father's house, with what ultimate intention I dare not think. Incredible as it must sound to modern ears, they were so far successful that for a whole week I was in ignorance of his whereabouts, while detectives were hunting for him up and down England. The abduction was carried out by young Lidderdale, with the assistance of a youth called Hacking, so coolly and skilfully as to indicate that the abettors behind the scenes are USED TO SUCH ABDUCTIONS. This, my lord, points to a very grave state of affairs in our midst. If the son of a Protestant clergyman like myself can be spirited away from a populous but nevertheless comparatively small town like Slowbridge, what must be going on in great cities like London? Moreover, everything is done to make it attractive for the unhappy youth who is thus lured away from his father's hearth. My own son is even now still impenitent, and I have the greatest fears for his moral and religious future, so rapid has been the corruption set up by evil companionship.

These, my lord, are the facts set out as shortly as possible and written on the eve of my departure in circumstances that militate against elegance of expression. I am, to tell the truth, still staggered by this affair, and if I make public my sorrow and my shame I do so in the hope that the Society of which your lordship is President, may see its way to take some kind of action that will make a repetition of such an outrage upon family life for ever impossible.

Believe me to be,
Your lordship's obedient servant,

Eustace Pomeroy.

The publication of this letter stirred England. *The Times* in a leading article demanded a full inquiry into the alleged circumstances.

The English Churchman said that nothing like it had happened since the days of Bloody Mary. Questions were asked in the House of Commons, and finally when it became known that Lord Danvers would ask a question in the House of Lords, Mr. Ogilvie took Mark to see Lord Hull who wished to be in possession of the facts before he rose to correct some misapprehensions of Lord Danvers. Mark also had to interview two Bishops, an Archdeacon, and a Rural Dean. He did not realize that for a few weeks he was a central figure in what was called THE CHURCH CRISIS. He was indignant at Mr. Pomeroy's exaggeration and perversions of fact, and he was so evidently speaking the truth that everybody from Lord Hull to a reporter of *The Sun* was impressed by his account of the affair, so that in the end the Pomeroy Abduction was decided to be less revolutionary than the Gunpowder Plot.

Mr. Lidderdale, however, believed that his nephew had deliberately tried to ruin him out of malice, and when two parents seized the opportunity of such a scandal to remove their sons from Haverton House without paying the terminal fees, Mr. Lidderdale told Mark that he should recoup himself for the loss out of the money left by his mother.

"How much did she leave?" his nephew asked.

"Don't ask impertinent questions."

"But it's my money, isn't it?"

"It will be your money in another six years, if you behave yourself. Meanwhile half of it will be devoted to paying your premium at the office of my friend Mr. Hitchcock."

"But I don't want to be a solicitor. I want to be a priest," said Mark.

Uncle Henry produced a number of cogent reasons that would make his nephew's ambition unattainable.

"Very well, if I can't be a priest, I don't want the money, and you can keep it yourself," said Mark. "But I'm not going to be a solicitor."

"And what are you going to be, may I inquire?" asked Uncle Henry.

"In the end I probably *shall* be a priest," Mark prophesied. "But I haven't quite decided yet how. I warn you that I shall run away."

"Run away," his uncle echoed in amazement. "Good heavens, boy, haven't you had enough of running away over this deplorable Pomeroy affair? Where are you going to run to?"

"I couldn't tell you, could I, even if I knew?" Mark asked as tactfully as he was able. "But as a matter of fact, I don't know. I only know that I won't go into Mr. Hitchcock's office. If you try to force me, I shall write to *The Times* about it."

Such a threat would have sounded absurd in the mouth of a schoolboy before the Pomeroy business; but now Mr. Lidderdale took it seriously and began to wonder if Haverton House would survive any more of such publicity. When a few days later Mr. Ogilvie, whom Mark had consulted about his future, wrote to propose that Mark should live with him and work under his superintendence with the idea of winning a scholarship at Oxford, Mr. Lidderdale was inclined to treat his suggestion as a solution of the problem, and he replied encouragingly:

Haverton House,
Slowbridge.
Jan. 15.

Dear Sir,

Am I to understand from your letter that you are offering to make yourself responsible for my nephew's future, for I must warn you that I could not accept your suggestion unless such were the case? I do not approve of what I assume will be the trend of your education, and I should have to disclaim any further responsibility in the matter of my nephew's future. I may inform you that I hold in trust for him until he comes of age the sum of £522 8s. 7d. which was left by his mother. The annual interest upon this I have used until now as a slight contribution to the expense to which I have been put on his account; but I have not thought it right to use any of the capital sum. This I am proposing to transfer to you. His mother did not execute any legal document and I have nothing more binding than a moral obligation. If you undertake the responsibility of looking after him until such time as he is able to earn his own living, I consider that you are entitled to use this money in any way you think right. I hope that the boy will reward your confidence more amply than he has rewarded mine. I need not allude to the Pomeroy business to you, for notwithstanding your public denials I cannot but consider that you were as deeply implicated in that disgraceful affair as he was. I note what you say about the admiration you had for my brother. I wish I could honestly say that I shared that admiration. But my brother and I were not on good terms, for which state of affairs he was entirely responsible. I am more ready to surrender to you all my authority over Mark because I am only too well aware how during the last year you have consistently undermined that authority and encouraged my nephew's rebellious spirit. I have had a great experience of boys during thirty-five years of schoolmastering, and I can assure you that I have never had to deal with a boy so utterly insensible to kindness as my nephew. His conduct toward his aunt I can only characterize as callous. Of his conduct towards me I prefer to say no more. I came forward at a moment when he was likely to be sunk in the most abject poverty, and my reward has been ingratitude. I pray that his dark and stubborn temperament may not turn to vice and folly as he grows older, but I have little hope of its not doing so. I confess that to me his future seems dismally black. You may have acquired some kind of influence over his emotions, if he has any emotions, but I am not inclined to suppose that it will endure.

On hearing from you that you persist in your offer to assume complete responsibility for my nephew, I will hand him over to your care at once. I cannot pretend that I shall be sorry to see the last of him, for I am not a hypocrite. I may add that his clothes are in rather a sorry state. I had intended to equip him upon his entering the office of my old friend Mr. Hitchcock and with that intention I have been letting him wear out what he has. This, I may say, he has done most effectually.

I am, Sir,
Yours faithfully,

Henry Lidderdale.

To which Mr. Ogilvie replied:

The Vicarage,
Meade Cantorum,
Bucks.
Jan. 16.

Dear Mr. Lidderdale,

I accept full responsibility for Mark and for Mark's money. Send both of them along whenever you like. I'm not going to embark on another controversy about the "rights" of boys. I've exhausted every argument on this subject since Mark involved me in his drastic measures of a month ago. But please let me assure you that I will do my best for him and that I am convinced he will do his best for me.

Yours truly,

Stephen Ogilvie.

CHAPTER XIII

WYCH-ON-THE-WOLD

Mark rarely visited his uncle and aunt after he went to live at Meade Cantorum; and the break was made complete soon afterward when the living of Wych-on-the-Wold was accepted by Mr. Ogilvie, so complete indeed that he never saw his relations again. Uncle Henry died five years later; Aunt Helen went to live at St. Leonard's, where she took up palmistry and became indispensable to the success of charitable bazaars in East Sussex.

Wych, a large village on a spur of the Cotswold hills, was actually in Oxfordshire, although by so bare a margin that all the windows looked down into Gloucestershire, except those in the Rectory; they looked out across a flat country of elms and willow-bordered streams to a flashing spire in Northamptonshire reputed to be fifty miles away. It was a high windy place, seeming higher and windier on account of the numbers of pigeons that were always circling round the church tower. There was hardly a house in Wych that did not have its pigeon-cote, from the great round columbary in the Rectory garden to the few holes in a gable-end of some steep-roofed cottage. Wych was architecturally as perfect as most Cotswold villages, and if it lacked the variety of Wychford in the vale below, that was because the exposed position had kept its successive builders too intent on solidity to indulge their fancy. The result was an austere uniformity of design that accorded fittingly with a landscape whose beauty was all of line and whose colour like the lichen on an old wall did not flauntingly reveal its gradations of tint to the transient observer. The bleak upland airs had taught the builders to be sparing with their windows; the result of such solicitude for the comfort of the inmates was a succession of blank spaces of freestone that delighted the eye with an effect of strength and leisure, of cleanliness and tranquillity.

The Rectory, dating from the reign of Charles II, did not arrogate to itself the right to retire behind trees from the long line of the single village street; but being taller than the other houses it brought the street to a dignified conclusion, and it was not unworthy of the noble church which stood apart from the village, a landmark for miles, upon the brow of the rolling wold. There was little traffic on the road that climbed up from Wychford in the valley of the swift Greenrush five miles away, and there was less traffic on the road beyond, which for eight miles sent branch after branch to remote farms and hamlets until itself became no more than a sheep track and faded out upon a hilly pasturage. Yet even this unfrequented road only bisected the village at the end of its wide street, where in the morning when the children were at school and the labourers at work in the fields the silence was cloistral, where one could stand listening to the larks high overhead, and where the lightest footstep aroused curiosity, so that one turned the head to peep and peer for the cause of so strange a sound.

Mr. Ogilvie's parish had a large superficial area; but his parishioners were not many outside the village, and in that country of wide pastures the whole of his cure did not include half-a-dozen farms. There was no doctor and no squire, unless Will Starling of Rushbrooke Grange could be counted as the squire.

Halfway to Wychford and close to the boundary of the two parishes an infirm signpost managed with the aid of a stunted hawthorn to keep itself partially upright and direct the wayfarer to Wych Maries. Without the signpost nobody would have suspected that the grassgrown track thus indicated led anywhere except over the top of the wold.

"You must go and explore Wych Maries," the Rector had said to Mark soon after they arrived. "You'll find it rather attractive. There's a disused chapel dedicated to St. Mary the Virgin and St. Mary Magdalene. My predecessor took me there when we drove round the parish on my first visit; but I haven't yet had time to go again. And you ought to have a look at the gardens of Rushbrooke Grange. The present squire is away. In the South Seas, I believe. But the housekeeper, Mrs. Honeybone, will show you round."

It was in response to this advice that Mark and Esther set out on a golden May evening to explore Wych Maries. Esther had continued to be friendly with Mark after the Pomeroy affair; and when he came to live at Meade Cantorum she had expressed her pleasure at the prospect of having him for a brother.

"But you'll keep off religion, won't you?" she had demanded.

Mark promised that he would, wondering why she should suppose that he was incapable of perceiving who was and who was not interested in it.

"I suppose you've guessed my fear?" she had continued. "Haven't you? Haven't you guessed that I'm frightened to death of becoming religious?"

The reassuring contradiction that one naturally gives to anybody who voices a dread of being overtaken by some misfortune might perhaps have sounded inappropriate, and Mark had held his tongue.

"My father was very religious. My mother is more or less religious. Stephen is religious. Miriam is religious. Oh, Mark, and I sometimes feel that I too must fall on my knees and surrender. But I won't. Because it spoils life. I shall be beaten in the end of course, and I'll probably get religious mania when I am beaten. But until then—" She did not finish her sentence; only her blue eyes glittered at the challenge of life.

That was the last time religion was mentioned between Mark and Esther, and since both of them enjoyed the country they became friends. On this May evening they stood by the signpost and looked across the shimmering grass to where the sun hung in his web of golden haze above the edge of the wold.

"If we take the road to Wych Maries," said Mark, "we shall be walking right into the sun."

Esther did not reply, but Mark understood that she assented to his truism, and they walked on as silent as the long shadows that followed them. A quarter of a mile from the high road the path reached the edge of the wold and dipped over into a wood which was sparse just below the brow, but which grew denser down the slope with many dark evergreens interspersed, and in the valley below became a jungle. After the bare upland country this volume of May verdure seemed indescribably rich and the valley beyond, where the Greenrush flowed through kingcups toward the sun, indescribably alluring. Esther and Mark forgot that they were exploring Wych Maries and thinking only of reaching that wide valley they ran down through the wood, rejoicing in the airy green of the ash-trees above them and shouting as they ran. But presently cypresses and sombre yews rose on either side of the path, and the road to Wych Maries was soft and silent, and the serene sun was lost, and their whispering footsteps forbade them to shout any more. At the bottom of the hill the trees increased in number and variety; the sun shone through pale oak-leaves and the warm green of sycamores. Nevertheless a sadness haunted the wood, where the red campions made only a mist of colour with no reality of life and flowers behind.

"This wood's awfully jolly, isn't it?" said Mark, hoping to gain from Esther's agreement the dispersal of his gloom.

"I don't care for it much," she replied. "There doesn't seem to be any life in it."

"I heard a cuckoo just now," said Mark.

"Yes, out of tune already."

"Mm, rather out of tune. Mind those nettles," he warned her.

"I thought Stephen said he drove here."

"Perhaps we've come the wrong way. I believe the road forked by the ash wood above. Anyway if we go toward the sun we shall come out in the valley, and we can walk back along the banks of the river to Wychford."

"We can always go back through the wood," said Esther.

"Yes, if you don't mind going back the way you came."

"Come on," she snapped. She was not going to be laughed at by Mark, and she dared him to deny that he was not as much aware as herself of an eeriness in the atmosphere.

"Only because it seems dark in here after that dazzling sunlight on the wold. Hark! I hear the sound of water."

They struggled through the undergrowth toward the sound; soon from a steep wooded bank they were gazing down into a millpool, the surface of which reflected with a gloomy deepening of their hue the colour but not the form of the trees above. Water was flowing through a rotten sluice gate down from the level of the stream upon a slimy water-wheel that must have been out of action for many years.

"The dark tarn of Auber in the misty mid region of Weir!" Mark exclaimed. "Don't you love *Ulalume*? I think it's about my favourite poem."

"Never heard of it," Esther replied indifferently. He might have taken advantage of this confession to give her a lecture on poetry, if the millpool and the melancholy wood had not been so affecting as to make the least attempt at literary exposition impertinent.

"And there's the chapel," Mark exclaimed, pointing to a ruined edifice of stone, the walls of which were stained with the damp of years rising from the pool. "But how shall we reach it? We must have come the wrong way."

"Let's go back! Let's go back!" Esther exclaimed, surrendering to the command of an intuition that overcame her pride. "This place is unlucky."

Mark looking at her wild eyes, wilder in the dark that came so early in this overshadowed place, was half inclined to turn round at her behest; but at that moment he perceived a possible path through the nettles and briers at the farther end of the pool and unwilling to go back to the Rectory without having visited the ruined chapel of Wych Maries he called on her to follow him. This she did fearfully at first; but gradually regaining her composure she emerged on the other side as cool and scornful as the Esther with whom he was familiar.

"What frightened you?" he asked, when they were standing on a grassgrown road that wound through a rank pasturage browsed on by a solitary black cow and turned the corner by a clump of cedars toward a large building, the presence of which was felt rather than seen beyond the trees.

"I was bored by the brambles," Esther offered for explanation.

"This must be the driving road," Mark proclaimed. "I say, this chapel is rather ripping, isn't it?"

But Esther had wandered away across the rank meadow, where her meditative form made the solitary black cow look lonelier than ever. Mark turned aside to examine the chapel. He had been warned by the Rector to look at the images of St. Mary the Virgin and St. Mary Magdalene that had survived the ruin of the holy place of which they were tutelary and to which they had given their name. The history of the chapel was difficult to trace. It was so small as to suggest that it was a chantry; but there was no historical justification for linking its fortunes with the Starlings who owned Rushbrooke Grange, and there was no record of any lost hamlet here. That it was called Wych Maries might show a connexion either with Wychford or with Wych-on-the-Wold; it lay about midway between the two, and in days gone by there had been controversy on this point between the two parishes. The question had been settled by a squire of Rushbrooke's buying it in the eighteenth century, since when a legend had arisen that it was built and endowed by some crusading Starling of the thirteenth century. There was record neither of its glory nor of its decline, nor of what manner of folk worshipped there, nor of those who destroyed it. The roofless haunt of bats and owls, preserved from complete collapse by the ancient ivy that covered its walls, the mortar between its stones the prey of briers, its floor a nettle bed, the chapel remained a mystery. Yet over the arch of the west door the two Maries gazed heavenward as they had gazed for six hundred years. The curiosity of the few antiquarians who visited the place and speculated upon its past had kept the images clear of the ivy that covered the rest of the fabric. Mark did not put this to the credit of the antiquarians; but now perceiving for the first time these two austere shapes of divine women under conditions of atmosphere that enhanced their austerity and unearthliness he ascribed their freedom from decay to the interposition of God. To Mark's imagination, fixed upon the images while Esther wandered solitary in the field beyond the chapel, there was granted another of those moments of vision which marked like milestones his spiritual progress. He became suddenly assured that he would neither marry nor beget children. He was astonished to find himself in the grip of this thought, for his mind had never until this evening occupied itself with marriage or children, nor even with love. Yet here he was obsessed by the conviction of his finite purpose in the scheme of the world. He could not, he said to himself, be considered credulous if he sought for the explanation of his state of mind in the images of the two Maries. He looked at them resolved to illuminate with reason's eye the fluttering shadows of dusk that gave to the stone an illusion of life's bloom.

"Did their lips really move?" he asked aloud, and from the field beyond the black cow lowed a melancholy negative. Whether the stone had spoken or not, Mark accepted the revelation of his future as a Divine favour, and thenceforth he regarded the ruined chapel of Wych Maries as the place where the vow he made on that Whit-sunday was accepted by God.

"Aren't you ever coming?" the voice of Esther called across the field, and Mark hurried away to rejoin her on the grassgrown drive that led round the cedar grove to Rushbrooke Grange.

"It's too late now to go inside," he objected.

They were standing before the house.

"It's not too late at all," she contradicted eagerly. "Down here it seems later than it really is."

Rushbrooke Grange lacked the architectural perfection of the average Cotswold manor. Being a one-storied building it occupied a large superficial area, and its tumbling irregular roofs of freestone, the outlines of which were blurred by the encroaching mist of vegetation that overhung them, gave the effect of water, as if the atmosphere of this dank valley had wrought upon the substance of the building and as if the architects themselves had been confused by the rivalry of the trees by which it was surrounded. The owners of Rushbrooke Grange had never occupied a prominent position in the county, and their estates had grown smaller with each succeeding generation. There was no conspicuous author of their decay, no outstanding gamester or libertine from whose ownership the family's ruin could be dated. There was indeed nothing of interest in their annals except an attack upon the Grange by a party of armed burglars in the disorderly times at the beginning of the nineteenth century, when the squire's wife and two little girls were murdered while the squire and his sons were drinking deep in the Stag Inn at Wychford four miles away. Mark did not feel much inclined to blunt his impression of the chapel by perambulating Rushbrooke Grange under the guidance of Mrs. Honeybone, the old housekeeper; but Esther perversely insisted upon seeing the garden at any rate, giving as her excuse that the Rector would like them to pay the visit. By now it was a pink and green May dusk; the air was plumy with moths' wings, heavy with the scent of apple blossom.

"Well, you must explain who we are," said Mark while the echoes of the bell died away on the silence within the house and they waited for the footsteps that should answer their summons. The answer came from a window above the porch where Mrs. Honeybone's face, wreathed in wistaria, looked down and demanded in accents that were harsh with alarm who was there.

"I am the Rector's sister, Mrs. Honeybone," Esther explained.

"I don't care who you are," said Mrs. Honeybone. "You have no business to go ringing the bell at this time of the evening. It frightened me to death."

"The Rector asked me to call on you," she pressed.

Mark had already been surprised by Esther's using her brother as an excuse to visit the house and he was still more surprised by hearing her speak so politely, so ingratiatingly, it seemed, to this grim woman embowered in wistaria.

"We lost our way," Esther explained, "and that's why we're so late. The Rector told me about the water-lily pool, and I should so much like to see it."

Mrs. Honeybone debated with herself for a moment, until at last with a grunt of disapproval she came downstairs and opened the front door. The lily pool, now a lily pool only in name, for it was covered with an integument of duckweed which in twilight took on the texture of velvet, was an attractive place set in an enclosure of grass between high grey walls.

"That's all there is to see," said Mrs. Honeybone.

"Mr. Starling is abroad?" Esther asked.

The housekeeper nodded.

"And when is he coming back?" she went on.

"That's for him to say," said the housekeeper disagreeably. "He might come back tonight for all I know."

Almost before the sentence was out of her mouth the hall bell jangled, and a distant voice shouted:

"Nanny, Nanny, hurry up and open the door!"

Mrs. Honeybone could not have looked more startled if the voice had been that of a ghost. Mark began to talk of going until Esther cut him short.

"I don't think Mr. Starling will mind our being here so much as that," she said.

135

Mrs. Honeybone had already hurried off to greet her master; and when she was gone Mark looked at Esther, saw that her face was strangely flushed, and in an instant of divination apprehended either that she had already met the squire of Rushbrooke Grange or that she expected to meet him here tonight; so that, when presently a tall man of about thirty-five with brick-dust cheeks came into the close, he was not taken aback when Esther greeted him by name with the assurance of old friendship. Nor was he astonished that even in the wan light those brick-dust cheeks should deepen to terra-cotta, those hard blue eyes glitter with recognition, and the small thin-lipped mouth lose for a moment its immobility and gape, yes, gape, in the amazement of meeting somebody whom he never could have expected to meet at such an hour in such a place.

"You," he exclaimed. "You here!"

By the way he quickly looked behind him as if to intercept a prying glance Mark knew that, whatever the relationship between Esther and the squire had been in the past, it had been a relationship in which secrecy had played a part. In that moment between him and Will Starling there was enmity.

"You couldn't have expected him to make a great fuss about a boy," said Esther brutally on their way back to the Rectory.

"I suppose you think that's the reason why I don't like him," said Mark. "I don't want him to take any notice of me, but I think it's very odd that you shouldn't have said a word about knowing him even to his housekeeper."

"It was a whim of mine," she murmured. "Besides, I don't know him very well. We met at Eastbourne once when I was staying there with Mother."

"Well, why didn't he say 'How do you do, Miss Ogilvie?' instead of breathing out 'you' like that?"

Esther turned furiously upon Mark.

"What has it got to do with you?"

"Nothing whatever to do with me," he said deliberately. "But if you think you're going to make a fool of me, you're not. Are you going to tell your brother you knew him?"

Esther would not answer, and separated by several yards they walked sullenly back to the Rectory.

CHAPTER XIV

ST. MARK'S DAY

Mark tried next day to make up his difference with Esther; but she repulsed his advances, and the friendship that had blossomed after the Pomeroy affair faded and died. There was no apparent dislike on either side, nothing more than a coolness as of people too well used to each other's company. In a way this was an advantage for Mark, who was having to apply himself earnestly to the amount of study necessary to win a scholarship at Oxford. Companionship with Esther would have meant considerable disturbance of his work, for she was a woman who depended on the inspiration of the moment for her pastimes and pleasures, who was impatient of any postponement and always avowedly contemptuous of Mark's serious side. His classical education at Haverton House had made little of the material bequeathed to him by his grandfather's tuition at Nancepean. None of his masters had been enough of a scholar or enough of a gentleman (and to teach Latin and Greek well one must be one or the other) to educate his taste. The result was an assortment of grammatical facts to which he was incapable of giving life. If the Rector of Wych-on-the-Wold was not a great scholar, he was at least able to repair the neglect of, more than the neglect of, the positive damage done to Mark's education by the meanness of Haverton House; moreover, after Mark had been reading with him six months he did find a really first-class scholar in Mr. Ford, the Vicar of Little Fairfield. Mark worked steadily, and existence in Oxfordshire went by without any great adventures of mind, body, or spirit. Life at the Rectory had a kind of graceful austerity like the well-proportioned Rectory itself. If Mark had bothered to analyze the cause of this graceful austerity, he might have found it in the personality of the Rector's elder sister Miriam. Even at Meade Cantorum, when he was younger, Mark had been fully conscious of her qualities; but here they found a background against which they could display themselves more perfectly. When they moved from Buckinghamshire and the new rector was seeing how much Miriam appreciated the new surroundings, he sold out some stock and presented her with enough ready money to express herself in the outward beauty of the Rectory's refurbishing. He was luckily not called upon to spend a great deal on the church, both his predecessors having maintained the fabric with care, and the fabric itself being sound enough and magnificent enough to want no more than that. Miriam, though shaking one of those capable and well-tended fingers at her beloved brother's extravagance, accepted the gift with an almost childish determination to give full value of beauty in return, so that there should not be a servant's bedroom nor a cupboard nor a corridor that did not display the evidence of her appreciation in loving care. The garden was handed over to Mrs. Ogilvie, who as soon as May warmed its high enclosures bloomed there like one of her own favourite peonies, rosy of face and fragrant, ample of girth, golden-hearted.

Outside the Rectory Mark spent most of his time with Richard Ford, the son of the Vicar of Little Fairfield, with whom he went to work in the autumn after his arrival in Oxfordshire. Here again Mark was lucky, for Richard, who was a year or two older than himself and a student at Cooper's Hill whence he would emerge as a civil engineer bound for India, was one of those entirely admirable young men who succeed in being saintly without any rapture or righteousness.

Mark said one day:

"Rector, you know, Richard Ford really is a saint; only for goodness' sake don't tell him I said so, because he'd be furious."

The Rector stopped humming a joyful *Miserere* to give Mark an assurance of his discretion. But Mark having said so much in praise of Richard could say no more, and indeed he would have found it hard to express in words what he felt about his friend.

Mark accompanied Richard on his visits to Wychford Rectory where in this fortunate corner of England existed a third perfect family. Richard was deeply in love with Margaret Grey, the second daughter, and if Mark had ever been intended to fall in love he would certainly have fallen in love with Pauline, the youngest daughter, who was fourteen.

"I could look at her for ever," he confided in Richard. "Walking down the road from Wych-on-the-Wold this morning I saw two blue butterflies on a wild rose, and they were like Pauline's eyes and the rose was like her cheek."

"She's a decent kid," Richard agreed fervently.

Mark had had such a limited experience of the world that the amenities of the society in which he found himself incorporated did not strike his imagination as remarkable. It was in truth one of those eclectic, somewhat exquisite, even slightly rarefied coteries which are produced partly by chance, partly by interests shared in common, but most of all, it would seem, by the very genius of the place. The genius of Cotswolds imparts to those who come beneath his influence the art of existing appropriately in the houses that were built at his inspiration. They do not boast of their privilege like the people of Sussex. They are not living up to a landscape so much as to an architecture, and their voices lowered harmoniously with the sigh of the wind through willows and aspens have not to compete with the sea-gales or the sea.

Mark accepted the manners of the society in which good fortune had set him as the natural expression of an inward orderliness, a traditional respect for beauty like the ritual of Christian worship. That the three daughters of the Rector of Wychford should be critical of those who failed to conform to their inherited refinement of life did not strike him as priggish, because it never struck him for a moment that any other standard than theirs existed. He felt the same about people who objected to Catholic ceremonies; their dislike of them did not present itself to him as arising out of a different religious experience from his own; but it appeared as a propensity toward unmannerly behaviour, as a kind of wanton disregard of decency and good taste. He was indeed still at the age when externals possess not so much an undue importance, but when they affect a boy as a mould through which the plastic experience of his youth is passed and whence it emerges to harden slowly to the ultimate form of the individual. In the case of Mark there was the revulsion from the arid ugliness of Haverton House and the ambition to make up for those years of beauty withheld, both of which urged him on to take the utmost advantage of this opportunity to expose the blank surface of those years to the fine etching of the present. Miriam at home, the Greys at Wychford, and in some ways most of all Richard Ford at Fairfield gave him in a few months the poise he would have received more gradually from a public school education.

So Mark read Greek with the Vicar of Little Fairfield and Latin with the Rector of Wych-on-the-Wold, who, amiable and holy man, had to work nearly twice as hard as his pupil to maintain his reserve of instruction. Mark took long walks with Richard Ford when Richard was home in his vacations, and long walks by himself when Richard was at Cooper's Hill. He often went to Wychford Rectory, where he learnt to enjoy Schumann and Beethoven and Bach and Brahms.

"You're like three Saint Cecilias," he told them. "Monica is by Luini and Margaret is by Perugino and Pauline . . ."

"Oh, who am I by?" Pauline exclaimed, clapping her hands.

"I give it up. You're just Saint Cecilia herself at fourteen."

"Isn't Mark foolish?" Pauline laughed.

"It's my birthday tomorrow," said Mark, "so I'm allowed to be foolish."

"It's my birthday in a week," said Pauline. "And as I'm two years younger than you I can be two years more foolish."

Mark looked at her, and he was filled with wonder at the sanctity of her maidenhood. Thenceforth meditating upon the Annunciation he should always clothe Pauline in a robe of white samite and set her in his mind's eye for that other maid of Jewry, even as painters found holy maids in Florence or Perugia for their bright mysteries.

While Mark was walking back to Wych and when on the brow of the first rise of the road he stood looking down at Wychford in the valley below, a chill lisping wind from the east made him shiver and he thought of the lines in Keats' *Eve of St. Mark*:

> *The chilly sunset faintly told*
> *Of unmatured green vallies cold,*
> *Of the green thorny bloomless hedge,*
> *Of rivers new with spring-tide sedge,*
> *Of primroses by shelter'd rills,*
> *And daisies on the aguish hills.*

The sky in the west was an unmatured green valley tonight, where Venus bloomed like a solitary primrose; and on the dark hills of Heaven the stars were like daisies. He turned his back on the little town and set off up the hill again, while the wind slipped through the hedge beside him in and out of the blackthorn boughs, lisping, whispering, snuffling, sniffing, like a small inquisitive animal. He thought of Monica, Margaret, and Pauline playing in their warm, candle-lit room behind him, and he thought of Miriam reading in her tall-back chair before dinner, for Evensong would be over by now. Yes, Evensong would be over, he remembered penitently, and he ought to have gone this evening, which was the vigil of St. Mark and of his birthday. At this moment he caught sight of the Wych Maries signpost black against that cold green sky. He gave a momentary start, because seen thus the signpost had a human look; and when his heart beat normally it was roused again, this time by the sight of a human form indeed, the form of Esther, the wind blowing her skirts before her, hurrying along the road to which the signpost so crookedly pointed. Mark who had been climbing higher and higher now felt the power of that wind full on his cheeks. It was as if it had found what it wanted, for it no longer whispered and lisped among the boughs of the blackthorn, but blew fiercely over the wide pastures, driving Esther before it, cutting through Mark like a sword. By the time he had reached the signpost she had disappeared in the wood.

Mark asked himself why she was going to Rushbrooke Grange.

"To Rushbrooke Grange," he said aloud. "Why should I think she is going to Rushbrooke Grange?"

Though even in this desolate place he would not say it aloud, the answer came back from this very afternoon when somebody had mentioned casually that the Squire was come home again. Mark half turned to follow Esther, but in the moment of turning he set his face resolutely in the direction of home. If Esther were really on her way to meet Will Starling, he would do more harm than good by appearing to pry.

Esther was the flaw in Mark's crystal clear world. When a year ago they had quarrelled over his avowed dislike of Will Starling, she had gone back to her solitary walks and he conscious, painfully conscious, that she regarded him as a young prig, had with that foolish pride of youth resolved to be so far as she was concerned what she supposed him to be. His admiration for the Greys and the Fords had driven her into jeering at them; throughout the year Mark and she had been scarcely polite to each other even in public. The Rector and Miriam probably excused Mark's rudeness whenever he let himself give way to it, because their sister did not spare either of them, and they were made aware with exasperating insistence of the dullness of the country and of the dreariness of everybody who lived in the neighbourhood. Yet, Mark could never achieve that indifference to her attitude either toward himself or toward other people that he wished to achieve. It was odd that this evening he should have beheld her in that relation to the wind, because in his thoughts about her she always appeared to him like the wind, restlessly sighing and fluttering round a comfortable house. However steady the candle-light, however bright the fire, however absorbing the book, however secure one may feel by the fireside, the wind is always there; and throughout these tranquil months Esther had always been most unmistakably there.

In the morning Mark went to Mass and made his Communion. It was a strangely calm morning; through the unstained windows of the clerestory the sun sloped quivering ladders of golden light. He looked round with half a hope that Esther was in the church; but she was absent, and throughout the service that brief vision of her dark transit across the cold green sky of yester eve kept recurring to his imagination, so that for all the rich peace of this interior he was troubled in spirit, and the intention to make this Mass upon his seventeenth birthday another spiritual experience was frustrated. In fact, he was worshipping mechanically, and it was only when Mass was over and he was kneeling to make an act of gratitude for his Communion that he began to apprehend how he was asking fresh favours from God without having moved a step forward to deserve them.

"I think I'm too pleased with myself," he decided, "I think I'm suffering from spiritual pride. I think . . ."

He paused, wondering if it was blasphemous to have an intuition that God was about to play some horrible trick on him. Mark discussed with the Rector the theological aspects of this intuition.

"The only thing I feel," said Mr. Ogilvie, "is that perhaps you are leading too sheltered a life here and that the explanation of your intuition is your soul's perception of this. Indeed, once or twice lately I have been on the point of warning you that you must not get into the habit of supposing you will always find the onset of the world so gentle as here."

"But naturally I don't expect to," said Mark. "I was quite long enough at Haverton House to appreciate what it means to be here."

"Yes," the Rector went on, "but even at Haverton House it was a passive ugliness, just as here it is a passive beauty. After our Lord had fasted forty days in the desert, accumulating reserves of spiritual energy, just as we in our poor human fashion try to accumulate in Lent reserves of spiritual energy that will enable us to celebrate Easter worthily, He was assailed by the Tempter more fiercely than ever during His life on earth. The history of all the early Egyptian monks, the history indeed of any life lived without losing sight of the way of spiritual perfection displays the same phenomena. In the action and reaction of experience, in the rise and fall of the tides, in the very breathing of the human lungs, you may perceive analogies of the divine rhythm. No, I fancy your intuition of this morning is nothing more than one of those movements which warn us that the sleeper will soon wake."

Mark went away from this conversation with the Rector dissatisfied. He wanted something more than analogies taken from the experience of spiritual giants, Titans of holiness whose mighty conquests of the flesh seemed as remote from him as the achievements of Alexander might appear to a captain of the local volunteers. What he had gone to ask the Rector was whether it was blasphemous to suppose that God was going to play a horrible trick on him. He had not wanted a theological discussion, an academic question and reply. Anything could be answered like that, probably himself in another twenty years, when he had preached some hundreds of sermons, would talk like that. Moreover, when he was alone Mark understood that he had not really wanted to talk about his own troubles to the Rector at all, but that his real preoccupation had been and still was Esther. He wondered, oh, how much he wondered, if her brother had the least suspicion of her friendship with Will Starling, or if Miriam had had the least inkling that Esther had not come in till nine o'clock last night because she had been to Wych Maries? Mark, remembering those wild eyes and that windblown hair when she stood for a moment framed in the doorway of the Rector's library, could not believe that none of her family had guessed that something more than the whim to wander over the hills had taken her out on such a night. Did Mrs. Ogilvie, promenading so placidly along her garden borders, ever pause in perplexity at her daughter's behaviour? Calling them all to mind, their attitudes, the expressions of their faces, the words upon their lips, Mark was sure that none of them had any idea what Esther was doing. He debated now the notion of warning Miriam in veiled language about her sister; but such an idea would strike Miriam as monstrous, as a mad and horrible nightmare. Mark shivered at the mere fancy of the chill that would come over her and of the disdain in her eyes. Besides, what right had he on the little he knew to involve Esther with her family? Superficially he might count himself her younger brother; but if he presumed too far, with what a deadly retort might she not annihilate his claim. Most certainly he was not entitled to intervene unless he intervened bravely and directly. Mark shook his head at the prospect of doing that. He could not imagine anybody's tackling Esther directly on such a subject. Seventeen today! He looked out of the window and felt that he was bearing upon his shoulders the whole of that green world outspread before him.

The serene morning ripened to a splendid noontide, and Mark who had intended to celebrate his birthday by enjoying every moment of it had allowed the best of the hours to slip away in a stupor of indecision. More and more the vision of Esther last night haunted him, and he felt that he could not go and see the Greys as he had intended. He could not bear the contemplation of the three girls with the weight of Esther on his mind. He decided to walk over to Little Fairfield and persuade Richard to make a journey of exploration up the Greenrush in a canoe. He would ask Richard his opinion of Will Starling. What a foolish notion! He knew perfectly well Richard's opinion of the Squire, and to lure him into a restatement of it would be the merest self-indulgence.

"Well, I must go somewhere today," Mark shouted at himself. He secured a packet of sandwiches from the Rectory cook and set out to walk away his worries.

"Why shouldn't I go down to Wych Maries? I needn't meet that chap. And if I see him I needn't speak to him. He's always been only too jolly glad to be offensive to me."

Mark turned aside from the high road by the crooked signpost and took the same path down under the ash-trees as he had taken with Esther for the first time nearly a year ago. Spring was much more like Spring in these wooded hollows; the noise of bees in the blossom of the elms was murmurous as limes in June. Mark congratulated himself on the spot in which he had chosen to celebrate this fine birthday, a day robbed from time like the day of a dream. He ate his lunch by the old mill dam, feeding the roach with crumbs until an elderly pike came up from the deeps and frightened the smaller fish away. He searched for a bullfinch's nest; but he did not find one, though he saw several of the birds singing in the snowberry bushes; round and ruddy as October apples they looked. At last he went to the ruined chapel, where after speculating idly for a little while upon its former state he fell as he usually did when he visited Wych Maries into a contemplation of the two images of the Blessed Virgin and St. Mary Magdalene. While he sat on a hummock of grass before the old West doorway he received an impression that since he last visited these forms of stone they had ceased to be mere relics of ancient worship unaccountably preserved from ruin, but that they had somehow regained their importance. It was not that he discerned in them any miraculous quality of living, still less of winking or sweating as images are reputed to wink and sweat for the faithful. No, it was not that, he decided, although by regarding them thus entranced as he was he could easily have brought himself to the point of believing in a supernatural manifestation. He was too well aware of this tendency to surrender to it; so, rousing himself from the rapt contemplation of them and forsaking the hummock of grass, he climbed up into the branches of a yew-tree that stood beside the chapel, that there and from that elevation, viewing the images and yet unviewed by them directly, he could be immune from the magic of fancy and discover why they should give him this impression of having regained their utility, yes, that was the word, utility, not importance. They were revitalized not from within, but from without; and even as his mind leapt at this explanation he perceived in the sunlight, beyond the shadowy yew-tree in which he was perched, Esther sitting upon that hummock of grass where but a moment ago he had himself been sitting.

For a moment, as if to contradict a reasonable explanation of the strange impression the images had made upon him, Mark supposed that she was come there for a tryst. This vanished almost at once in the conviction that Esther's soul waited there either in question or appeal. He restrained an impulse to declare his presence, for although he felt that he was intruding upon a privacy of the soul, he feared to destroy the fruits of that privacy by breaking in. He knew that Esther's pride would be so deeply outraged at having been discovered in a moment of weakness thus upon her knees, for she had by now fallen upon her knees in prayer, that it might easily happen she would never in all her life pray more. There was no escape for Mark without disturbing her, and he sat breathless in the yew-tree, thinking that soon she must perceive his glittering eye in the depths of the dark foliage as in passing a hedgerow one may perceive the eye of a nested bird. From his position he could see the images, and out of the spiritual agony of Esther kneeling there, the force of which was communicated to himself, he watched them close, scarcely able to believe that they would not stoop from their pedestals and console the suppliant woman with benediction of those stone hands now clasped aspiringly to God, themselves for centuries suppliant like the woman at their feet. Mark could think of nothing better to do than to turn his face from Esther's face and to say for her many *Paternosters* and *Aves*. At first he thought that he was praying in a silence of nature; but presently the awkwardness of his position began to affect his concentration, and he found that he was saying the words mechanically, listening the while to the voices of birds. He compelled his attention to the prayers; but the birds were too loud. The *Paternosters* and the *Aves* were absorbed in their singing and chirping and twittering, so that Mark gave up to them and wished for a rosary to help his feeble attention. Yet could he have used a rosary without falling out of the yew-tree? He took his hands from the bough for a moment and nearly overbalanced. *Make not your rosary of yew berries*, he found himself saying. Who wrote that? *Make not your rosary of yew berries*. Why, of course, it was Keats. It was the first line of the *Ode to Melancholy*. Esther was still kneeling out there in the sunlight. And how did the poem continue? *Make not your rosary of yew berries*. What was the second line? It was ridiculous to sit astride a bough and say *Paternosters* and *Aves*. He could not sit there much longer. And then just as he was on the point of letting go he saw that Esther had risen from her knees and that Will Starling was standing in the doorway of the chapel looking at her, not speaking but waiting for her to speak, while he wound a strand of ivy round his fingers and unwound it again, and wound it round again until it broke and he was saying:

"I thought we agreed after your last display here that you'd give this cursed chapel the go by?"

"I can't escape from it," Esther cried. "You don't understand, Will, what it means. You never have understood."

"Dearest Essie, I understand only too well. I've paid pretty handsomely in having to listen to reproaches, in having to dry your tears and stop your sighs with kisses. Your damned religion is a joke. Can't you grasp that? It's not my fault we can't get married. If I were really the scoundrel you torment yourself into thinking I am, I would have married and taken the risk of my strumpet of a wife turning up. But I've treated you honestly, Essie. I can't help loving you. I went away once. I went away again. And a third time I went just to relieve your soul of the sin of loving me. But I'm sick of suffering for the sake of a myth, a superstition."

Esther had moved close to him, and now she put a hand upon his arm.

"To you, Will. Not to me."

"Look here, Essie," said her lover. "If you knew that you were liable to these dreadful attacks of remorse and penitence, why did you ever encourage me?"

"How dare you say I encouraged you?"

"Now don't let your religion make you dishonest," he stabbed. "No man seduces a woman of your character without as much goodwill as deserves to be called encouragement, and by God *is* encouragement," he went on furiously. "Let's cut away some of the cant before we begin arguing again about religion."

"You don't know what a hell you're making for me when you talk like that," she gasped. "If I did encourage you, then my sin is a thousand times blacker."

"Oh, don't exaggerate, my dear girl," he said wearily. "It isn't a sin for two people to love each other."

"I've tried my best to think as you do, but I can't. I've avoided going to church. I've tried to hate religion, I've mocked at God . . ." she broke off in despair of explaining the force of grace, against the gift of which she had contended in vain.

"I always thought you were brave, Essie. But you're a real coward. The reason for all this is your fear of being pitchforked into a big bonfire by a pantomime demon with horns and a long tail." He laughed bitterly. "To think that you, my adored Essie, should really have the soul of a Sunday school teacher. You, a Bacchante of passion, to be puling about your sins. You! You! Girl, you're mad! I tell you there is no such thing as damnation. It's a bogey invented by priests to enchain mankind. But if there is and if that muddle-headed old gentleman you call God really exists and if he's a just God, why then let him damn me and let him give you your harp and your halo while I burn for both. Essie, my mad foolish frightened Essie, can't you understand that if you give me up for this God of yours you'll drive me to murder. If I must marry you to hold you, why then I'll kill that cursed wife of mine . . ."

It was his turn now to break off in despair of being able to express his will to keep Esther for his own, and because argument seemed so hopeless he tried to take her in his arms, whereupon Mark who was aching with the effort to maintain himself unobserved upon the bough of the yew-tree said his *Paternosters* and *Aves* faster than ever, that she might have the strength to resist that scoundrel of Rushbrooke Grange. He longed to have the eloquence to make some wonderful prayer to the Blessed Virgin and St. Mary Magdalene so that a miracle might happen and their images point accusing hands at the blasphemer below.

And then it seemed as if a miracle did happen, for out of the jangle of recriminations and appeals that now signified no more than the noise of trees in a storm he heard the voice of Esther gradually gain its right to be heard, gradually win from its rival silence until the tale was told.

"I know that I am overcome by the saving grace of God," she was saying. "And I know that I owe it to them." She pointed to the holy women above the door. The squire shook his fist; but he still kept silence. "I have run away from God since I knew you, Will. I have loved you as much as that. I have gone to church only when I had to go for my brother's sake, but I have actually stuffed my ears with cotton wool so that no word there spoken might shake my faith in my right to love you. But it was all to no purpose. You know that it was you who told me always to come to our meetings through the wood and past the chapel. And however fast I went and however tight I shut myself up in thoughts of you and your love and my love I have always felt that these images spoke to me reproachfully in passing. It's not mere imagination, Will. Why, before we came to Wych-on-the-Wold when you went away to the Pacific that I might have peace of mind, I used always to be haunted by the idea that God was calling me back to Him, and I would run, yes, actually run through the woods until my legs have been torn by brambles."

"Madness! Madness!" cried Starling.

"Let it be madness. If God chooses to pursue a human soul with madness, the pursuit is not less swift and relentless for that. And I shook Him off. I escaped from religion; I prayed to the Devil to keep me wicked, so utterly did I love you. Then when my brother was offered Wych-on-the-Wold I felt that the Devil had heard my prayer and had indeed made me his own. That frightened me for a moment. When I wrote to you and said we were coming here and you hurried back, I can't describe to you the fear that overcame me when I first entered this hollow where you lived. Several times I'd tried to come down before you arrived here, but I'd always been afraid, and that was why the first night I brought Mark with me."

"That long-legged prig and puppy," grunted the squire.

Mark could have shouted for joy when he heard this, shouted because he was helping with his *Paternosters* and his *Aves* to drive this ruffian out of Esther's life for ever, shouted because his long legs were strong enough to hold on to this yew-tree bough.

"He's neither a prig nor a puppy," Esther said. "I've treated him badly ever since he came to live with us, and I treated him badly on your account, because whenever I was with him I found it harder to resist the pursuit of God. Now let's leave Mark out of this. Everything was in your favour, I tell you. I was sure that the Devil . . ."

"The Devil!" Starling interrupted. "Your Devil, dear Essie, is as ridiculous as your God. It's only your poor old God with his face painted black like the bogey man of childhood."

"I was sure that the Devil," Esther repeated without seeming to hear the blasphemy, "had taken me for his own and given us to each other. You to me. Me to you, my darling. I didn't care. I was ready to burn in Hell for you. So, don't call me coward, for mad though you think me I was ready to be damned for you, and *I* believe in damnation. You don't. Yet the first time I passed by this chapel on my way to meet you again after that endless horrible parting I had to run away from the holy influence. I remember that there was a black cow in the field near the gates of the Grange, and I waited there while Mark poked about in this chapel, waited in the twilight afraid to go back and tell him to hurry in case I should be recaptured by God and meet you only to meet you never more."

"I suppose you thought my old Kerry cow was the Devil, eh?" he sneered.

She paid no attention, but continued enthralled by the passion of her spiritual adventure.

"It was no use. I couldn't come by here every day and not go back. Why, once I opened the Bible at hazard just to show my defiance and I read *Her sins which are many are forgiven for she loved much.* This must be the end of our love, my lover, for I can't go on. Those two stone Maries have brought me back to God. No more with you, my own beloved. No more, my darling, no more. And yet if even now with one kiss you could give me strength to sin I should rejoice. But they have made my lips as cold as their own, and my arms that once knew how to clasp you to my heart they have lifted up to Heaven like their own. I am going into a convent at once, where until I die I shall pray for you, my own love."

The birds no longer sang nor twittered nor cheeped in the thickets around, but all passion throbbed in the voice of Esther when she spoke these words. She stood there with her hair in disarray transfigured like a tree in autumn on which the sunlight shines when the gale has died, but from which the leaves will soon fall because winter is at hand. Yet her lover was so little moved by her ordeal that he went back to mouthing his blasphemies.

"Go then," he shouted. "But these two stone dolls shall not have power to drive my next mistress into folly. Wasn't Mary Magdalene a sinner? Didn't she fall in love with Christ? Of course, she did! And I'll make an example of her just as Christians make an example of all women who love much."

The squire pulled himself up by the ivy and struck the image of St. Mary Magdalene on the face.

"When you pray for me, dear Essie, in your convent of greensick women, don't forget that your patron saint was kicked from her pedestal by your lover."

Starling was as good as his word; but the effort he made to overthrow the saint carried him with it; his foot catching in the ivy fell head downward and striking upon a stone was killed.

Mark hesitated before he jumped down from his bough, because he dreaded to add to Esther's despair the thought of his having overheard all that went before. But seeing her in the sunlight now filled again with the voices of birds, seeing her blue eyes staring in horror and the nervous twitching of her hands he felt that the shock of his irruption might save her reason and in a moment he was standing beside her looking down at the dead man.

"Let me die too," she cried.

Mark found himself answering in a kind of inspiration:

"No, Esther, you must live to pray for his soul."

"He was struck dead for his blasphemy. He is in Hell. Of what use to pray for his soul?"

"But Esther while he was falling, even in that second, he had time to repent. Live, Esther. Live to pray for him."

Mark was overcome with a desire to laugh at the stilted way in which he was talking, and, from the suppression of the desire, to laugh wildly at everything in the scene, and not least at the comic death of Will Starling, even at the corpse itself lying with a broken neck at his feet. By an effort of will he regained control of his muscles, and the tension of the last half hour finding no relief in bodily relaxation was stamped ineffaceably upon his mind to take its place with that afternoon in his father's study at the Lima Street Mission which first inspired him with dread of the sexual relation of man to woman, a dread that was now made permanent by what he had endured on the bough of that yew-tree.

Thanks to Mark's intervention the business was explained without scandal; nobody doubted that the squire of Rushbrooke Grange died a martyr to his dislike of ivy's encroaching upon ancient images. Esther's stormy soul took refuge in a convent, and there it seemed at peace.

CHAPTER XV

THE SCHOLARSHIP

The encounter between Esther and Will Starling had the effect of strengthening Mark's intention to be celibate. He never imagined himself as a possible protagonist in such a scene; but the impression of that earlier encounter between his mother and father which gave him a horror of human love was now renewed. It was renewed, moreover, with the light of a miracle to throw it into high relief. And this miracle could not be explained away as a coincidence, but was an old-fashioned miracle that required no psychical buttressing, a hard and fast miracle able to withstand any criticism. It was a pity that out of regard for Esther he could not publish it for the encouragement of the faithful and the confusion of the unbelievers.

The miracle of St. Mary Magdalene's intervention on his seventeenth birthday was the last violent impression of Mark's boyhood. Thenceforward life moved placidly through the changing weeks of a country calendar until the date of the scholarship examination held by the group of colleges that contained St. Mary's, the college he aspired to enter, but for which he failed to win even an exhibition. Mr. Ogilvie was rather glad, for he had been worried how Mark was going to support himself for three or four years at an expensive college like St. Mary's. But when Mark was no more successful with another group of colleges, his tutors began to be alarmed, wondering if their method of teaching Latin and Greek lacked the tradition of the public school necessary to success.

"Oh, no, it's obviously my fault," said Mark. "I expect I go to pieces in examinations, or perhaps I'm not intended to go to Oxford."

"I beg you, my dear boy," said the Rector a little irritably, "not to apply such a loose fatalism to your career. What will you do if you don't go to the University?"

"It's not absolutely essential for a priest to have been to the University," Mark argued.

"No, but in your case I think it's highly advisable. You haven't had a public school education, and inasmuch as I stand to you *in loco parentis* I should consider myself most culpable if I didn't do everything possible to give you a fair start. You haven't got a very large sum of money to launch yourself upon the world, and I want you to spend what you have to the best advantage. Of course, if you can't get a scholarship, you can't and that's the end of it. But, rather than that you should miss the University I will supplement from my own savings enough to carry you through three years as a commoner."

Tears stood in Mark's eyes.

"You've already been far too generous," he said. "You shan't spend any more on me. I'm sorry I talked in that foolish way. It was really only a kind of affectation of indifference. I'm feeling pretty sore with myself for being such a failure; but I'll have another shot and I hope I shall do better."

Mark as a last chance tried for a close scholarship at St. Osmund's Hall for the sons of clergymen.

"It's a tiny place of course," said the Rector. "But it's authentic Oxford, and in some ways perhaps you would be happier at a very small college. Certainly you'd find your money went much further."

The examination was held in the Easter vacation, and when Mark arrived at the college he found only one other candidate besides himself. St. Osmund's Hall with its miniature quadrangle, miniature hall, miniature chapel, empty of undergraduates and with only the Principal and a couple of tutors in residence, was more like an ancient almshouse than an Oxford college. Mark and his rival, a raw-boned youth called Emmett who was afflicted with paroxysms of stammering, moved about the precincts upon tiptoe like people trespassing from a high road.

On their first evening the two candidates were invited to dine with the Principal, who read second-hand book catalogues all through dinner, only pausing from their perusal to ask occasionally in a courtly tone if Mr. Lidderdale or Mr. Emmett would not take another glass of wine. After dinner they sat in his library where the Principal addressed himself to the evidently uncongenial task of estimating the comparative fitness of his two guests to receive Mr. Tweedle's bounty. The Reverend Thomas Tweedle was a benevolent parson of the eighteenth century who by his will had provided the money to educate the son of one indigent clergyman for four years. Mark was shy enough under the Principal's courtly inquisition, but poor Emmett had a paroxysm each time he was asked the simplest question about his tastes or his ambitions. His tongue appearing like a disturbed mollusc waved its tip slowly round in an agonized endeavour to give utterance to such familiar words as "yes" or "no." Several times Mark feared that he would never get it back at all and that Emmett would either have to spend the rest of his life with it protruding before him or submit it to amputation and become a mute. When the ordeal with the Principal was over and the two guests were strolling back across the quadrangle to their rooms, Emmett talked normally and without a single paroxysm about the effect his stammer must have had upon the Principal. Mark did his best to reassure poor Emmett.

"Really," he said, "it was scarcely noticeable to anybody else. You noticed it, because you felt your tongue getting wedged like that between your teeth; but other people would hardly have noticed it at all. When the Principal asked you if you were going to take Holy Orders yourself, I'm sure he only thought you hadn't quite made up your mind yet."

"But I'm sure he did notice something," poor Emmett bewailed. "Because he began to hum."

"Well, but he was always humming," said Mark. "He hummed all through dinner while he was reading those book catalogues."

"It's very kind of you, Lidderdale," said Emmett, "to make the best of it for me, but I'm not such a fool as I look, and the Principal certainly hummed six times as loud whenever he asked me a question as he did over those catalogues. I know what I look like when I get into one of those states. I once caught sight of myself in a glass by accident, and now whenever my tongue gets caught up like that I'm wondering all the time why everybody doesn't get up and run out of the room."

"But I assure you," Mark persisted, "that little things like that—"

"Little things like that!" Emmett interrupted furiously. "It's all very well for you, Lidderdale, to talk about little things like that. If you had a tongue like mine which seems to get bigger instead of smaller every year, you'd feel very differently."

"But people always grow out of stammering," Mark pointed out.

"Thanks very much," said Emmett bitterly, "but where shall I be by the time I've grown out of it? You don't suppose I shall win this scholarship, do you, after they've seen me gibbering and mouthing at them like that? But if only I could manage somehow to get to Oxford I should have a chance of being ordained, and—" he broke off, perhaps unwilling to embarrass his rival by any more lamentations.

"Do forget about this evening," Mark begged, "and come up to my room and have a talk before you turn in."

"No, thanks very much," said Emmett. "I must sit up and do some work. We've got that general knowledge paper tomorrow morning."

"But you won't be able to acquire much more general knowledge in one evening," Mark protested.

"I might," said Emmett darkly. "I noticed a Whitaker's almanack in the rooms I have. My only chance to get this scholarship is to do really well in my papers; and though I know it's no good and that this is my last chance, I'm not going to neglect anything that could possibly help. I've got a splendid memory for statistics, and if they'll only ask a few statistics in the general knowledge paper I may have some luck tomorrow. Goodnight, Lidderdale, I'm sorry to have inflicted myself on you like this."

Emmett hurried away up the staircase leading to his room and left his rival standing on the moonlit grass of the quadrangle. Mark was turning toward his own staircase when he heard a window open above and Emmett's voice:

"I've found another Whitaker of the year before," it proclaimed. "I'll read that, and you'd better read this year's. If by any chance I did win this scholarship, I shouldn't like to think I'd taken an unfair advantage of you, Lidderdale."

"Thanks very much, Emmett," said Mark. "But I think I'll have a shot at getting to bed early."

"Ah, you're not worrying," said Emmett gloomily, retiring from the window.

When Mark was sitting by the fire in his room and thinking over the dinner with the Principal and poor Emmett's stammering and poor Emmett's words in the quad afterwards, he began to imagine what it would mean to poor Emmett if he failed to win the scholarship. Mark had not been so successful himself in these examinations as to justify a grand self-confidence; but he could not regard Emmett as a dangerous competitor. Had he the right in view of Emmett's handicap to accept this scholarship at his expense? To be sure, he might urge on his own behalf that without it he should himself be debarred from Oxford. What would the loss of it mean? It would mean, first of all, that Mr. Ogilvie would make the financial effort to maintain him for three years as a commoner, an effort which he could ill afford to make and which Mark had not the slightest intention of allowing him to make. It would mean, next, that he should have to occupy himself during the years before his ordination with some kind of work among people. He obviously could not go on reading theology at Wych-on-the-Wold until he went to Glastonbury. Such an existence, however attractive, was no preparation for the active life of a priest. It would mean, thirdly, a great disappointment to his friend and patron, and considering the social claims of the Church of England it would mean a handicap for himself. There was everything to be said for winning this scholarship, nothing to be said against it on the grounds of expediency. On the grounds of expediency, no, but on other grounds? Should he not be playing the better part if he allowed Emmett to win? No doubt all that was implied in the necessity for him to win a scholarship was equally implied in the necessity for Emmett to win one. It was obvious that Emmett was no better off than himself; it was obvious that Emmett was competing in a kind of despair. Mark remembered how a few minutes ago his rival had offered him this year's Whitaker, keeping for himself last year's almanack. Looked at from the point of view of Emmett who really believed that something might be gained at this eleventh hour from a study of the more recent volume, it had been a fine piece of self-denial. It showed that Emmett had Christian talents which surely ought not to be wasted because he was handicapped by a stammer.

The spell that Oxford had already cast on Mark, the glamour of the firelight on the walls and raftered ceiling of this room haunted by centuries of youthful hope, did not persuade him how foolish it was to surrender all this. On the contrary, this prospect of Oxford so beautiful in the firelight within, so fair in the moonlight without, impelled him to renounce it, and the very strength of his temptation to enjoy all this by winning the scholarship helped him to make up his mind to lose it. But how? The obvious course was to send in idiotic answers for the rest of his papers. Yet examinations were so mysterious that when he thought he was being most idiotic he might actually be gaining his best marks. Moreover, the examiners might ascribe his answers to ill health, to some sudden attack of nerves, especially if his papers today had been tolerably good. Looking back at the Principal's attitude after dinner that night, Mark could not help feeling that there had been something in his manner which had clearly shown a determination not to award the scholarship to poor Emmett if it could possibly be avoided. The safest way would be to escape tomorrow morning, put up at some country inn for the next two days, and go back to Wych-on-the-Wold; but if he did that, the college authorities might write to Mr. Ogilvie to demand the reason for such extraordinary behaviour. And how should he explain it? If he really intended to deny himself, he must take care that nobody knew he was doing so. It would give him an air of unbearable condescension, should it transpire that he had deliberately surrendered his scholarship to Emmett. Moreover, poor Emmett would be so dreadfully mortified if he found out. No, he must complete his papers, do them as badly as he possibly could, and leave the result to the wisdom of God. If God wished Emmett to stammer forth His praises and stutter His precepts from the pulpit, God would know how to manage that seemingly so intractable Principal. Or God might hear his prayers and cure poor Emmett of his impediment. Mark wondered to what saint was entrusted the patronage of stammerers; but he could not remember. The man in whose rooms he was lodging possessed very few books, and those few were mostly detective stories.

It amused Mark to make a fool of himself next morning in the general knowledge paper. He flattered himself that no candidate for a scholarship at St. Osmund's Hall had ever shown such black ignorance of the facts of every-day life. Had he been dropped from Mars two days before, he could scarcely have shown less knowledge of the Earth. Mark tried to convey an impression that he had been injudiciously crammed with Latin and Greek, and in the afternoon he produced a Latin prose that would have revolted the easy conscience of a fourth form boy. Finally, on the third day, in an unseen passage set from the Georgics he translated *tonsisque ferunt mantelia villis* by *having pulled down the villas (i. e. literally shaved) they carry off the mantelpieces* which he followed up with translating *Maeonii carchesia Bacchi* as the *lees of Maeonian wine (i.e. literally carcases of Maeonian Bacchus)*.

"I say, Lidderdale," said Emmett, when they came out of the lecture room where the examination was being held. "I had a tremendous piece of luck this afternoon."

"Did you?"

"Yes, I've just been reading the fourth Georgics last term, and I don't think I made a single mistake in that unseen."

"Good work," said Mark.

"I wonder when they'll let us know who's got the scholarship," said Emmett. "But of course you've won," he added with a sigh.

"I did very badly both yesterday and today."

"Oh, you're only saying that to encourage me," Emmett sighed. "It sounds a dreadful thing to say and I ought not to say it because it'll make you uncomfortable, but if I don't succeed, I really think I shall kill myself."

"All right, that's a bargain," Mark laughed; and when his rival shook hands with him at parting he felt that poor Emmett was going home to Rutland convinced that Mark was just as hard-hearted as the rest of the world and just as ready to laugh at his misfortune.

It was Saturday when the examination was finished, and Mark wished he could be granted the privilege of staying over Sunday in college. He had no regrets for what he had done; he was content to let this experience be all that he should ever intimately gain of Oxford; but he should like to have the courage to accost one of the tutors and to tell him that being convinced he should never come to Oxford again he desired the privilege of remaining until Monday morning, so that he might crystallize in that short space of time an impression which, had he been successful in gaining the scholarship, would have been spread over four years. Mark was not indulging in sentiment; he really felt that by the intensity of the emotion with which he would live those twenty-four hours he should be able to achieve for himself as much as he should achieve in four years. So far as the world was concerned, this experience would be valueless; for himself it would be beyond price. So far as the world was concerned, he would never have been to Oxford; but could he be granted this privilege, Oxford would live for ever in his heart, a refuge and a meditation until the grave. Yet this coveted experience must be granted from without to make it a perfect experience. To ask and to be refused leave to stay till Monday would destroy for him the value of what he had already experienced in three days' residence; even to ask and to be granted the privilege would spoil it in retrospect. He went down the stairs from his room and stood in the little quadrangle, telling himself that at any rate he might postpone his departure until twilight and walk the seven miles from Shipcot to Wych-on-the-Wold. While he was on his way to notify the porter of the time of his departure he met the Principal, who stopped him and asked how he had got on with his papers. Mark wondered if the Principal had been told about his lamentable performance and was making inquiries on his own account to find out if the unsuccessful candidate really was a lunatic.

"Rather badly, I'm afraid, sir."

"Well, I shall see you at dinner tonight," said the Principal dismissing Mark with a gesture before he had time even to look surprised. This was a new perplexity, for Mark divined from the Principal's manner that he had entirely forgotten that the scholarship examination was over and that the candidates had already dined with him. He went into the lodge and asked the porter's advice.

"The Principal's a most absent-minded gentleman," said the porter. "Most absent-minded, he is. He's the talk of Oxford sometimes is the Principal. What do you think he went and did only last term. Why, he was having some of the senior men to tea and was going to put some coal on the fire with the tongs and some sugar in his cup. Bothered if he didn't put the sugar in the fire and a lump of coal in his cup. It didn't so much matter him putting sugar in the fire. That's all according, as they say. But fancy—well, I tell

159

you we had a good laugh over it in the lodge when the gentlemen came out and told me."

"Ought I to explain that I've already dined with him?" Mark asked.

"Are you in any what you might call immediate hurry to get away?" the porter asked judicially.

"I'm in no hurry at all. I'd like to stay a bit longer."

"Then you'd better go to dinner with him again tonight and stay in college over the Sunday. I'll take it upon myself to explain to the Dean why you're still here. If it had been tea I should have said 'don't bother about it,' but dinner's another matter, isn't it? And he always has dinner laid for two or more in case he's asked anybody and forgotten."

Thus it came about that for the second time Mark dined with the Principal, who disconcerted him by saying when he arrived:

"I remember now that you dined with me the night before last. You should have told me. I forget these things. But never mind, you'd better stay now you're here."

The Principal read second-hand book catalogues all through dinner just as he had done two nights ago, and he only interrupted his perusal to inquire in courtly tones if Mark would take another glass of wine. The only difference between now and the former occasion was the absence of poor Emmett and his paroxysms. After dinner with some misgivings if he ought not to leave his host to himself Mark followed him upstairs to the library. The principal was one of those scholars who live in an atmosphere of their own given off by old calf-bound volumes and who apparently can only inhale the air of the world in which ordinary men move when they are smoking their battered old pipes. Mark sitting opposite to him by the fireside was tempted to pour out the history of himself and Emmett, to explain how he had come to make such a mess of the examination. Perhaps if the Principal had alluded to his papers Mark would have found the courage to talk about himself; but the Principal was apparently unaware that his guest had any ambitions to enter St. Osmund's Hall, and whatever questions he asked related to the ancient folios and quartos he took down in turn from his shelves. A clock struck ten in the moonlight without, and Mark rose to go. He felt a pang as he walked from the cloudy room and looked for the last time at that tall remote scholar, who had forgotten his guest's existence at the moment he ceased to shake his hand and who by the time he had reached the doorway was lost again in the deeps of the crabbed volume resting upon his knees. Mark sighed as he closed the library door behind him, for he knew that he was shutting out a world. But when he stood in the small silver quadrangle Mark was glad that he had not given way to the temptation of confiding in the Principal. It would have been a feeble end to his first denial of self. He was sure that he had done right in surrendering his place to Emmett, for was not the unexpected opportunity to spend these few more hours in Oxford a sign of God's approval? *Bright as the glimpses of eternity to saints accorded in their mortal hour.* Such was Oxford tonight.

Mark sat for a long while at the open window of his room until the moon had passed on her way and the quadrangle was in shadow; and while he sat there he was conscious of how many people had inhabited this small quadrangle and of how they too had passed on their way like the moon, leaving behind them no more than he should leave behind from this one hour of rapture, no more than the moon had left of her silver upon the dim grass below.

Mark was not given to gazing at himself in mirrors, but he looked at himself that night in the mirror of the tiny bedroom, into which the April air came up sweet and frore from the watermeadows of the Cherwell close at hand.

"What will you do now?" he asked his reflection. "Yet, you have such a dark ecclesiastical face that I'm sure you'll be a priest whether you go to Oxford or not."

Mark was right in supposing his countenance to be ecclesiastical. But it was something more than that: it was religious. Even already, when he was barely eighteen, the high cheekbones and deepset burning eyes gave him an ascetic look, while the habit of prayer and meditation had added to his expression a steadfast purpose that is rarely seen in people as young as him. What his face lacked were those contours that come from association with humanity; the ripeness that is bestowed by long tolerance of folly, the mellowness that has survived the icy winds of disillusion. It was the absence of these contours that made Mark think his face so ecclesiastical; however, if at eighteen he had possessed contours and soft curves, they would have been nothing but the contours and soft curves of that rose, youth; and this ecclesiastical bonyness would not fade and fall as swiftly as that.

Mark turned from the glass in sudden irritation at his selfishness in speculating about his appearance and his future, when in a short time he should have to break the news to his guardian that he had thrown away for a kindly impulse the fruit of so many months of diligence and care.

"What am I going to say to Ogilvie?" he exclaimed. "I can't go back to Wych and live there in pleasant idleness until it's time to go to Glastonbury. I must have some scheme for the immediate future."

In bed when the light was out and darkness made the most fantastic project appear practical, Mark had an inspiration to take the habit of a preaching friar. Why should he not persuade Dorward to join him? Together they would tramp the English country, compelling even the dullest yokels to hear the word of God . . . discalced . . . over hill, down dale . . . telling stories of the saints and martyrs in remote inns . . . deep lanes . . . the butterflies and the birds . . . Dorward should say Mass in the heart of great woods . . . over hill, down dale . . . discalced . . . preaching to men of Christ . . .

Mark fell asleep.

In the morning Mark heard Mass at the church of the Cowley Fathers, a strengthening experience, because the Gregorian there so strictly and so austerely chanted without any consideration for sentimental humanity possessed that very effect of liberating and purifying spirit held in the bonds of flesh which is conveyed by the wind blowing through a grove of pines or by waves quiring below a rocky shore.

If Mark had had the least inclination to be sorry for himself and indulge in the flattery of regret, it vanished in this music. Rolling down through time on the billows of the mighty Gregorian it were as grotesque to pity oneself as it were for an Arctic explorer to build a snowman for company at the North Pole.

Mark came out of St. John's, Cowley, into the suburban prettiness of Iffley Road, where men and women in their Sunday best tripped along in the April sunlight, tripped along in their Sunday best like newly hatched butterflies and beetles. Mark went in and out of colleges all day long, forgetting about the problem of his immediate future just as he forgot that the people in the sunny streets were not really butterflies and beetles. At twilight he decided to attend Evensong at St. Barnabas'. Perhaps the folk in the sunny April streets had turned his thoughts unconsciously toward the simple aspirations of simple human nature. He felt when he came into the warm candle-lit church like one who has voyaged far and is glad to be at home again. How everybody sang together that night, and how pleasant Mark found this congregational outburst. It was all so jolly that if the organist had suddenly turned round like an Italian organ-grinder and kissed his fingers to the congregation, his action would have seemed perfectly appropriate. Even during the *Magnificat*, when the altar was being censed, the tinkling of the thurible reminded Mark of a tambourine; and the lighting and extinction of the candles was done with as much suppressed excitement as if the candles were going to shoot red and green stars or go leaping and cracking all round the chancel.

It happened this evening that the preacher was Father Rowley, that famous priest of the Silchester College Mission in the great naval port of Chatsea. Father Rowley was a very corpulent man with a voice of such compassion and with an eloquence so simple that when he ascended into the pulpit, closed his eyes, and began to speak, his listeners involuntarily closed their eyes and followed that voice whithersoever it led them. He neither changed the expression of his face nor made use of dramatic gestures; he scarcely varied his tone, yet he could keep a congregation breathlessly attentive for an hour. Although he seemed to be speaking in a kind of trance, it was evident that he was unusually conscious of his hearers, for if by chance some pious woman coughed or turned the pages of a prayer-book he would hold up the thread of his sermon and without any change of tone reprove her. It was strange to watch him at such a moment, his eyes still tightly shut and yet giving the impression of looking directly at the offending member of the congregation. This evening he was preaching about a naval disaster which had lately occurred, the sinking of a great battleship by another great battleship through a wrong signal. He was describing the scene when the news reached Chatsea, telling of the sweethearts and wives of the lost bluejackets who waited hoping against hope to hear that their loved ones had escaped death and hearing nearly always the worst news.

"So many of our own dear bluejackets and marines, some of whom only last Christmas had been eating their plum duff at our Christmas dinner, so many of my own dear boys whom I prepared for Confirmation, whose first Confession I had heard, and to whom I had given for the first time the Body and Blood of Our Lord Jesus Christ."

He spoke too of what it meant in the future of material suffering on top of their mental agony. He asked for money to help these women immediately, and he spoke fiercely of the Admiralty red tape and of the obstruction of the official commission appointed to administer the relief fund.

The preacher went on to tell stories from the lives of these boys, finding in each of them some illustration of a Christian virtue and conveying to his listeners a sense of the extraordinary preciousness of human life, so that there was no one who heard him but was fain to weep for those young bluejackets and marines taken in their prime. He inspired in Mark a sense of shame that he had ever thought of people in the aggregate, that he had ever walked along a crowded street without perceiving the importance of every single human being that helped to compose its variety. While he sat there listening to the Missioner and watching the large tears roll slowly down his cheeks from beneath the closed lids, Mark wondered how he could have dared to suppose last night that he was qualified to become a friar and preach the Gospel to the poor. While Father Rowley was speaking, he began to apprehend that before he could aspire to do that he must himself first of all learn about Christ from those very poor whom he had planned to convert.

This sermon was another milestone in Mark's religious life. It discovered in him a hidden treasure of humility, and it taught him to build upon the rock of human nature. He divined the true meaning of Our Lord's words to St. Peter: *Thou art Peter and on this rock I will build my church and the gates of Hell shall not prevail against it.* John was the disciple whom Jesus loved, but he chose Peter with all his failings and all his follies, with his weakness and his cowardice and his vanity. He chose Peter, the bedrock of human nature, and to him he gave the keys of Heaven.

Mark knew that somehow he must pluck up courage to ask Father Rowley to let him come and work under him at Chatsea. He was sure that if he could only make him grasp the spirit in which he would offer himself, the spirit of complete humility devoid of any kind of thought that he was likely to be of the least use to the Mission, Father Rowley might accept his oblation. He would have liked to wait behind after Evensong and approach the Missioner directly, so that before speaking to Mr. Ogilvie he might know what chance the offer had of being accepted; but he decided against this course, because he felt that Father Rowley's compassion might be embarrassed if he had to refuse his request, a point of view that was characteristic of the mood roused in him by the sermon. He went back to sleep for the last time in an Oxford college, profoundly reassured of the rightness of his action in giving up the scholarship to Emmett, although, which was characteristic of his new mood, he had by this time begun to tell himself that he had really done nothing at all and that probably in any case Emmett would have been the chosen scholar.

If Mark had still any doubts of his behaviour, they would have vanished when on getting into the train for Shipcot he found himself in an otherwise empty third-class smoking carriage opposite Father Rowley himself, who with a small black bag beside him, so small that Mark wondered how it could possibly contain the night attire of so fat a man, was sitting back in the corner with a large pipe in his mouth. He was wearing one of those square felt hats sometimes seen on the heads of farmers, and if one had only seen his head and hat without the grubby clerical attire beneath one might have guessed him to be a farmer. Mark noticed now that his eyes of a limpid blue were like a child's, and he realized that in his voice while he was preaching there had been the same sweet gravity of childhood. Just at this moment Father Rowley caught sight of someone he knew on the platform and shouting from the window of the compartment he attracted the attention of a young man wearing an Old Siltonian tie.

"My dear man," he cried, "how are you? I've just made a most idiotic mistake. I got it into my head that I should be preaching here on the first Sunday in term and was looking forward to seeing so many Silchester men. I can't think how I came to make such a muddle."

Father Rowley's shoulders filled up all the space of the window, so that Mark only heard scattered fragments of the conversation, which was mostly about Silchester and the Siltonians he had hoped to see at Oxford.

"Goodbye, my dear man, goodbye," the Missioner shouted, as the train moved out of the station. "Come down and see us soon at Chatsea. The more of you men who come, the more we shall be pleased."

Mark's heart leapt at these words, which seemed of good omen to his own suit. When Father Rowley was ensconced in his corner and once more puffing away at his pipe, Mark thought how ridiculous it would sound to say that he had heard him preach last night at St. Barnabas' and that, having been much moved by the sermon, he was anxious to be taken on at St. Agnes' as a lay helper. He wished that Father Rowley would make some remark to him that would lead up to his request, but all that Father Rowley said was:

"This is a slow train to Birmingham, isn't it?"

This led to a long conversation about trains, and slow though this one might be it was going much too fast for Mark, who would be at Shipcot in another twenty minutes without having taken any advantage of his lucky encounter.

"Are you up at Oxford?" the priest at last inquired.

It was now or never; and Mark took the opportunity given him by that one question to tell Father Rowley twenty disjointed facts about his life, which ended with a request to be allowed to come and work at Chatsea.

"You can come and see us whenever you like," said the Missioner.

"But I don't want just to come and pay a visit," said Mark. "I really do want to be given something to do, and I shan't be any expense. I only want to keep enough money to go to Glastonbury in four years' time. If you'd only see how I got on for a month. I don't pretend I can be of any help to you. I don't suppose I can. But I do so tremendously want you to help me."

"Who did you say your father was?"

"Lidderdale, James Lidderdale. He was priest-in-charge of the Lima Street Mission, which belonged to St. Simon's, Notting Hill, in those days. St. Wilfred's, Notting Dale, it is now."

"Lidderdale," Father Rowley echoed. "I knew him. I knew him well. Lima Street. Viner's there now, a dear good fellow. So you're Lidderdale's son?"

"I say, here's my station," Mark exclaimed in despair, "and you haven't said whether I can come or not."

"Come down on Tuesday week," said Father Rowley. "Hurry up, or you'll get carried on to the next station."

Mark waved his farewell, and he knew, as he drove back on the omnibus over the rolling wold to Wych that he had this morning won something much better than a scholarship at St. Osmund's Hall.

CHAPTER XVI

CHATSEA

When Mark had been exactly a week at Chatsea he celebrated his eighteenth birthday by writing a long letter to the Rector of Wych:

St. Agnes' House,
Keppel Street,
Chatsea.
St. Mark's Day.

My dear Rector,

Thank you very much for sending me the money. I've handed it over to a splendid fellow called Gurney who keeps all the accounts (private or otherwise) in the Mission House. Poor chap, he's desperately ill with asthma, and nobody thinks he can live much longer. He suffers tortures, particularly at night, and as I sleep in the next room I can hear him.

You mustn't think me inconsiderate because I haven't written sooner, but I wanted to wait until I had seen a bit of this place before I wrote to you so that you might have some idea what I was doing and be able to realize that it is the one and only place where I ought to be at the moment.

But first of all before I say anything about Chatsea I want to try to express a little of what your kindness has meant to me during the last two years. I look back at myself just before my sixteenth birthday when I was feeling that

I should have to run away to sea or do something mad in order to escape that solicitor's office, and I simply gasp! What and where should I be now if it hadn't been for you? You have always made light of the burden I must have been, and though I have tried to show you my gratitude I'm afraid it hasn't been very successful. I'm not being very successful now in putting it into words. I know my failure to gain a scholarship at Oxford has been a great disappointment to you, especially after you had worked so hard yourself to coach me. Please don't be anxious about my letting my books go to the wall here. I had a talk about this with Father Rowley, who insisted that anything I am allowed to do in the district must only be done when I have a good morning's work with my books behind me. I quite realize the importance of a priest's education. One of the assistant priests here, a man called Snaith, took a good degree at Cambridge both in classics and theology, so I shall have somebody to keep me on the lines. If I stay here three years and then have two years at Glastonbury I don't honestly think that I shall start off much handicapped by having missed both public school and university. I expect you're smiling to read after one week of my staying here three years! But I assure you that the moment I sat down to supper on the evening of my arrival I felt at home. I think at first they all thought I was an eager young Ritualist, but when they found that they didn't get any rises out of ragging me, they shut up.

This house is a most extraordinary place. It is an old Congregational chapel with a gallery all round which has been made into cubicles, scarcely one of which is ever empty or ever likely to be empty so far as I can see! I should think it must be rather like what the guest house of a monastery used to be like in the old days before the Reformation. The ground floor of the chapel has been turned into a gymnasium, and twice a week the apparatus is cleared away and we have a dance. Every other evening it's used furiously by Father Rowley's "boys." They're such a jolly lot, and most of them splendid gymnasts. Quite a few have become professional acrobats since they opened the gymnasium. The first morning after my arrival I asked

Father Rowley if he'd got anything special for me to do and he told me to catalogue the books in his library. Everybody laughed at this, and I thought at first that some joke was intended, but when I got to his room I found it really was in utter confusion with masses of books lying about everywhere. So I set to work pretty hard and after about three days I got them catalogued and in good order. When I told him I had finished he looked very surprised, and a solemn visit of inspection was ordered. As the room was looking quite tidy at last, I didn't mind. I've realized since that Father Rowley always sets people the task of cataloguing and arranging his books when he doubts if they are really worth their salt, and now he complains that I have spoilt one of his best ordeals for slackers. I said to him that he needn't be afraid because from what I could see of the way he treated books they would be just as untidy as ever in another week. Everybody laughed, though I was afraid at first they might consider it rather cheek my talking like this, but you've got to stand up for yourself here because there never was such a place for turning a man inside out. It's a real discipline, and I think if I manage to deserve to stay here three years I shall have the right to feel I've had the finest training for Holy Orders anybody could possibly have.

You know enough about Father Rowley yourself to understand how impossible it would be for me to give any impression of his personality in a letter. I have never felt so strongly the absolute goodness of anybody. I suppose that some of the great mediæval saints like St. Francis and St. Anthony of Padua must have been like that. One reads about them and what they did, but the facts one reads don't really tell anything. I always feel that what we really depend on is a kind of tradition of their absolute saintliness handed on from the people who experienced it. I suppose in a way the same applies to Our Lord. I always feel it wouldn't matter a bit to me if the four Gospels were proved to be forgeries tomorrow, because I should still be convinced that Our Lord was God. I know this is a platitude, but I don't think until I met Father Rowley that I ever realized the force and power that goes with exceptional goodness.

There are so many people who are good because they were born good. Richard Ford, for example, he couldn't have ever been anything else but good, but I always feel that people like him remain practically out of reach of the ordinary person and that the goodness is all their own and dies with them just as it was born with them. What I feel about a man like Father Rowley is that he probably had a tremendous fight to be good. Of course, I may be perfectly wrong and he may have had no fight at all. I know one of the people at the Mission House told me that, though there is nobody who likes smoking better than he or more enjoys a pint of beer with his dinner, he has given up both at St. Agnes merely to set an example to weak people. I feel that his goodness was with such energy fought for that it now exists as a kind of complete thing and will go on existing when Father Rowley himself is dead. I begin to understand the doctrine of the treasury of merit. I remember you once told me how grateful I ought to be to God because I had apparently escaped the temptations that attack most boys. I am grateful; but at the same time I can't claim any merit for it! The only time in my life when I might have acquired any merit was when I was at Haverton House. Instead of doing that, I just dried up, and if I hadn't had that wonderful experience at Whitsuntide in Meade Cantorum church nearly three years ago I should be spiritually dead by now.

This is a very long letter, and I don't seem to have left myself any time to tell you about St. Agnes' Church. It reminds me of my father's mission church in Lima Street, and oddly enough a new church is being built almost next door just as one was being built in Lima Street. I went to the children's Mass last Sunday, and I seemed to see him walking up and down the aisle in his alb, and I thought to myself that I had never once asked you to say Mass for his soul. Will you do so now next time you say a black Mass? This is a wretched letter, and it doesn't succeed in the least in expressing what I owe to you and what I already owe to Father Rowley. I used to think that the Sacred Heart was a rather material device for attracting the multitude, but I'm beginning to realize in the atmosphere of St. Agnes' that it is a gloriously simple devotion and that it is human nature's attempt to express the inexpressible. I'll write to you again next week. Please give my love to everybody at the Rectory.

Always your most affectionate

Mark.

Father Rowley had been at St. Agnes' seven or eight years when Mark found himself attached to the Mission, in which time he had transformed the district completely. It was a small parish (actually of course it was not a parish at all, although it was fast qualifying to become one) of something over a thousand small houses, few of which were less than a century old. The streets were narrow and crooked, mostly named after bygone admirals or forgotten sea-fights; the romantic and picturesque quarter of a great naval port to the casual glance of a passer-by, but heartbreaking to any except the most courageous resident on account of its overcrowded and tumbledown condition. Yet it lacked the dreariness of an East End slum, for the sea winds blew down the narrowest streets and alleys, sailors and soldiers were always in view, and the windows of the pawnbrokers were filled with the relics of long voyages, with idols and large shells, with savage weapons and the handiwork of remote islands.

When Mark came to live in Keppel Street, most of the brothels and many of the public houses had been eliminated from the district, and in their place flourished various clubs and guilds. The services in the church were crowded: there was a long roll of communicants; the civilization of the city of God was visible in this Chatsea slum. One or two of the lay helpers used to horrify Mark with stories of early days there, and when he seemed inclined to regret that he had arrived so late upon the scene, they used to tease him about his missionary spirit.

"If he can't reform the people," said Cartwright, one of the lay helpers, a tall thin young man with a long nose and a pleasant smile, "he still has us to reform."

"Come along, Mark Anthony," said Warrender, another lay helper, who after working for seven years among the poor had at last been charily accepted by the Bishop for ordination. "Come along. Why don't you try your hand on us?"

"You people seem to think," said Mark, "that I've got a mania for reforming. I don't mean that I should like to see St. Agnes' where it was merely for my own personal amusement. The only thing I'm sorry about is that I didn't actually see the work being done."

Father Rowley came in at this moment, and everybody shouted that Mark was going to preach a sermon.

"Splendid," said the Missioner whose voice when not moved by emotion was rich in a natural unction that encouraged everyone round to suppose he was being successfully humorous, such a savour did it add to the most innutritious chaff. Those who were privileged to share his ordinary life never ceased to wonder how in the pulpit or in the confessional or at prayer this unction was replaced by a remote beauty of tone, a plangent and thrilling compassion that played upon the hearts of all who heard him.

"Now really, Father Rowley," Mark protested. "Do I preach a great deal? I'm always being chaffed by Cartwright and Warrender about an alleged mania for reforming people, which only exists in their imagination."

Indeed Mark had long ago grown out of the desire to reform or to convert anybody, although had he wished to keep his hand in, he could have had plenty of practice among the guests of the Mission House. Nobody had ever succeeded in laying down the exact number of casual visitors that could be accommodated therein. However full it appeared, there was always room for one more. Taking an average, day in, day out through the year, one might fairly say that there were always eight or nine casual guests in addition to the eight or nine permanent residents, of whom Mark was soon glad to be able to count himself one. The company was sufficiently mixed to have been offered as a proof to the sceptical that there was something after all in simple Christianity. There would usually be a couple of prefects from Silchester, one or two 'Varsity men, two or three bluejackets or marines, an odd soldier or so, a naval officer perhaps, a stray priest sometimes, an earnest seeker after Christian example often, and often a drunkard who had been dumped down at the door of St. Agnes' Mission House in the hope that where everybody else had failed Father Rowley might succeed. Then there were the tramps, some who had heard of a comfortable night's lodging, some who came whining and cringing with a pretence of religion. This last class was discouraged as much as possible, for one of the first rules of the Mission House was to show no favour to any man who claimed to be religious, it being Father Rowley's chief dread to make anybody's religion a paying concern. Sometimes a jailbird just released from prison would find in the Mission House an opportunity to recover his self-respect. But whoever the guest was, soldier, sailor, tinker, tailor, apothecary, ploughboy, or thief, he was judged at the Mission House as a man. Some of the visitors repaid their host by theft or fraud; but when they did, nobody uttered proverbs or platitudes about mistaken kindness. If one lame dog bit the hand that was helping him over the stile, the next dog that came limping along was helped over just as freely.

"What right has one miserable mortal to be disillusioned by another miserable mortal?" Father Rowley demanded. "Our dear Lord when he was nailed to the cross said 'Father, forgive them, for they know not what they do.' He did not say, 'I am fed up with these people I have come down from Heaven to save. I've had enough of it. Send an angel with a pair of pincers to pull out these nails.'"

If the Missioner's patience ever failed, it was when he had to deal with High Church young men who made pilgrimages to St. Agnes' because they had heard that this or that service was conducted there with a finer relish of Romanism than anywhere else at the moment in England. On one occasion a pietistic young creature, who brought with him his own lace cotta but forgot to bring his nightshirt, begged to be allowed the joy of serving Father Rowley at early Mass next morning. When they came back and were sitting round the breakfast table, this young man simpered in a ladylike voice:

"Oh, Father, couldn't you keep your fingers closed when you give the *Dominus vobiscum*?"

"Et cum spiritu tuo," shouted Father Rowley. "I can keep my fingers closed when I box your ears."

And he proved it.

It was a real box on the ears, so hard a blow that the ladylike young man burst into tears to the great indignation of a Chief Petty Officer staying in the Mission House, who declared that he was half in a mind to catch the young swab such a snitch on the conk as really would give him something to blubber about. Father Rowley evidently had no remorse for his violence, and the young man went away that afternoon saying how sorry he was that the legend of the good work being done at St. Agnes' had been so much exaggerated.

Mark wrote an account of this incident, which had given him intense pleasure, to Mr. Ogilvie. Perhaps the Rector was afraid that Mark in his ambition to avoid "churchiness" was inclining toward the opposite extreme; or perhaps, charitable and saintly man though he was, he felt a pang of jealousy at Mark's unbounded admiration of his new friend; or perhaps it was merely that the east wind was blowing more sharply than usual that morning over the wold into the Rectory garden. Whatever the cause, his answering letter made Mark feel that the Rector did not appreciate Father Rowley as thoroughly as he ought.

The Rectory,
Wych-on-the-Wold.
Oxon.
Dec. 1.

My dear Mark,

I was glad to get your long and amusing letter of last week. I am delighted to think that as the months go by you are finding work among the poor more and more congenial. I would not for the world suggest your coming back here for Christmas after what you tell me of the amount of extra work it will entail for everybody in the Mission House; at the same time it would be useless to pretend that we shan't all be disappointed not to see you until the New Year.

On reading through your last letter again I feel just a little worried lest, in the pleasure you derive from Father Rowley's treatment of what was no doubt a very irritating young man, you may be inclined to go to the opposite extreme and be too ready to laugh at real piety when it is not accompanied by geniality and good fellowship, or by an obvious zeal for good works. I know you will acquit me of any desire to defend extreme "churchiness," and I have no doubt you will remember one or two occasions in the past when I was rather afraid that you were tending that way yourself. I am not in the least criticizing Father Rowley's method of dealing with it, but I am a trifle uneasy at the inordinate delight it seems to have afforded you. Of course, it is intolerable for any young man serving a priest at Mass to watch his fingers all the time, but I don't think you have any right to assume because on this occasion the young man showed himself so sensitive to mere externals that he is always aware only of externals. Unfortunately a very great deal of true and fervid piety exists under this apparent passion for externals. Remember that the ordinary criticism by the man in the street of Catholic ceremonies and of Catholic methods of worship involves us all in this condemnation. I suppose that you would consider yourself justified, should the circumstances permit (which in this case of course they do not), in protesting against a priest's not taking the Eastward Position when he said Mass. I was talking to Colonel Fraser the other day, and he was telling me how much he had enjoyed the ministrations of the Reverend Archibald Tait, the Leicestershire cricketer, who throughout the "second service" never once turned his back on the congregation, and, so far as I could gather from the Colonel's description, conducted this "second service" very much as a conjuror performs his tricks. When I ventured to argue with the Colonel, he said to me: "That is the worst of you High Churchmen, you make the ritual more important than the Communion itself." All human judgments, my dear Mark, are relative, and I have no doubt that this unpleasant young man (who, as I have already said, was no doubt justly punished by Father Rowley) may have felt the same kind of feeling in a different degree that I should feel if I assisted at the jugglery of the Reverend Archibald Tait. At any rate you, my dear boy, are bound to credit this young man with as much sincerity as yourself, otherwise you commit a sin against charity. You must acquire at least as much toleration for the Ritualist as I am glad to notice you are acquiring for the thief. When you are a priest yourself, and in a comparatively short time you will be a priest, I do hope you won't, without

his experience, try to imitate Father Rowley too closely in
his summary treatment of what I have already I hope made
myself quite clear in believing to be in this case a most
insufferable young man. Don't misunderstand this letter. I
have such great hopes of you in the stormy days to come,
and the stormy days are coming, that I should feel I was
wrong if I didn't warn you of your attitude towards the
merest trifles, for I shall always judge you and your conduct
by standards that I should be very cautious of setting for
most of my penitents.

> Your ever affectionate,
>
> Stephen Ogilvie.

My mother and Miriam send you much love. We miss you
greatly at Wych. Esther seems happy in her convent and will soon
be clothed as a novice.

When Mark read this letter, he was prompt to admit himself
in the wrong; but he could not bear the least implied criticism of
Father Rowley.

St. Agnes' House,
Keppel Street,
Chatsea.
Dec. 3.

My dear Mr. Ogilvie,

I'm afraid I must have expressed myself very badly in
my last letter if I gave you the least idea that Father Rowley
was not always charity personified. He had probably come
to the conclusion that the young man was not much good
and no doubt he deliberately made it impossible for him
to stay on at the Mission House. We do get an awful lot
of mere loafers here; I don't suppose that anybody who
keeps open house can avoid getting them. After all, if
the young man had been worth anything he would have
realized that he had made a fool of himself and by the way
he took his snubbing have re-established himself. What he

actually did was to sulk and clear out with a sneer at the work done here. I'm sorry I gave you the impression that I was triumphing so tremendously over his discomfiture. By writing about it I probably made the incident appear much more important than it really was. I've no doubt I did triumph a little, and I'm afraid I shall never be able not to feel rather glad when a fellow like that is put in his place. I am not for a moment going to try to argue that you can carry Christian charity too far. The more one meditates on the words, and actions of Our Lord, the more one grasps how impossible it is to carry charity too far. All the same, one owes as much charity to Father Rowley as to the young man. This sounds now I have written it down as if I were getting in a hit at you, and that is the worst of writing letters to justify oneself. What I am trying to say is that if I were to have taken up arms for the young man and supposed him to be ill-used or misjudged I should be criticizing Father Rowley. I think that perhaps you don't quite realize what a saint he is in every way. This is my fault, no doubt, because in my letters to you I have always emphasized anything that would bring into relief his personality. I expect that I've been too much concerned to draw a picture of him as a man, in doing which I've perhaps been unsuccessful in giving you a picture of him as a priest. It's always difficult to talk or write about one's intimate religious feelings, and you've been the only person to whom I ever have been able to talk about them. However much I admire and revere Father Rowley I doubt if I could talk or write to him about myself as I do to you.

Until I came here I don't think I ever quite realized all that the Blessed Sacrament means. I had accepted the Sacrifice of the Mass as one accepts so much in our creed, without grasping its full implication. If anybody were to have put me through a catechism about the dogma I should have answered with theological exactitude, without any appearance of misapprehending the meaning of it; but it was not until I came here that its practical reality—I don't know if I'm expressing myself properly or not, I'm pretty sure I'm not; I don't mean practical application and I don't mean any kind of addition to my faith; perhaps what I mean is that I've learnt to grasp the mystery of the Mass outside myself, outside that is to say my own devotion, my own awe, as a practical fact alive to these people here. Sometimes when I go to Mass I feel as people who watched Our Lord with His disciples and followers must have felt. I feel like one of those people who ran after Him and asked Him what they could do to be saved. I feel when I look at what has been done here as if I must go to each of these poor people in turn and beg them to bring me to the feet of Christ, just as I suppose on the shores of the sea of Galilee people must have begged St. Peter or St. Andrew or St. James or St. John to introduce them, if one can use such a word for such an occasion. This seems to me the great work that Father Rowley has effected in this parish. I have only had one rather shy talk with him about religion, and in the course of it I said something in praise of what his personality had effected.

"My personality has effected nothing," he answered. "Everything here is effected by the Blessed Sacrament."

That is why he surely has the right without any consideration for the dignity of churchy young men to box their ears if they question his outward respect for the Blessed Sacrament. Even Our Lord found it necessary at least on one occasion to chase the buyers and sellers out of the Temple, and though it is not recorded that He boxed the ears of any Pharisee, it seems to me quite permissible to believe that He did! He lashed them with scorn anyway.

To come back to Father Rowley, you know the great cry of the so-called Evangelical party "Jesus only"? Well, Father Rowley has really managed to make out of what was becoming a sort of ecclesiastical party cry something that really is evangelical and at the same time Catholic. These people are taught to make the Blessed Sacrament the central fact of their lives in a way that I venture to say no Welsh revivalist or Salvation Army captain has ever made Our Lord the central fact in the lives of his converts, because with the Blessed Sacrament continually before them, Which is Our Lord Jesus Christ, their conversion endures. I could fill a book with stories of the wonderful behaviour of these poor souls. The temptation is to say of a man like Father Rowley that he has such a natural spring of human charity flowing from his heart that by offering to the world a Christlike example he converts his flock. Certainly he does give a Christlike example and undoubtedly that must have a great influence on his people; but he does not believe, and I don't believe, that a Christlike example is of any use without Christ, and he gives them Christ. Even the Bishop of Silchester had to admit the other day that Vespers of the Blessed Sacrament as held at St. Agnes' is a perfectly scriptural service. Father Rowley makes of the Blessed Sacrament Christ Himself, so that the poor people may flock round Him. He does not go round arguing with them, persuading them, but in the crises of their lives, as the answer to every question, as the solution of every difficulty and doubt, as the consolation in every sorrow, he offers them the Blessed Sacrament. All his prayers (and he makes a great use of extempore prayer, much to the annoyance of the Bishop, who considers it ungrammatical), all his sermons, all his actions revolve round that one great fact. "Jesus Christ is what you need," he says, "and Jesus Christ is here in your church, here upon your altar."

You can't go into the little church without finding fifty people praying before the Blessed Sacrament. The other day when the "King Harry" was sunk by the "Trafalgar," the people here subscribed I forget how many pounds for the widows and children of the bluejackets and marines of the Mission who were drowned, and when it was finished and the subscription list was closed, they subscribed all over again to erect an altar at which to say Masses for the dead. And the old women living in Father Rowley's free houses that were once brothels gave up their summer outing so that the money spent on them might be added to the fund. When the Bishop of Silchester came here last week for Confirmation he asked Father Rowley what that altar was.

"That is the ugliest thing I've ever seen," he said. But when Father Rowley told him about the poor people and the old women who had no money of their own, he said: "That is the most beautiful thing I've ever heard."

I am beginning to write as if it was necessary to convince you of the necessity of making the Blessed Sacrament the central feature of the religious life today and for ever until the end of the world. But, I know you won't think I'm doing anything of the kind, for really I am only trying to show you how much my faith has been strengthened and how much my outlook has deepened and how much more than ever I long to be a priest to be able to give poor people Jesus Christ in the Blessed Sacrament.

Your ever affectionate

Mark.

CHAPTER XVII

THE DRUNKEN PRIEST

Gradually, Mark found to his pleasure and his pride that he was becoming, if not indispensable to Father Rowley (the Missioner found no human being indispensable) at any rate quite evidently useful. Perhaps Father Rowley though that in allowing himself to rely considerably upon Mark's secretarial talent he was indulging himself in a luxury to which he was not entitled. That was Father Rowley's way. The moment he discovered himself enjoying anything too much, whether it was a cigar or a secretary, he cut himself off from it, and this not in any spirit of mortification for mortification's sake, but because he dreaded the possibility of putting the slightest drag upon his freedom to criticize others. He had no doubt at all in his own mind that he was perfectly justified in making use of Mark's intelligence and energy. But in a place like the Mission House, where everybody from lay helper to casual guest was supposed to stand on his own feet, the Missioner himself felt that he must offer an example of independence.

"You're spoiling me, Mark Anthony," he said one day. "There's nothing for me to do this evening."

"I know," Mark agreed contentedly. "I want to give you a rest for once."

"Rest?" the priest echoed. "You don't seriously expect a fat man like me to sit down in an armchair and rest, do you? Besides, you've got your own reading to do, and you didn't come to Chatsea as my punkah walla."

Mark insisted that he was getting along in his own way quite fast enough, and that he had plenty of time on his hands to keep Father Rowley's correspondence in some kind of order.

"All these other people have any amount to do," said Mark. "Cartwright has his boys every evening and Warrender has his men."

"And Mark Anthony has nothing but a fat, poverty-stricken, slothful mission priest," Father Rowley gurgled.

"Yes, and you're more trouble than all the rest put together. Look here, I've written to the Bishop's chaplain about that confirmation; I explained why we wanted to hold a special confirmation for these two boys we are emigrating, and he has written back to say that the Bishop has no objection to a special confirmation's being held by the Bishop of Matabeleland when he comes to stay here next week. At the same time, he says the Bishop doesn't want it to become a precedent."

"No. I can quite understand that," Father Rowley chuckled. "Bishops are haunted by the creation of precedents. A precedent in the life of a bishop is like an illegitimate child in the life of a respectable churchwarden. No, the only thing I fear is that if I devour all your spare time you won't get quite what you wanted to get by coming to live with us."

He laid a fat hand on Mark's shoulder.

"Please don't bother about me," said Mark. "I get all I want and more than I expected if I can be of the least use to you. I know I'm rather disappointing you by not behaving like half the people who come down here and want to get up a concert on Monday, a dance on Tuesday, a conjuring entertainment on Wednesday, a street procession on Thursday, a day of intercession on Friday, and an amateur dramatic entertainment on Saturday, not to mention acting as ceremonarius on Sunday. I know you'd like me to propose all sorts of energetic diversions, so that you could have the pleasure of assuring me that I was only proposing them to gratify my own vanity, which of course would be perfectly true. Luckily I'm of a retiring disposition, and I don't want to do anything to help the ten thousand benighted parishioners of Saint Agnes', except indirectly by striving to help in my own feeble way the man who really is helping them. Now don't throw that inkpot at me, because the room's quite dirty enough already, and as I've made you sit still for five minutes I've achieved something this evening that mighty few people have achieved in Keppel Street. I believe the only time you really rest is in the confessional box."

"Mark Anthony, Mark Anthony," said the priest, "you talk a great deal too much. Come along now, it's bedtime."

One of the rules of the Mission House was that every inmate should be in bed by ten o'clock and all lights out by a quarter past. The day began with Mass at seven o'clock at which everybody was expected to be present; and from that time onward everybody was so fully occupied that it was essential to go to bed at a reasonable hour. Guests who came down for a night or two were often apt to forget how much the regular workers had to do and what a tax it put upon the willing servants to manage a house of which nobody could say ten minutes before a meal how many would sit down to it, nor even until lights out for how many people beds must be made. In case any guest should forget this rule by coming back after ten o'clock, Father Rowley made a point of having the front door bell to ring in his bedroom, so that he might get out of bed at any hour of the night and admit the loiterer. Guests were warned what would be the effect of their lack of consideration, and it was seldom that Father Rowley was disturbed.

Among the guests there was one class of which a representative was usually to be found at the Mission House. This was the drunken clergyman, which sounds as if there was at this date a high proportion of drunken clergymen in the Church of England; but which means that when one did come to St. Agnes' he usually stayed for a long time, because he would in most cases have been sent there when everybody else had despaired of him to see what Father Rowley could effect.

About the time when Mark was beginning to be recognized as Father Rowley's personal vassal, it happened that the Reverend George Edward Mousley who had been handed on from diocese to diocese during the last five years had lately reached the Mission House. For more than two months now he had spent his time inconspicuously reading in his own room, and so well had he behaved, so humbly had he presented himself to the notice of his fellow guests, that Father Rowley was moved one afternoon to dictate a letter about him to Mark, who felt that the Missioner by taking him so far into his confidence had surrendered to his pertinacity and that thenceforth he might consider himself established as his private secretary.

"The letter is to the Lord Bishop Suffragan of Warwick, St. Peter's Rectory, Warwick," Father Rowley began. "My dear Bishop of Warwick, I have now had poor Mousley here for two months. It is not a long time in which to effect a lasting reformation of one who has fallen so often and so grievously, but I think you know me well enough not to accuse me of being too sanguine about drunken priests. I have had too many of them here for that. In his case however I do feel justified in asking you to agree with me in letting him have an opportunity to regain the respect due to himself and the reverence due to his priesthood by being allowed once more to the altar. I should not dream of allowing him to officiate without your permission, because his sad history has been so much a personal burden to yourself. I'm afraid that after the many disappointments he has inflicted upon you, you will be doubtful of my judgment. Yet I do think that the critical moment has arrived when by surprising him thus we might clinch the matter of his future behaviour once and for all. His conduct here has been so humble and patient and in every way exemplary that my heart bleeds for him. Therefore, my dear Bishop of Warwick, I hope you will agree to what I firmly trust will be the completion of his spiritual cure. I am writing to you quite impersonally and informally, as you see, so that in replying to me you will not be involving yourself in the affairs of another diocese. You will, of course, put me down as much a Jesuit as ever in writing to you like this, but you will equally, I know, believe me to be, Yours ever affectionately in Our Blessed Lord.

"And I'll sign it as soon as you can type it out," Father Rowley wound up.

"Oh, I do hope he will agree," Mark exclaimed.

"He will," the Missioner prophesied. "He will because he is a wise and tender and godly man and therefore will never be more than a Bishop Suffragan as long as he lives. Mark!"

Mark looked up at the severity of the tone.

"Mark! Correct me when I fall into the habit of sneering at the episcopate."

That night Father Rowley was attending a large temperance demonstration in the Town Hall for the purpose of securing if possible a smaller proportion of public houses than one for every eighty of the population, which was the average for Chatsea. The meeting lasted until nearly ten o'clock; and it had already struck the hour when Father Rowley with Mark and two or three others got back to Keppel Street. There was nothing Father Rowley disliked so much as arriving home himself after ten, and he hurried up to his room without inquiring if everybody was in.

Mark's window looked out on Keppel Street; and the May night being warm and his head aching from the effects of the meeting, he sat for nearly an hour at the open window gazing down at the passers by. There was not much to see, nothing more indeed than couples wandering home, a bluejacket or two, an occasional cat, and a few women carrying jugs of beer. By eleven o'clock even this slight traffic had ceased, and there was nothing down the silent street except a salt wind from the harbour that roused a memory of the beach at Nancepean years ago when he had sat there watching the glow-worm and decided to be a lighthouse-keeper keeping his lamps bright for mariners homeward bound. It was of streets like Keppel Street that they would have dreamed, with the Stag Light winking to port, and the west wind blowing strong astern. What a lighthouse-keeper Father Rowley was! How except by the grace of God could one explain such goodness as his? Fashions in saintliness might change, but there was one kind of saint that always and for every creed spoke plainly of God's existence, such saints as St. Francis of Assisi or St. Anthony of Padua, who were manifestly the heirs of Christ. With what a tender cynicism Our Lord had called St. Peter to be the foundation stone of His Church, with what a sorrowful foreboding of the failure of Christianity. Such a choice appeared as the expression of God's will not to be let down again as He was let down by Adam. Jesus Christ, conscious at the moment of what He must shortly suffer at the hands of mankind, must have been equally conscious of the failure of Christianity two thousand years beyond His Agony and Bloody Sweat and Crucifixion. Why, within a short time after His life on earth it was necessary for that light from heaven to shine round about Saul on the Damascus road, because already scoffers, while the disciples were still alive, may have been talking about the failure of Christianity. It must have been another of God's self-imposed limitations that He did not give to St. John that capacity of St. Paul for organization which might have made practicable the Christianity of the master Who loved him. *Woman, behold thy son! Behold thy mother!* That dying charge showed that Our

Lord considered John the most Christlike of His disciples, and he remained the most Christlike man until twelve hundred years later St. Francis was born at Assisi. St. Paul, St. Augustine, St. Dominic, if Christianity could only produce mighty individualists of Faith like them, it could scarcely have endured as it had endured. *And now abideth faith, hope, charity, these three; but the greatest of these is charity.* There was something almost wistful in those words coming from the mouth of St. Paul. It was scarcely conceivable that St. John or St. Francis could ever have said that; it would scarcely have struck either that the three virtues were separable.

Keppel Street was empty now. Mark's headache had been blown away by the night wind with his memories and the incoherent thoughts which had gathered round the contemplation of Father Rowley's character. He was just going to draw away from the window and undress when he caught sight of a figure tacking from one pavement to the other up Keppel Street. Mark watched its progress, amused at the extraordinary amount of trouble it was giving itself, until one tack was brought to a sharp conclusion by a lamp-post to which the figure clung long enough to be recognized as that of the Reverend George Edward Mousley, who had been tacking like this to make the harbour of the Mission House. Mark, remembering the letter which had been written to the Bishop of Warwick, wondered if he could not at any rate for tonight spare Father Rowley the disappointment of knowing that his plea for re-instatement was already answered by the drunken priest himself. He must make up his mind quickly, because even with the zigzag course Mousley was taking he would soon be ringing the bell of the Mission House, which meant that Father Rowley would be woken up and go down to let him in. Of course, he would have to know all about it in the morning, but tonight when he had gone to bed tired and full of hope for temperance in general and the reformation of Mousley in particular it was surely right to let him sleep in ignorance. Mark decided to take it upon himself to break the rules of the house, to open the door to Mousley, and if possible to get him upstairs to bed quietly. He went down with a lighted candle, crept across the gymnasium, and opened the door. Mousley was still tacking from pavement to pavement and making very little headway against a strong current of drink. Mark thought he had better go out and offer his services as pilot, because Mousley was beginning to sing an extraordinary song in which the tune and the words of *Goodbye, Dolly, I must leave you*, had got mixed up with *O happy band of pilgrims*.

"Look here, Mr. Mousley, you mustn't sing now," said Mark taking hold of the arm with which the drunkard was trying to beat time. "It's after eleven o'clock, and you're just outside the Mission House."

"I've been just outside the Mission House for an hour and three quarters, old chap," said Mr. Mousley solemnly. "Most incompatible thing I've ever known. I got back here at a quarter past nine, and I was just going to walk in when the house took two paces to the rear, and I've been walking after it the whole evening. Most incompatible thing I've ever known. Most incompatible thing that's ever happened to me in my life, Lidderdale. If I were a superstitious man, which I'm not, I should say the house was bewitched. If I had a moment to spare, I should sit down at once and write an account of my most incompatible experience to the Society of Psychical Research, if I were a superstitious man, which I'm not. Yes . . ."

Mr. Mousley tried to focus his glassy eyes upon the arcana of spiritualism, rocking ambiguously the while upon the kerb. Mark murmured something more about the need for going in quietly.

"It's very kind of you to come out and talk to me like this," the drunken priest went on. "But what you ought to have done was to have kept hold of the house for a minute or two so as to give me time to get in quietly. Now we shall probably both be out here all night trying to get in quietly. It's impossible to keep warm by this lamp-post. Most inadequate heating arrangement. It is a lamp-post, isn't it? Yes, I thought it was. I had a fleeting impression that it was my bedroom candle, but I see now that I was mistaken, I see now perfectly clearly that it is a lamp-post, if not two. Of course, that may account for my not being able to get into the Mission House. I was trying to decide which front door I should go in by, and while I was waiting I think I must have gone in by the wrong one, for I hit my nose a most severe blow on the nose. One has to remember to be very careful with front doors. Of course, if it was my own house I should have used a latch-key instanter; for I inevitably, I mean invariably, carry a latch-key about with me and when it won't open my front door I use it to wind my watch. You know, it's one of those small keys you can wind up watches with, if you know the kind of key I mean. I'd draw you a picture of it if I had a pencil, but I haven't got a pencil."

"Now don't stay talking here," Mark urged. "Come along back, and do try to come quietly. I keep telling you it's after eleven o'clock, and you know Father Rowley likes everybody to be in by ten."

"That's what I've been saying to myself the whole evening," said Mr. Mousley. "Only what happened, you see, was that I met the son of a man who used to know my father, a very nice fellow indeed, a very intellectual fellow. I never remember spending a more intellectual evening in my life. A feast of reason and a flowing bowl, I mean soul, s-o-u-l, not b-o-u-l. Did I say bowl? Soul . . . Soul . . ."

"All right," said Mark. "But if you've had such a jolly evening, come in now and don't make a noise."

"I'll come in whenever you like," Mr. Mousley offered. "I'm at your disposition entirely. The only request I have to make is that you will guarantee that the house stays where it was built. It's all very fine for an ordinary house to behave like this, but when a mission house behaves like this I call it disgraceful. I don't know what I've done to the house that it should conceive such a dislike to me. I say, Lidderdale, have they been taking up the drains or something in this street? Because I distinctly had an impression just then that I put my foot into a hole."

"The street's perfectly all right," said Mark. "Nothing has been done to it."

"There's no reason why they shouldn't take up the drains if they want to, I'm not complaining. Drains have to be taken up and I should be the last man to complain; but I merely asked a question, and I'm convinced that they have been taking up the drains. Yes, I've had a very intellectual evening. My head's whirling with philosophy. We've talked about everything. My friend talked a good deal about Buddhism. And I made rather a good joke about Confucius being so confusing, at which I laughed inordinately. Inordinately, Lidderdale. I've had a very keen sense of humour ever since I was a baby. I say, Lidderdale, you certainly know your way about this street. I'm very much obliged to me for meeting you. I shall get to know the street in time. You see, my object was to get beyond the house, because I said to myself 'the house is in Keppel Street, it can dodge about *in*

Keppel Street, but it can't be in any other street,' so I thought that if I could dodge it into the corner of Keppel Street—you follow what I mean? I may be talking a bit above your head, we've been talking philosophy all the evening, but if you concentrate you'll follow my meaning."

"Here we are," said Mark, for by this time he had persuaded Mr. Mousley to put his foot upon the step of the front door.

"You managed the house very well," said the clergyman. "It's extraordinary how a house will take to some people and not to others. Now I can do anything I like with dogs, and you can do anything you like with houses. But it's no good patting or stroking a house. You've got to manage a house quite differently to that. You've got to keep a house's accounts. You haven't got to keep a dog's accounts."

They were in the gymnasium by now, which by the light of Mark's small candle loomed as vast as a church.

"Don't talk as you go upstairs," Mark admonished.

"Isn't that a dog I see there?"

"No, no, no," said Mark. "It's the horse. Come along."

"A horse?" Mousley echoed. "Well, I can manage horses too. Come here, Dobbin. If I'd known we were going to meet a horse I should have brought back some sugar with me. I suppose it's too late to go back and buy some sugar now?"

"Yes, yes," said Mark impatiently. "Much too late. Come along."

"If I had a piece of sugar he'd follow us upstairs. You'll find a horse will go anywhere after a piece of sugar. It is a horse, isn't it? Not a donkey? Because if it was a donkey he would want a thistle, and I don't know where I can get a thistle at this time of night. I say, did you prod me in the stomach then with anything?" asked Mr. Mousley severely.

"No, no," said Mark. "Come along, it was the parallel bars."

"I've not been near any bars tonight, and if you are suggesting that I've been in bars you're making an insinuation which I very much resent, an insinuation which I resent most bitterly, an insinuation which I should not allow anybody to make without first pointing out that it was an insinuation."

"Do come down off that ladder," Mark said.

"I beg your pardon, Lidderdale. I was under the impression for the moment that I was going upstairs. I have really been so confused by Confucius and by the extraordinary behaviour of the house tonight, recoiling from me as it did, that for the moment I was under the impression that I was going upstairs."

At this moment Mr. Mousley fell from the ladder, luckily on one of the gymnasium mats.

"I do think it's a most ridiculous habit," he said, "not to place a doormat in what I might describe as a suitable cavity. The number of times in my life that I've fallen over doormats simply because people will not take the trouble to make the necessary depression in the floor with which to contain such a useful domestic receptacle you would scarcely believe. I must have fallen over thousands of doormats in my life," he shouted at the top of his voice.

"You'll wake everybody up in the house," Mark exclaimed in an agony. "For heaven's sake keep quiet."

"Oh, we are in the house, are we?" said Mr. Mousley. "I'm very much relieved to hear you say that, Lidderdale. For a brief moment, I don't know why, I was almost as confused as Confucius as to where we were."

At this moment, candle in hand, and in a white flannel nightgown looking larger than ever, Father Rowley appeared in the gallery above and leaning over demanded who was there.

"Is that Father Rowley?" Mr. Mousley inquired with intense courtesy. "Or do my eyes deceive me? You'll excuse me from replying to your apparently simple question, Father Rowley, but I have met such a number of people tonight including the son of a man who used to know my father that I really don't know who *is* there, although I'm inclined to think that *I* am here. But I've had a series of such a remarkable series of adventures tonight that I should like your advice about them. I've been spending a very intellectual evening, Father Rowley."

"Go to bed," said the mission priest severely. "I'll speak to you in the morning."

"Father Rowley isn't annoyed with me, is he?" Mr. Mousley asked.

"I think he's rather annoyed at your being so late," said Mark.

"Late for what?"

"Is that you, Mark, down there?" asked the Missioner.

"I'm lighting Mr. Mousley across the gymnasium," Mark explained. "I think I'd better take him up to his room."

"If your young friend is as clever at managing rooms as he is at managing houses we shall get on splendidly, Father Rowley. I have perfect confidence in his manner with rooms. He soothed this house in the most remarkable way. It was jumping about like a pea in a pod till he caught hold of the reins."

"Mark, go to bed. I will see Mr. Mousley to his room."

"Several years ago," said the drunken priest. "I went with an old friend to see Miss Ellen Terry as Lady Macbeth. The resemblance between Father Rowley and Miss Ellen Terry is very remarkable. Goodnight, Lidderdale, I am perfectly comfortable on this mat. Goodnight."

In the gallery above Mark, who had not dared to disobey Father Rowley's orders, asked him what was to be done to get Mr. Mousley to bed.

"Go and wake Cartwright and Warrender to help me to get him upstairs," the Missioner commanded.

"I can help you . . ." Mark began.

"Do what I say," said the Missioner curtly.

In the morning Father Rowley sent for Mark to give his account of what had happened the night before, and when Mark had finished his tale, the priest sat for a while in silence.

"Are you going to send him away?" Mark asked.

"Send him away?" Father Rowley repeated. "Where would I send him? If he can't keep off drink in this house and in these surroundings where else will he keep off drink? No, I'm only amused at my optimism."

There was a knock on the door.

"I expect that is Mr. Mousley," said Mark. "I'll leave you with him."

"No, don't go away," said the Missioner. "If Mousley didn't mind your seeing him as he was last night, there's no reason why this morning he should mind your hearing my comments upon his behaviour."

The tap on the door was repeated.

"Come in, come in, Mousley, and take a seat."

Mr. Mousley walked timidly across the room and sat on the very edge of the chair offered him by Father Rowley. He was a quiet, rather drab little man, the kind of little man who always loses his seat in a railway carriage and who always gets pushed further up in an omnibus, one of life's pawns. The presence of Mark did not seem to affect him, for no sooner was he seated than he began to apologize with suspicious rapidity, as if by now his apologies had been reduced to a formula.

"I really must apologize, Father Rowley, for my lateness last night and for coming in, I fear, slightly the worse for liquor. The fact is I had a little headache and went to the chemist for a pick-me-up, on top of which I met an old college friend, and though I don't think I had more than two glasses of beer I may have had three. They didn't seem to go very well with the pick-me-up. I assure you—"

"Stop," said Father Rowley. "The only assurance of any value to me will be your behaviour in the future."

"Oh, then I'm not to leave this morning?" Mr. Mousley gasped with open mouth.

"Where would you go if you left here?"

"Well, to tell you the truth," Mr. Mousley admitted, "I have been rather worried over that little problem ever since I woke up this morning. I scarcely expected that you would tolerate my presence any longer in this house. You will excuse me, Father Rowley, but I am rather overwhelmed for the moment by your kindness. I scarcely know how to express what I feel. I have usually found people so very impatient of my weakness. Do you seriously mean I needn't go away this morning?"

"You have already been sufficiently punished, I hope," said the Missioner, "by the humiliations you have inflicted on yourself both outside and inside this house."

"My thoughts are always humiliating," said Mr. Mousley. "I think perhaps that nowadays these humiliating thoughts are my chief temptation to drink. Since I have been here and shared in your hospitality I have felt more sharply than ever my disgrace. I have several times been on the point of asking you to let me be given some kind of work, but I have always been too much ashamed when it came to the point to express my aspirations in words."

"Only yesterday afternoon," said Father Rowley, "I wrote to the Bishop of Warwick, who has continued to interest himself in you notwithstanding the many occasions you have disappointed him, yes, I wrote to the Bishop of Warwick to say that since you came to St. Agnes' your behaviour had justified my suggesting that you should once again be allowed to say Mass."

"You wrote that yesterday afternoon?" Mr. Mousley exclaimed. "And the instant afterwards I went out and got drunk?"

"You mean you took a pick-me-up and two glasses of beer," corrected Father Rowley.

"No, no, no, it wasn't a pick-me-up. I went out and got drunk on brandy quite deliberately."

Father Rowley looked quickly across at Mark, who hastily left the two priests together. He divined from the Missioner's quick glance that he was going to hear Mr. Mousley's confession. A week later Mr. Mousley asked Mark if he would serve at Mass the next morning.

"It may seem an odd request," he said, "but inasmuch as you have seen the depths to which I can sink, I want you equally to see the heights to which Father Rowley has raised me."

CHAPTER XVIII

SILCHESTER COLLEGE MISSION

It was never allowed to be forgotten at St. Agnes' that the Mission was the Silchester College Mission; and there were few days in the year on which it was possible to visit the Mission House without finding there some member of the College past or present. Every Sunday during term two or three prefects would sit down to dinner; masters turned up during the holidays; even the mighty Provost himself paid occasional visits, during which he put off most of his majesty and became as nearly human as a facetious judge. Nor did Father Rowley allow Silchester to forget that it had a Mission. He was not at all content with issuing a half yearly report of progress and expenses, and he had no intention of letting St. Agnes' exist as a subject for an occasional school sermon or a religious tax levied on parents. From the first moment he had put foot in Chatsea he had done everything he could to make St. Agnes' be what it was supposed to be—the Silchester College Mission. He was particularly anxious that the new church should be built and beautified with money from Silchester sources, even if he also accepted money for this purpose from outside. Soon after Mark had become recognized as Father Rowley's confidential secretary, he visited Silchester for the first time in his company.

It was the custom during the summer for the various guilds and clubs connected with the parish to be entertained in turn at the College. It had never happened that Mark had accompanied any of these outings, which in the early days of St. Agnes' had been regarded with dread by the College authorities, so many flowers were picked, so much fruit was stolen, but which now were as orderly and respectable excursions as you could wish to see. Mark's first visit to Silchester was on the occasion of Father Rowley's terminal sermon in the June after he was nineteen. He found the experience intimidating, because he was not yet old enough to have learnt self-confidence and he had never passed through the ordeal either of a first term at a public school or of a first term at the University. Boys are always critical, and at Silchester with the tradition of six hundred years to give them a corporate self-confidence, the judgment of outsiders is more severe than anywhere in the world, unless it might be in the New Hebrides. Added to their critical regard was a chilling politeness which would have made downright insolence appear cordial in comparison. Mark felt like Gulliver in the presence of the Houyhnms. These noble animals, so graceful, so clean, so condescending, appalled him. Yet he had found the Silchester men who came to visit the Mission easy enough to get on with. No doubt they, without their background were themselves a little shy, although their shyness never mastered them so far as to make them ill at ease. Here, however, they seemed as imperturbable and unbending as the stone saints, row upon row on the great West front of the Cathedral. Mark apprehended more clearly than ever the powerful personality of Father Rowley when he found that these noble young animals accorded to him the same quality of respect that they gave to a popular master or even to a popular athlete. The Missioner seemed able to understand their intimate and allusive conversation, so characteristic of a small and highly developed society; he seemed able to chaff them at the right moment; to take them seriously when they ought to be taken seriously; in a word to have grasped without being a Siltonian the secret of Silchester. He and Mark were staying at a house which possessed super-imposed upon the Silchester tradition a tradition of its own extending over the forty years during which the Reverend William Jex Monkton had been a house master. It was difficult for Mark, who had nothing but the traditions of Haverton House for a standard to understand how with perfect respect the boys could address their master by his second name without prejudice to discipline. Yet everybody in Jex's house called him Jex; and when you looked at that delightful old gentleman himself with his criss-cross white tie and curly white hair, you realized how impossible it was for him to be called anything else except Jex.

For the first time since Mark, brooding upon the moonlit quadrangle of St. Osmund's Hall, bade farewell to Oxford, he regretted for a while his surrender of the scholarship to Emmett. What was Emmett doing now? Had his stammer improved in the confidence that his success must surely have brought him? Mark made an excuse to forsake the company of the four or five men in whose charge he had been left. He was tired of being continually rescued from drowning in their conversation. Their intentional courtesy galled him. He felt like a negro chief being shown the sights of England by a tired equerry. It was a fine summer day, and he went down to the playing fields to watch the cricket match. He sat down in the shade of an oak tree on the unfrequented side, unable in the mood he was in to ask against whom the College was playing or which side was in. Players and spectators alike appeared unreal, a mirage of the sunlight; the very landscape ceased to be anything more substantial than a landscape perceived by dreamers in the clouds. The trees and towers of Silchester, the bald hills of Berkshire on the horizon, the cattle in the meadows, the birds in the air exasperated Mark with his inability to put himself in the picture. The grass beneath the oak was scattered with a treasury of small suns minted by the leaves above, trembling patens and silver disks that Mark set himself to count.

"Trying not to yearn and trying not to yawn," he muttered. "Forty-four, forty-five, forty-six."

"You're ten out," said a voice. "We want fifty-six to tie, fifty-seven to win."

Mark looked up and saw that a Silchester man whom he remembered seeing once at the Mission was preparing to sit down beside him. He was a tall youth, fair and freckled and clear cut, perfectly self-possessed, but lacking any hint of condescension in his manner.

"Didn't you come over with Rowley?" he inquired.

Mark was going to explain that he was working at the Mission when it struck him that a Silchester man might have the right to resent that, and he gave no more than a simple affirmative.

"I remember seeing you at the Mission," he went on. "My name's Hathorne. Oh, well hit, sir, well hit!"

Hathorne's approbation of the batsman made the match appear even more remote. It was like the comment of a passer-by upon a well-designed figure in a tapestry. It was an expression of his own æsthetic pleasure, and bore no relation to the player he applauded.

"I've only been down to the Mission once," he continued, turning to Mark. "I felt rather up against it there."

"Well, I feel much more up against it in Silchester," replied Mark.

"Yes, I can understand that," Hathorne nodded. "But you're only up against form: I was up against matter. It struck me when I was down there what awful cheek it was for me to be calmly going down to Chatsea and supposing that I had a right to go there, because I had contributed a certain amount of money belonging to my father, to help spiritually a lot of people who probably need spiritual help much less than I do myself. Of course, with anybody else except Rowley in charge the effect would be damnable. As it is, he manages to keep us from feeling as if we'd paid to go and look at the Zoo. You're a lucky chap to be working there without the uncomfortable feeling that you're just being tolerated because you're a Siltonian."

"I was thinking," said Mark, "that I was only being tolerated here because I happened to come with Rowley. It's impossible to visit a place like this and not regret that one must remain an outsider."

"It depends on what you want to do," said Hathorne. "I want to be a parson. I'm going up to the Varsity in October, and I am beginning to wonder what on earth good I shall be at the end of it all."

He gave Mark an opportunity to comment on this announcement; but Mark did not know what to say and remained silent.

"I see you're not in the mood to be communicative," Hathorne went on with a smile. "I don't blame you. It's impossible to be communicative in this place; but some time, when I'm down at the Mission again, I'd like to have what is called a heart-to-heart talk. That was a good boundary. We shall win quite comfortably. So long!"

The tall, fair youth passed on; and although Mark never had that heart-to-heart talk with him in the Mission, because he was killed in a mountaineering accident in Switzerland that August, the memory of him sitting there under the oak tree on that fine summer afternoon remained with Mark for ever; and after that brief conversation he lost most of his shyness, so that he came to enjoy his visits to Silchester as much as the Missioner himself did.

As the new church drew near its completion, Mark apprehended why Father Rowley attached so much importance to as much of the money for it as possible coming directly from Silchester. He apprehended how the Missioner felt that he was building Silchester in a Chatsea slum; and from that moment that landscape like a mirage of the sunlight, that landscape into which he had been unable to fit himself when he first beheld it became his own, for now beyond the chimneypots he could always see the bald hills of Berkshire and the trees and towers of Silchester, and at the end of all the meanest alleys there were cattle in the meadows and birds in the air above.

Silchester was not the only place that Mark visited with Father Rowley. It became a recognized custom for him to travel up to London whenever the Missioner was preaching, and in London he was once more struck by the variety of Father Rowley's worldly knowledge and secular friends. One week-end will serve as a specimen of many. They left Chatsea on a Saturday morning travelling up to town in a third class smoker full of bluejackets and soldiers on leave. None of them happened to know the Missioner, and for a time they talked surlily in undertones, evidently viewing with distaste the prospect of having a Holy Joe in their compartment all the way to London; but when Father Rowley pulled out his pipe, for always when he was away from St. Agnes' he allowed himself the privilege of smoking, and began to talk to them about their ships and their regiments with unquestionable knowledge, they unbent, so that long before Waterloo was reached it must have been the jolliest compartment in the whole train. It was all done so easily, and yet without any of that deliberate descent from a pedestal, which is the democratic manner of so many parsons; there was none of that Friar Tuck style of aggressive laymanhood, nor that subtler way of denying Christ (of course with the best intentions) which consists of salting the conversation with a few "damns" and peppering it with a couple of "bloodies" to show that a parson may be what is called human. Father Rowley was simply himself; and a month later two of the bluejackets in that compartment and one of the soldiers were regular visitors to the Mission House, and what is more regular visitors to the Blessed Sacrament.

They reached London soon after midday and went to lunch at a restaurant in Jermyn Street famous for a Russian salad that Father Rowley sometimes spoke of with affection in Chatsea. After lunch they went to a matinée of *Pelleas and Mélisande*, the Missioner having been given two stalls by an actor friend. Mark enjoyed the play and was being stirred by the imagination of old, unhappy, far off things until his companion began to laugh. Several clever women who looked as if they had been dragged through a hedge said "Hush!"; even Mark, compassionate of the players' feelings should they hear Father Rowley laugh at the poignant nonsense they were uttering on the stage, begged him to control himself.

"But this is most unending rubbish," he said. "I've never heard anything so ridiculous in my life. Terrible."

The curtain fell on the act at this moment, so that Father Rowley was able to give louder voice to his opinions.

"This is unspeakable bosh," he repeated. "I can't understand anything at all that is going on. People run on and run off again and make the most idiotic remarks. I really don't think I can stand any more of this."

The clever women rattled their beads and writhed their necks like angry snakes without effect upon the Missioner.

"I don't think I can stand any more of this," he repeated. "I shall have apoplexy if this goes on."

The clever women hissed angrily about the kind of people that came to theatres nowadays.

"This man Maeterlinck must have escaped from an asylum," Father Rowley went on. "I never heard such deplorable nonsense in my life."

"I shall ask an attendant if we can change our seats," snapped one of the clever women in front. "That's the worst of coming to a Saturday afternoon performance, such extraordinary people come up to town on Saturdays."

"There you are," exclaimed Father Rowley loudly, "even that poor woman in front thinks they're extraordinary."

"She's talking about you," said Mark, "not about the people in the play."

"My good woman," said Father Rowley, leaning over and tapping her on the shoulder. "You don't think that you really enjoy this rubbish, do you?"

One of her friends who was near the gangway called out to a programme seller:

"Attendant, attendant, is it possible for my friends and myself to move into another row? We are being pestered with a running commentary by that stout clergyman behind that lady in green."

"Don't disturb yourselves, you foolish geese," said Father Rowley rising. "I'm not going to sit through another act. Come along, Mark, come along, come along. I am not happy. I am not happy," he cried in an absurd falsetto.

Then roaring with laughter at his own imitation of Mélisande, he went rolling out of the theatre and sniffed contentedly the air of the Strand.

"I told Lady Pechell we shouldn't arrive till tea-time, so we'd better go and ride on the top of a bus as far as the city."

It was an exhilarating ride, although Mark found that Father Rowley occupied much more than half of the seat for two. About five o'clock they came to the shadowy house in Portman Square in which they were to stay till Monday. The Missioner was as much at home here as he was at Silchester College or in a railway compartment full of bluejackets. He knew as well how to greet the old butler as Lady Pechell and her sister Mrs. Mannakay, to all of whom equally his visit was an obvious delight. Not even Father Rowley's bulk could dwarf the proportions of that double drawing-room or of that heavy Victorian furniture. He took his place among the cases of stuffed humming birds and glass-topped tables of curios, among the brocade curtains with shaped vallances and golden tassels, among the chandeliers and lacquered cabinets and cages of avadavats, sitting there like a great Buddha while he chatted to the two old ladies of a society that seemed to Mark as remote as the people in *Pelleas and Mélisande*. From time to time one of the old ladies would try to draw Mark into the conversation; but he preferred listening and let them think that his monosyllabic answers signified a shyness that did not want to be conspicuous. Soon they appeared to forget his existence. Deep in the lap of an armchair covered with a glazed chintz of Sèvres roses and sable he was enthralled by that chronicle of phantoms, that frieze of ghosts passing before his eyes, while the present faded away upon the growing quiet of the London evening and became remote as the distant roar of the traffic, which itself was remote as the sound of the sea in a shell. Fox-hunting squires caracoled by with the air of paladins; and there was never a lady mentioned that did not take the fancy like a princess in an old tale.

"He's universal," Mark thought. "And that's one of the secrets of being a great priest. And that's why he can talk about Heaven and make you feel that he knows what he's talking about. And if I can discern what he is," Mark went on to himself, "I can be what he is. And I will be," he vowed in the rapture of a sudden revelation.

On Sunday morning Father Rowley preached in the fashionable church of St. Cyprian's, South Kensington, after which they lunched at the vicarage. The Reverend Drogo Mortemer was a dapper little bachelor (it would be inappropriate to call such a worldly little fellow a celibate) who considered himself the leader of the most advanced section of the Catholic Party in the Church of England. He certainly had a finger in the pie of every well-cooked intrigue, knew everybody worth knowing in London, and had the private ears of several bishops. No more skilful place-finder existed, and any member of the advanced section who wanted a place for himself or for a friend had recourse to Mortemer.

"But the little man is all right," Father Rowley had told Mark. "Many people would have used his talents to further himself. He has every qualification for the episcopate except one—he believes in the Sacraments."

Mr. Mortemer was the only son of James Mortimer of the famous firm of Hadley and Mortimer. His father had become rich before he married the youngest daughter of an ancient but impoverished house, and soon after his marriage he died. Mrs. Mortemer brought up her son to forget that his father had been a tradesman and to remember that he was rich. In order to dissociate herself from a partnership which now existed only in name above the plate glass of the enormous shop in Oxford Street Mrs. Mortemer took to spelling her name with an "e," which as she pointed out was the original spelling. She had already gratified her romantic fancy by calling her son Drogo. Harrow and Cambridge completed what Mrs. Mortemer began, and if Drogo had not developed what his mother spoke of as a "mania for religion" there is no reason to suppose that he would not one day have been a cabinet minister. However, as it was, Mrs. Mortemer died cherishing with her last breath a profound conviction that her son would soon be a bishop. That he was not likely to become a bishop was due to the fact that with all his worldliness, with all his wealth, with all his love of wire-pulling, with all his respect for rank he held definite opinions and was not afraid to belong to a minority unpopular in high places. He had too a simple piety that made his church a power in spite of fashionable weddings and exorbitant pew rents.

"The sort of thing we're trying to do here in a small way," he said to Father Rowley at lunch, "is what the Jesuits are doing at Farm Street. My two assistant priests are both rather brilliant young people, and I'm always on the look out to get more young men of the right type."

"You'd better offer Lidderdale a title when he's ready to be ordained."

"Why, of course I will," said the dapper little vicar with a courteous smile for Mark. "Do take some more claret, Father Rowley. It's rather a specialty of ours here. We have a friend in Bordeaux who buys for us."

It was typical of Mr. Mortemer to use the plural.

"There you are, Mark Anthony. I've secured you a title."

"Mr. Mortemer is only being polite," said Mark.

"No, no, my dear boy, on the contrary I meant absolutely what I said."

He seemed worried by Mark's distrust of his sincerity, and for the rest of lunch he laid himself out to entertain his less important guest, talking with a slight excess of charm about the lack of vitality, loss of influence, and oriental barbarism of the Orthodox Church.

"*Enfin*, Asiatic religion," he said. "Don't you agree with me, Mr. Lidderdale? And our Philorthodox brethren who would like to bring about reunion with such a Church . . . the result would be dreadful . . . Eurasian . . . yes, I must confess that sometimes I sympathize with the behaviour of the Venetians in the Fourth Crusade."

Father Rowley looked at his watch and announced that it was time to start for Poplar, where he was to address a large gathering of Socialists in the Town Hall. Mr. Mortemer made a *moue*.

"Nevertheless I'm bound to admit that you have a strong case. Perhaps I'm like the young man with large possessions," he burst out with a sudden intense gravity. "Perhaps after all the St. Cyprian's religion isn't Christianity at all. Just Catholicism. Nothing else."

"You'd better come down to Poplar with Mark and me," Father Rowley suggested.

But Mr. Mortemer shook his head with a smile.

The Poplar meeting was crowded. In an atmosphere of good fellowship one speaker after another got up and denounced the present order. It was difficult to follow the arguments of the speakers, because the audience cheered so many isolated statements. A number of people shook hands with Father Rowley when he had finished his speech and wished that there were more parsons like him. Father Rowley had not indulged in political attacks, but had contented himself with praise of the poor. He had spoken movingly, but Mark was not moved by his words. He had a vague feeling that Father Rowley was being exploited. He was dazed by the exuberance of the meeting and was glad when it was over and he was back in Portman Square talking to Lady Pechell and Mrs. Mannakay while Father Rowley rested for an hour before he walked round the corner to preach in old Jamaica Chapel, a galleried Georgian conventicle that was now the Church of the Visitation, but was still generally known as Jamaica Chapel. Evensong was half over when the preacher arrived, and the church being full Mark was given a chair by the sidesman in a dark corner, which presently became darker when Father Rowley went up into the pulpit, for all the lights were lowered except those above the preacher's head, and nothing was visible in the church except the luminous crucifix upon the High Altar. The warmth and darkness brought out the scent of the many women gathered together; the atmosphere was charged with human emotion so that Mark sitting in his corner could fancy that he was lost in the sensuous glooms behind some *Mater Addolorata* of the seventeenth century. He longed to be back in Chatsea. He was dismayed at the prospect of one day perhaps having to cope with this quality of devotion. He shuddered at the thought, and for the first time he wondered if he had not a vocation for the monastic life. But was it a vocation if one longed to escape the world? Must not a true vocation be a longing to draw nearer to

God? Oh, this nauseating bouquet of feminine perfumes . . . it was impossible to pay attention to the sermon.

Mark went to bed early with a headache; but in the morning he woke refreshed with the knowledge that they were going back to Chatsea, although before they reached home the journey had to be broken at High Thorpe whither Father Rowley had been summoned to an interview by the Bishop of Silchester on account of refusing to communicate some people at the mid-day celebration. Dr. Crawshay was at that time so ill that he received the Chatsea Missioner in bed, and on hearing that he was accompanied by a young man who hoped to take Holy Orders the Bishop sent word for Mark to come up to his bedroom, where he gave him his blessing. Mark never forgot the picture of the Bishop lying there under a chequered coverlet looking like an old ivory chessman, a white bishop that had been taken in the game and put off the board.

"And now, Mr. Rowley," Dr. Crawshay began when he had motioned Mark to a chair. "To return to the subject under discussion between us. How can you justify by any rubric of the Book of Common Prayer non-communicating attendance?"

"I don't justify it by any rubric," the Missioner replied.

"Oh, you don't, don't you?"

"I justify it by the needs of human nature," the Missioner continued. "In order to provide the necessary three communicants for the mid-day Mass . . ."

"One moment, Mr. Rowley," the Bishop interrupted. "I beg you most earnestly to avoid that word. You know my old-fashioned Protestant notions," he added, and his eyes so tired with pain twinkled for a moment. "To me there is always something distasteful about that word."

"What shall I substitute, my lord?" the Missioner asked. "Do you object to the word 'Eucharist'?"

"No, I don't object to that, though why you should want a Greek name when we have a beautiful English name like the Lord's Supper, why you should want to employ such a barbarism as 'Eucharist' I don't know. However, if you must use Eucharist, use Eucharist. And now, by wandering off into a discussion of terminology I forget where we were. Oh yes, you were on the point of justifying non-communicating attendance by the needs of human nature."

"I am afraid, my lord, that in a district like St. Agnes' it is impossible always to ensure communicants for sometimes as many as four early Lord's Suppers said by visiting priests."

The Bishop's eyes twinkled again.

"Yes, there you rather have me, Mr. Rowley. Four early Lord's Suppers does sound, I must admit, a little odd."

"Four early Eucharists followed by another for children at half-past nine, and the parochial sung Mass—sung Eucharist."

"Children?" Dr. Crawshay repeated. "You surely don't let children go to the Celebration?"

"*Suffer little children to come unto Me, and forbid them not, for of such is the Kingdom of Heaven,*" Father Rowley reminded the Bishop.

"Yes, yes, I happen to have heard that text before. But the devil, Mr. Rowley, can cite Scripture to his purpose."

"In the last letter I wrote to your lordship about the services at St. Agnes' I particularly mentioned our children's Eucharist."

"Did you, Mr. Rowley, did you? I had quite forgotten that."

Father Rowley turned to Mark for verification.

"Oh, if Mr. Rowley remembers that he did write, there is no need to call witnesses. I have had to complain a good deal of him, but I have never had to complain of his frankness. It must be my fault, but I certainly hadn't understood that there was definitely a children's Eucharist. This then, I fancy, must be the service at which those three ladies complained of your treatment of them."

"What three ladies?" asked the priest.

"Dear me, I'm growing very unbusinesslike, I'm afraid. I thought I had enclosed you a copy of their letter to me when I wrote to invite an explanation of your high-handed action."

The Bishop sighed. The details of these ecclesiastical squabbles distracted him at a time when he should soon leave this fretful earth behind him. He continued wearily:

"These were the three ladies who were refused communion by you at, as I understood, the mid-day Celebration, which now turns out to be what you call the children's Eucharist."

"It is perfectly true, my lord," Father Rowley admitted, "that on Sunday week three women did present themselves from a neighbouring parish."

"Ah, they were not parishioners?"

"Certainly not, my lord."

"Which is a point in your favour."

"Throughout the service they sat looking through opera-glasses at Snaith who was officiating, and greatly scandalizing the children, who are not used to such behaviour in church."

"Such behaviour was certainly most objectionable," the Bishop agreed.

"I happened to be sitting at the back of the church, thinking out my sermon, and their behaviour annoyed me so much that I sent for the sacristan to go and order a cab. I then went up and whispered to them that inasmuch as they were strangers it would be better if they went and made their Communion in the next parish where the service would be more lenient to their theory of worship. I took one of them by the arm, led her gently down the aisle and out into the street, and handed her into the cab. Her two companions followed her; I paid the cabman; and that was the end of the matter."

The Bishop lay back on the pillows and thought for a moment or two in silence.

"Yes," he said finally, "I think that in this case you were justified. At the same time your justification by the Book of Common Prayer lay in the fact that these women did not give you notice beforehand of their intention to communicate. I think I must insist that in future you make some arrangement with your workers and helpers to secure the requisite minimum of communicants for every celebration. Personally, I think six on a Sunday and four on a week-day far too many. I think the repetition has a tendency to cheapen the Sacrament."

"*By Him therefore let us offer the sacrifice of praise to God continually,*" Father Rowley quoted from the Epistle to the Hebrews.

"Yes, yes, I know," said the Bishop. "But I wish you wouldn't drag in these texts. They really have nothing whatever to do with the point in question. Please realize, Mr. Rowley, that I allow you a great deal of latitude at St. Agnes' because I am aware of what a great influence for good you have been among these poor people."

"Your lordship has always been consideration itself."

"If that be your opinion, I want you to obey my ruling in this small matter. I am continually being involved in correspondence on your account with Vigilance Societies of the type of the Protestant Alliance, and I shall give myself the pleasure of answering their complaints without at the same time not, as I hope, impeding your splendid work. I wish also, if God allows me to leave this bed again, to take the next Confirmation in St. Agnes' myself. My presence there will afford you a measure of official support which will not, I venture to believe, be a disadvantage to your work. I do not expect you to modify your method of conducting the service too much. That would savour of hypocrisy, both on your side and on mine. But there are one or two things which I should prefer not to see again. Last time you dressed a number of your choir-boys in red cassocks."

"The servers, you mean, my lord?"

"Whatever you call them, they wear red cassocks, red slippers, and red skull caps. That I really cannot stand. You must put them into black cassocks and leave their caps and slippers in the vestry cupboard. Further, I do not wish that most conspicuous processional crucifix to be carried about in front of me wherever I go."

"Would you like the crucifix to be taken down from the altar as well?" Father Rowley asked.

"No, that can stay: I shan't see that one."

"What date will suit your lordship for the Confirmation?"

"Ought not the question to have been rather what date will suit you, for I have never yet been fortunate enough, and I never hope to be fortunate enough, to fix upon a date straight off that will suit you, Mr. Rowley. Let me know that later. In any case, my presence must depend, alas, upon the state of my health. Now, how are you getting on with your new church?"

"We shall be ready to open it in the spring of next year if all goes well. Do you think that a new licence will be required? The new St. Agnes' is joined to the present church by the sacristy."

The Bishop considered the question for a moment.

"No, I think that the old licence will serve. There is no prospect yet of making St. Agnes' into a parish, and I would rather take advantage of the technicality, all things being considered. Goodbye, Mr. Rowley. God bless you."

The Bishop raised his thin arm.

"God bless your lordship."

"You are always in my prayers, Mr. Rowley. I think much about you lying here on the threshold of Eternal Life."

The Bishop turned to Mark who knelt beside the bed.

"Young man, I would fain be spared long enough to ordain you to the service of Almighty God, but you are still young and I am very near to death. You could not have before you a better example of a Christian gentleman than your friend and my friend Mr. Rowley. I shall say nothing about his example as a clergyman of the Church of England. Remember me, both of you, in your prayers."

The Bishop sank back exhausted, and his visitors went quietly out of the room.

CHAPTER XIX

THE ALTAR FOR THE DEAD

All went as well with the new St. Agnes' as the Bishop had hoped. Columns of red brick were covered in marble and alabaster by the votive offerings of individuals or the subscriptions of different Silchester Houses; the baldacchino was given by one rich old lady, the pavement of the church by another; the Duke of Birmingham contributed a thurible; Oxford Old Siltonians decorated the Lady Chapel; Cambridge Old Siltonians found the gold mosaic for the dome of the apse. Father Rowley begged money for the fabric far and wide, and the architect, the contractors, and the workmen, all Chatsea men, gave of their best and asked as little as possible in return. The new church was to be opened on Easter morning. But early in Lent the Bishop of Silchester died in the bed from which he had never risen since the day Father Rowley and Mark received his blessing. The diocese mourned him, for he was a gentle scholar, wise in his knowledge of men, simple and pious in his own life.

Dr. Harvard Cheesman, the new Bishop, was translated from the see of Ipswich to which he had been preferred from the Chapel Royal in the Savoy. Bishop Cheesman possessed all the episcopal qualities. He had the hands of a physician and the brow of a scholar. He was filled with a sense of the importance of his position, and in that perhaps was included n sense of the importance of himself. He was eloquent in public, grandiloquent in private. To him Father Rowley wrote shortly after his enthronement.

St. Agnes' House,
Keppel Street,
Chatsea.
March 24.

My Lord Bishop,

I am unwilling to trouble you at a moment when you must be unusually busy; but I shall be glad to hear from you about the opening of the new church of the Silchester College Mission, which was fixed for Easter Sunday. Your predecessor, Bishop Crawshay, did not think that any new licence would be necessary, because the new St. Agnes' is joined by the sacristy to the old mission church. There is no idea at present of asking you to constitute St. Agnes' a parish and therefore the question of consecration does not arise. I regret to say that Bishop Crawshay thoroughly disapproved of our services and ritual, and I think he may have felt unwilling to commit himself to endorsing them by the formal grant of a new licence. May I hear from you at your convenience, and may I respectfully add that your lordship has the prayers of all my people?

I am your lordship's obedient servant,

John Rowley.

To which the Lord Bishop of Silchester replied as follows:

High Thorpe Castle.
March 26.

Dear Mr. Rowley,

As my predecessor Bishop Crawshay did not think a new licence would be necessary I have no doubt that you can go ahead with your plan of opening the new St. Agnes' on Easter Sunday. At the same time I cannot help feeling that a new licence would be desirable and I am asking Canon Whymper as Rural Dean to pay a visit and make the necessary report. I have heard much of your work, and I pray that it may be as blessed in my time as it was in the time of my predecessor. I am grateful to your people for their prayers and I am, my dear Mr. Rowley,

Yours very truly,

Harvard Silton.

Canon Whymper, the Rector of Chatsea and Rural Dean, visited the new church on the Monday of Passion week. On Saturday Father Rowley received the following letter from the Bishop:

High Thorpe Castle.
April 9.

Dear Mr. Rowley,

I have just received Canon Whymper's report upon the new church of the Silchester College Mission, and I think before you open the church on Easter Sunday I should like to talk over one or two comparatively unimportant details with you personally. Moreover, it would give me pleasure to make your acquaintance and hear something of your method of work at St. Agnes'. Perhaps you will come to High Thorpe on Monday. There is a train which arrives at High Thorpe at 2.36. So I shall expect you at the Castle at 2.42.

Yours very truly,

Harvard Silton.

Mark paid his second visit to High Thorpe Castle on one of those serene April mornings that sail like swans across the lake of time. The episcopal standard on the highest turret hung limp; the castle quivered in the sunlight; the lawns wearing their richest green seemed as far from being walked upon as the blue sky above them. Whether it was that Mark was nervous about the result of the coming interview or whether it was that his first visit to High

Thorpe had been the climax of so many new experiences, he was certainly much more sharply aware on this occasion of what the Castle stood for. Looking back to the morning when he and Father Rowley sat with Bishop Crawshay in his bedroom, he realized how much the personality of the dead bishop had dominated his surroundings and how little all this dignity and splendour, which must have been as imposing then as it was now, had impressed his imagination. There came over Mark, when he and Father Rowley were walking silently along the drive, such a foreboding of the result of this visit that he almost asked the priest why they bothered to continue their journey, why they did not turn round immediately and take the next train back to Chatsea. But before he had time to say anything Father Rowley had pulled the chain of the door bell, the butler had opened the door, and they were waiting the Bishop's pleasure in a room that smelt of the best leather and the best furniture polish. It was a room that so long as Dr. Cheesman held the see of Silchester would be given over to the preliminary nervousness of the diocesan clergy, who would one after another look at that steel engraving of Jesus Christ preaching by the Sea of Galilee, and who when they had finished looking at that would look at those two oil paintings of still life, those rich and sombre accumulations of fish, fruit and game, that glowed upon the walls with a kind of sinister luxury. Waiting rooms are all much alike, the doctor's, the dentist's, the bishop's, the railway-station's; they may differ slightly in externals, but they all possess the same atmosphere of transitory discomfort. They have all occupied human beings with the perusal of books they would never otherwise have dreamed of opening, with the observation of pictures they would never otherwise have thought of regarding twice.

"Would you step this way," the butler requested. "His lordship is waiting for you in the library."

The two culprits, for by this time Mark was oblivious of every other emotion except one of profound guilt, guilt of what he could not say, but most unmistakably guilt, walked along toward the Bishop's library—Father Rowley like a fat and naughty child who knows he is going to be reproved for eating too many tarts.

There was a studied poise in the attitude of the Bishop when they entered. One shapely leg trailed negligently behind his chair ready at any moment to serve as the pivot upon which its owner could swing round again into the every-day world; the other leg firmly wedged against the desk supported the burden of his concentration. The Bishop swung round on the shapely leg in attendance, and in a single sweeping gesture blotted the last page of the letter he had been writing and shook Father Rowley by the hand.

"I am delighted to have an opportunity of meeting you, Mr. Rowley," he began, and then paused a moment with an inquiring look at Mark.

"I thought you wouldn't mind, my lord, if I brought with me young Lidderdale, who is reading for Holy Orders and working with us at St. Agnes'. I am apt to forget sometimes exactly to what I have and have not committed myself and I thought your lordship would not object . . ."

"To a witness?" interposed the Bishop in a tone of courtly banter. "Come, come, Mr. Rowley, had I known you were going to be so suspicious of me I should have asked my domestic chaplain to be present on my side."

Mark, supposing that the Bishop was annoyed by his presence at the interview, made a movement to retire, whereupon the Bishop tapped him paternally upon the shoulder and said:

"Nonsense, non-sense, I was merely indulging in a mild pleasantry. Sit down, Mr. Rowley. Mr. Lidderdale I think you will find that chair quite comfortable. Well, Mr. Rowley," he began, "I have heard much of you and your work. Our friend Canon Whymper spoke of it with enthusiasm. Yes, yes, with enthusiasm. I often regret that in the course of my ministry I have never had the good fortune to be called to work among the poor, the real poor. You have been privileged, Mr. Rowley, if I may be allowed to say so, greatly, immensely privileged. You find a wilderness, and you make of it a garden. Wonderful. Wonderful."

Mark began to feel uncomfortable, and he thought by the way Father Rowley was puffing his cheeks that he too was beginning to feel uncomfortable. The Missioner looked as if he was blowing away the lather of the soap that the Bishop was using upon him so prodigally.

"Some other time, Mr. Rowley, when I have a little leisure . . . I perceive the need of making myself acquainted with every side of my new diocese—a little leisure, yes . . . sometime I should like to have a long talk with you about all the details of your work at Chatsea, of which as I said Canon Whymper has spoken to me most enthusiastically. The question, however, immediately before us this morning is the licence of your new church. Since writing to you first I have thought the matter over most earnestly. I have given the matter the gravest consideration. I have consulted Canon Whymper and I have come to the conclusion that bearing all the circumstances in mind it will be wiser for you to apply, and I hope be granted, a new licence. With this decision in my mind I asked Canon Whymper in his capacity as Rural Dean to report upon the new church. Mr. Rowley, his report is extremely favourable. He writes to me of the noble fabric, noble is the actual epithet he employs, yes, the very phrase. He expresses his conviction that you are to be congratulated, most warmly congratulated, Mr. Rowley, upon your vigorous work. I believe I am right in saying that all the money necessary to erect this noble edifice has been raised by yourself?"

"Not all of it," said Father Rowley. "I still owe £3,000."

"A mere trifle," said the Bishop, dismissing the sum with the airy gesture of a conjurer who palms a coin. "A mere trifle compared with what you have already raised. I know that at the moment there is no question of constituting as a parish what is at present merely a district; but such a contingency must be borne in mind by both of us, and inasmuch as that would imply consecration by myself I am unwilling to prejudice any decision I might have to take later, should the necessity for consecration arise, by allowing you at the moment a wider latitude than I might be prepared to allow you in the future. Yes, Canon Whymper writes most enthusiastically of the noble fabric." The Bishop paused, drummed with his fingers on the arm of his chair as if he were testing the pitch of his instrument, and then taking a deep breath boomed forth: "But Mr. Rowley, in his report he informs me that in the middle of the south aisle exists an altar or Holy Table expressly and exclusively designed for what he was told are known as masses for the dead."

"That is perfectly true," said Father Rowley.

"Ah," said the Bishop, shaking his head gravely. "I did not indeed imagine that Canon Whymper would be misinformed about such an important feature; but I did not think it right to act without ascertaining first from you that such is indeed the case. Mr. Rowley, it would be difficult for me to express how grievously it pains me to have to seem to interfere in the slightest degree with the successful prosecution of your work among the poor of Chatsea, especially to make such interference one of the first of my actions in a new diocese; but the responsibilities of a bishop are grave. He cannot lightly endorse a condition of affairs, a method of services which in his inmost heart after the deepest confederation he feels is repugnant to the spirit of the Church Of England . . ."

"I question that opinion, my lord," said the Missioner.

"Mr. Rowley, pray allow me to finish. We have little time at our disposal for a theological argument which would in any case be fruitless, for as I told you I have already examined the question with the deepest consideration from every standpoint. Though I may respect your opinions in my private capacity, for I do not wish to impugn for one moment the sincerity of your beliefs, in my episcopal, or what I may call my public character, I can only condemn them utterly. Utterly, Mr. Rowley, and completely."

"But this altar, my lord," shouted Father Rowley, springing to his feet, to the alarm of Mark, who thought he was going to shake his fist in the Bishop's face, "this altar was subscribed for by the poor of St. Agnes', by all the poor of St. Agnes', as a memorial of the lives of sailors and marines of St. Agnes' lost in the sinking of the *King Harry*. Your predecessor, Bishop Crawshay, knew of its existence, actually saw it and commented on its ugliness; yet when I told him the circumstances in which it had been erected he was deeply moved by the beautiful idea. This altar has been in use for nearly three years. Masses for the dead have been said there time after time. This altar is surrounded by memorials of my dead people. It is one of the most vital factors in my work there. You ask me to remove it, before you have been in the diocese a month, before you have had time to see with your own eyes what an influence for good it has on the daily lives of the poor people who built it. My lord, I will not remove the altar."

While Father Rowley was speaking the Bishop of Silchester had been looking like a man on a railway platform who has been ambushed by a whistling engine.

"Mr. Rowley, Mr. Rowley," he said, "I pray you to control yourself. I beg you to understand that this is not a mere question of red tape, if I may use the expression, of one extra altar or Holy

Table, but it is a question of the services said at that altar or Holy Table."

"That is precisely what I am trying to point out to your lordship," said Father Rowley angrily.

"You yourself told me when you wrote to me that Bishop Crawshay disapproved of much that was done at St. Agnes'. It was you who put it into my head at the beginning of our correspondence that you were not asking me formally to open the new church, because you were doubtful of the effect your method of worship might have upon me. I don't wish for a moment to suggest that you were trying to bundle on one side the question of the licence, before I had had a moment to look round me in my new diocese, I say I do *not* think this for a moment; but inasmuch as the question has come before me officially, as sooner or later it must have come before me officially, I cannot allow my future action to be prejudiced by giving you liberties now that I may not be prepared to allow you later on. Suppose that in three years' time the question of consecrating the new St. Agnes' arises and the legality of this third altar or Holy Table is questioned, how should I be able to turn round and forbid then what I have not forbidden now?"

"Your lordship prefers to force me to resign?"

"Force you to resign, Mr. Rowley?" the Bishop repeated in aggrieved accents. "What can I possibly have said that could lead you to suppose for one moment that I was desirous of forcing you to resign? I make allowance for your natural disappointment. I make every allowance. Otherwise Mr. Rowley I should be tempted to characterize such a statement as cruel. As cruel, Mr. Rowley."

"What other alternative have I?"

"I should have said, Mr. Rowley, that you have one other very obvious alternative, and that is to accept my ruling upon the subject of this third altar or Holy Table. When I shall receive an assurance that you will do so, I shall with pleasure, with great pleasure, give you a new licence."

"I could not possibly do that," said the Missioner. "I could not possibly go back to my people tonight and tell them this Holy Week that what I have been teaching them for ten years is a lie. I would rather resign a thousand times."

"That is a far more accurate statement than your previous assertion that I was forcing you to resign."

"When will you have found a priest to take my place temporarily?" the Missioner asked in a chill voice. "It is unlikely that the Silchester College authorities will find another missioner at once, and I think it rests with your lordship to find a locum tenens. I do not wish to disappoint my people about the date of the opening of their new church. They have been looking forward to this Easter for so long now. Poor dears!"

Father Rowley sighed out the last ejaculation to himself, and his sigh ran through the Bishop's opulent library like a dull wind. Mark had a mad impulse to tell the Bishop the story of his father and the Lima Street Mission. His father had resigned on Palm Sunday. Oh, this ghastly dream . . . Father Rowley leave Chatsea! It was unimaginable . . .

But the Bishop was overthrowing the work of ten years with apparently as little consciousness of the ruin he was creating as a boar that has rooted up an ant-heap with his snout.

"Quite so. Quite so, Mr. Rowley. I certainly see your point," the Bishop declared. "I will do my best to secure a priest, but meanwhile . . . let me see. I need scarcely say how painful your decision has been, what pain it has caused me. Let me see, yes, in the circumstances I agree with you that it would be inadvisable to postpone the opening. I think from every point of view it would be wisest to proceed according to schedule. Could not this altar or Holy Table be railed off temporarily, I do not say muffled up, but could not some indication be given of the fact that I do not sanction its use? In that case I should have no objection, indeed on the contrary I should be only too happy for you to carry on with your work either until I can find a temporary substitute or until the Silchester College authorities can appoint a new missioner. Dear me, this is dreadfully painful for me."

Father Rowley stared at the Bishop in astonishment.

"You want me to continue?" he asked. "Really, my lord, you will excuse my plain speaking if I tell you that I am amazed at your point of view. A moment ago you told me that I must either remove this altar or resign."

"Pardon me, Mr. Rowley. I did not mention the word 'resign.'"

"And now," the Missioner went on without paying any attention to the interruption. "You are ready to let me stay at St.

Agnes' until a successor can conveniently be found. If my teaching is as pernicious as you think, I cannot understand your lordship's tolerating my officiating for another hour in your diocese."

"Mr. Rowley, you are introducing into this unhappy affair a great deal of extraneous feeling. I do not reproach you. I know that you are labouring under the stress of strong emotion. I overlook the manner which you have adopted towards me. I overlook it, Mr. Rowley. Before we close this interview, which I must once more assure you is as painful for me as for you, I want you to understand how deeply I regret having been forced to take the action I have. I ask your prayers, Mr. Rowley, and please be sure that you always have and always will have my prayers. Have you anything more you would like to say? Do not let me give you the impression from my alluding to the heavy work of entering upon the duties and responsibilities of a new diocese that I desire to hurry you in any way this afternoon. You will want to catch the 4.10 back to Chatsea I have no doubt. Too early perhaps for tea. Goodbye, Mr. Rowley. Goodbye, Mr . . ." the Bishop paused and looked inquiringly at Mark. "Lidderdale, ah, yes," he said. "For the moment I forgot. Goodbye, Mr. Lidderdale. A simple railing will, I think be sufficient for the altar in question, Mr. Rowley. I perfectly appreciate your motive in asking the Bishop of Barbadoes to officiate at the opening. I quite see that you did not wish to commit me to an approval of a ritual which might be more advanced than I might consider proper in my diocese . . . Goodbye, goodbye."

Father Rowley and Mark found themselves once more in the drive. The episcopal standard floated in the wind, which had sprung up while they were with the Bishop. They walked silently to the railway station under a fast clouding sky.

CHAPTER XX

FATHER ROWLEY

The first episcopal act of the Bishop of Silchester drove many poor souls away from God. It was a time of deep emotional stress for all the St. Agnes' workers, and Father Rowley could not show himself in Keppel Street without being surrounded by a crowd of supplicants who with tears and lamentations begged him to give up the new St. Agnes' and to remain in the old mission church rather than be lost to them for ever. There were some who even wished him to surrender the Third Altar; but in his last sermon preached on the Sunday night before he left Chatsea, he spoke to them and said:

"In the name of the Father and of the Son and of the Holy Ghost. Amen. The 15th verse of the 21st Chapter of the Holy Gospel according to Saint John: *Feed my lambs*.

"It is difficult for me, dear people, to preach to you this evening for the last time as your missioner, to preach, moreover, the last sermon that will ever be preached in this little mission church which has meant so much to you and so much to me. By the mercy of God man does not realize at the moment all that is implied by an occasion like this. He speaks with his mouth words of farewell; but his heart still beats to what was and what is, rather than to what will be.

"When I took as my text tonight those three words of Our Lord to St. Peter, *Feed my Lambs*, I took them as words that might be applied, first to the Lord Bishop of this diocese, secondly to the priest who will take my place in this Mission, and thirdly and perhaps most poignantly of all to myself. I cannot bring myself to suppose that in this moment of grief, in this moment of bitterness, almost of despair I am able to speak fairly of the Bishop of Silchester's action in compelling me to resign what has counted for all that is most precious in my life on earth. And already, in saying that the Bishop has compelled me to resign, I am not speaking with perfect accuracy, inasmuch as if I had been willing to surrender what I considered one of the essential articles of our belief, the Bishop would have been glad to licence the new St. Agnes' and to give his countenance and his support to me, the unworthy priest in charge of it.

"I want you therefore, dear people, to try to look at the matter from the standpoint of the Bishop. I want you to try to understand that in objecting to our little altar for the dead he is objecting not so much to the altar itself as to the services said at that altar. If it had merely been a question between us of a third altar, whether here or in the new St. Agnes', I should have found it possible, however unwillingly, to ask you—you, who out of your hard-earned savings built that altar—to allow it to be removed. Yes, I should have been selfish enough to ask you to make that great sacrifice on my account. But when the Bishop insisted that I and the priests who have borne with me and worked with me and preached with me and prayed with me all these years should abstain from saying those Masses which we believe and which you believe help our dear ones waiting for the Day of Judgment—why, then, I felt that my surrender would have been a denial of our dear Lord, such a denial as St. Peter himself uttered in the hall of the high-priest's house. But the Bishop does not believe that our prayers here below have any efficacy or can in any way help the blessed dead. He does not believe in such prayers, and he believes that those who do believe in such prayers are wrong, not merely according to the teaching of the Prayer Book, but also according to the revelation of Almighty God. I do not want you to say, as you will be tempted to say, that the Bishop of Silchester in condemning our method of services at St. Agnes' is condemning them with an eye to public opinion or to political advantage. Alas, I have myself been tempted to say bitter words about him, to think bitter thoughts; but at this moment, with that last *Nunc Dimittis* ringing in my ears, *Lord now lettest Thou Thy servant depart in peace*, I realize that the Bishop is acting honestly and sincerely, however much he may be acting wrongly and hastily. It is dreadful for me at this moment of parting to feel that some of you here tonight may be turned from the face of God because you are angered against one of God's ministers. If any poor words of mine have power to touch your hearts, I beg you to believe that in giving us this great trial of our faith God is acting with that mysterious justice and omniscience of which we speak idly without in the least apprehending what He means. I shall say no more in defence and explanation of the Bishop's action, and if he should consider my defence and explanation of it a piece of presumption I send him at this solemn moment of farewell a message that I shall never cease to pray that he may long guide you on the way that leads up to eternal happiness.

"I can speak more freely of what your attitude should be towards Father Hungerford, the priest who is coming to take my place and who is going with God's help to do far more for you here than ever I have been able to do. I want you all to put yourselves in his place; I want you all to think of him tonight wondering, fearing, doubting, hoping, and praying. I want you to imagine how difficult he must be feeling the situation is for him. He will come here tomorrow conscious that there is nobody in this district of ours who does not feel, whether he be a communicant or not, that the Bishop had no right to intervene so soon and without greater knowledge of his new diocese in a district like ours. I cannot help knowing how much I myself am to blame in this particular; but, my dear people, it has been very hard for me during these last two weeks always to be brave and hopeful. Often I have found those entreaties on my doorstep almost more than I could endure to hear, those letters on my desk almost more than I could bear to read. So, if you want to do the one thing that can comfort me in this bitter hour of mine I entreat you to show Father Hungerford that your faith and your hope and your love do not depend on your affection for an unworthy priest, but upon that deeper, greater, nobler affection for the word of God. There is only one way in which you can show Father Hungerford that Jesus Christ lives in your hearts, and that is by going to Confession and to Communion and by hearing Mass as you have done all this time. Show him by your behaviour in the street, by your kindness and consideration at home, by your devotion and reverence in church, that you appreciate the mercies of God, that you appreciate what it means to have Jesus Christ upon your altar, that you are, in a word, Christians.

"And now at last I must think of those words of our dear Lord as they apply to myself: *Feed my lambs*. And as I repeat them, I ask myself again if I have done right, for I am troubled in spirit, and I wonder if I ought to have given up that third altar and to have remained here. But even as I wonder this, even as at this moment I stand in this pulpit for the last time, a voice within me forbids me to doubt. No, my dear folk, I cannot surrender that altar. I cannot come to you and say that what I have been teaching for ten years was of so little value, of so little importance, of so little worth, that for the sake of policy it can be abandoned with a stroke of the pen or a nod of the head. I stand here looking out into the future, hearing like angelic trumpets those three words sounding and resounding upon the great void of time: *Feed my lambs!* I ask myself what work lies before me, what lambs I shall have to feed elsewhere; I ask myself in my misery whether God has found me unworthy of the trust He gave me. I feel that if I leave St. Agnes' tomorrow with the thought that you still cherish angry and resentful feelings I shall sink to a lower depth of humiliation and depression than I have yet reached. But if I can leave St. Agnes' with the assurance that my work here will go steadily forward to the glory of God from the point at which I renounced it, I shall know that God must have some other purpose for the remainder of my life, some other mission to which He intends to call me. To you, my dear people, to you who have borne with me patiently, to you who have tolerated so sweetly my infirmities, to you who have been kind to my failings, to you who have taught me so much more of our dear Lord Jesus Christ than I have been able to teach you, to you I say goodbye. I cannot harrow your feelings or my own by saying any more. In the name of the Father, and of the Son, and of the Holy Ghost. Amen."

Notwithstanding these words, the first episcopal act of the Bishop of Silchester drove many poor souls away from God.

The effect upon Mark, had his religion been merely a pastime of adolescence, would have been disastrous. Owing to human nature's respect for the conspicuous there is nothing so demoralizing to faith as the failure of a leader of religion to set forth in his own actions the word of God. Mark, however, looked at the whole business more from an ecclesiastical angle. He had reason to condemn the Bishop for unchristian behaviour; but he preferred to condemn him for uncatholic behaviour. Dr. Cheesman and the many other Dr. Cheesmans of whom the Anglican episcopate was at this period composed never succeeded in shaking his belief in Christ; they did succeed in shaking for a short time his belief in the Church of England. There are few Anglo-Catholics, whether priests or laymen, who have never doubted the right of their Church to proclaim herself a branch of the Holy Catholic Church. This phase of doubt is indeed so common that in ecclesiastical circles it has come to be regarded as a kind of mental chicken-pox, not very alarming if it catches the patient when young, but growing more dangerous in proportion to the lateness of its attack. Mark had his attack young. When Father Rowley left Chatsea, he was anxious to accompany him on what he knew would be an exhausting time of travelling round to preach and collect the necessary money to pay off what was actually a personal debt. It seemed that there must be something fundamentally wrong with a Church that allowed a man to perambulate England in an endeavour to pay off the debt upon a building from ministrating in which he had been debarred. This debt, moreover, was presumably going to be paid by people who fully subscribed to teaching which had been officially condemned.

When Mark commented on this, Father Rowley pointed out that as a matter of fact a great deal of money had been sent by people who admired the practical side, or what they would have called the practical side of his work among the poor, but who at the same time thoroughly disapproved of its ecclesiastical form.

"In justice to the poor old Church of England," he said to Mark, "it must be pointed out that a good deal of this money has been given by devout Anglicans under protest."

"Yes, but that doesn't seriously affect the argument," said Mark. "You collect I don't know how many thousands of pounds to put up a magnificent church from which the Bishop of Silchester sees fit to turn you out, but for the debt on which you are still personally responsible. It's fantastic!"

"Mark Anthony," the priest said with a laugh, "you lack the legal mind. The Bishop did not turn me out. The Bishop can perfectly well say I turned myself out."

"It is all too subtle for me," said Mark. "But I'm not going to worry you with any more arguments. You've had enough of them to last you for ever. I do wish you'd let me stick to you personally and help you in any way possible."

"No, Mark Anthony," the priest replied. "I've done my work at St. Agnes', and you've done yours. Your business now is to take advantage of what has happened and to get back to your books, which whatever you may say have been more and more neglected lately. You'll find it of enormous help to be a good theologian. I have never ceased to regret my own shortcomings in that respect. Besides, I think you ought to spend a certain amount of time with Ogilvie before you go to Glastonbury. There is quite a lot of work to do if you look for it in a country parish like—what's the name of the place? Wych. Oh, yes, quite a lot of work. Don't bother your head about Anglican Orders and Roman Claims and the Catholicity of the Church of England. Your business is to save souls, your own included. Go back and read and get to know the people in Ogilvie's parish. Anybody can tackle a district like St. Agnes'; anybody that is who has the suitable personality. How many people can tackle an English country parish? I hardly know one. I should like to have you with me. I'm fond of you, and you're useful; but at your age to travel round from town to town listening to my begging would be all wrong. I might even go to America. I've had most cordial invitations from several American bishops, and if I can't raise the money in England I shall have to go there. If God has any more work for me to do I shall be offered a cure some day somewhere. I want you to be one of my assistant priests, and if you're going to be useful to me as an assistant priest, you really must have some theology behind you. These bishops get more and more difficult to deal with every year. Now, it's no good arguing. My mind's made up. I won't take you with me."

So Mark went back to Wych-on-the-Wold and brooded upon the non-Catholic aspects of the Anglican Church.

CHAPTER XXI

POINTS OF VIEW

Mark did not find that his guardian was much disturbed by his doubts of the validity of Anglican Orders nor much alarmed by his suspicion that the Establishment had no right to be considered a branch of the Holy Catholic Church.

"The crucial point in the Roman position is their doctrine of intention," said Mr. Ogilvie. "It always seems to me that this doctrine is a particularly dangerous one for them to play with and one that may recoil at any moment upon their own heads. There has been a great deal of super-subtle dividing of intentions into actual, virtual, habitual, and interpretative; but if you are going to take your stand on logic you must be ready to face a logical conclusion. Let us agree for a moment that Barlow and the other bishops who consecrated Matthew Parker had no intention of consecrating him as a bishop for the purpose of ordaining priests in the sense in which Catholics understand the word priest. Do the Romans expect us to believe that all their prelates in the time of the Renaissance had a perfect intention when they were consecrating? Or leave on one side for a moment the sacrament of Orders; the validity of other sacraments is affected by their extension of the doctrine beyond the interpretation of St. Thomas Aquinas. However improbable it may be that at one moment all the priests of the Catholic Church should lack the intention let us say of absolution, it *is* a *logical* possibility, in which case all the faithful would logically speaking be damned. It was in order to guard against this kind of logical catastrophe that the first split between an actual intention and a virtual intention was made. The Roman Church teaches that the virtual intention is enough; but if we argue that a virtual intention might be ascribed to the bishops who consecrated Parker, the Roman controversialists present us with another subdivision—the habitual intention, which is one that formerly existed, but of the present continuance of which there is no trace. Now really, my dear Mark, you must admit that we've reached a point very near to nonsense if this kind of logical subtlety is to control Faith."

"As a matter of fact," said Mark, "I don't think I should ever want to 'vert over the question of the validity of Anglican Orders. I haven't any doubts now of their validity, and I think it's improbable that I shall have any doubts after I'm ordained. At the same time, there *is* something wrong with the Church of England if a situation like that in Chatsea can be created by the whim of a bishop. Our unhappy union between Church and State has created a class of bishops which has no parallel anywhere else in Christendom. In order to become a bishop in England, at any rate of the kind that has a seat in the House of Lords, it is necessary to be a gentleman, or rather to have the outward and visible signs of being a gentleman, to be a scholar, or to be a diplomat. Of course, there will be exceptions; but if you look at almost all our bishops, you will find they have reached their dignity by social attainments or by political utility or sometimes by intellectual distinction, but hardly ever by religious fervour, or spiritual honesty, or fearless opinion. I can sympathize with the dissenters of the seventeenth century in blaming the episcopate for all spiritual maladies. I expect there were a good many Dr. Cheesmans in the days of Defoe. Look back and see how the bishops have always voted in the House of Lords with enthusiastic unanimity against every proposal of reform that was ever put forward. I wonder what will happen when they are called upon to face a real national crisis."

"I'm perfectly ready to agree with everything you say about bishops," the Rector volunteered. "But more or less, I'm sorry to add, it is a criticism that can be applied to all the orders of the priesthood everywhere in Christendom. What can we, what dare we say in favour of priests when we remember Our Lord?"

"When a man does try to follow the Gospel a little more closely than the rest," Mark raged, "the bishops down him. They exist to maintain the safety of their class. They have reached their present position by knowing the right people, by condemning the wrong people, and by balancing their fat bottoms on fences. Sometimes when their political patrons quarrel over a pair of mediocrities, a saintly man who is either very old or very ill like Bishop Crawshay is appointed as a stop-gap."

"Yes," the Rector agreed. "But our present bishops are only one more aspect of Victorian materialism. The whole of contemporary society can be criticized in the same way. After all, we get the bishops we deserve, just as we get the politicians we deserve and the generals we deserve and the painters we deserve."

"I don't think that's any excuse for the bishops. I sometimes dream of worming myself up and stopping at nothing in order to be made a bishop, and then when I have the mitre at last of appearing in my true colours."

"Our Protestant brethren think that is what many of our right reverend fathers in God do now," the Rector laughed.

These discussions might have continued for ever without taking Mark any further. His failure to experience Oxford had deprived him of the opportunity to whet his opinions upon the grindstone of debate, and there had been no time for academic argument in the three years of Keppel Street. In Wych-on-the-Wold there never seemed much else to do but argue. It was one of the effects of leaving, or rather of seeing destroyed, a society that was obviously performing useful work and returning to a society that, so far as Mark could observe performed no kind of work whatever. He was loath to criticize the Rector; but he felt that he was moving along in a rut that might at any moment deepen to a chasm in which he would be spiritually lost. He seemed to be taking his priestly responsibilities too lightly, to be content with gratifying his own desire to worship Almighty God without troubling about his parishioners. Mark did not like to make any suggestions about parochial work, because he was afraid of the Rector's retorting with an implied criticism of St. Agnes'; and that would have involved him in a bitter argument for which he would afterward be sorry. Nor was it only in his missionary duties that he felt his old friend was allowing himself to rust. Three years ago the Rector had said a daily Mass. Now he was content with one on Thursdays except on festivals. Mark began to take walks far afield, which was a sign of irritation with the inaction of the life round him rather than the expression of an interest in the life beyond. On one of these walks he found himself at Wield in the diocese of Kidderminster thirty miles or more away from home. He had spent the night in a remote Cotswold village, and all the morning he had been travelling through the level vale of Wield which, beautiful at the time of blossom, was now at midsummer a landscape without line, monotonously green, prosperous and complacent. While he was eating his bread and cheese at the public bar of the principal inn, he picked up one of the local newspapers and reading it, as one so often reads in such surroundings, with much greater particularity than the journal of a metropolis, he came upon the following letter:

To the Editor of the WIELD OBSERVER AND SOUTH WORCESTERSHIRE COURANT,

SIR,—The leader in your issue of last Tuesday upon my sermon in St. Andrew's Church on the preceding Sunday calls for some corrections. The action of the Bishop of Kidderminster in inhibiting Father Rowley from accepting an invitation to preach in my church is due either to his ignorance of the facts of the case, to his stupidity in appreciating them, or, I must regretfully add, to his natural bias towards persecution. These are strong words for a parish priest to use about his diocesan; but the Bishop of Kidderminster's consistent support of latitudinarianism and his consistent hostility towards any of his clergy who practise the forms of worship which they feel they are bound to practise by the rubrics of the Book of Common Prayer call for strong words. The Bishop in correspondence with me declined to give any reason for his inhibition of Father Rowley beyond a general disapproval of his teaching. I am informed privately that the Bishop is suffering from a delusion that Father Rowley disobeyed the Bishop of Silchester, which is of course perfectly untrue and which is only one more sign of how completely out of accord our bishops are with what is going on either in their own diocese or in any other. My own inclination was frankly to defy his Lordship and insist upon Father Rowley's fulfilling his engagement. I am not sure that I do not now regret that I allowed my church-wardens to overpersuade me on this point. I take great exception to your statement that the offertories both in the morning and in the evening were sent by me to Father Rowley regardless of the wishes of my parishioners. That there are certain parishioners of St. Andrew's who objected I have no doubt. But when I send you the attached list of parishioners who subscribed no less than £18 to be added to the two collections, you will I am sure courteously admit that in this case the opinion of the parishioners of St. Andrew's was at one with the opinion of their Vicar.—I am, Sir, your obedient servant,

ADRIAN FORSHAW.

Mark was so much delighted by this letter that he went off at once to call on Mr. Forshaw, but did not find him at home; he was amused to hear from the housekeeper that his reverence had been summoned to an interview with the Bishop of Kidderminster. Mark fancied that it would be the prelate who would have the unpleasant quarter of an hour. Presently he began to ponder what it meant for such a letter to be written and published; his doubts about the Church of England returned; and in this condition of mind he found himself outside a small Roman Catholic church dedicated to St. Joseph, where hopeful of gaining the Divine guidance within he passed through the door. It may be that he was in a less receptive mood than he thought, for what impressed him most was the Anglican atmosphere of this Italian outpost. The stale perfume of incense on stone could not eclipse that authentic perfume of respectability which has been acquired by so many Roman Catholic churches in England. There were still hanging on the pillars the framed numbers of Sunday's hymns. Mark pictured the choir boy who must have slipped the cards in the frame with anxious and triumphant and immemorial Anglican zeal; and while he was contemplating this symbolical hymn-board, over his shoulder floated an authentic Anglican voice, a voice that sounded as if it was being choked out of the larynx by the clerical collar. It was the Rector, a stumpy little man with the purple stock of a monseigneur, who showed the stranger round his church and ended by inviting him to lunch. Mark, wondering if he had reached a crossroad in his progress, accepted the invitation, and prepared himself reverently to hear the will of God. Monseigneur Cripps lived in a little Gothic house next to St.

Joseph's, a trim little Gothic house covered with the oiled curls of an ampelopsis still undyed by autumn's henna.

"You've chosen a bad day to come to lunch," said Monseigneur with a warning shake of the head. "It's Friday, you know. And it's hard to get decent fish away from the big towns."

While his host went off to consult the housekeeper about the extra place for lunch, a proceeding which induced him to make a joke about extra 'plaice' and extra 'place,' at which he laughed heartily, Mark considered the most tactful way of leading up to a discussion of the position of the Anglican Church in regard to Roman claims. It should not be difficult, he supposed, because Monseigneur at the first hint of his guest's desire to be converted would no doubt welcome the topic. But when Monseigneur led the way to his little Gothic dining-room full of Arundel prints, Mark soon apprehended that his host had evidently not had the slightest notion of offering an *ad hoc* hospitality. He paid no attention to Mark's tentative advances, and if he was willing to talk about Rome, it was only because he had just paid a visit there in connexion with a school of which he was a trustee and out of which he wanted to make one kind of school and the Roman Catholic Bishop of Dudley wanted to make another.

"I had to take the whole question to headquarters," Monseigneur explained impressively. "But I was disappointed by Rome, oh yes, I was very disappointed. When I was a young man I saw it *couleur de rose*. I did enjoy one thing though, and that was going round the Vatican. Yes, they looked remarkably smart, the Papal Guards; as soon as they saw I was *Monsignore*, they turned out and presented arms. I'm bound to admit that I *was* impressed by that. But on the way down I lost my pipe in the train. And do you think I could buy a decent pipe in Rome? I actually had to pay five *lire*—or was it six?—for this inadequate tube."

He produced from his pocket the pipe he had been compelled to buy, a curved briar all varnish and gold lettering.

"I've been badly treated in Wield. Certainly, they made me Monseigneur. But then they couldn't very well do less after I built this church. We've been successful here. And I venture to think popular. But the Bishop is in the hands of the Irish. He cannot grasp that the English people will not have Irish priests to rule them. They don't like it, and I don't blame them. You're not Irish, are you?"

Mark reassured him.

"This plaice isn't bad, eh? I ordered turbot, but you never get the fish you order in these Midland towns. It always ends in my having plaice, which is good for the soul! Ha-ha! I hate the Irish myself. This school of which I am the chief trustee was intended to be a Catholic reformatory. That idea fell through, and now my notion is to turn it into a decent school run by secular clergy. All the English Catholic schools are in the hands of the regular clergy, which is a mistake. It puts too much power in the hands of the Benedictines and the Jesuits and the rest of them. After all, the great strength of the Catholic Church in England will always be the secular clergy. And what do we get now? A lot of objectionable Irishmen in Trilby hats. Last time I saw the Bishop I gave him my frank opinion of his policy. I told him my opinion to his face. He won't get me to kowtow to him. Yes, I said to him that, if he handed over this school to the Dominicans, he was going to spoil one of the finest opportunities ever presented of educating the sons of decent English gentlemen to be simple parish priests. But the Bishop of Dudley is an Irishman himself. He can't think of anything educationally better than Ushaw. And, as I was telling you, I saw there was nothing for it but to take the whole matter right up to headquarters, that is to Rome. Did I tell you that the Papal Guards turned out and presented arms? Ah, I remember now, I did mention it. I was extraordinarily impressed by them. A fine body. But generally speaking, Rome disappointed me after many years. Of course we English Catholics don't understand that way of worshipping. I'm not criticizing it. I realize that it suits the Italians. But suppose I started clearing my throat in the middle of Mass? My congregation would be disgusted, and rightly. It's an astonishing thing that I couldn't buy a good pipe in Rome, don't you think? I must have lost mine when I got out of the carriage to look at the leaning tower of Pisa, and my other one got clogged up with some candle grease. I couldn't get the beastly stuff out, so I had to give the pipe to a porter. They're keen on English pipes, those Italian porters. Poor devils, I'm not surprised. Of course, I need hardly say that in Rome they promised to do everything for me; but you can't trust them when your back is turned, and I need hardly add that the Bishop was pulling strings all the time. They showed me one of his letters, which was a tissue of mis-statements—a regular tissue. Now, suppose you had a son and you wanted him to be a priest? You don't necessarily want him to become a Jesuit or a Benedictine or a Dominican. Where can you send him now? Stonyhurst, Downside, Beaumont. There isn't a single decent school run by the secular clergy. You know what I mean? A school for the sons of gentlemen—a public school. We've got magnificent buildings, grounds, everything you could wish. I've been promised all the money necessary, and then the Bishop of Dudley steps in and says that these Dominicans ought to take it on."

"I'm afraid I've somehow given you a wrong impression," Mark interposed when Monseigneur Cripps at last filled his mouth with plaice. "I'm not a Roman Catholic."

"Oh, aren't you?" said Monseigneur indifferently. "Never mind, I expect you see my point about the necessity for the school to be run by secular clergy. Did I tell you how I got the land for my church here? That's rather an interesting story. It belonged to Lord Evesham who, as perhaps you may know, is very anti-Catholic, but a thorough good sportsman. We always get on capitally together. Well, one day I said to his agent, Captain Hart: 'What about this land, Hart? Don't you think you could get it out of his lordship?' 'It's no good, Father Cripps,' said Hart—I wasn't Monseigneur then of course—'It's no good,' he said, 'his lordship absolutely declines to let his land be used for a Catholic church.' 'Come along, Hart,' I said, 'let's have a round of golf.' Well, when we got to the eighteenth hole we were all square, and we'd both of us gone round three better than bogie and broken our own records. I was on the green with my second shot, and holed out in three. 'My game,' I shouted because Hart had foozled his drive and wasn't on the green. 'Not at all,' he said. 'You shouldn't be in such a hurry. I may hole out in one,' he laughed. 'If you do,' I said, 'you ought to get Lord Evesham to give me that land.' 'That's a bargain,' he said, and he took his mashie. Will you believe it? He did the hole in two, sir, won the game, and beat the record for the course! And that's how I got the land to build my church. I was delighted! I was delighted! I've told that story everywhere to show what sportsmen are. I told it to the Bishop, but of course he being an Irishman didn't see anything

233

funny in it. If he could have stopped my being made Monseigneur, he'd have done so. But he couldn't."

"You seem to have as much trouble with your bishops as we do with ours in the Anglican Church," said Mark.

"We shouldn't, if we made the right men bishops," said Monseigneur. "But so long as they think at Westminster that we're going to convert England with a tagrag and bobtail mob of Irish priests, we never shall make the right men. You were looking round my church just now. Didn't it remind you of an English church?"

Mark agreed that it did very much.

"That's my secret: that's why I've been the most successful mission priest in this diocese. I realize as an Englishman that it is no use to give the English Irish Catholicism. When I was in Rome the other day I was disgusted, I really was. I was disgusted. I thoroughly sympathize with Protestants who go there and are disgusted. You cannot expect a decent English family to confess to an Irish peasant. It's not reasonable. We want to create an English tradition."

"What between the Roman party in the Anglican Church and the Anglican party in the Roman Church," said Mark, "It seems a pity that some kind of reunion cannot be effected."

"So it could," Monseigneur declared. "So it could, if it wasn't for the Irish. Look at the way we treat our English converts. The clergy, I mean. Why? Because the Irish do not want England to be converted."

Mark did not raise with Monseigneur Cripps the question of his doubts. Indeed, before the plaice had been taken away he had decided that they no longer existed. It became clear to him that the English Church was England; and although he knew in his heart that Monseigneur Cripps was suffering from a sense of grievance and that his criticism of Roman policy was too obviously biased, it pleased him to believe that it was a fair criticism.

Mark thanked Monseigneur Cripps for his hospitality and took a friendly leave of him. An hour later he was walking back through the pleasant vale of Wield toward the Cotswolds. As he went his way among the green orchards, he thought over his late impulse to change allegiance, marvelling at it now and considering it irrational, like one astonished at his own behaviour in a dream. There came into his mind a story of George Fox who drawing near to the city of Lichfield took off his shoes in a meadow and cried three times in a loud voice "Woe unto the bloody city of Lichfield," after which he put on his shoes again and proceeded into the town. Mark looked back in amazement at his lunch with Monseigneur Cripps and his own meditated apostasy. To his present mood that intention to forsake his own Church appeared as remote from actuality as the malediction of George Fox upon the city of Lichfield.

Here among these green orchards in the heart of England Roman Catholicism presented itself to Mark's imagination as an exotic. The two words "Roman Catholicism" uttered aloud in the quiet June sunlight gave him the sensation of an allamanda or of a gardenia blossoming in an apple-tree. People who talked about bringing the English Church into line with the trend of Western Christianity lacked a sense of history. Apart from the question whether the English Church before the Reformation had accepted the pretensions of the Papacy, it was absurd to suppose that contemporary Romanism had anything in common with English Catholicism of the early sixteenth century. English Catholicism long before the Reformation had been a Protestant Catholicism, always in revolt against Roman claims, always preserving its insularity. It was idle to question the Catholic intentions of a priesthood that could produce within a century of the Reformation such prelates as Andrews and Ken. It was ridiculous at the prompting of the party in the ascendancy at Westminster to procure a Papal decision against English Orders when two hundred and fifty years ago there was a cardinal's hat waiting for Laud if he would leave the Church of England. And what about Paul IV and Elizabeth? Was he not willing to recognize English Orders if she would recognize his headship of Christendom?

But these were controversial arguments, and as Mark walked along through the pleasant vale of Wield with the Cotswold hills rising taller before him at every mile he apprehended that his adhesion to the English Church had been secured by the natural scene rather than by argument. Nevertheless, it was interesting to speculate why Romanism had not made more progress in England, why even now with a hierarchy and with such a distinguished line of converts beginning with Newman it remained so completely out of touch with the national life of the country. While the Romans converted one soul to Catholicism, the inheritors of the Oxford Movement were converting twenty. Catholicism must be accounted a disposition of mind, an attitude toward life that did not necessarily imply all that was implied by Roman Catholicism. What was the secret of the Roman failure? Everywhere else in the world Roman Catholicism had known how to adapt itself to national needs; only in England did it remain exotic. It was like an Anglo-Indian magnate who returns to find himself of no importance in his native land, and who but for the flavour of his curries and perhaps a black servant or two would be utterly inconspicuous. He tries to fit in with the new conditions of his readopted country, but he remains an exotic and is regarded by his neighbours as one to whom the lesson must be taught that he is no longer of importance. What had been the cause of this breach in the Roman Catholic tradition, this curious incompetency, this Anglo-Indian conservatism and pretentiousness? Perhaps it had begun when in the seventeenth century the propagation of Roman Catholicism in England was handed over to the Jesuits, who mismanaged the country hopelessly. By the time Rome had perceived that the conversion of England could not be left to the Jesuits the harm was done, so that when with greater toleration the time was ripe to expand her organization it was necessary to recruit her priests in Ireland. What the Jesuits had begun the Irish completed. It had been amusing to listen to the lamentations of Monseigneur Cripps; but Monseigneur Cripps had expressed, however ludicrous his egoism, the failure of his Church in England.

Mark's statement of the Anglican position with nobody to answer his arguments except the trees and the hedgerows seemed flawless. The level road, the gentle breeze in the orchards on either side, the scent of the grass, and the busy chirping of the birds coincided with the main point of his argument that England was most inexpressibly Anglican and that Roman Catholicism was most unmistakably not. His arguments were really hasty footnotes to his convictions; if each one had separately been proved wrong, that would have had no influence on the point of view he had reached. He forgot that this very landscape that was seeming incomparable England herself had yesterday appeared complacent and monotonous. In fact he was as bad as George Fox, who after taking off his shoes to curse the bloody city of Lichfield should only have put them on again to walk away from it.

The grey road was by now beginning to climb the foothills of the Cotswolds; a yellow-hammer, keeping always a few paces ahead, twittered from quickset boughs nine encouraging notes that drowned the echoes of ancient controversies. In such a countryside no claims papal or episcopal possessed the least importance; and Mark dismissed the subject from his mind, abandoning himself to the pleasure of the slow ascent. Looking back after a while he could see the town of Wield riding like a ship in a sea of verdure, and when he surveyed thus England asleep in the sunlight, the old ambition to become a preaching friar was kindled again in his heart. He would re-establish the extinct and absolutely English Order of St. Gilbert so that there should be no question of Roman pretensions. Doubtless, St. Francis himself would understand a revival of his Order without reference to existing Franciscans; but nobody else would understand, and it would be foolish to insist upon being a Franciscan if the rest of the Order disowned him and his followers. If anybody had asked Mark at that moment why he wanted to restore the preaching friars, he might have found it difficult to answer. He was by no means imbued with the missionary spirit just then; his experience at Chatsea had made him pessimistic about missionary effort in the Church of England. If a man like Father Rowley had failed to win the support of his ecclesiastical superiors, Mark, who possessed more humility than is usual at twenty-one, did not fancy that he should be successful. The ambition to become a friar was revived by an incomprehensible, or if not incomprehensible, certainly by an inexplicable impulse to put himself in tune with the landscape, to proclaim as it were on behalf of that dumb heart of England beating down there in the flowery Vale of Wield: *God rest you merry gentlemen, let nothing you dismay!* There was revealed to him with the assurance of absolute faith that all the sorrows, all the ugliness, all the soullessness (no other word could be found) of England in the first year of the twentieth century was due to the Reformation; the desire to become a preaching friar was the dramatic expression of this inspired conviction. Before his journey through the Vale of Wield Mark in any discussion would have been ready to argue the mistake of the Reformation: but now there was no longer room for argument. What formerly he thought now he knew. The song of the yellow-hammer was louder in the quickset hedge; the trees burned with a sharper green; the road urged his feet.

"If only everybody in England could move as I am moving now," he thought. "If only I could be granted the power to show a few people, so that they could show others, and those others show all the world. How confidently that yellow-hammer repeats his song! How well he knows that his song is right! How little he envies the linnet and how little the linnet envies him! The fools that talk of nature's cruelty, the blind fatuous sentimental coxcombs!"

Thus apostrophizing, Mark came to a wayside inn; discovering that he was hungry, he took his seat at a rustic table outside and called for bread and cheese and beer. While he was eating, a vehicle approached from the direction in which he would soon be travelling. He took it at first for a caravan of gipsies, but when it grew near he saw that it was painted over with minatory texts and was evidently the vehicle of itinerant gospellers. Two young men alighted from the caravan when it pulled up before the door of the inn. They were long-nosed sallow creatures with that expression of complacency which organized morality too often produces, and in this quiet countryside they gave an effect of being overgrown Sunday-school scholars upon their annual outing. Having cast a censorious glance in the direction of Mark's jug of ale, they sat down at the farther end of the bench and ordered food.

"The preaching friars of today," Mark thought gloomily.

"Excuse me," said one of the gospellers. "I notice you've been looking very hard at our van. Excuse me, but are you saved?"

"No, are you?" Mark countered with an angry blush.

"We are," the gospeller proclaimed. "Or I and Mr. Smillie here," he indicated his companion, "wouldn't be travelling round trying to save others. Here, read this tract, my friend. Don't hurry over it. We can wait all day and all night to bring one wandering soul to Jesus."

Mark looked at the young men curiously; perceiving that they were sincere, he accepted the tract and out of courtesy perused it. The tale therein enfolded reminded him of a narrative testifying to the efficacy of a patent medicine. The process of conversation followed a stereotyped formula.

For three and a half years I was unable to keep down any sins for more than five minutes after I had committed the last one. I had a dizzy feeling in the heart and a sharp pain in the small of the soul. A friend of mine recommended me to try the good minister in the slum . . . After the first text I was able to keep down my sins for six minutes . . . after twenty-two bottles I am as good as I ever was . . . I ascribe my salvation entirely to . . . Mark handed back the tract with a smile.

"Do you convert many people with this literature?" he asked.

"We don't often convert a soul right off," said Mr. Smillie. "But we sow the good seed, if you follow my meaning; and we leave the rest to Jesus. Mr. Bullock and I have handed over seven hundred tracts in three weeks, and we know that they won't all fall on stony ground or be choked by tares and thistles."

"Do you mind my asking you a question?" Mark said.

The gospel bearers craned their necks like hungry fowls in their eagerness to peck at any problems Mark felt inclined to scatter before them. A ludicrous fancy passed through his mind that much of the good seed was pecked up by the scatterers.

"What are you trying to convert people to?" Mark solemnly inquired.

"What are we trying to convert people to?" echoed Mr. Bullock and Mr. Smillie in unison. Then the former became eloquent. "We're trying to wash ignorant people in the blood of the Lamb. We're converting them from the outer darkness, where there is weeping and wailing and gnashing of teeth, to be rocked safe for ever in the arms of Jesus. If you'd have read that tract I handed you a bit more slowly and a bit more carefully, you wouldn't have had any call to ask a question like that."

"Perhaps I framed my question rather badly," Mark admitted. "I understand that you want to bring people to believe in Our Lord; but when by a tract or by a personal exhortation or by an emotional appeal you've induced them to suppose that they are converted, or as you put it saved, what more do you give them?"

"What more do we give them?" Mr. Smillie shrilled. "What more can we give them after we've given them Christ Jesus? We're sitting here offering you Christ Jesus at this moment. You're sitting there mocking at us. But Mr. Bullock and me don't mind how much you mock. We're ready to stay here for hours if we can bring you safe to the bosom of Emmanuel."

"Yes, but suppose I told you that I believe in Our Lord Jesus Christ without any persuasion from you?" Mark inquired.

239

"Well, then you're saved," said Mr. Bullock decidedly. "And you can ask the landlord for our bill, Mr. Smillie."

"But is nothing more necessary?" Mark persisted.

"*By faith are ye justified*," Mr. Bullock and Mr. Smillie shouted simultaneously.

Mark paused for a moment to consider whether argument was worth while, and then he returned to the attack.

"I'm afraid I think that people like you do a great deal of damage to Christianity. You only flatter human conceit. You get hold of some emotional creature and work upon his feelings until in an access of self-absorption he feels that the universe is standing still while the necessary measures are taken to secure his personal salvation. You flatter this poor soul, and then you go away and leave him to work out his own salvation."

"If you're dwelling in Christ Jesus and Christ Jesus is dwelling in you, you haven't got to work out your own salvation. He worked out your salvation on the Cross," said Mr. Bullock contemptuously.

"And you think that nothing more is necessary from a man? It seems to me that the religion you preach is fatal to human character. I'm not trying to be offensive when I tell you that it's the religion of a tapeworm. It's a religion for parasites. It's a religion which ignores the Holy Ghost."

"Perhaps you'll explain your assertion a little more fully?" Mr. Bullock invited with a scowl.

"What I mean is that, if Our Lord's Atonement removed all responsibility from human nature, there doesn't seem much for the Holy Ghost to do, does there?"

"Well, as it happens," said Mr. Bullock sarcastically, "Mr. Smillie and I here do most of our work with the help of the Holy Ghost, so you've hit on a bad example to work off your sneers on."

"I'm not trying to sneer," Mark protested. "But strangely enough just before you came along I was thinking to myself how much I should like to travel over England preaching about Our Lord, because I think that England has need of Him. But I also think, now you've answered my question, that *you* are doing more harm than good by your interpretation of the Holy Ghost."

"Mr. Smillie," interrupted Mr. Bullock in an elaborately offhand voice, "if you've counted the change and it's all correct, we'd better get a move on. Let's gird up our loins, Mr. Smillie, and not sit wrestling here with infidels."

"No, really, you must allow me," Mark persisted. "You've had it so much your own way with your tracts and your talks this last few weeks that by now you must be in need of a sermon yourselves. The gospel you preach is only going to add to the complacency of England, and England is too complacent already. All Northern nations are, which is why they are Protestant. They demand a religion which will truckle to them, a religion which will allow them to devote six days of the week to what is called business and on the seventh day to rest and praise God that they are not as other men."

"*Render unto Cæsar the things that are Cæsar's and unto God the things that are God's*," said Mr. Smillie, putting the change in his pocket and untying the nosebag from the horse.

"*Ye cannot serve God and mammon*," Mark retorted. "And I wish you'd let me finish my argument."

"Mr. Smillie and I aren't touring the Midlands trying to find grapes on thorns and figs on thistles," said Mr. Bullock scathingly. "We'd have given you a chance, if you'd have shown any fruits of the Spirit."

"You've just said you weren't looking for grapes or figs," Mark laughed. "I'm sorry I've made you so cross. But you began the argument by asking me if I was saved. Think how annoyed you would have been if I had begun a conversation by asking you if you were washed."

"My last words to you is," said Mr. Bullock solemnly, looking out of the caravan window, "my last words to you are," he corrected himself, "is to avoid beer. You can touch up the horse, Mr. Smillie."

"I'll come and touch you up, you big-mouthed Bible thumpers," a rich voice shouted from the inn door. "Yes, you sit outside my public-house and swill minerals when you're so full of gas already you could light a corporation gasworks. Avoid beer, you walking bellows? Step down out of that travelling menagerie, and I'll give you 'avoid beer.' You'll avoid more than beer before I've finished with you."

But the gospel bearers without paying any attention to the tirade went on their way; and Mark who did not wait to listen to the innkeeper's abuse of all religion and all religious people went on his way in the opposite direction.

Swinging homeward over the Cotswolds Mark flattered himself on a victory over heretics, and he imagined his adversaries entering Wield that afternoon, the prey of doubt and mortification. At the highest point of the road he even ventured to suppose that they might find themselves at Evensong outside St. Andrew's Church and led within by the grace of the Holy Spirit that they might renounce their errors before the altar. Indeed, it was not until he was back in the Rectory that the futility of his own bearing overwhelmed him with shame. Anxious to atone for his self-conceit, Mark gave the Rector an account of the incident.

"It seems to me that I behaved very feebly, don't you think?"

"That kind of fellow is a hard nut to crack," the Rector said consolingly. "And you can't expect just by quoting text against text to effect an instant conversion. Don't forget that your friends are in their way as great enthusiasts probably as yourself."

"Yes, but it's humiliating to be imagining oneself leading a revival of the preaching friars and then to behave like that. What strikes me now, when it's too late, is that I ought to have waited and taken the opportunity to tackle the innkeeper. He was just the ordinary man who supposes that religion is his natural enemy. You must admit that I missed a chance there."

"I don't want to check your missionary zeal," said the Rector. "But I really don't think you need worry yourself about an omission of that kind so long before you are ordained. If I didn't know you as well as I do, I might even be inclined to consider such a passion for souls at your age a little morbid. I wish with all my heart you'd gone to Oxford," he added with a sigh.

"Well, really, do you know," said Mark, "I don't regret that. Whatever may be the advantages of a public school and university, the education hampers one. One becomes identified with a class; and when one has finished with that education, the next two or three years have to be spent in discovering that public school and university men form a very small proportion of the world's population. Sometimes I almost regret that my mother did not let me acquire that Cockney accent. You can say a lot of things in a Cockney accent which said without any accent sound priggish. You must admit, Rector, that your inner comment on my tale of the gospellers and the innkeeper is 'Dear me! I am afraid Mark's turning into a prig.'"

"No, no. I laid particular stress on the point that if I didn't know you as well as I do I might perhaps have thought that," the Rector protested.

"I don't think I am a prig," Mark went on slowly. "I don't think I have enough confidence in myself to be a prig. I think the way I argued with Mr. Bullock and Mr. Smillie was a bit priggish, because at the back of my head all the time I was talking I felt in addition to the arrogance of faith a kind of confounded snobbishness; and this sense of superiority came not from my being a member of the Church, but from feeling myself more civilized than they were. Looking back now at the conversation, I can remember that actually at the very moment I was talking of the Holy Ghost I was noticing how Mr. Bullock's dicky would keep escaping from his waistcoat. I wonder if the great missionary saints of the middle ages had to contend with this accumulation of social conventions with which we are faced nowadays. It seems to me that in everything—in art, in religion, in mere ordinary everyday life and living—man is adding daily to the wall that separates him from God."

"H'm, yes," said the Rector, "all this only means that you are growing up. The child is nearer to God than the man. Wordsworth said it better than I can say it. Similarly, the human race must grow away from God as it takes upon itself the burden of knowledge. That surely is inherent in the fall of man. No philosopher has yet improved upon the first chapter of Genesis as a symbolical explanation of humanity's plight. When man was created—or if you like to put it evolved—there must have been an exact moment at which he had the chance of remaining where he was—in other words, in the Garden of Eden—or of developing further along his own lines with free will. Satan fell from pride. It is natural to assume that man, being tempted by Satan, would fall from the same sin, though the occasion, of his fall might be the less heroic sin of curiosity. Yes, I think that first chapter of Genesis, as an attempt to sum up the history of millions of years, is astoundingly complete. Have you ever thought how far by now the world would have grown away from God without the Incarnation?"

"Yes," said Mark, "and after nineteen hundred years how little nearer it has grown."

"My dear boy," said the Rector, "if man has not even yet got rid of rudimentary gills or useless paps he is not going to grow very visibly nearer to God in nineteen hundred years after growing away from God for ninety million. Yet such is the mercy of our Father in Heaven that, infinitely remote as we have grown from Him, we are still made in His image, and in childhood we are allowed a few years of blessed innocency. To some children—and you were one of them—God reveals Himself more directly. But don't, my dear fellow, grow up imagining that these visions you were accorded as a boy will be accorded to you all through your life. You may succeed in remaining pure in act, but you will find it hard to remain pure in heart. To me the most frightening beatitude is *Blessed are the pure in heart, for they shall see God*. What your present state of mind really amounts to is lack of hope, for as soon as you find yourself unable to be as miraculously eloquent as St. Anthony of Padua you become the prey of despair."

"I am not so foolish as that," Mark replied. "But surely, Rector, it behoves me during these years before my ordination to criticize myself severely."

"As severely as you like," the Rector agreed, "provided that you only criticize yourself, and don't criticize Almighty God."

"But surely," Mark went on, "I ought to be asking myself now that I am twenty-one how I shall best occupy the next three years?"

"Certainly," the Rector assented. "Think it over, and be sure that, when you have thought it over and have made your decision with the help of prayer, I shall be the first to support that decision in every way possible. Even if you decide to be a preaching friar," he added with a smile. "And now I have some news for you. Esther arrives here tomorrow to stay with us for a fortnight before she is professed."

CHAPTER XXII

SISTER ESTHER MAGDALENE

Esther's novitiate in the community of St. Mary Magdalene, Shoreditch, had lasted six months longer than was usual, because the Mother Superior while never doubting her vocation for the religious life had feared for her ability to stand the strain of that work among penitents to which the community was dedicated. In the end, her perseverance had been rewarded, and the day of her profession was at hand.

During the whole of her nearly four years' novitiate Esther had not been home once; although Mark and she had corresponded at long intervals, their letters had been nothing more than formal records of minor events, and on St. John's eve he drove with the dogcart to meet her, wondering all the way how much she would have changed. The first thing that struck him when he saw her alight from the train on Shipcot platform was her neatness. In old days with windblown hair and clothes flung on anyhow she had belonged so unmistakably to the open air. Now in her grey habit and white veil of the novice she was as tranquil as Miriam, and for the first time Mark perceived a resemblance between the sisters. Her complexion, which formerly was flushed and much freckled by the open air, was now like alabaster; and although her auburn hair was hidden beneath the veil Mark was aware of it like a hidden fire. He had in the very moment of welcoming her a swift vision of that auburn hair lying on the steps of the altar a fortnight hence, and he was filled with a wild desire to be present at her profession and gathering up the shorn locks to let them run through his fingers like flames. He had no time to be astonished at himself before they were shaking hands.

"Why, Esther," he laughed, "you're carrying an umbrella."

"It was raining in London," she said gravely.

He was on the point of exclaiming at such prudence in Esther when he blushed in the remembrance that she was a nun. During the drive back they talked shyly about the characters of the village and the Rectory animals.

"I feel as if you'd just come back from school for the holidays," he said.

"Yes, I feel as if I'd been at school," she agreed. "How sweet the country smells."

"Don't you miss the country sometimes in Shoreditch?" he asked.

She shook her head and looked at him with puzzled eyes.

"Why should I miss anything in Shoreditch?"

Mark was abashed and silent for the rest of the drive, because he fancied that Esther might have supposed that he was referring to the past, rather than give which impression he would have cut out his tongue. When they reached the Rectory, Mark was moved almost to tears by the greetings.

"Dear little sister," Miriam murmured. "How happy we are to have you with us again."

"Dear child," said Mrs. Ogilvie. "And really she does look like a nun."

"My dearest girl, we have missed you every moment of these four years," said the Rector, bending to kiss her. "How cold your cheek is."

"It was quite chilly driving," said Mark quickly, for there had come upon him a sudden dismay lest they should think she was a ghost. He was relieved when Miriam announced tea half an hour earlier than usual in honour of Esther's arrival; it seemed to prove that to her family she was still alive.

"After tea I'm going to Wych Maries to pick St. John's wort for the church. Would you like to walk as far?" Mark suggested, and then stood speechless, horrified at his want of tact. He had the presence of mind not to excuse himself, and he was grateful to Esther when she replied in a calm voice that she should like a walk after tea.

When the opportunity presented itself, Mark apologized for his suggestion.

"By why apologize?" she asked. "I assure you I'm not at all tired and I really should like to walk to Wych Maries."

He was amazed at her self-possession, and they walked along with unhastening conventual steps to where the St. John's wort grew amid a tangle of ground ivy in the open spaces of a cypress grove, appearing most vividly and richly golden like sunlight breaking from black clouds in the western sky.

"Gather some sprays quickly, Sister Esther Magdalene," Mark advised. "And you will be safe against the demons of this night when evil has such power."

"Are we ever safe against the demons of the night?" she asked solemnly. "And has not evil great power always?"

"Always," he assented in a voice that trembled to a sigh, like the uncertain wind that comes hesitating at dusk in the woods. "Always," he repeated.

As he spoke Mark fell upon his knees among the holy flowers, for there had come upon him temptation; and the sombre trees standing round watched him like fiends with folded wings.

"Go to the chapel," he cried in an agony.

"Mark, what is the matter?"

"Go to the chapel. For God's sake, Esther, don't wait."

In another moment he felt that he should tear the white veil from her forehead and set loose her auburn hair.

"Mark, are you ill?"

"Oh, do what I ask," he begged. "Once I prayed for you here. Pray for me now."

At that moment she understood, and putting her hands to her eyes she stumbled blindly toward the ruined church of the two Maries, heavily too, because she was encumbered by her holy garb. When she was gone and the last rustle of her footsteps had died away upon the mid-summer silence, Mark buried his body in the golden flowers.

"How can I ever look any of them in the face again?" he cried aloud. "Small wonder that yesterday I was so futile. Small wonder indeed! And of all women, to think that I should fall in love with Esther. If I had fallen in love with her four years ago . . . but now when she is going to be professed . . . suddenly without any warning . . . without any warning . . . yet perhaps I did love her in those days . . . and was jealous . . ."

247

And even while Mark poured forth his horror of himself he held her image to his heart.

"I thought she was a ghost because she was dead to me, not because she was dead to them. She is not a ghost to them. And is she to me?"

He leapt to his feet, listening.

"Should she come back," he thought with beating heart. "Should she come back . . . I love her . . . she hasn't taken her final vows . . . might she not love me? No," he shouted at the top of his voice. "I will not do as my father did . . . I will not . . . I will not . . ."

Mark felt sure of himself again: he felt as he used to feel as a little boy when his mother entered on a shaft of light to console his childish terrors. When he came to the ruined chapel and saw Esther standing with uplifted palms before the image of St. Mary Magdalene long since put back upon the pedestal from which it had been flung by the squire of Rushbrooke Grange, Mark was himself again.

"My dear," Esther cried, impulsively taking his hand. "You frightened me. What was the matter?"

He did not answer for a moment or two, because he wanted her to hold his hand a little while longer, so much time was to come when she would never hold it.

"Whenever I dip my hand in cold water," he said at last, "I shall think of you. Why did you say that about the demons of the night?"

She dropped his hand in comprehension.

"You're disgusted with me," he murmured. "I'm not surprised."

"No, no, you mustn't think of me like that. I'm still a very human Esther, so human that the Reverend Mother has made me wait an extra year to be professed. But, Mark dear, can't you understand, you who know what I endured in this place, that I am sometimes tempted by memories of him, that I sometimes sin by regrets for giving him up, my dead lover so near to me in this place. My dead love," she sighed to herself, "to whose memory in my pride of piety I thought I should be utterly indifferent."

A spasm of jealousy had shaken Mark while Esther was speaking, but by the time she had finished he had fought it down.

"I think I must have loved you all this time," he told her.

"Mark dear, I'm ten years older than you. I'm going to be a nun for what of my life remains. And I can never love anybody else. Don't make this visit of mine a misery to me. I've had to conquer so much and I need your prayers."

"I wish you needed my kisses."

"Mark!"

"What did I say? Oh, Esther, I'm a brute. Tell me one thing."

"I've already told you more than I've told anyone except my confessor."

"Have you found happiness in the religious life?"

"I have found myself. The Reverend Mother wanted me to leave the community and enter a contemplative order. She did not think I should be able to help poor girls."

"Esther, what a stupid woman! Why surely you would be wonderful with them?"

"I think she is a wise woman," said Esther. "I think since we came picking St. John's wort I understand how wise she is."

"Esther, dear dear Esther, you make me feel more than ever ashamed of myself. I entreat you not to believe what the Reverend Mother says."

"You have only a fortnight to convince me," said Esther.

"And I will convince you."

"Mark, do you remember when you made me pray for his soul telling me that in that brief second he had time to repent?"

Mark nodded grimly.

"You still do think that, don't you?"

"Of course I do. He must have repented."

She thanked him with her eyes; and Mark looking into their depths of hope unfathomable put away from him the thought that the damned soul of Will Starling was abroad tonight with power of evil. Yes, he put this thought behind him; but carrying an armful of St. John's wort to hang in sprays above the doors of the church he could not rid himself of the fancy that his arms were filled with Esther's auburn hair.

CHAPTER XXIII

MALFORD ABBEY

Mark left Wych-on-the-Wold next day; although he did not announce that he should be absent from home so long, he intended not to return until Esther had gone back to Shoreditch. He hoped that he was not being cowardly in thus running away; but after having assured Esther that she could count on his behaving normally for the rest of her visit, he found his sleep that night so profoundly disturbed by feverish visions that when morning came he dreaded his inability to behave as both he would wish himself and she would wish him to behave. Flight seemed the only way to find peace. He was shocked not so much by being in love with Esther, but by the suddenness with which his desires had overwhelmed him, desires which had never been roused since he was born. If in an instant he could be turned upside down like that, could he be sure that upon the next occasion, supposing that he fell in love with somebody more suitable, he should be able to escape so easily? His father must have married his mother out of some such violent impulse as had seized himself yesterday afternoon, and resentment about his weakness had spoilt his whole life. And those dreams! How significant now were the words of the Compline hymn, and how much it behoved a Christian soul to vanquish these ill dreams against beholding which the defence of the Creator was invoked. He had vowed celibacy; yet already, three months after his twenty-first birthday, after never once being troubled with the slightest hint that the vow he had taken might be hard to keep, his security had been threatened. How right the Rector had been about that frightening beatitude.

Mark had taken the direction of Wychford, and when he reached the bridge at the bottom of the road from Wych-on-the-Wold he thought he would turn aside and visit the Greys whom he had not seen for a long time. He was conscious of a curiosity to know if the feelings aroused by Esther could be aroused by Monica or Margaret or Pauline. He found the dear family unchanged and himself, so far as they were concerned, equally unchanged and as much at his ease as he had ever been.

"And what are you going to do now?" one of them asked.

"You mean immediately?"

Mark could not bring himself to say that he did not know, because such a reply would have seemed to link him with the state of mind in which he had been thrown yesterday afternoon.

"Well, really, I was thinking of going into a monastery," he announced.

Pauline clapped her hands.

"Now I think that is just what you ought to do," she said.

Then followed questions about which Order he proposed to join; and Mark ashamed to go back on what he had said lest they should think him flippant answered that he thought of joining the Order of St. George.

"You know—Father Burrowes, who works among soldiers."

When Mark was standing by the cross-roads above Wychford and was wondering which to take, he decided that really the best thing he could do at this moment was to try to enter the Order of St. George. He might succeed in being ordained without going to a theological college, or if the Bishop insisted upon a theological course and he found that he had a vocation for the religious life, he could go to Glastonbury and rejoin the Order when he was a priest. It was true that Father Rowley disapproved of Father Burrowes; but he had never expressed more than a general disapproval, and Mark was inclined to attribute his attitude to the prejudice of a man of strong personality and definite methods against another man of strong personality and definite methods working on similar lines among similar people. Mark remembered now that there had been a question at one time of Father Burrowes' opening a priory in the next parish to St. Agnes'. Probably that was the reason why Father Rowley disapproved of him. Mark had heard the monk preach on one occasion and had liked him. Outside the pulpit, however, he

251

knew nothing more of him than what he had heard from soldiers staying in the Keppel Street Mission House, who from Aldershot had visited Malford Abbey, the mother house of the Order. The alternative to Malford was Clere Abbey on the Berkshire downs where Dom Cuthbert Manners ruled over a small community of strict Benedictines. Had Mark really been convinced that he was likely to remain a monk for the rest of his life, he would have chosen the Benedictines; but he did not feel justified in presenting himself for admission to Clere on what would seem impulse. He hoped that if he was accepted by the Order of St. George he should be given an opportunity to work at one of the priories in Aldershot or Sandgate, and that the experience he might expect to gain would help him later as a parish priest. He could not confide in the Rector his reason for wanting to subject himself to monastic discipline, and he expected a good deal of opposition. It might be better to write from whatever village he stayed in tonight and make the announcement without going back at all. And this is what in the end he decided to do.

> The Sun Inn,
> Ladingford.
> June 24.
>
> My dear Rector,
>
> I expect you gathered from our talk the day before yesterday that I was feeling dissatisfied with myself, and you must know that the problem of occupying my time wisely before I am ordained has lately been on my mind. I don't feel that I could honestly take up a profession to which I had no intention of sticking, and though Father Rowley recommended me to stay at home and work with the village people I don't feel capable of doing that yet. If it was a question of helping you by taking off your shoulders work that I could do it would be another matter. But you've often said to me that you had more time on your hands than you cared for since you gave up coaching me for an Oxford scholarship, and so I don't think I'm wrong in supposing that you would find it hard to discover for me any parochial

routine work. I'm not old enough yet to fish for souls, and I have no confidence in my ability to hook them. Besides, I think it would bore you if I started "missionizing" in Wych-on-the-Wold.

I've settled therefore to try to get into the Order of St. George. I don't think you know Father Burrowes personally, but I've always heard that he does a splendid work among soldiers, and I'm hoping that he will accept me as a novice.

Latterly, in fact since I left Chatsea, I've been feeling the need of a regular existence, and, though I cannot pretend that I have a vocation for the monastic life in the highest sense, I do feel that I have a vocation for the Order of St. George. You will wonder why I have not mentioned this to you, but the fact is—and I hope you'll appreciate my frankness—I did not think of the O.S.G. till this morning. Of course they may refuse to have me. But I shall present myself without a preliminary letter, and I hope to persuade Father Burrowes to have me on probation. If he once does that, I'm sure that I shall satisfy him. This sounds like the letter of a conceited clerk. It must be the fault of this horrible inn pen, which is like writing with a tooth-pick dipped in a puddle! I thought it was best not to stay at the Rectory, with Esther on the verge of her profession. It wouldn't be fair to her at a time like this to make my immediate future a matter of prime importance. So do forgive my going off in this fashion. I suppose it's just possible that some bishop will accept me for ordination from Malford, though no doubt it's improbable. This will be a matter to discuss with Father Burrowes later.

Do forgive what looks like a most erratic course of procedure. But I really should hate a long discussion, and if I make a mistake I shall have had a lesson. It really is essential for me to be tremendously occupied. I cannot say more than this, but I do beg you to believe that I'm not taking this apparently unpremeditated step without a very strong reason. It's a kind of compromise with my ambition to re-establish in the English Church an order of preaching friars. I haven't yet given up that idea, but I'm sure that I ought not to think about it seriously until I'm a priest.

I'm staying here tonight after a glorious day's tramp, and tomorrow morning I shall take the train and go by Reading and Basingstoke to Malford. I'll write to you as soon as I know if I'm accepted. My best love to everybody, and please tell Esther that I shall think about her on St. Mary Magdalene's Day.

Yours always affectionately,

Mark.

To Esther he wrote by the same post:

My dear Sister Esther Magdalene,

Do not be angry with me for running away, and do not despise me for trying to enter a monastery in such a mood. I'm as much the prey of religion as you are. And I am really horrified by the revelation of what I am capable of. I saw in your eyes yesterday the passion of your soul for Divine things. The memory of them awes me. Pray for me, dear sister, that all my passion may be turned to the service of God. Defend me to your brother, who will not understand my behaviour.

Mark.

Three days later Mark wrote again to the Rector:

The Abbey,
Malford,
Surrey.
June 27th.

My dear Rector,

I do hope that you're not so much annoyed with me that you don't want to hear anything about my monastic adventures. However, if you are you can send back this long letter unopened. I believe that is the proper way to show one's disapproval by correspondence.

I reached Malford yesterday afternoon, and after a jolly walk between high hazel hedges for about two miles I reached the Abbey. It doesn't quite fulfil one's preconceived ideas of what an abbey should look like, but I suppose it is the most practicable building that could be erected with the amount of money that the Order had to spare for what in a way is a luxury for a working order like this. What it most resembles is three tin tabernacles put together to form three sides of a square, the fourth and empty side of which is by far the most beautiful, because it consists of a glorious view over a foreground of woods, a middle-distance of park land, and on the horizon the Hampshire downs.

I am an authority on this view, because I had to gaze at it for about a quarter of an hour while I was waiting for somebody to open the Abbey door. At last the porter, Brother Lawrence, after taking a good look at me through the grill, demanded what I wanted. When I said that I wanted to be a monk, he looked very alarmed and hurried away, leaving me to gaze at that view for another ten minutes. He came back at last and let me in, informing me in a somewhat adenoidish voice that the Reverend Brother was busy in the garden and asking me to wait until he came in. Brother Lawrence has a large, pock-marked face, and while he is talking to anybody he stands with his right hand in his left sleeve and his left hand in his right sleeve like a Chinese mandarin or an old washer-woman with her arms folded under her apron. You must make the most of my descriptions in this letter, because if I am accepted as a probationer I shan't be able to indulge in any more personalities about my brethren.

The guest-room like everything else in the monastery is match-boarded; and while I was waiting in it the noise was terrific, because some corrugated iron was being nailed on the roof of a building just outside. I began to regret that Brother Lawrence had opened the door at all and that he had not left me in the cloisters, as by the way I discovered that the space enclosed by the three tin tabernacles is called! There was nothing to read in the guest-room except one sheet of a six months' old newspaper which had been spread on the table presumably for a guest to mend something with glue. At last the Reverend Brother, looking most beautiful in a white habit with a zucchetto of mauve velvet, came in and welcomed me with much friendliness. I was surprised to find somebody so young as Brother Dunstan in charge of a monastery, especially as he said he was only a novice as yet. It appears that all the bigwigs—or should I say big-cowls?—are away at the moment on business of the Order and that various changes are in the offing, the most important being the giving up of their branch in Malta and the consequent arrival of Brother George, of whom Brother Dunstan spoke in a hushed voice. Father Burrowes, or the Reverend Father as he is called, is preaching in the north of England at the moment, and Brother Dunstan tells me it is quite impossible for him to say anything, still less to do anything, about my admission. However, he urged me to stay on for the present as a guest, an invitation which I accepted without hesitation. He had only just time to show me my cell and the card of rules for guests when a bell rang and, drawing his cowl over his head, he hurried off.

After perusing the rules, I discovered that this was the bell which rings a quarter of an hour before Vespers for solemn silence. I hadn't the slightest idea where the chapel was, and when I asked Brother Lawrence he glared at me and put his finger to his mouth. I was not to be discouraged, however, and in the end he showed me into the ante-chapel which is curtained off from the quire. There was only one other person in the ante-chapel, a florid, well-dressed man with a rather mincing and fussy way of worshipping. The monks led by Brother Lawrence (who is not even a novice yet, but a postulant and wears a black habit, without a hood, tied round the waist with a rope) passed from the refectory through the ante-chapel into the quire, and Vespers began. They used an arrangement called "The Day Hours of the English Church," but beyond a few extra antiphons there was very little difference from ordinary Evening Prayer. After Vespers I had a simple and solemn meal by myself, and I was wondering how I should get hold of a book to pass away the evening, when Brother Dunstan came in and asked me if I'd like to sit with the brethren in the library until the bell rang for simple silence a quarter of an hour before Compline at 9.15, after which everybody—guests and monks—are expected to go to bed in solemn silence. The difference between simple silence and solemn silence is that you may ask necessary questions and get necessary replies during simple silence; but as far as I can make out, during solemn silence you wouldn't be allowed to tell anybody that you were dying, or if you did tell anybody, he wouldn't be able to do anything about it until solemn silence was over.

The other monks are Brother Jerome, the senior novice after Brother Dunstan, a pious but rather dull young man with fair hair and a squashed face, and Brother Raymond, attractive and bird-like, and considered a great Romanizer by the others. There is also Brother Walter, who is only a probationer and is not even allowed wide sleeves and a habit like Brother Lawrence, but has to wear a very moth-eaten cassock with a black band tied round it. Brother Walter had been marketing in High Thorpe (I wonder what the Bishop of Silchester thought if he saw him in the neighbourhood of the episcopal castle!) and having lost himself on the way home he had arrived back late for Vespers and was tremendously teased by the others in consequence. Brother Walter is a tall excitable awkward creature with black hair that sticks up on end and wide-open frightened eyes. His cassock is much too short for him both in the arms and in the legs; and as he has very large hands and very large feet, his hands and feet look still larger in consequence. They didn't talk about much that was interesting during recreation. Brother Dunstan and Brother Raymond were full of monkish jokes, at all of which Brother Walter laughed in a very high voice—so loudly once that Brother Jerome asked him if he would mind making less noise, as he was reading Montalembert's Monks of the West, at which Brother Walter fell into an abashed gloom.

I asked who the visitor in the ante-chapel was and was told that he was a Sir Charles Horner who owns the whole of Malford and who has presented the Order with the thirty acres on which the Abbey is built. Sir Charles is evidently an ecclesiastically-minded person and, I should imagine, rather pleased to be able to be the patron of a monastic order.

I will write you again when I have seen Father Burrowes. For the moment I'm inclined to think that Malford is rather playing at being monks; but as I said, the bigwigs are all away. Brother Dunstan is a delightful fellow, yet I shouldn't imagine that he would make a successful abbot for long.

I enjoyed Compline most of all my experiences during the day, after which I retired to my cell and slept without turning till the bell rang for Lauds and Prime, both said as one office at six o'clock, after which I should have liked a conventual Mass. But alas, there is no priest here and I have been spending the time till breakfast by writing you this endless letter.

Yours ever affectionately,

Mark.

P.S. They don't say Mattins, which I'm inclined to think rather slack. But I suppose I oughtn't to criticize so soon.

To those two letters of Mark's, the Rector replied as follows:

The Rectory,
Wych-on-the-Wold,
Oxon.
June 29th.

My dear Mark,

I cannot say frankly that I approve of your monastic scheme. I should have liked an opportunity to talk it over with you first of all, and I cannot congratulate you on your good manners in going off like that without any word. Although you are technically independent now, I think it would be a great mistake to sink your small capital of £500 in the Order of St. George, and you can't very well make use of them to pass the next two or three years without contributing anything.

The other objection to your scheme is that you may not get taken at Glastonbury. In any case the Glastonbury people will give the preference to Varsity men, and I'm not sure that they would be very keen on having an ex-monk. However, as I said, you are independent now and can choose yourself what you do. Meanwhile, I suppose it is possible that Burrowes may decide you have no vocation, in which case I hope you'll give up your monastic ambitions and come back here.

Yours affectionately,

Stephen Ogilvie.

Mark who had been growing bored in the guest-room of Malford Abbey nearly said farewell to it for ever when he received the Rector's letter. His old friend and guardian was evidently wounded by his behaviour, and Mark considering what he owed him felt that he ought to abandon his monastic ambitions if by doing so he could repay the Rector some of his kindness. His hand was on the bell that should summon the guest-brother (when the bell was working and the guest-brother was not) in order to tell him that he had been called away urgently and to ask if he might have the Abbey cart to take him to the station; but at that moment Sir Charles Horner came in and began to chat affably to Mark.

"I've been intending to come up and see you for the last three days. But I've been so confoundedly busy. They wonder what we country gentlemen do with ourselves. By gad, they ought to try our life for a change."

Mark supposed that the third person plural referred to the whole body of Radical critics.

"You're the son of Lidderdale, I hear," Sir Charles went on without giving Mark time to comment on the hardship of his existence. "I visited Lima Street twenty-five years ago, before you were born that was. Your father was a great pioneer. We owe him a lot. And you've been with Rowley lately? That confounded bishop. He's our bishop, you know. But he finds it difficult to get at Burrowes except by starving him for priests. The fellow's a timeserver, a pusher . . ."

Mark began to like Sir Charles; he would have liked anybody who would abuse the Bishop of Silchester.

"So you're thinking of joining my Order," Sir Charles went on without giving Mark time to say a word. "I call it my Order because I set them up here with thirty acres of uncleared copse. It gives the Tommies something to do when they come over here on furlough from Aldershot. You've never met Burrowes, I hear."

Mark thought that Sir Charles for a busy man had managed to learn a great deal about an unimportant person like himself.

"Will Father Burrowes be here soon?" Mark inquired.

"'Pon my word, I don't know. Nobody knows when he'll be anywhere. He's preaching all over the place. He begs the deuce of a lot of money, you know. Aren't you a friend of Dorward's? You were asking Brother Dunstan about him. His parish isn't far from here. About fifteen miles, that's all. He's an amusing fellow, isn't he? Has tremendous rows with his squire, Philip Iredale. A pompous ass whose wife ran away from him a little time ago. Served him right, Dorward told me in confidence. You must come and have lunch with me. There's only Lady Landells. I can't afford to live in the big place. Huge affair with Doric portico and all that, don't you know. It's let to Lord Middlesborough, the shipping man. I live at Malford Lodge. Quite a jolly little place I've made of it. Suits me better than that great gaunt Georgian pile. You'd better walk down with me this morning and stop to lunch."

Mark, who was by now growing tired of his own company in the guest-room, accepted Sir Charles' invitation with alacrity; and they walked down from the Abbey to the village of Malford, which was situated at the confluence of the Mall and the Nodder, two diminutive tributaries of the Wey, which itself is not a mighty stream.

"A rather charming village, don't you think?" said Sir Charles, pointing with his tasselled cane to a particularly attractive rose-hung cottage. "It was lucky that the railway missed us by a couple of miles; we should have been festering with tin bungalows by now on any available land, which means on any land that doesn't belong to me. I don't offer to show you the church, because I never enter it."

Mark had paused as a matter of course by the lychgate, supposing that with a squire like Sir Charles the inside should be of unusual interest.

"My uncle most outrageously sold the advowson to the Simeon Trustees, it being the only part of my inheritance he could alienate from me, whom he loathed. He knew nothing would enrage me more than that, and the result is that I've got a fellow as vicar who preaches in a black gown and has evening communion twice a month. That is why I took such pleasure in planting a monastery in the parish; and if only that old time-server the Bishop of Silchester would licence a chaplain to the community, I should get my Sunday Mass in my own parish despite my uncle's simeony, as I call it. As it is with Burrowes away all the time raising funds, I don't get a Mass at the Abbey and I have to go to the next parish, which is four miles away and appears highly undignified for the squire."

"And you can't get him out?" said Mark.

"If I did get him out, I should be afflicted with another one just as bad. The Simeon Trustees only appoint people of the stamp of Mr. Choules, my present enemy. He's a horrid little man with a gaunt wife six feet high who beats her children and, if village gossip be true, her husband as well. Now you can see Malford Place, which is let to Middlesborough, as I told you."

Mark looked at the great Georgian house with its lawns and cedars and gateposts surmounted by stone wyverns. He had seen many of these great houses in the course of his tramping; but he had never thought of them before except as natural features in the landscape; the idea that people could consider a gigantic building like that as much a home as the small houses in which Mark had spent his life came over him now with a sense of novelty.

"Ghastly affair, isn't it?" said the owner contemptuously. "I'd let it stand empty rather than live in it myself. It reeks of my uncle's medicine and echoes with his gouty groans. Besides what is there in it that's really mine?"

Mark who had been thinking what an easy affair life must be for Sir Charles was struck by his tone of disillusionment. Perhaps all people who inherited old names and old estates were affected by their awareness of transitory possession. Sir Charles could not alienate even a piece of furniture. A middle-aged bachelor and a cosmopolitan, he would have moved about the corridors and halls of that huge house with less permanency than Lord Middlesborough who paid him so well to walk about in it in his stead, and who was no more restricted by the terms of his lease than was his landlord by the conditions of the entail. Mark began to feel sorry for him; but without cause, for when Sir Charles came in sight of Malford Lodge where he lived, he was full of enthusiasm. It was indeed a pretty little house of red brick, dating from the first quarter of the nineteenth century and like so many houses of that period built close to the road, surrounded too on three sides by a verandah of iron and copper in the pagoda style, thoroughly ugly, but by reason of the mellow peacock hues time had given its roof, full of personality and charm. They entered by a green door in the brick wall and crossed a lawn sloping down to the little river to reach the shade of a tulip tree in full bloom, where seated in one of those tall wicker garden chairs shaped like an alcove was an elderly lady as ugly as Priapus.

"There's Lady Landells, who's a poetess, you know," said Sir Charles gravely.

Mark accepted the information with equal gravity. He was still unsophisticated enough to be impressed at hearing a woman called a poetess.

"Mr. Lidderdale is going to have lunch with us, Lady Landells," Sir Charles announced.

"Oh, is he?" Lady Landells replied in a cracked murmur of complete indifference.

"He's a great admirer of your poems," added Sir Charles, hearing which Lady Landells looked at Mark with her cod's eyes and by way of greeting offered him two fingers of her left hand.

"I can't read him any of my poems today, Charles, so pray don't ask me to do so," the poetess groaned.

"I'm going to show Mr. Lidderdale some of our pictures before lunch," said Sir Charles.

Lady Landells paid no attention; Mark, supposing her to be on the verge of a poetic frenzy, was glad to leave her in that wicker alcove under the tulip tree and to follow Sir Charles into the house.

It was an astonishing house inside, with Gothic carving everywhere and with ancient leaded casements built inside the sashed windows of the exterior.

"I took an immense amount of trouble to get this place arranged to my taste," said Sir Charles; and Mark wondered why he had bothered to retain the outer shell, since that was all that was left of the original. In every room there were copies, excellently done of pictures by Botticelli and Mantegna and other pre-Raphaelite painters; the walls were rich with antique brocades and tapestries; the ceilings were gilded or elaborately moulded with fan traceries and groining; great candlesticks stood in every corner; the doors were all old with floriated hinges and huge locks—it was the sort of house in which Victor Hugo might have put on his slippers and said, "I am at home."

"I admit nothing after 1520," said Sir Charles proudly.

Mark wondered why so fastidious a medievalist allowed the Order of St. George to erect those three tin tabernacles and to matchboard the interior of the Abbey. But perhaps that was only another outer shell which would gradually be filled.

Lunch was a disappointment, because when Sir Charles began to talk about the monastery, which was what Mark had been wanting to talk about all the morning, Lady Landells broke in:

"I am sorry, Charles, but I'm afraid that I must beg for complete silence at lunch, as I'm in the middle of a sonnet."

The poetess sighed, took a large mouthful of food, and sighed again.

After lunch Sir Charles took Mark to see his library, which reminded him of a Rossetti interior and lacked only a beautiful long-necked creature, full-lipped and auburn-haired, to sit by the casement languishing over a cithern or gazing out through bottle-glass lights at a forlorn and foreshortened landscape of faerie land.

"Poor Lady Landells was a little tiresome at lunch," said Sir Charles half to himself. "She gets moods. Women seem never to grow out of getting moods. But she has always been most kind to me, and she insists on giving me anything I want for my house. Last year she was good enough to buy it from me as it stands, so it's really her house, although she has left it back to me in her will. She took rather a fancy to you by the way."

Mark, who had supposed that Lady Landells had regarded him with aversion and scorn, stared at this.

"Didn't she give you her hand when you said goodbye?" asked Sir Charles.

"Her left hand," said Mark.

"Oh, she never gives her right hand to anybody. She has some fad about spoiling the magnetic current of Apollo or something. Now, what about a walk?"

Mark said he should like to go for a walk very much, but wasn't Sir Charles too busy?

"Oh, no, I've nothing to do at all."

Yet only that morning he had held forth to Mark at great length on the amount of work demanded for the management of an estate.

"Now, why do you want to join Burrowes?" Sir Charles inquired presently.

"Well, I hope to be a priest, and I think I should like to spend the next two years out of the world."

"Yes, that is all very well," said Sir Charles, "but I don't know that I altogether recommend the O.S.G. I'm not satisfied with the way things are being run. However, they tell me that this fellow Brother George has a good deal of common-sense. He has been running their house in Malta, where he's done some good work. I gave them the land to build a mother house so that they could train people for active service, as it were; but Burrowes keeps chopping and changing and sending untrained novices to take charge of an important branch like Sandgate, and now since Rowley left he talks of opening a priory in Chatsea. That's all very well, and it's quite right of him to bear in mind that the main object of the Order is to work among soldiers; but at the same time he leaves this place to run itself, and whenever he does come down here he plans some hideous addition, to pay for which he has to go off preaching for another three months, so that the Abbey gets looked after by a young novice of twenty-five. It's ridiculous, you know. I was grumbling at the Bishop; but really I can understand his disinclination to countenance Burrowes. I have hopes of Brother George, and I shall take an early opportunity of talking to him."

Mark was discouraged by Sir Charles' criticism of the Order; and that it could be criticized like this through the conduct of its founder accentuated for him the gulf that lay between the English Church and the rest of Catholic Christendom.

It was not much solace to remember that every Benedictine community was an independent congregation. One could not imagine the most independent community's being placed in charge of a novice of twenty-five. It made Mark's proposed monastic life appear amateurish; and when he was back in the matchboarded guest-room the impulse to abandon his project was revised. Yet he felt it would be wrong to return to Wych-on-the-Wold. The impulse to come here, though sudden, had been very strong, and to give it up without trial might mean the loss of an experience that one day he should regret. The opinion of Sir Charles Horner might or might not be well founded; but it was bound to be a prejudiced opinion, because by constituting himself to the extent he had a patron of the Order he must involuntarily expect that it should be conducted according to his views. Sir Charles himself, seen in perspective, was a tolerably ridiculous figure, too much occupied with the paraphernalia of worship, too well pleased with himself, a man of rank and wealth who judged by severe standards was an old maid, and like all old maids critical, but not creative.

CHAPTER XXIV

THE ORDER OF ST. GEORGE

The Order of St. George was started by the Reverend Edward Burrowes six years before Sir Charles Horner's gift of land for a Mother House led him to suppose that he had made his foundation a permanent factor in the religious life of England.

Edward Burrowes was the only son of a band-master in the Royal Artillery who at an impressionable moment in the life of his son was stationed at Malta. The religious atmosphere of Malta combined with the romantic associations of chivalry and the influence of his mother determined the boy's future. The band-master was puzzled and irritated by his son's ecclesiastical bias. He thought that so much church-going argued an unhealthy preoccupation, and as for Edward's rhapsodies about the Auberge of Castile, which sheltered the Messes of the Royal Artillery and the Royal Engineers, they made him sick, to use his own expression.

"You make me sick, Ted," he used to declare. "The sooner I get quit of Malta and quartered at Woolwich again, the better I shall be pleased."

When at last the band-master was moved to Woolwich, he hoped that the effect of such prosaic surroundings would put an end to Ted's mooning, and that he would settle down to a career more likely to reward him in this world rather than in that ambiguous world beyond to which his dreams aspired. Edward, who was by this time seventeen and who had so far submitted to his father's wishes as to be working in a solicitor's office, found that the effect of being banished from Malta was to stimulate him into a practical attempt to express his dreams of religious devotion. He hired a small room over a stable in a back street and started a club for the sons of soldiers. The band-master would not have minded this so much, especially when he was congratulated on his son's enterprise by the wife of the Colonel. Unfortunately this was not enough for Edward, who having got the right side of an unscrupulously romantic curate persuaded him to receive his vows of a Benedictine oblate. The band-master, proud and fond though he might be of his own uniform, objected to his son's arriving home from business and walking about the house in a cassock. He objected equally to finding that his own musical gifts had with his son degenerated into a passion for playing Gregorian chants on a vile harmonium. It was only consideration for his delicate wife that kept the band-master from pitching both cassock and harmonium into the street. The amateur oblate regretted his father's hostility; but he persevered with the manner of life he had marked out for himself, finding much comfort and encouragement in reading the lives of the saintly founders of religious orders.

At last, after a long struggle against the difficulties that friends and father put in his way, Edward Burrowes managed at the age of twenty-seven to get ordained in Canada, whither, in despair of escaping otherwise from the solicitor's office, he had gone to seek his own fortune. He took with him the oblate's cassock; but he left behind the harmonium, which his father kicked to pieces in rage at not being able to kick his son. Burrowes worked as a curate in a dismal lakeside town in Ontario, consoling himself with dreams of monasticism and chivalry, and gaining a reputation as a preacher. His chief friend was a young farmer, called George Harvey, whom he succeeded in firing with his own enthusiasm and whom he managed to persuade—which shows that Burrowes must have had great powers of persuasion—to wear the habit of a Benedictine novice, when he came to spend Saturday night to Monday morning with his friend. By this time Burrowes had passed beyond the oblate stage, for having found a Canadian bishop willing to dispense him from that portion of the Benedictine rule which was incompatible with his work as a curate in Jonesville, Ontario, he got himself clothed as a novice. About this period a third man joined Burrowes and Harvey in their spare-time monasticism. This was John Holcombe, who had emigrated from Dorsetshire after an unfortunate love affair and who had been taken on by George Harvey as a carter. Holcombe was the son of a yeoman farmer that owned several hundred acres of land. He had been educated at Sherborne, and soon by his capacity and attractive personality he made himself so indispensable to his employer that George Harvey's farm was turned into a joint concern. No doubt Harvey's example was the immediate cause of Holcombe's associating himself with the little community: but it still says much for Burrowes' powers of persuasion that he should have been able to impress this young Dorset farmer with the serious possibility of leading the monastic life in Ontario.

When another year had passed, an opportunity arose of acquiring a better farm in Alberta. It was the Bishop of Alberta who had been so sympathetic with Burrowes' monastic aspirations; and, when Harvey and Holcombe decided to move to Moose Rib, Burrowes gave up his curacy to lead a regular monastic life, so far as one could lead a regular monastic life on a farm in the Northwest.

Two more years had gone by when a letter arrived from England to tell George Harvey that he was the heir to £12,000. Burrowes had kept all his influence over the young farmer, and he was actually able to persuade Harvey to devote this fortune to founding the Order of St. George for mission work among soldiers. There was some debate whether Father Burrowes, Brother George, and Brother Birinus should take their final vows immediately; but in the end Father Burrowes had his way, and they were all three professed by the sympathetic Bishop of Alberta, who granted them a constitution subject to the ratification of the Archbishop of Canterbury. Father Burrowes was elected Father Superior, Brother George was made Assistant Superior, and Brother Birinus had to concentrate in his person various monastic offices just as on the Moose Rib Farm he had combined in his person the duties of the various hands.

The immediate objective of the new community was Malta, where it was proposed to open their first house and where, in despite of the outraged dignity of innumerable real monks already there, they made a successful beginning. A second house was opened at Gibraltar and put in charge of Brother Birinus. Neither Malta nor Gibraltar provided much of a field for reinforcing the Order, which, if it was to endure, required additional members. Father Burrowes proposed that he should go to England and open a house at Aldershot, and that, if he could obtain a hearing as a preacher, he should try to raise enough funds for a house at Sandgate as well. Brother George and Brother Birinus in a solemn chapter of three accepted the proposal; the house at Gibraltar was given up; the Father Superior went to seek the fortunes of the Order in England, while the other two remained at their work in Malta. Father Burrowes was even more successful as a preacher than he hoped; ascribing the steady flow of offertories to Divine favour, he instituted during the next four years, priories at Aldershot and Sandgate. He began to feel the need of a Mother House, having now more than enough candidates for the Order of Saint George, where the novices could be suitably trained to meet the stress of active mission work. One of his moving appeals for this object was heard by Sir Charles Horner who, for reasons he had already explained to Mark and because underneath all his ecclesiasticism there did exist a genuine desire for the glory of God, had presented the land at Malford to the Order. Father Burrowes preached harder than ever, addressed drawing-room meetings, and started a monthly magazine called *The Dragon* to raise the necessary money to build a mighty abbey. Meanwhile, he had to be contented with those three tin tabernacles. Brother George, who had remained all these years in Malta, suggested that it was time for somebody else to take his place out there, and the Father Superior, although somewhat unwillingly, had agreed to his coming to Malford. Not having heard of anybody whom at the moment he considered suitable to take charge of what was now a distant outpost of the Order, he told Brother George to close the house. It was at this stage in the history of the Order that Mark presented himself as a candidate for admission.

Father Burrowes arrived unexpectedly two days after the lunch at Malford Lodge; and presently Brother Dunstan came to tell Mark that the Reverend Father would see him in the Abbott's Parlour immediately after Nones. Mark thought that Sir Charles might have given a mediæval lining to this room at least, which with its roll-top desk looked like the office of the clerk of the works.

"So you want to be a monk?" said Father Burrowes contemptuously. "Want to dress up in a beautiful white habit, eh?"

"I really don't mind what I wear," said Mark, trying not to appear ruffled by the imputation of wrong motives. "But I do want to be a monk, yes."

"You can't come here to play at it," said the Superior, looking keenly at Mark from his bright blue eyes and lighting up a large pipe.

"Curiously enough," said Mark, who had forgotten the Benedictine injunction to discourage newcomers that seek to enter a community, "I wrote to my guardian a few days ago that my impression of Malford Abbey was rather that it was playing at being monks."

The Superior flushed to a vivid red. He was a burly man of fair complexion, inclined to plumpness, and with a large mobile mouth eloquent and sensual. His hands were definitely fat, the backs of them covered with golden hairs and freckles.

"So you're a critical young gentleman, are you? I suppose we're not Catholic enough for you. Well," he snapped, "I'm afraid you won't suit us. We don't want you. Sorry."

"I'm sorry too," said Mark. "But I thought you would prefer frankness. If you will spare me a few minutes, I'll explain why I want to join the Order of St. George. If when you've heard what I have to say you still think that I'm not suitable, I shall recognize your right to be of that opinion from your experience of many young men like myself who have been tried and found wanting."

"Did you learn that speech by heart?" the Superior inquired, raising his eyebrows mockingly.

"I see you're determined to find fault," Mark laughed. "But, Reverend Father, surely you will listen to my reasons before deciding against them or me?"

"My instinct tells me you'll be no good to us. But if you insist on wasting my time, fire ahead. Only please remember that, though I may be a monk, I'm a very busy man."

Mark gave a full account of himself until the present and wound up by saying:

"I don't think I have any sentimental reasons for wanting to enter a monastery. I like working among soldiers and sailors. I am ready to put down £200 and I hope to be of use. I wish to be a priest, and if you find or I find that when the time comes for me to be ordained I shall make a better secular priest, at any rate, I shall have had the advantage of a life of discipline and you, I promise, will have had a novice who will have regarded himself as such, but yet will have learnt somehow to have justified your confidence."

The Superior looked down at his desk pondering. Presently he opened a letter and threw a quick suspicious glance at Mark.

"Why didn't you tell me that you had an introduction from Sir Charles Horner?"

"I didn't know that I had," Mark answered in some astonishment. "I only met him here a few days ago for the first time. He invited me to lunch, and he was very pleasant; but I never asked him to write to you, nor did he suggest doing so."

"Have you any vices?" Father Burrowes asked abruptly.

"I don't think—what do you mean exactly?" Mark inquired.

"Drink?"

"No, certainly not."

"Women?"

Mark flushed.

"No." He wondered if he should speak of the episode of St. John's eve such a short time ago; but he could not bring himself to do so, and he repeated the denial.

"You seem doubtful," the Superior insisted.

"As a matter of fact," said Mark, "since you press this point I ought to tell you that I took a vow of celibacy when I was sixteen."

Father Burrowes looked at him sharply.

"Did you indeed? That sounds very morbid. Don't you like women?"

"I don't think a priest ought to marry. I was told by Sir Charles that you vowed yourself to the monastic life when you were not much more than seventeen. Was that morbid?"

The Superior laughed boisterously, and Mark glad to have put him in a good humour laughed with him. It was only after the interview was over that the echo of that laugh sounded unpleasantly in the caves of memory, that it rang false somehow like a denial of himself.

"Well, I suppose we must try you as a probationer at any rate," said the Superior. And suddenly his whole manner changed. He became affectionate and sentimental as he put his hand on Mark's shoulder.

"I hope, dear lad, that you will find a vocation to serve our dear Lord in the religious life. God bless you and give you endurance in the path you have chosen."

Mark reproached himself for his inclination to dislike the Reverend Father to whom he now owed filial affection, piety, and respect, apart from what he owed him as a Christian of Christian charity. He should gain but small spiritual benefit from his self-chosen experiment if this was the mood in which he was beginning his monastic life; and when Brother Jerome, who was acting novice-master, began to instruct him in his monastic duty, he made up his mind to drive out that demon of criticism or rather to tame it to his own service by criticizing himself. He wrote on markers for his favourite devotional books:

Observe at every moment of the day the good in others, the evil in thyself; and when thou liest awake in the night remember only what good thou hast found in others, what evil in thyself.

This was Mark's addition to Thomas a Kempis, to Mother Juliana of Norwich, to Jeremy Taylor and William Law; this was Mark's sprout of holy wisdom among the Little Flowers of Saint Francis.

The Rule of Malford was not a very austere adaptation of the Rule of Saint Benedict; and, with the Reverend Father departing after Mark had been admitted as a probationer and leaving the administration of the Abbey to the priority of Brother Dunstan, a good deal of what austerity had been retained was now relaxed.

The Night Office was not said at Malford, where the liturgical worship of the day began with Lauds and Prime at six. On Mark devolved the duty of waking the brethren in the morning, which was done by striking the door of each cell with a hammer and saying: *The Lord be with you*, whereupon the sleeping brother must rise from his couch and open the door of his cell to make the customary response. After Lauds and Prime, which lasted about half an hour, the brethren retired to their cells to put them in order for the day and to meditate until seven o'clock, unless they had been given tasks out of doors. At seven o'clock, if there was a priest in the monastery, Mass was said; otherwise meditation and study was prolonged until eight o'clock, when breakfast was eaten. Those who had work in the fields or about the house departed after breakfast to their tasks. At nine Terce was said, which was not attended by the brethren working out of doors; at twelve Sext was said attended by all the brethren, and at twelve-fifteen dinner was eaten. After dinner, the brethren retired to their cells and meditated until one o'clock, when their various duties were resumed, interrupted only in the case of those working indoors by the office of None at three o'clock. At a quarter to five the bell rang for tea. Simple silence was relaxed, and the brethren enjoyed their recreation until six-fifteen when the bell rang for a quarter of an hour's solemn silence before Vespers. Supper was eaten after Vespers, and after supper, which was finished about eight o'clock, there was reading and recreation until the bell rang for Compline at nine-fifteen. This office said, solemn silence was not broken until the response to the *dominus vobiscum* in the morning. The rule of simple silence was not kept very strictly at this period. Two brethren working in the garden in these hot July days found that permitted conversation about the immediate matter in hand, say the whereabouts of a trowel or a hoe, was easily extended into observations about the whereabouts of Brother So-and-So during Terce or the way Brother Somebody-else was late with the antiphon. From the little incidents of the Abbey's daily round the conversation was easily extended into a discussion of the policy of the Order in general. Speculations where the Reverend Father was preaching that evening or that morning and whether his offertories would be as large during the summer as they had been during the spring were easily amplified from discussions about the general policy of the Order into discussions about the general policy of Christendom, the pros and cons of the Roman position, the disgraceful latitudinarianism of bishops and deans; and still more widely amplified from remarks upon the general policy of Christendom into arguments about the universe and the great philosophies of humanity. Thus Mark, who was an ardent Platonist, would find himself at odds with Brother Jerome who was an equally ardent Aristotelian, while the weeds, taking advantage of the philosophic contest, grew faster than ever.

Whatever may have been Brother Dunstan's faults of indulgence, they sprang from a debonair and kindly personality which shone like a sun upon the little family and made everybody good-humoured, even Brother Lawrence, who was apt to be cross because he had been kept a postulant longer than he expected. But perhaps the happiest of all was Brother Walter, who though still a probationer was now the senior probationer, a status which afforded him the most profound satisfaction and gave him a kindly feeling toward Mark who was the cause of promotion.

"And the Reverend Father has promised me that I shall be clothed as a postulant on August 10th when Brother Lawrence is to be clothed as a novice. The thought makes me so excited that I hardly know what to do sometimes, and I still don't know what saint's name I'm going to take. You see, there was some mystery about my birth, and I was called Walter because I was found by a policeman in Walter Street, and as ill-luck would have it there's no St. Walter. Of course, I know I have a very wide choice of names, but that is what makes it so difficult. I had rather a fancy to be Peter, but he's such a very conspicuous saint that it struck me as being a little presumptuous. Of course, I have no doubt whatever that St. Peter would take me under his protection, for if you remember he was a modest saint, a very modest saint indeed who asked to be crucified upside down, not liking to show the least sign of competition with our dear Lord. I should very much like to call myself Brother Paul, because at the school I was at we were taken twice a year to see St. Paul's Cathedral and had toffee when we came home. I look back to those days as some of the happiest of my life. There again it does seem to be putting yourself up rather to take the name of a great saint like St. Paul. Then I thought of taking William after the little St. William of Norwich who was murdered by the Jews. That seems going to the other extreme, doesn't it, for though I know that out of the mouths of babes and sucklings shall come forth praise, one would like to feel one had for a patron saint somebody a little more conspicuous than a baby. I wish you'd give me a word of advice. I think about this problem until sometimes my head's in a regular whirl, and I lose my place in the Office. Only yesterday at Sext, I found myself saying the antiphon proper to St. Peter a fortnight after St. Peter's day had passed and gone, which seems to show that my mind is really set upon being Brother Peter, doesn't it? And yet I don't know. He is so very conspicuous all through the Gospels, isn't he?"

"Then why don't you compromise," suggested Mark, "and call yourself Brother Simon?"

"Oh, what a splendid idea!" Brother Walter exclaimed, clapping his hands. "Oh, thank you, Brother Mark. That has solved all my difficulties. Oh, do let me pull up that thistle for you."

Brother Walter the probationer resumed his weeding with joyful ferocity of purpose, his mind at peace in the expectation of shortly becoming Brother Simon the postulant.

What Mark enjoyed most in his personal relations with the community were the walks on Sunday afternoons. Sir Charles Horner made a habit of joining these to obtain the Abbey gossip and also because he took pleasure in hearing himself hold forth on the management of his estate. Most of his property was woodland, and the walks round Malford possessed that rich intimacy of the English countryside at its best. Mark was not much interested in what Sir Charles had to ask or in what Sir Charles had to tell or in what Sir Charles had to show, but to find himself walking with his monastic brethren in their habits down glades of mighty oaks, or through sparse plantations of birches, beneath which grew brakes of wild raspberries that would redden with the yellowing corn, gave him as assurance of that old England before the Reformation to which he looked back as to a Golden Age. Years after, when much that was good and much that was bad in his monastic experience had been forgotten, he held in his memory one of these walks on a fine afternoon at July's end within the octave of St. Mary Magdalene. It happened that Sir Charles had not accompanied the monks that Sunday; but in his place was an old priest who had spent the week-end as a guest in the Abbey and who had said Mass for the brethren that morning. This had given Mark deep pleasure, because it was the Sunday after Esther's profession, and he had been able to make his intention her present joy and future happiness. He had been silent throughout the walk, seeming to listen in turn to Brother Dunstan's rhapsodies about the forthcoming arrival of Brother George and Brother Birinus with all that it meant to him of responsibility more than he could bear removed from his shoulders; or to Brother Raymond's doubts if it should not be made a rule that when no priest was in the Abbey the brethren ought to walk over to Wivelrod, the church Sir Charles attended four miles away, or to Brother Jerome's disclaimer of Roman sympathies in voicing his opinion that the Office should be said in Latin. Actually he paid little attention to any of them, his thoughts being far away with Esther. They had chosen Hollybush Down for their walk that Sunday, because they thought that the view over many miles of country would please the ancient priest. Seated on the short aromatic grass in the shade of a massive hawthorn full-berried with tawny fruit, the brethren looked down across a slope dotted with junipers to the view outspread before them. None spoke, for it had been warm work in their habits to climb the burnished grass. It would have been hard to explain the significance of that group, unless it were due to some haphazard achievement of perfect form; yet somehow for Mark that moment was taken from time and placed in eternity, so that whenever afterward in his life he read about the Middle Ages he was able to be what he read, merely by re-conjuring that monkish company in the shade of that hawthorn tree.

On their way back to the Abbey Mark found himself walking with Mr. Lamplugh, the ancient priest, who turned out to have known his father.

"Dear me, are you really the son of James Lidderdale? Why, I used to go and preach at Lima Street in old days long before your father married. And so you're Lidderdale's son. Now I wonder why you want to be a monk."

Mark gave an account of himself since he left school and tried to give some good reasons why he was at Malford.

"And so you were with Rowley? Well, really you ought to know something about missions by now. But perhaps you're tired of mission work already?" the old priest inquired with a quick glance at Mark as if he would see how much of the real stuff existed underneath that probationer's cassock.

"This is an active Order, isn't it?" Mark countered. "Of course, I'm not tired of mission work. But after being with Father Rowley and being kept busy all the time I found that being at home in the country made me idle. I told the Reverend Father that I hoped to be ordained as a secular priest and that I did not imagine I had any vocation for the contemplative life. I have as a matter of fact a great longing for it. But I don't think that twenty-one is a good age for being quite sure if that longing is not mere sentiment. I suppose you think I'm just indulging myself with the decorative side of religion, Father Lamplugh? I really am not. I can assure you that I'm far too much accustomed to the decorative side to be greatly influenced by it."

The old priest laid a thin hand on Mark's sleeve.

"To tell the truth, my dear boy, I was on the verge of violating the decencies of accepted hospitality by criticizing the Order of which you have become a probationer. I am just a little doubtful about the efficacy of its method of training young men. However, it really is not my business, and I hope that I am wrong. But I *am* a little doubtful if all these excellent young brethren are really desirous . . . no, I'll not say another word, I've already disgracefully exceeded the limitations to criticism that courtesy alone demands of me. I was carried away by my interest in you when I heard whose son you were. What a debt we owe to men like your father and Rowley! And here am I at seventy-six after a long and useless life presuming to criticize other people. God forgive me!" The old man crossed himself.

That afternoon and evening recreation was unusually noisy, and during Vespers one or two of the brethren were seized with an attack of giggles because Brother Lawrence, who was in a rapt condition of mind owing to the near approach of St. Lawrence's day when he was to be clothed as a novice, tripped while he was holding back the cope during the censing of the *Magnificat* and falling on his knees almost upset Father Lamplugh. There was no doubt that the way Brother Lawrence stuck out his lower jaw when he was self-conscious was very funny; but Mark wished that the giggling had not occurred in front of Father Lamplugh. He wished too that during recreation after supper Brother Raymond would be less skittish and Brother Dunstan less arch in the manner of reproving him.

"Holy simplicity is all very well," Mark thought. "But holy imbecility is a great bore, especially when there is a stranger present."

Luckily Father Burrowes came back the following week, and Mark's deepening impression of the monastery's futility was temporarily obliterated by the exciting news that the Bishop of Alberta whom the brethren were taught to reverence as a second founder would be the guest of the Order on St. Lawrence's day and attend the profession of Brother Anselm. Mark had not yet seen Brother Anselm, who was the brother in charge of the Aldershot priory, and he welcomed the opportunity of witnessing those solemn final vows. He felt that he should gain much from meeting Brother Anselm, whose work at Aldershot was considered after the Reverend Father's preaching to be the chief glory of the Order. Brother Lawrence was a little jealous that his name day, on which he was to be clothed in Chapter as a novice, should be chosen for the much more important ceremony, and he spoke sharply to poor Brother Walter when the latter rejoiced in the added lustre Brother Anselm's profession would shed upon his own promotion.

"You must remember, Brother," he said, "that you'll probably remain a postulant for a very long time."

"But not for ever," replied poor Brother Walter in a depressed tone of voice.

"There may not be time to attend to you," said Brother Lawrence spitefully. "You may have to wait until the Bishop has gone."

"Oh dear, oh dear," sighed Brother Walter looking woeful. "Brother Mark, do you hear what they say?"

"Never mind," said Mark, "we'll take our final vows together when Brother Lawrence is still a doddering old novice."

Brother Lawrence clicked his tongue and bit his under lip in disgust at such a flippant remark.

"What a thing to say," he muttered, and burying his hands in his sleeves he walked off disdainfully, his jaw thrust before him.

"Like a cow-catcher," Mark thought with a smile.

The Bishop of Alberta was a dear old gentleman with silvery hair and a complexion as fresh and pink as a boy's. With his laced rochet and purple biretta he lent the little matchboarded chapel an exotic splendour when he sat in a Glastonbury chair beside the altar during the Office. The more ritualistic of the brethren greatly enjoyed giving him reverent genuflexions and kissing his episcopal ring. Brother Raymond's behaviour towards him was like that of a child who has been presented with a large doll to play with, a large doll that can be dressed and undressed at the pleasure of its owner with nothing to deter him except a faint squeak of protest such as the Bishop himself occasionally emitted.

CHAPTER XXV

SUSCIPE ME, DOMINE

Brother Anselm was to arrive on the vigil of St. Lawrence. Normally Brother Walter would have been sent to meet him with the Abbey cart at the station three miles away. But Brother Walter was in a state of such excitement over his near promotion to postulant that it was not considered safe to entrust him with the pony. So Mark was sent in his place. It was a hot August evening with thunder clouds lying heavy on the Malford woods when Mark drove down the deep lanes to the junction, wondering what Brother Anselm would be like and awed by the imagination of Brother Anselm's thoughts in the train that was bringing him from Aldershot to this momentous date of his life's history. Almost before he knew what he was saying Mark was quoting from *Romeo and Juliet*:

> *My mind misgives*
> *Some consequence, yet hanging in the stars,*
> *Shall bitterly begin his fearful date*
> *With this night's revels.*

"Now why should I have thought that?" he asked himself, and he was just deciding that it was merely a verbal sequence of thought when the first far-off peal of thunder muttered a kind of menacing contradiction of so easy an explanation. It would be raining soon; Mark thumped the pony's angular haunches, and tried to feel cheerful in the oppressive air.

Brother Anselm did not appear as Mark had pictured him. Instead of the lithe enthusiast with flaming eyes he saw a heavily built man with blunted features, wearing powerful horn spectacles, his expression morose, his movements ungainly. He had, however, a mellow and strangely sympathetic voice, in which Mark fancied that he perceived the power he was reputed to wield over the soldiers for whose well-being he fought so hard. Mark would have liked to ask him about life in the Aldershot priory; perhaps if Brother Anselm had been less taciturn, he would have broken if not the letter at any rate the spirit of the Rule by begging the senior to ask for his services in the Priory. But no sooner were they jogging back to Malford than the rain came down in a deluge, and Brother Anselm, pulling the hood of his frock over his head, was more unapproachable than ever. Mark wished that he had a novice's frock and hood, for the rain was pouring down the back of his neck and the threadbare cassock he wore was already drenched.

"Thank you, Brother," said the new-comer when the Abbey was attained.

It was dark by now, and, with nothing visible of the speaker except his white habit in the gloom, the voice might have been the voice of a heavenly visitant, so rarely sweet, so gentle and harmonious were the tones. Mark was much moved by that brief recognition of himself.

The wind rose high during the night; listening to it roaring through the coppice in which the Abbey was built, Mark lay awake for a long time in mute prayer that Brother Anselm might find peace and felicity in his new state. And while he prayed for Brother Anselm he prayed for Esther in Shoreditch. In the morning when Mark went from cell to cell, rousing the brethren from sleep with his hammer and salutation, the sun was climbing a serene and windless sky. The familiar landscape was become a mountain top. Heaven was very near.

Mark was glad that the day was so fair for the profession of Brother Anselm, and at Lauds the antiphon, versicle, and response proper to St. Lawrence appealed to him by their fitness to the occasion,

Gold is tried in the fire: and acceptable men in the furnace of adversity.

V. The Righteous shall grow as a lily.
R. He shall flourish for ever before the Lord.

Mark concerned himself less with his own reception as a postulant. The distinction between a probationer and a postulant was very slight, really an arbitrary one made by Father Burrowes for his own convenience, and until he had to decide whether he should petition to be clothed as a novice Mark did not feel that he was called upon to take himself too seriously as a monk. For that reason he did not change his name, but preferred to stay Brother Mark. The little ceremony of reception was carried through in Chapter before the brethren went into the Oratory to say Terce, and Brother Walter was so much excited when he heard himself addressed as Brother Simon that for a moment it seemed doubtful if he would be sufficiently calm to attend the profession of Brother Anselm at the conventual Mass. However, during the clothing of Brother Lawrence as a novice Brother Simon quieted down, and even gave over counting the three knots in the rope with which he had been girdled. Ordinarily, Brother Lawrence would have been clothed after Mass, but this morning it was felt that such a ceremony coming after the profession of Brother Anselm would be an anti-climax, and it was carried through in Chapter. It took Brother Lawrence all he had ever heard and read about humility and obedience not to protest at the way his clothing on his own saint's day, for which he had been made to wait nearly a year, was being carried through in such a hole in the corner fashion. But he fixed his mind upon the torments of the blessed archdeacon on the gridiron and succeeded in keeping his temper.

Mark felt that the profession of Brother Anselm lost some of its dignity by the absence of Brother George and Brother Birinus, the only other professed members of the Order apart from Father Burrowes himself. It struck him as slightly ludicrous that a few young novices and postulants should represent the venerable choir-monks whom one pictured at such a ceremony from one's reading of the Rule of St. Benedict. Moreover, Father Burrowes never presented himself to Mark's imagination as an authentic abbot. Nor indeed was he such. Malford Abbey was a courtesy title, and such monastic euphemisms as the Abbot's Parlour and the Abbot's Lodgings to describe the matchboarded apartments sacred to the Father Superior, while they might please such ecclesiastical enthusiasts as Brother Raymond, appealed to Mark as pretentious and somewhat silly. In fact, if it had not been for the presence of the Bishop of Alberta in cope and mitre Mark would have found it hard, when after Terce the brethren assembled in the Chapter-room to hear Brother Anselm make his final petition, to believe in the reality of what was happening, to believe, when Brother Anselm in reply to the Father Superior's exhortation chose the white cowl and scapular (which in the Order of St. George differentiated the professed monk from the novice) and rejected the suit of dittos belonging to his worldly condition, that he was passing through moments of greater spiritual importance than any since he was baptized or than any he would pass through before he stood upon the threshold of eternity.

But this was a transient scepticism, a fleeting discontent, which vanished when the brethren formed into procession and returned to the oratory singing the psalm: *In Convertendo*.

> *When the Lord turned again the captivity of Sion: then were we like unto them, that dream.*
> *Then was our mouth filled with laughter: and our tongue with joy.*
> *Then said they among the heathen: The Lord hath done great things for them.*
> *Yea, the Lord hath done great things for us already: whereof we rejoice.*
> *Turn our captivity, O Lord: as the rivers in the south.*
> *They that sow in tears: shall reap in joy.*
> *He that now goeth on his way weeping, and beareth forth good seed: shall doubtless come again with joy, and bring his sheaves with him.*

The Father Superior of the Order sang the Mass, while the Bishop of Alberta seated in his Glastonbury chair suffered with an expression of childlike benignity the ritualistic ministrations of Brother Raymond, the ceremonial doffing and donning of his mitre. It was very still in the little Oratory, for it was the season when birds are hushed; and even Sir Charles Horner who was all by himself in the ante-chapel did not fidget or try to peep through the heavy brocaded curtains that shut out the quire. Mark dared not look up when at the offertory Brother Anselm stood before the Altar and answered the solemn interrogations of the Father Superior, question after question about his faith and endurance in the life he desired to enter. And to every question he answered clearly *I will*. The Father Superior took the parchment on which were written the vows and read aloud the document. Then it was placed upon the Altar, and there upon that sacrificial stone Brother Anselm signed his name to a contract with Almighty God. The holy calm that shed itself upon the scene was like a spell on every heart that was beating there in unison with the heart of him who was drawing nearer to Heaven. Prostrating himself, the professed monk prayed first to God the Father:

O receive me according to thy word that I may live; and let me not be disappointed of my hope.

The hearts that beat in unison with his took up the prayer, and the voices of his brethren repeated it word for word. And now the professed monk prayed to God the Son:

O receive me according to thy word that I may live; and let me not be disappointed of my hope.

Once more his brethren echoed the entreaty.

And lastly the professed monk prayed to God the Holy Ghost:

O receive me according to thy word that I may live; and let me not be disappointed of my hope.

For the third time his brethren echoed the entreaty, and then one and all in that Oratory cried:

Glory be to the Father and to the Son and to the Holy Ghost; as it was in the beginning, is now, and ever shall be, world without end. Amen.

There followed prayers that the peace of God might be granted to the professed monk to enable him worthily to perform the vows which he had made, and before the blessing and imposition of the scapular the Bishop rose to speak in tones of deep emotion:

"Brethren, I scarcely dared to hope, when, now nearly ten years ago, I received the vows of your Father Superior as a novice, that I should one day be privileged to be present at this inspiring ceremony. Nor even when five years ago in the far north-west of Canada I professed your Father Superior and those two devoted souls who will soon be with you, now that their work in Malta is for the time finished, did I expect to find myself in this beautiful Oratory which your Order owes to the generosity of a true son of the Church. My heart goes out to you, and I thank God humbly that He has vouchsafed to hear my prayers and bless the enterprise from which I had indeed expected much, but which Almighty God has allowed to prosper more, far more, than I ventured to hope. All my days I have longed to behold the restoration of the religious life to our country, and now when my eyes are dim with age I am granted the ineffable joy of beholding what for too long in my weakness and lack of faith I feared was never likely to come to pass.

"The profession of our dear brother this morning is, I pray, an earnest of many professions at Malford. May these first vows placed upon the Altar of this Oratory be blessed by Almighty God! May our brother be steadfast and happy in his choice! Brethren, I had meant to speak more and with greater eloquence, but my heart is too full. The Lord be with you."

Now Brother Anselm was clothed in the blessed habit while the brethren sang:

Come, Holy Ghost, our souls inspire,
And lighten with celestial fire.

The Father Superior of the Order gave him the paternal kiss. He begged the prayers of his brethren there assembled, and drawing the hood of his cowl over his head prostrated himself again before the Altar. The Mass proceeded.

If the strict Benedictine usage had been followed at Malford, Brother Anselm would have remained apart from the others for three days ofter his profession, wrapped in his cowl, alone with God. But he was anxious to go back to Aldershot that very afternoon, excusing himself because Brother Chad, left behind in charge of the Priory, would be overwhelmed by his various responsibilities.

Brother Dunstan, who had wept throughout the ceremony of the profession, was much upset by Brother Anselm's departure. He had hoped to achieve great exaltation of spirit by Brother Anselm's silent presence. He began to wonder if the newly professed monk appreciated his position. Had himself been granted what Brother Anselm had been granted, he should have liked to spend a week in contemplation of the wonder which had befallen him. Brother Dunstan asked himself if his thoughts were worthy of a senior novice, of one who had for a while acted as Prior and been accorded the address of Reverend Brother. He decided that they were not, and as a penance he begged for the nib with which Brother Anselm had signed his profession. This he wore round his neck as an amulet against unbrotherly thoughts and as a pledge of his own determination to vow himself eternally to the service of God.

Mark was glad that Brother Anselm was going back so soon to his active work. It was an assurance that the Order of St. George did have active work to do; and when he was called upon to drive Brother Anselm to the station he made up his mind to conquer his shyness and hint that he should be glad to serve the Order in the Priory at Aldershot.

This time, notwithstanding that he had a good excuse to draw his hood close, Brother Anselm showed himself more approachable.

"If the Reverend Father suggests your name," he promised Mark, "I shall be glad to have you with us. Brother Chad is simply splendid, and the Tommies are wonderful. It's quite right of course to have a Mother House, but . . ." He broke off, disinclined to criticize the direction of the Order's policy to a member so junior as Mark.

"Oh, I'm not asking you to do anything yet awhile," Mark explained. "I quite realize that I have a great deal to learn before I should be any use at Aldershot or Sandgate. I hope you don't mind my talking like this. But until this morning I had not really intended to remain in the Order. My hope was to be ordained as soon as I was old enough. Now since this morning I feel that I do long for the spiritual support of a community for my own feeble aspirations. The Bishop's words moved me tremendously. It wasn't what he said so much, but I was filled with all his faith and I could have cried out to him a promise that I for one would help to carry on the restoration. At the same time, I know that I'm more fitted for active work, not by any good I expect to do, but for the good it will do me. I suppose you'd say that if I had a true vocation I shouldn't be thinking about what part I was going to play in the life of the Order, but that I should be content to do whatever I was told. I'm boring you?" Mark broke off to inquire, for Brother Anselm was staring in front of him through his big horn spectacles like an owl.

"No, no," said the senior. "But I'm not the novice-master. Who is, by the way?"

"Brother Jerome."

The other did not comment on this information, but Mark was sure that he was trying not to look contemptuous.

Soon the junction came in sight, and from down the line the white smoke of a train approaching.

"Hurry, Brother, I don't want to miss it."

Mark thumped the haunches of the pony and drove up just in time for Brother Anselm to escape.

"Thank you, Brother," said that same voice which yesterday, only yesterday night, had sounded so rarely sweet. Here on this mellow August afternoon it was the voice of the golden air itself, and the shriek of the engine did not drown its echoes in Mark's soul where all the way back to Malford it was chiming like a bell.

CHAPTER XXVI

ADDITION

Mark's ambition to go and work at Aldershot was gratified before the end of August, because Brother Chad fell ill, and it was considered advisable to let him spend a long convalescence at the Abbey.

The Priory,
17, Farnborough Villas,
Aldershot.
St. Michael and All Angels.

My dear Rector,

I don't think you'll be sorry to read from the above address that I've been transferred from Malford to one of the active branches of the Order. I don't accept your condemnation of the Abbey as pseudo-monasticism, though I can quite well understand that my account of it might lead you to make such a criticism. The trouble with me is that my emotions and judgment are always quarrelling. I suppose you might say that is true of most people. It's like the palmist who tells everybody that he is ruled by his head or his heart, as the case may be. But when one approaches the problem of religion (let alone what is called the religious life) one is terribly perplexed to know which is to be obeyed. I don't think that you can altogether rule out emotion as a touchstone of truth. The endless volumes of St. Thomas Aquinas, through which I've been wading, do not cope with the fact that the whole of his vast intellectual and severely logical structure is built up on the assumption of faith, which is the gift of emotion, not judgment. The whole system is a petitio principii really.

I did not mean to embark on a discussion of the question of the Ultimate Cause of religion, but to argue with you about the religious life! The Abbot Paphnutius told Cassian that there were three sorts of vocation—ex Deo, per hominem, and ex necessitate. Now suppose I have a vocation, mine is obviously per hominem. I inherit the missionary spirit from my father. That spirit was fostered by association with Rowley. My main object in entering the Order of St. George was to work among soldiers, not because I felt that soldiers needed "missionizing" more than any other class, but because the work at Chatsea brought me into contact with both sailors and soldiers, and turned my thoughts in their direction. I also felt the need of an organization behind my efforts. My first impulse was to be a preaching friar, but that would have laid too much on me as an individual, and from lack of self-confidence, youthfulness, want of faith perhaps, I was afraid. Well, to come back to the Abbot Paphnutius and his three vocations—it seems fairly clear that the first, direct from God, is a better vocation than the one which is inspired by human example, or the third, which arises from the failure of everything else. At the same time they ARE all three genuine vocations. What applies to the vocation seems to me to apply equally to the community. What you stigmatize as our pseudo-monasticism is still experimental, and I think I can see the Reverend Father's idea. He has had a great deal of experience with an Order which began so amateurishly, if I may use the word, that nobody could have imagined that it would grow to the size and strength it has reached in ten years. The Bishop of Alberta revealed much to us of our beginnings during his stay at the Abbey, and after I had listened to him I felt how presumptuous it was for me to criticize the central source of the religious life we are hoping to spread. You see, Rector, I must have criticized it implicitly in my letters to you, for your objections are simply the expression of what I did not like to say, but what I managed to convey through the medium of would-be humorous description. One hears of the saving grace of humour, but I'm not sure that humour is a saving grace. I rather wish that I had no sense of humour. It's a destructive quality. All the great sceptics have been humourists. Humour is really a device to secure human comfort. Take me. I am inspired to become a preaching friar. I instantly perceive the funny side of setting out to be a preaching friar. I tell myself that other people will perceive the funny side of it, and that consequently I shall do no good as a preaching friar. Yes, humour is a moisture which rusts everything except gold. As a nation the Jews have the greatest sense of humour, and they have been the greatest disintegrating force in the history of mankind. The Scotch are reputed to have no sense of humour, and they are morally the most impressive nation in the world. What humour is allowed them is known as dry humour. The corroding moisture has been eliminated. They are still capable of laughter, but never so as to interfere with their seriousness in the great things of life. I remember I once heard a tiresome woman, who was striving to be clever, say that Our Lord could not have had much sense of humour or He would not have hung so long on the Cross. At the time I was indignant with the silly blasphemy, but thinking it over since I believe that she was right, and that, while her only thought had been to make a remark that would create a sensation in the room, she had actually hit on the explanation of some of Our Lord's human actions. And his lack of humour is the more conspicuous because he was a Jew. I was reading the other day a book of essays by one of our leading young latitudinarian divines, in which he was most anxious to prove that Our Lord had all the graces of a well-bred young man about town, including a pretty wit. He actually claimed that the pun on Peter's name was an example of Our Lord's urbane and genial humour! It gives away the latitudinarian position completely. They're really ashamed of Christianity. They want to bring it into line with modern thought. They hope by throwing overboard the Incarnation, the Resurrection of the Body, and the Ascension, to lighten the ship so effectually that it will ride buoyantly over the billows of modern knowledge. But however lightly the ship rides, she will still be at sea, and it would be the better if she struck on the rock of Peter and perished than that she should ride buoyantly but aimlessly over the uneasy oceans of knowledge.

I've once more got a long way from the subject of my letter, but I've always taken advantage of your patience to air my theories, and when I begin to write to you my pen runs away with me. The point I want to make is that unless there is a mother house which is going to create a reserve of spiritual energy, the active work of the Order is going to suffer. The impulse to save souls might easily exhaust itself in the individual. A few disappointments, unceasing hard work, the interference of a bishop, the failure of financial support, a long period in which his work seems to have come to a standstill, all these are going to react on the individual missioner who depends on himself. Looking back now at the work done by my father, and by Rowley at Chatsea, I'm beginning to understand how dangerous it is for one man to make himself the pivot of an enterprise. I only really know about my father's work at second hand, but look at Chatsea. I hear now that already the work is falling to pieces. Although that may not justify the Bishop of Silchester, I'm beginning to see that he might argue that if Rowley had shown himself sufficiently humble to obey the forces of law and order in the Church, he would have had accumulated for him a fresh store of energy from which he might have drawn to consolidate his influence upon the people with whom he worked. Anyway, that's what I'm going to try to acquire from the pseudo-monasticism of Malford. I'm determined to dry up the critical and humorous side of myself. Half of it is nothing more than arrogance. I'm grateful for being sent to Aldershot, but I'm going to make my work here depend on the central source of energy and power. I'm going to say that my work is per hominem, but that the success of my work is ex Deo. You may tell me that any man with the least conception of Christian Grace would know that. Yes, he may know it intellectually, but does he know it emotionally? I confess I don't yet awhile. But I do know that if the Order of St. George proves itself a real force, it will not be per hominem, it will not be by the Reverend Father's eloquence in the pulpit, but by the vocation of the community ex Deo.

Meanwhile, here I am at Aldershot. Brother Chad, whose place I have taken, was a character of infinite sweetness and humility. All our Tommies speak of him in a sort of protective way, as if he were a little boy they had adopted. He had—has, for after all he's only gone to the Abbey to get over a bad attack of influenza on top of months of hard work—he has a strangely youthful look, although he's nearly thirty. He hails from Lichfield. I wonder what Dr. Johnson would have made of him. I've already told you about Brother Anselm. Well, now that I've seen him at home, as it were, I can't discover the secret of his influence with our men. He's every bit as taciturn with them as he was with me on that drive from the station, and yet there is not one of them that doesn't seem to regard him as an intimate friend. He's extraordinarily good at the practical side of the business. He makes the men comfortable. He always knows just what they're wanting for tea or for supper, and the games always go well when Brother Anselm presides, much better than they do when I'm in charge! I think perhaps that's because I play myself, and want to win. It infects the others. And yet we ought to want to win a game—otherwise it's not worth playing. Also, I must admit that there's usually a row in the billiard room on my nights on duty. Brother Anselm makes them talk better than I do, and I don't think he's a bit interested in their South African experiences. I am, and they won't say a word about them to me. I've been here a month now, so they ought to be used to me by this time.

We've just heard that the guest-house for soldiers at the Abbey will be finished by the middle of next month, so we're already discussing our Christmas party. The Priory, which sounds so grand and gothic, is really the corner house of a most depressing row of suburban villas, called Glenview and that sort of thing. The last tenant was a traveller in tea and had a stable instead of the usual back-garden. This we have converted into a billiard room. An officer in one of the regiments quartered here told us that it was the only thing in Aldershot we had converted. The authorities aren't very fond of us. They say we encourage the men to grumble and give them too great idea of their own importance. Brother Anselm asked a general once with whom we fell out if it was possible to give a man whose profession it was to defend his country too great an idea of his own importance. The general merely blew out his cheeks and looked choleric. He had no suspicion that he had been scored off. We don't push too much religion into the men at present. We've taught them to respect the Crucifix on the wall in the dining-room, and sometimes they attend Vespers. But they're still rather afraid of chaff, such as being called the Salvation Army by their comrades. Well, here's an end to this long letter, for I must write now to Brother Jerome, whose name-day it is tomorrow. Love to all at the Rectory.

Your ever affectionate

Mark.

Mark remained at Aldershot until the week before Christmas, when with a party of Tommies he went back to the Abbey. He found that Brother Chad's convalescence had been seriously impeded in its later stages by the prospect of having to remain at the Abbey as guest-master, and though Mark was sorry to leave Aldershot he saw by the way the Tommies greeted their old friend that he was dear to their hearts. When after Christmas Brother Chad took the party back, Mark made up his mind that the right person was going.

Mark found many changes at the Abbey during the four months he had been away. The greatest of all was the presence of Brother George as Prior. The legend of him had led Mark to expect someone out of the ordinary; but he had not been prepared for a personality as strong as this. Brother George was six feet three inches tall, with a presence of great dignity and much personal beauty. He had an aquiline nose, strong chin, dark curly hair and bright imperious eyes. His complexion, burnt by the Mediterranean sun, made him seem in his white habit darker than he really was. His manner was of one accustomed to be immediately obeyed. Mark could scarcely believe when he saw Brother Dunstan beside

Brother George that only last June Brother Dunstan was acting as Prior. As for Brother Raymond, who had always been so voluble at recreation, one look from Brother George sent him into a silence that was as solemn as the disciplinary silence imposed by the rule. Brother Birinus, who was Brother George's right hand in the Abbey as much as he had been his right hand on the Moose Rib farm, was even taller than the Prior; but he was lanky and raw-boned, and had not the proportions of Brother George. He was of a swarthy complexion, not given to talking much, although when he did speak he always spoke to the point. He and Brother George were hard at work ploughing up some derelict fields which they had persuaded Sir Charles Horner to let to the Abbey rent free on condition that they were put back into cultivation. The patron himself had gone away for the winter to Rome and Florence, and Mark was glad that he had, for he was sure that otherwise his inquisitiveness would have been severely snubbed by the Prior. Father Burrowes went away as usual to preach after Christmas; but before he went Mark was clothed as a novice together with two other postulants who had been at Malford since September. Of these Brother Giles was a former school-master, a dried-up, tobacco-coloured little man of about fifty, with a quick and nervous, but always precise manner. Mark liked him, and his manual labour was done under the direction of Brother Giles, who had been made gardener, a post for which he was well suited. The other new novice was Brother Nicholas whom, had Mark not been the fellow-member of a community, he would have disliked immensely. Brother Nicholas was one of those people who are in a perpetual state of prurient concern about the sexual morality of the human race. He was impervious to snubs, of which he received many from Brother George, and he had somehow managed to become a favourite of the Reverend Father, so that he had been appointed guest-master, a post that was always coveted, and one for which nobody felt Brother Nicholas was suited.

Besides the increase of numbers there had been considerable additions made to the fabric of the Abbey, if such a word as fabric may be applied to matchboard, felt, and corrugated iron. Mention has already been made of the new Guest-house, which accommodated not only soldiers invited to spend their furloughs at the Abbey, but also tramps who sought a night's lodging. Mark, as Porter, found his time considerably taken up with these casuals, because as soon as the news spread of a comfortable lodging they came begging for shelter in greater numbers than had been anticipated. A rule was made that they should pay for their entertainment by doing a day's work, and it was one of Mark's duties to report on the qualifications of these casuals to Brother George, whose whole life was occupied with the farm that he was creating out of those derelict fields.

"There's a black man just arrived, Reverend Brother. He says he lost his ship at Southampton through a boiler explosion, and is tramping to Cardiff," Mark would report.

"Can he plough a straight furrow?" the Prior would demand.

"I doubt it," Mark would answer with a smile. "He can't walk straight across the dormitory."

"What's he been drinking?"

"Rum, I fancy."

"Why did you let him in?"

"It's such a stormy night."

"Well, send him along to me tomorrow after Lauds, and I'll put him to cleaning out the pigsties."

Mark only had to deal with these casuals. Regular guests like the soldiers, who were always welcome, and ecclesiastically minded inquirers were looked after by Brother Nicholas. One of the things for which Mark detested Brother Nicholas was the habit he had of showing off his poor casuals to the paying guests. It took Mark a stern reading of St. Benedict's Rule and the observations therein upon humility and obedience not to be rude to Brother Nicholas sometimes.

"Brother," he asked one day. "Have you ever read what our Holy Father says about gyrovagues and sarabaites?"

Brother Nicholas, who always thought that any long word with which he was unfamiliar referred to sexual perversion, asked what such people were.

"You evidently haven't," said Mark. "Our Holy Father disapproves of them."

"Oh, so should I, Brother Mark," said Brother Nicholas quickly. "I hate anything like that."

"It struck me," Mark went on, "that most of our paying guests are gyrovagues and sarabaites."

"What an accusation to make," said Brother Nicholas, flushing with expectant curiosity and looking down his long nose to give the impression that it was the blush of innocence and modesty.

When, an hour or so later, he had had leisure to discover the meaning of both terms, he came up to Mark and exclaimed:

"Oh, brother, how could you?"

"How could I what?" Mark asked.

"How could you let me think that it meant something much worse? Why, it's nothing really. Just wandering monks."

"They annoyed our Holy Father," said Mark.

"Yes, they did seem to make him a bit ratty. Perhaps the translation softened it down," surmised Brother Nicholas. "I'll get a dictionary tomorrow."

The bell for solemn silence clanged, and Brother Nicholas must have spent his quarter of an hour in most unprofitable meditation.

Another addition to the buildings was a wide, covered verandah, which had been built on in front of the central block, and which therefore extended the length of the Refectory, the Library, the Chapter Room, and the Abbot's Parlour. The last was now the Prior's Parlour, because lodgings for Father Burrowes were being built in the Gatehouse, the only building of stone that was being erected.

This Gatehouse was to be finished as an Easter offering to the Father Superior from devout ladies, who had been dismayed at the imagination of his discomfort. The verandah was granted the title of the Cloister, and the hours of recreation were now spent here instead of in the Library as formerly, which enabled studious brethren to read in peace.

The Prior made a rule that every Sunday afternoon all the brethren should assemble in the Cloister at tea, and spend the hour until Vespers in jovial intercourse. He did not actually specify that the intercourse was to be jovial, but he look care by judicious teazing to see that it was jovial. In his anxiety to bring his farm into cultivation, Brother George was apt to make any monastic duty give way to manual labour on those thistle-grown fields, and it was seldom that there were more than a couple of brethren to say the Office between Lauds and Vespers. The others had to be content with crossing themselves when they heard the bell for

Terce or None, and even Sext was sparingly attended after the Prior instituted the eating of the mid-day meal in the fields on fine days. Hence the conversation in the Cloister on Sunday afternoons was chiefly agricultural.

"Are you going to help me drill the ten-acre field tomorrow, Brother Giles?" the Prior asked one grey Sunday afternoon in the middle of March.

"No, I'm certainly not, Reverend Brother, unless you put me under obedience to do so."

"Then I think I shall," the Prior laughed.

"If you do, Reverend Brother," the gardener retorted, "you'll have to put my peas under obedience to sow themselves."

"Peas!" the Prior scoffed. "Who cares about peas?"

"Oh, Reverend Brother!" cried Brother Simon, his hair standing up with excitement. "We couldn't do without peas."

Brother Simon was assistant cook nowadays, a post he filled tolerably well under the supervision of the one-legged soldier who was cook.

"We couldn't do without oats," said Brother Birinus severely.

He spoke so seldom at these gatherings that when he did few were found to disagree with him, because they felt his words must have been deeply pondered before they were allowed utterance.

"Have you any flowers in the garden for St. Joseph?" asked Brother Raymond, who was sacristan.

"A few daffodils, that's all," Brother Giles replied.

"Oh, I don't think that St. Joseph would like daffodils," exclaimed Brother Raymond. "He's so fond of white flowers, isn't he?"

"Good gracious!" the Prior thundered. "Are we a girls' school or a company of able-bodied men?"

"Well, St. Joseph is always painted with lilies, Reverend Brother," said the sacristan, rather sulkily.

He disapproved of the way the Prior treated what he called his pet saints.

"We're not an agricultural college either," he added in an undertone to Brother Dunstan, who shook his finger and whispered "hush."

"I doubt if we ought to keep St. Joseph's Day," said the Prior truculently. There was nothing he enjoyed better on these Sunday afternoons than showing his contempt for ecclesiasticism.

"Reverend Brother!" gasped Brother Dunstan. "Not keep St. Joseph's Day?"

"He's not in our calendar," Brother George argued. "If we're going to keep St. Joseph, why not keep St. Alo—what's his name and Philip Neri and Anthony of Padua and Bernardine of Sienna and half-a-dozen other Italian saints?"

"Why not?" asked Brother Raymond. "At any rate we have to keep my patron, who was a dear, even if he was a Spaniard."

The Prior looked as if he were wondering if there was a clause in the Rule that forbade a prior to throw anything within reach at an imbecile sacristan.

"I don't think you can put St. Joseph in the same class as the saints you have just mentioned," pompously interposed Brother Jerome, who was cellarer nowadays and fancied that the continued existence of the Abbey depended on himself.

"Until you can learn to harness a pair of horses to the plough," said the Prior, "your opinions on the relative importance of Roman saints will not be accepted."

"I've never been used to horses," said Brother Jerome.

"And you have been used to saints?" the Prior laughed, raising his eyebrows.

Brother Jerome was silent.

"Well, Brother Lawrence, what do you say?"

Brother Lawrence stuck out his lower jaw and assumed the expression of the good boy in a Sunday School class.

"St. Joseph was the foster-father of Our Blessed Lord, Reverend Brother," he said primly. "I think it would be most disrespectful both to Our Blessed Lord and to Our Blessed Lady if we didn't keep his feast-day, though I am sure St. Joseph would have no objection to daffodils. No objections at all. His whole life and character show him to have been a man of the greatest humility and forbearance."

The Prior rocked with laughter. This was the kind of speech that sometimes rewarded his teasing.

"We always kept St. Joseph's day at the Visitation, Hornsey," Brother Nicholas volunteered. "In fact we always made it a great feature. We found it came as such a relief in Lent."

The Prior nodded his head mockingly.

"These young folk can teach us a lot about the way to worship God, Brother Birinus," he commented.

Brother Birinus scowled.

"I broke three shares ploughing that bad bit of ground by the fir trees," he announced gloomily. "I think I'll drill in the oats tomorrow in the ten-acre. It's no good ploughing deep," he added reproachfully.

"Well, I believe in deep ploughing," the Prior argued.

Mark realized that Brother Birinus had deliberately brought back the conversation to where it started in order to put an end to the discussion about St. Joseph. He was glad, because he himself was the only one of the brethren who had not yet been called upon to face the Prior's contemptuous teasing. He wondered if he should have had the courage to speak up for St. Joseph's Day. He should have found it difficult to oppose Brother George, whom he liked and revered. But in this case he was wrong, and perhaps he was also wrong to make the observation of St. Joseph's Day a cudgel with which to belabour the brethren.

The following afternoon Mark had two casuals who he fancied might be useful to the Prior, and leaving the ward of the gate to Brother Nicholas he took them down with him through the coppice to where over the bleak March furrows Brother George was ploughing that rocky strip of bad land by the fir trees. The men were told to go and report themselves to Brother Birinus, who with Brother Dunstan to feed the drill was sowing oats a field or two away.

"I don't think Brother Birinus will be sorry to let Brother Dunstan go back to his domestic duties," the Prior commented sardonically.

Mark was turning to go back to *his* domestic duties when Brother George signed to him to stop.

"I suppose that like the rest of them you think I've no business to be a monk?" Brother George began.

Mark looked at him in surprise.

"I don't believe that anybody thinks that," he said; but even as he spoke he looked at the Prior and wondered why he had become a monk. He did not appear, standing there in breeches and gaiters, his shirt open at the neck, his hair tossing in the wind, his face and form of the soil like a figure in one of Fred Walker's pictures, no, he certainly did not appear the kind of man who could be led away by Father Burrowes' eloquence and persuasiveness into choosing the method of life he had chosen. Yes, now that the question had been put to him Mark wondered why Brother George was a monk.

"You too are astonished at me," said the Prior. "Well, in a way I don't blame you. You've only seen me on the land. This comes of letting myself be tempted by Horner's offer to give us this land rent free if I would take it in hand. And after all," he went on talking to the wide grey sky rather than to Mark, "the old monks were great tillers of the soil. It's right that we should maintain the tradition. Besides, all those years in Malta I've dreamed just this. Brother Birinus and I have stewed on those sun-baked heights above Valetta and dreamed of this. What made you join our Order?" he asked abruptly.

Mark told him about himself.

"I see, you want to keep your hand in, eh? Well, I suppose you might have done worse for a couple of years. Now, I've never wanted to be a priest. The Reverend Father would like me to be ordained, but I don't think I should make a good priest. I believe if I were to become a priest, I should lose my faith. That sounds a queer thing to say, and I'd rather you didn't repeat it to any of those young men up there."

The monastery bell sounded on the wind.

"Three o'clock already," exclaimed the Prior. And crossing himself he said the short prayer offered to God instead of the formal attendance at the Office.

"Well, I mustn't let the horses get chilled. You'd better get back to your casuals. By the way, I'm going to have Brother Nicholas to work out here awhile, and I want you to act as guest-master. Brother Raymond will be porter, and I'm going to send Brother Birinus off the farm to be sacristan. I shall miss him out here, of course."

The Prior put his hand once more to the plough, and Mark went slowly back to the Abbey. On the brow of the hill before he plunged into the coppice he turned to look down at the distant figure moving with slow paces across the field below.

"He's wrestling with himself," Mark thought, "more than he's wrestling with the soil."

CHAPTER XXVII

MULTIPLICATION

At Easter the Abbey Gatehouse was blessed by the Father Superior, who established himself in the rooms above and allowed himself to take a holiday from his labour of preaching. Mark expected to be made porter again, but the Reverend Father did not attempt to change the posts assigned to the brethren by the Prior, and Mark remained guest-master, a duty that was likely to give him plenty of occupation during the summer months now close at hand.

On Low Sunday the Father Superior convened a full Chapter of the Order, to which were summoned Brother Dominic, the head of the Sandgate house, and Brother Anselm. When the brethren, with the exception of Brother Simon, who was still a postulant, were gathered together, the Father Superior addressed them as follows:

"Brethren, I have called this Chapter of the Order of St. George to acquaint you with our financial position, and to ask you to make a grave decision. Before I say any more I ought to explain that our three professed brethren considered that a Chapter convened to make a decision such as I am going to ask you to make presently should not include the novices. I contended that in the present state of our Order where novices are called upon to fill the most responsible positions it would be unfair to exclude them; and our professed brethren, like true sons of St. Benedict, have accepted my ruling. You all know what great additions to our Mother House we have made during the past year, and you will all realize what a burden of debt this has laid upon the Order and on myself what a weight of responsibility. The closing of our Malta

Priory, which was too far away to interest people in England, eased us a little. But if we are going to establish ourselves as a permanent force in modern religious life, we must establish our Mother House before anything. You may say that the Order of St. George is an Order devoted to active work among soldiers, and that we are not concerned with the establishment of a partially contemplative community. But all of you will recognize the advantage it has been to you to be asked to stay here and prepare yourselves for active work, to gather within yourselves a great store of spiritual energy, and hoard within your hearts a mighty treasure of spiritual strength. Brethren, if the Order of St. George is to be worthy of its name and of its claim we must not rest till we have a priory in every port and garrison, and in every great city where soldiers are stationed. Even if we had the necessary funds to endow these priories, have we enough brethren to take charge of them? We have not. I cannot help feeling that I was too hasty in establishing active houses both at Aldershot and at Sandgate, and I have convened you today to ask you to vote in Chapter that the house at Sandgate be temporarily given up, great spiritual influence though it has proved itself under our dear Brother Dominic with the men of Shorncliffe Camp, not only that we may concentrate our resources and pay our debts, but also that we may have the help of Brother Dominic himself, and of Brother Athanasius, who has remained behind in charge and is not here today."

The Father Superior then read a statement of the Order's financial liabilities, and invited any Brother who wished, to speak his mind. All waited for the Prior, who after a short silence rose:

"Reverend Father and Brethren, I don't think that there is much to say. Frankly, I am not convinced that we ought to have spent so much on the Abbey, but having done so, we must obviously try and put ourselves on a sound financial basis. I should like to hear what Brother Dominic has to say."

Brother Dominic was a slight man with black hair and a sallow complexion, whose most prominent feature was an, immense hooked nose with thin nostrils. Whether through the associations with his name saint, or merely by his personality, Mark considered that he looked a typical inquisitor. When he spoke, his lips seemed to curl in a sneer. The expression was probably quite accidental, perhaps caused by some difficulty in breathing, but the effect was sinister, and his smooth voice did nothing to counteract the unpleasant grimace. Mark wondered if he was really successful with the men at Shorncliffe.

"Reverend Father, Reverend Brother, and Brethren," said Brother Dominic, "you can imagine that it is no easy matter for me to destroy with a few words a house that in a small way I had a share in building up."

"The lion's share," interposed the Father Superior.

"You are too generous, Reverend Father," said Brother Dominic. "We could have done very little at Sandgate if you had not worked so hard for us throughout the length and breadth of England. And that is what personally I do feel, Brethren," he continued in more emphatic tones. "I do feel that the Reverend Father knows better than we what is the right policy for us to adopt. I will not pretend that I shall be anything but loath to leave Sandgate, but the future of the whole order depends on the ability of brethren like myself," Brother Dominic paused for the briefest instant to flash a quick glance at Brother Anselm, "to recognize that our usefulness to the soldiers among whom we are proud and happy to spend our lives is bounded by our usefulness to the Order of St. George. I give my vote without hesitation in favour of closing the Priory at Sandgate, and abandoning temporarily the work at Shorncliffe Camp."

Nobody else spoke when Brother Dominic sat down, and everybody voted in favour of the course of action proposed by the Father Superior.

Brother Dominic, in addition to his other work, had been editing *The Dragon*, the monthly magazine of the Order, and it was now decided to print this in future at the Abbey, some constant reader having presented a fount of type. The opening of a printing-press involved housing room, and it was decided to devote the old kitchens to this purpose, so that new kitchens could be built, a desirable addition in view of the increasing numbers in the Abbey and the likelihood of a further increase presently.

Mark had not been touched by the abandonment of the Sandgate priory until Brother Athanasius arrived. Brother Athanasius was a florid young man with bright blue eyes, and so much pent-up energy as sometimes to appear blustering. He lacked any kind of ability to hide his feelings, and he was loud in his denunciation of the Chapter that abolished his work. His criticisms were so loud, aggressive, and blatant, that he was nearly ordered to retire from the Order altogether. However, the Father Superior went away to address a series of drawing-room meetings in London, and Brother George, with whom Brother Athanasius, almost alone of the brethren, never hesitated to keep his end up, discovering that he was as ready to stick up to horses and cows, did not pay attention to the Father Superior's threat that, if Brother Athanasius could not keep his tongue quiet, he must be sent away. Mark made friends with him, and when he found that, in spite of all his blatancy and self-assertion, Brother Athanasius could not keep the tears from his bright blue eyes whenever he spoke of Shorncliffe, he was sorry for him and vexed with himself for accepting the surrender of Sandgate priory so much as a matter of course, because he had no personal experience of its work.

"But was Brother Dominic really good with the men?" Mark asked.

"Oh, Brother Dominic was all right. Don't you try and make me criticize Brother Dominic. He bought the gloves and I did the fighting. Good man of business was Brother D. I wish we could have some boxing here. Half the brethren want punching about in my opinion. Old Brother Jerome's face is squashed flat like a prize-fighter's, but I bet he's never had the gloves on in his life. I'm fond of old Brother J. But, my word, wouldn't I like to punch into him when he gives us that pea-soup more than four times a week. Chronic, I call it. Well, if he doesn't give us a jolly good blow out on my name-day next week I really will punch into him. Old Brother Flatface, as I called him the other day. And he wasn't half angry either. Didn't we have sport last second of May! I took a party of them all round Hythe and Folkestone. No end of a spree!"

Mark was soon too much occupied with his duties as guestmaster to lament with Brother Athanasius the end of the Sandgate priory. The Reverend Father's drawing-room addresses were sending fresh visitors down every week to see for themselves the size of the foundation that required money, and more money, and more money still to keep it going. In the old Chatsea days guests who visited the Mission House were expected to provide entertainment for their hosts. It mattered not who they were, millionaires or paupers, parsons or laymen, undergraduates or board-school boys, they had to share the common table, face the common teasing, and help the common task. Here at the Abbey, although the guests had much more opportunity of intercourse with the brethren than would have been permitted in a less novel monastic house, they were definitely guests, from whom nothing was expected beyond observance of the rules for guests. They were of all kinds, from the distinguished lay leaders of the Catholic party to young men who thought emotionally of joining the Order.

Mark tried to conduct himself as impersonally as possible, and in doing so he managed to impress all the visitors with being a young man intensely preoccupied with his vocation, and as such to be treated with gravity and a certain amount of deference. Mark himself was anxious not to take advantage of his position, and make friends with people that otherwise he might not have met. Had he been sure that he was going to remain in the Order of St. George, he would have allowed himself a greater liberty of intercourse, because he would not then have been afraid of one day seeing these people in the world. He desired to be forgotten when they left the Abbey, or if he was remembered to be remembered only as a guestmaster who tried to make the Monastery guests comfortable, who treated them with courtesy, but also with reserve.

None of the young men who came down to see if they would like to be monks got as far as being accepted as a probationer until the end of May, when a certain Mr. Arthur Yarrell, an undergraduate from Keble College, Oxford, whose mind was a dictionary of ecclesiastical terms, was accepted and a month later became a postulant as Brother Augustine, to the great pleasure of Brother Raymond, who said that he really thought he should have been compelled to leave the Order if somebody had not joined it with an appreciation of historic Catholicism. Early in June Sir Charles Horner introduced another young man called Aubrey Wyon, whom he had met at Venice in May.

"Take a little trouble over entertaining him," Sir Charles counselled. And then, looking round to see that no thieves or highwaymen were listening, he whispered to Mark that Wyon had money. "He would be an asset, I fancy. And he's seriously thinking of joining you," the baronet declared.

To tell the truth, Sir Charles who was beginning to be worried by the financial state of the Order of St. George, would at this crisis have tried to persuade the Devil to become a monk if the Devil would have provided a handsome dowry. He had met Aubrey Wyon at an expensive hotel, had noticed that he was expensively dressed and drank good wine, had found that he was interested in ecclesiastical religion, and, having bragged a bit about the land he had presented to the Order of St. George, had inspired Wyon to do some bragging of what he had done for various churches.

"If I could find happiness at Malford," Wyon had said, "I would give them all that I possess."

Sir Charles had warned the Father Superior that he would do well to accept Wyon as a probationer, should he propose himself; and the Father Superior, who was by now as anxious for money as a company-promoter, made himself as pleasant to Wyon as he knew how, flattering him carefully and giving voice to his dreams for the great stone Abbey to be built here in days to come.

Mark took an immediate and violent dislike to the newcomer, which, had he been questioned about it, he would have attributed to his elaborate choice of socks and tie, or to his habit of perpetually tightening the leather belt he wore instead of braces, as if he would compel that flabbiness of waist caused by soft living to vanish; but to himself he admitted that the antipathy was deeper seated.

"It's like the odour of corruption," he murmured, though actually it was the odour of hair washes and lotions and scents that filled the guest's cell.

However, Aubrey Wyon became for a week a probationer, ludicrously known as Brother Aubrey, after which he remained a postulant only a fortnight before he was clothed as a novice, having by then taken the name of Anthony, alleging that the inspiration to become a monk had been due to the direct intervention of St. Anthony of Padua on June 13th.

Whether Brother Anthony turned the Father Superior's head with his promises of what he intended to give the Order when he was professed, or whether having once started he was unable to stop, there was continuous building all that summer, culminating in a decision to begin the Abbey Church.

Mark wondered why Brother George did not protest against the expenditure, and he came to the conclusion that the Prior was as much bewitched by ambition for his farm as the head of the Order was by his hope of a mighty fane.

Thus things drifted during the summer, when, since the Father Superior was not away so much, his influence was exerted more strongly over the brethren, though at the same time he was not attracting as much money as was now always required in ever increasing amounts.

Such preaching as he did manage later on during the autumn was by no means so financially successful as his campaign of the preceding year at the same time. Perhaps the natural buoyancy of his spirit led Father Burrowes in his disappointment to place more trust than he might otherwise have done in Brother Anthony's plan for the benefit of the Order. The cloister became like Aladdin's Cave whenever there were enough brethren assembled to make an audience for his luscious projects and prefigurations. Sundays were the days when Brother Anthony was particularly eloquent, and one Sunday in mid-September—it was the Feast of the Exaltation of the Holy Cross—he surpassed himself.

"My notion would be to copy," he proclaimed, "with of course certain improvements, the buildings on Monte Cassino. We are not quite so high here; but then on the other hand that is an advantage, because it will enable us to allot less space to the superficial area. Yes, I have a very soft spot for the cloisters of Monte Cassino."

Brother Anthony gazed round for the approbation of the assembled brethren, none of whom had the least idea what the cloisters of Monte Cassino looked like.

"And I think some of our altar furniture is a little mean," Brother Anthony continued. "I'm not advocating undue ostentation; but there is room for improvement. They understood so well in the Middle Ages the importance of a rich equipment. If I'd only known when I was in Sienna this spring that I was coming here, I should certainly have bought a superb reredos that was offered to me comparatively cheap. The columns were of malachite and porphyry, and the panels of *rosso antico* with scrolls of *lumachella*. They only asked 15,000 lire. It was absurdly cheap. However, perhaps it would be wiser to wait till we finish the Abbey Church before we decide on the reredos. I'm very much in favour of beaten gold for the tabernacle. By the way, Reverend Father, have you decided to build an ambulatory round the clerestory? I must say I think it would be effective, and of course for meditation unique. I shall have to find if my money will run to it. Oh, and Brother Birinus, weren't you saying the other day that the green vestments were rather faded? Don't worry. I'm only waiting to make up my mind between velvet and brocade for the purple set to order a completely new lot, including a set in old rose damask for mid-Lent. It always seems to me such a mistake not to take advantage of that charming use."

Father Burrowes was transported to the days of his youth at Malta when his own imagination was filled with visions of precious metals, of rare fabrics and mighty architecture.

"A silver chalice of severe pattern encrusted round the stem with blue zircons," Brother Anthony was chanting in his melodious voice, his eyes bright with the reflection of celestial splendours. "And perhaps another in gold with the sacred monogram wrought on the cup in jacinths and orange tourmalines. Yes, I'll talk it over with Sir Charles and get him to approve the design."

The next morning two detectives came to Malford Abbey, and arrested Aubrey Wyon alias Brother Anthony for obtaining money under false pretences in various parts of the world. With them he departed to prison and a life more ascetic than any he had hitherto known. Brother Anthony departed indeed, but he was not discredited until it was too late. His grandiose projects and extravagant promises had already incited Father Burrowes to launch out on several new building operations that the Order could ill afford.

Perhaps the cloister had been less like the Cave of Aladdin than the Cave of the Forty Thieves.

After Christmas another Chapter was convened, to which Brother Anselm and Brother Chad were both bidden. The Father Superior addressed the brethren as he had addressed them a year ago, and finished up his speech by announcing that, deeply as he regretted it, he felt bound to propose that the Aldershot priory should be closed.

"What?" shouted Brother Anselm, leaping to his feet, his eyes blazing with wrath through his great horn spectacles.

The Prior quickly rose to say that he could not agree to the Reverend Father's suggestion. It was impossible for them any longer to claim that they were an active Order if they confined themselves entirely to the Abbey. He had not opposed the shutting down of the Sandgate priory, nor, he would remind the Reverend Father, had he offered any resistance to the abandonment of Malta.

But he felt obliged to give his opinion strongly in favour of making any sacrifice to keep alive the Aldershot priory.

Brother George had spoken with force, but without eloquence; and Mark was afraid that his speech had not carried much weight.

The next to rise was Brother Birinus, who stood up as tall as a tree and said:

"I agree with Brother George."

And when he sat down it was as if a tree had been uprooted.

There was a pause after this, while every brother looked at his neighbour, waiting for him to rise at this crisis in the history of the Order. At last the Father Superior asked Brother Anselm if he did not intend to speak.

"What can I say?" asked Brother Anselm bitterly. "Last year I should have been true to myself and voted against the closing of the Sandgate house. I was silent then in my egoism. I am not fit to defend our house now."

"But I will," cried Brother Chad, rising. "Begging your pardon, Reverend Father and Brethren, if I am speaking too soon, but I cannot believe that you seriously consider closing us down. We're just beginning to get on well with the authorities, and we've a regular lot of communicants now. We began as just a Club, but we're something more than a Club now. We're bringing men to Our Lord, Brethren. You will do a great wrong if you let those poor souls think that for the sake of your own comfort you are ready to forsake them. Forgive me, Reverend Father. Forgive me, dear Brethren, if I have said too much and spoken uncharitably."

"He has not spoken uncharitably enough," Brother Athanasius shouted, rising to his feet, and as he did so unconsciously assuming the attitude of a boxer. "If I'd been here last year, I should have spoken much more uncharitably. I did not join this Order to sit about playing with vestments. I wanted to bring soldiers to God. If this Order is to be turned into a kind of male nunnery, I'm off tomorrow. I'm boiling over, that's what I am, boiling over. If we can't afford to do what we should be doing, we can't afford to build gatehouses, and lay out flower-beds, and sit giggling in tin cloisters. It's the limit, that's what it is, the limit."

Brother Athanasius stood there flushed with defiance, until the Father Superior told him to sit down and not make a fool of himself, a command which, notwithstanding that the feeling of the Chapter had been so far entirely against the head of the Order, such was the Father Superior's authority, Brother Athanasius immediately obeyed.

Brother Dominic now rose to try, as he said, to bring an atmosphere of reasonableness into the discussion.

"I do not think that I can be accused of inconsistency," he pointed out smoothly, "when we look back to our general Chapter of a year ago. Whatever my personal feelings were about closing the Sandgate priory, I recognized at once that the Reverend Father was right. There is really no doubt that we must be strong at the roots before we try to grow into a tall tree. However flourishing the branches, they will wither if the roots are not fed. The Reverend Father has no desire, as I understand him, to abandon the activity of the Order. He is merely anxious to establish us on a firm basis. The Reverend Brother said that we should make any sacrifice to maintain the Aldershot house. I have no desire to accuse the Reverend Brother of inconsistency, but I would ask him if he is willing to give up the farm, which, as you know, has cost so far a great deal more than we could afford. But of course the Reverend Brother would give up the farm. At the same time, we do not want him to give it up. We realize that under his capable guidance that farm will presently be a source of profit. Therefore, I beg the Reverend Brother to understand that I am making a purely rhetorical point when I ask him if he is prepared to give up the farm. I repeat, we do not want the farm given up.

"Another point which I feel has been missed. In giving up Aldershot, we are not giving up active work entirely. We have a good deal of active work here. We have our guest-house for casuals, and we are always ready to feed, clothe, and shelter any old soldiers who come to us. We are still young as an Order. We have only four professed monks, including the Reverend Father. We want to have more than that before we can consider ourselves established. I for one should hesitate to take my final vows until I had spent a long time in strict religious preparation, which in the hurry and scurry of active work is impossible. We have listened to a couple of violent speeches, or at any rate to one violent speech by a brother who was for a year in close touch with myself. I appeal to him not to drag the discussion down to the level of lay politics. We are free, we novices, to leave tomorrow. Let us remember that, and do not let us take advantage of our freedom to impart to this Mother House of ours the atmosphere of the world to which we may return when we will.

"And let us remember when we oppose the judgment of the Reverend Father that we are exalting ourselves without reason. Let us remember that it is he who by his eloquence and by his devotion and by his endurance and by his personality, has given us this wonderful house. Are we to turn round and say to him who has worked so hard for us that we do not want his gifts, that we are such wonderful fishers of men that we can be independent of him? Oh, my dear Brethren, let me beg you to vote in favour of abandoning all our dependencies until we are ourselves no longer dependent on the Reverend Father's eloquence and devotion and endurance and personality. God has blessed us infinitely. Are we to fling those blessings in His face?"

Brother Dominic sat down; after him in succession Brother Raymond, Brother Dunstan, Brother Lawrence, Brother Jerome, Brother Nicholas, and Brother Augustine spoke in support of the Father Superior. Brother Giles refused to speak, and though Mark's heart was thundering in his mouth with unuttered eloquence, at the moment he should rise he could not find a word, and he indicated with a sign that like Brother Giles, he had nothing to say.

"The voting will be by ballot," the Reverend Father announced. "It is proposed to give up the Priory at Aldershot. Let those brethren who agree write Yes on a strip of paper. Let those who disagree write No."

All knelt in silent prayer before they inscribed their will; after which they advanced one by one to the ballot-box, into which under the eyes of a large crucifix they dropped their papers. The Father Superior did not vote. Brother Simon, who was still a postulant, and not eligible to sit in Chapter, was fetched to count the votes. He was much excited at his task, and when he announced that seven papers were inscribed Yes, that six were inscribed No, and that one paper was blank, his teeth were chattering.

"One paper blank?" somebody repeated.

"Yes, really," said Brother Simon. "I looked everywhere, and there's not a mark on it."

All turned involuntarily toward Mark, whose paper in fact it was, although he gave no sign of being conscious of the ownership.

"In a General Chapter of the Order of St. George, held upon the Vigil of the Epiphany of our Lord Jesus Christ, in the year of Grace, 1903, it was resolved to close the Priory of the Order in the town of Aldershot."

The Reverend Father, having invoked the Holy Trinity, declared the Chapter dissolved.

CHAPTER XXVIII

DIVISION

Mark was vexed with himself for evading the responsibility of recording his opinion. His vote would not have changed the direction of the policy; but if he had voted against giving up the house at Aldershot, the Father Superior would have had to record the casting vote in favour of his own proposal, and whatever praise or blame was ultimately awarded to the decision would have belonged to him alone, who as head of the Order was best able to bear it. Mark's whole sympathy had been on the side of Brother George, and as one who had known at first hand the work in Aldershot, he did feel that it ought not to be abandoned so easily. Then when Brother Athanasius was speaking, Mark, in his embarrassment at such violence of manner and tone, picked up a volume lying on the table by his elbow that by reading he might avoid the eyes of his brethren until Brother Athanasius had ceased to shout. It was the Rule of St. Benedict which, with a print of Fra Angelico's Crucifixion and an image of St. George, was all the decoration allowed to the bare Chapter Room, and the page at which Mark opened the leather-bound volume was headed: DE PRAEPOSITO MONASTERII.

> *'It happens too often that through the appointment of the Prior grave scandals arise in monasteries, since some there be who, puffed up with a malignant spirit of pride, imagining themselves to be second Abbots, and assuming unto themselves a tyrannous authority, encourage scandals and create dissensions in the community . . .*
>
> *'Hence envy is excited, strife, evil-speaking, jealousy, discord, confusion; and while the Abbot and the Prior run counter to each*

other, by such dissension their souls must of necessity be imperilled; and those who are under them, when they take sides, are travelling on the road to perdition...

"On this account we apprehend that it is expedient for the preservation of peace and good-will that the management of his monastery should be left to the discretion of the Abbot...

"Let the Prior carry out with reverence whatever shall be enjoined upon him by his Abbot, doing nothing against the Abbot's will, nor against his orders..."

Mark could not be otherwise than impressed by what he read.

Ii qui sub ipsis sunt, dum adulantur partibus, eunt in perditionem... Nihil contra Abbatis voluntatem faciens...

Mark looked up at the figure of St. Benedict standing in that holy group at the foot of the Cross.

Ideoque nos proevidemus expedire, propter pacis caritatisque custodiam, in Abbatis pendere arbitrio ordinationem monasterii sui...

St. Benedict had more than apprehended; he had actually foreseen that the Abbot ought to manage his own monastery. It was as if centuries ago, in the cave at Subiaco, he had heard that strident voice of Brother Athanasius in this matchboarded Chapter-room, as if he had beheld Brother Dominic, while apparently he was striving to persuade his brethren to accept the Father Superior's advice, nevertheless taking sides, and thereby travelling along the road that leads toward destruction. This was the thought that paralyzed Mark's tongue when it was his turn to speak, and this was why he would not commit himself to an opinion. Afterward, his neutrality appeared to him a weak compromise, and he regretted that he had not definitely allied himself with one party or the other.

The announcement in *The Dragon* that the Order had been compelled to give up the Aldershot house produced a large sum of sympathetic contributions; and when the Father Superior came back just before Lent, he convened another Chapter, at which he told the Community that it was imperative to establish a priory in London before they tried to reopen any houses elsewhere. His argument was cogent, and once again there was the appearance of unanimity among the Brethren, who all approved of the proposal. It had always been the custom of Father Burrowes to preach his hardest during Lent, because during that season of self-denial he was able to raise more money than at any other time, but until now he had never failed to be at the Abbey at the beginning of Passion Week, nor to remain there until Easter was over.

The Feast of St. Benedict fell upon the Saturday before the fifth Sunday in Lent, and the Father Superior, who had travelled down from the North in order to be present, announced that he considered it would be prudent, so freely was the money flowing in, not to give up preaching this year during Passion Week and Holy Week. Naturally, he did not intend to leave the Community without a priest at such a season, and he had made arrangements with the Reverend Andrew Hett to act as chaplain until he could come back into residence himself.

Brother Raymond and Brother Augustine were particularly thrilled by the prospect of enjoying the ministrations of Andrew Hett, less perhaps because they would otherwise be debarred from their Easter duties than because they looked forward to services and ceremonies of which they felt they had been robbed by the austere Anglicanism of Brother George.

"Andrew Hett is famous," declared Brother Raymond at the pitch of exultation. "It was he who told the Bishop of Ipswich that if the Bishop made him give up Benediction he would give up singing Morning and Evening Prayer."

"That must have upset the Bishop," said Mark. "I suppose he resigned his bishopric."

"I should have thought that you, Brother Mark, would have been the last one to take the part of a bishop when he persecutes a Catholic priest!"

"I'm not taking the part of the Bishop," Mark replied. "But I think it was a silly remark for a curate to make. It merely put him in the wrong, and gave the Bishop an opportunity to score."

The Prior had questioned the policy of engaging Andrew Hett as Chaplain, even for so brief a period as a month. He argued that, inasmuch as the Bishop of Silchester had twice refused to licence him to parishes in the diocese, it would prejudice the Bishop against the Order of St. George, and might lead to his inhibiting the Father Superior later on, should an excuse present itself.

"Nonsense, my dear Brother George," said the Reverend Father. "He won't know anything about it officially, and in any case ours is a private oratory, where refusals to licence and episcopal inhibitions have no effect."

"That's not my point," argued Brother George. "My point is that any communication with a notorious ecclesiastical outlaw like this fellow Hett is liable to react unfavourably upon us. Why can't we get down somebody else? There must be a number of unemployed elderly priests who would be glad of the holiday."

"I'm afraid that I've offered Hett the job now, so let us make up our minds to be content."

Mark, who was doing secretarial work for the Reverend Father, happened to be present during this conversation, which distressed him, because it showed him that the Prior was still at variance with the Abbot, a state of affairs that was ultimately bound to be disastrous for the Community. He withdrew almost immediately on some excuse to the Superior's inner room, whence he intended to go downstairs to the Porter's Lodge until the Prior was gone. Unfortunately, the door of the inner room was locked, and before he could explain what had happened, a conversation had begun which he could not help overhearing, but which he dreaded to interrupt.

"I'm afraid, dear Brother George," the Reverend Father was saying, "I'm very much afraid that you are beginning to think I have outlived my usefulness as Superior of the Order."

"I've never suggested that," Brother George replied angrily.

"You may not have meant to give that impression, but certainly that is what you have succeeded in making me feel personally," said the Superior.

"I have been associated with you long enough to be entitled to express my opinion in private."

"In private, yes. But are you always careful only to do so in private? I'm not complaining. My only desire is the prosperity and health of the Order. Next Christmas I am ready to resign, and let the brethren elect another Superior-general."

"That's talking nonsense," said the Prior. "You know as well as I do that nobody else except you could possibly be Superior. But recently I happen to have had a better opportunity than you to criticize our Mother House, and frankly I'm not satisfied with the men we have. Few of them will be any use to us. Birinus, Anselm, Giles, Chad, Athanasius if properly suppressed, Mark, these in varying degrees, have something in them, but look at the others! Dominic, ambitious and sly, Jerome, a pompous prig, Dunstan, a nincompoop, Raymond, a milliner, Nicholas, a—well, you know what I think Nicholas is, Augustine, another nincompoop, Lawrence, still at Sunday School, and poor Simon, a clown. I've had a dozen probationers through my hands, and not one of them was as good as what we've got. I'm afraid I'm less hopeful of the future than I was in Canada."

"I notice, dear Brother George," said the Father Superior, "that you are prejudiced in favour of the brethren who follow your lead with a certain amount of enthusiasm. That is very natural. But I'm not so pessimistic about the others as you are. Perhaps you feel that I am forgetting how much the Order owes to your generosity in the past. Believe me, I have forgotten nothing. At the same time, you gave your money with your eyes open. You took your vows without being pressed. Don't you think you owe it to yourself, if not to the Order or to me personally, to go through with what you undertook? Your three vows were Chastity, Poverty, and Obedience."

There was no answer from the Prior; a moment later he shut the door behind him, and went downstairs alone. Mark came into the room at once.

"Reverend Father," he said. "I'm sorry to have to tell you that I overheard what you and the Reverend Brother were saying." He went on to explain how this had happened, and why he had not liked to make his presence known.

"You thought the Reverend Brother would not bear the mortification with as much fortitude as myself?" the Father Superior suggested with a faint smile.

It struck Mark how true this was, and he looked in astonishment at Father Burrowes, who had offered him the key to his action.

"Well, we must forget what we heard, my son," said the Father Superior. "Sit down, and let's finish off these letters."

An hour's work was done, at the end of which the Reverend Father asked Mark if his had been the blank paper when the votes were counted in Chapter, and when Mark admitted that it had been, he pressed him for the reason of his neutrality.

"I'm not sure that it oughtn't to be called indecision," said Mark. "I was personally interested in the keeping on of Aldershot, because I had worked there."

"Then why not have voted for doing so?" the Superior asked, in accents that were devoid of the least grudge against Mark for disagreeing with himself.

"I tried to get rid of my personal opinion," Mark explained. "I tried to look at the question strictly from the standpoint of the member of a community. As such I felt that the Reverend Brother was wrong to run counter to his Superior. At the same time, if you'll forgive me for saying so, I felt that you were wrong to give up Aldershot. I simply could not arrive at a decision between the two opinions."

"I do not blame you, my son, for your scrupulous cast of mind. Only beware of letting it chill your enthusiasm. Satan may avail himself of it one day, and attack your faith. Solomon was just. Our Blessed Lord, by our cowardly standards, was unjust. Remembering the Gadarene swine, the barren fig-tree, the parable of the wedding-guest without a garment, Martha and Mary..."

"Martha and Mary!" interrupted Mark. "Why, that was really the point at issue. And the ointment that might have been sold for the benefit of the poor. Yes, Judas would have voted with the Reverend Brother."

"And Pontius Pilate would have remained neutral," added Father Burrowes, his blue eyes glittering with delight at the effect upon Mark of his words.

But when Mark was walking back to the Abbey down the winding drive among the hazels, he wished that he and not the Reverend Father had used that illustration. However, useless regrets for his indecision in the matter of the priory at Aldershot were soon obliterated by a new cause of division, which was the arrival of the Reverend Andrew Hett on the Vigil of the Annunciation, just in time to sing first Vespers.

It fell to Mark's lot to entertain the new chaplain that evening, because Brother Jerome who had become guest-master when

Brother Anselm took his place as cellarer was in the infirmary. Mark was scarcely prepared for the kind of personality that Hett's proved to be. He had grown accustomed during his time at the Abbey to look down upon the protagonists of ecclesiastical battles, so little else did any of the guests who visited them want to discuss, so much awe was lavished upon them by Brother Raymond and Brother Augustine. It did not strike Mark that the fight at St. Agnes' might appear to the large majority of people as much a foolish squabble over trifles, a cherishing of the letter rather than the spirit of Christian worship, as the dispute between Mr. So-and-so and the Bishop of Somewhere-or-other in regard to his use of the Litany of the Saints in solemn procession on high days and holy days.

Andrew Hett revived in Mark his admiration of the bigot, which would have been a dangerous thing to lose in one's early twenties. The chaplain was a young man of perhaps thirty-five, tall, raw-boned, sandy-haired, with a complexion of extreme pallor. His light-blue eyes were very red round the rims, and what eyebrows he possessed slanted up at a diabolic angle. His voice was harsh, high, and rasping as a guinea fowl's. When Mark brought him his supper, Hett asked him several questions about the Abbey time-table, and then said abruptly:

"The ugliness of this place must be soul-destroying."

Mark looked at the Guest-chamber with new eyes. There was such a force of assertion in Hett's tone that he could not contradict him, and indeed it certainly was ugly.

"Nobody can live with matchboarded walls and ceilings and not suffer for it," Hett went on. "Why didn't you buy an old tithe barn and live in that? It's an insult to Almighty God to worship Him in such surroundings."

"This is only a beginning," Mark pointed out.

"A very bad beginning," Hett growled. "Such brutalizing ugliness would be inexcusable if you were leading an active life. But I gather that you claim to be contemplative here. I've been reading your ridiculous monthly paper *The Dragon*. Full of sentimental bosh about bringing back the glories of monasticism to England. Tintern was not built of tin. How can you contemplate Almighty God here? It's not possible. What Divine purpose is served by collecting men under hundreds of square feet of corrugated iron? I'm astonished at Charles Horner. I thought he knew better than to encourage this kind of abomination."

There was only one answer to make to Hett, which was that the religious life of the Community did not depend upon any externals, least of all upon its lodging; but when Mark tried to frame this answer, his lips would not utter the words. In that moment he knew that it was time for him to leave Malford and prepare himself to be a priest elsewhere, and otherwise than by what the Rector had stigmatized as the pseudo-monastic life.

Mark wondered when he had left the chaplain to his ferocious meditations what would have been the effect of that diatribe upon some of his brethren. He smiled to himself, as he sat over his solitary supper in the Refectory, to picture the various expressions he could imagine upon their faces when they came hotfoot from the Guest-chamber with the news of what manner of priest was in their midst. And while he was sipping his bowl of pea-soup, he looked up at the image of St. George and perceived that the dragon's expression bore a distinct resemblance to that of the Reverend Andrew Hett. That night it seemed to Mark, in one of those waking trances that occur like dreams between one disturbed sleep and another, that the presence of the chaplain was shaking the flimsy foundations of the Abbey with such ruthlessness that the whole structure must soon collapse.

"It's only the wind," he murmured, with that half of his mind which was awake. "March is going out like a dragon."

After Mass next day, when Mark was giving the chaplain his breakfast, the latter asked who kept the key of the tabernacle.

"Brother Birinus, I expect. He is the sacristan."

"It ought to have been given to me before Mass. Please go and ask for it," requested the chaplain.

Mark found Brother Birinus in the Sacristy, putting away the white vestments in the press. When Mark gave him the chaplain's message, Brother Birinus told him that the Reverend Brother had the key.

"What does he want the key for?" asked Brother George when Mark had repeated to him the chaplain's request.

"He probably wishes to change the Host," Mark suggested.

"There is no need to do that. And I don't believe that is the reason. I believe he wants to have Benediction. He's not going to have Benediction here."

Mark felt that it was not his place to argue with the Reverend Brother, and he merely asked him what reply he was to give to the chaplain.

"Tell him that the key of the Tabernacle is kept by me while the Reverend Father is away, and that I regret I cannot give it to him."

The priest's eyes blazed with anger when Mark returned without the key.

"Who is the Reverend Brother?" he rasped.

"Brother George."

"Yes, but what is he? Apothecary, tailor, ploughboy, what?"

"Brother George is the Prior."

"Well, please tell the Prior that I should like to speak to him instantly."

When Mark found Brother George he had already doffed his habit, and was dressed in his farmer's clothes to go working on the land.

"I'll speak to Mr. Hett before Sext. Meanwhile, you can assure him that the key of the Tabernacle is perfectly safe. I wear it round my neck."

Brother George pulled open his shirt, and showed Mark the golden key hanging from a cord.

On receiving the Prior's message, the chaplain asked for a railway time-table.

"I see there is a fast train at 10.30. Please order the trap."

"You're not going to leave us?" Mark exclaimed.

"Do you suppose, Brother Mark, that no bishop in the Establishment will receive me in his diocese because I am accustomed to give way? I should not have asked for the key of the Tabernacle unless I thought that it was my duty to ask for it. I cannot take it from the Reverend Brother's neck. I will not stay here without its being given up to me. Please order the trap in time to catch the 10.30 train."

"Surely you will see the Reverend Brother first," Mark urged. "I should have made it clear to you that he is out in the fields, and that all the work of the farm falls upon his shoulders. It cannot make any difference whether you have the key now or before Sext. And I'm sure the Reverend Brother will see your point of view when you put it to him."

"I am not going to argue about the custody of God," said the chaplain. "I should consider such an argument blasphemy, and I consider the Prior's action in refusing to give up the key sacrilege. Please order the trap."

"But if you sent a telegram to the Reverend Father . . . Brother Dominic will know where he is . . . I'm sure that the Reverend Father will put it right with Brother George, and that he will at once give you the key."

"I was summoned here as a priest," said the chaplain. "If the amateur monk left in charge of this monastery does not understand the prerogatives of my priesthood, I am not concerned to teach him except directly."

"Well, will you wait until I've found the Reverend Brother and told him that you intend to leave us unless he gives you the key?" Mark begged, in despair at the prospect of what the chaplain's departure would mean to a Community already too much divided against itself.

"It is not one of my prerogatives to threaten the prior of a monastery, even if he is an amateur," said the chaplain. "From the moment that Brother George refuses to recognize my position, I cease to hold that position. Please order the trap."

"You won't have to leave till half-past nine," said Mark, who had made up his mind to wrestle with Brother George on his own initiative, and if possible to persuade him to surrender the key to the chaplain of his own accord. With this object he hurried out, to find Brother George ploughing that stony ground by the fir-trees. He was looking ruefully at a broken share when Mark approached him.

"Two since I started," he commented.

But he was breaking more precious things than shares, thought Mark, if he could but understand.

"Let the fellow go," said Brother George coldly, when Mark had related his interview with the chaplain.

"But, Reverend Brother, if he goes we shall have no priest for Easter."

"We shall be better off with no priest than with a fellow like that."

"Reverend Brother," said Mark miserably, "I have no right to remonstrate with you, I know. But I must say something. You are making a mistake. You will break up the Community. I am not speaking on my own account now, because I have already made up my mind to leave, and get ordained. But the others! They're not all strong like you. They really are not. If they feel that they have been deprived of their Easter Communion by you . . . and have you the right to deprive them? After all, Father Hett has reason on his side. He is entitled to keep the key of the Tabernacle. If he wishes to hold Benediction, you can forbid him, or at least you can forbid the brethren to attend. But the key of the Tabernacle belongs to him, if he says Mass there. Please forgive me for speaking like this, but I love you and respect you, and I cannot bear to see you put yourself in the wrong."

The Prior patted Mark on the shoulder.

"Cheer up, Brother," he said. "You mustn't mind if I think that I know better than you what is good for the Community. I have had a longer time to learn, you must remember. And so you're going to leave us?"

"Yes, but I don't want to talk about that now," Mark said.

"Nor do I," said Brother George. "I want to get on with my ploughing."

Mark saw that it was as useless to argue with him as attempt to persuade the chaplain to stay. He turned sadly away, and walked back with heavy steps towards the Abbey. Overhead, the larks, rising and falling upon their fountains of song, seemed to mock the way men worshipped Almighty God.

CHAPTER XXIX

SUBTRACTION

Mark had not spent a more unhappy Easter since the days of Haverton House. He was oppressed by the sense of excommunication that brooded over the Abbey, and on the Saturday of Passion Week the versicles and responses of the proper Compline had a dreadful irony.

V. O King most Blessed, govern Thy servants in the right way.
R. Among Thy Saints, O King most Blessed.
V. By holy fasts to amend our sinful lives.
R. O King most Blessed, govern Thy Saints in the right way.
V. To duly keep Thy Paschal Feast.
R. Among Thy Saints, O King most Blessed.

"Brother Mark," said Brother Augustine, on the morning of Palm Sunday, "*did* you notice that ghastly split infinitive in the last versicle at Compline? *To duly keep.* I can't think why we don't say the Office in Latin."

Mark felt inclined to tell Brother Augustine that if nothing more vital than an infinitive was split during this holy season, the Community might have cause to congratulate itself. Here now was Brother Birinus throwing away as useless the bundle of palms that lacked the blessing of a priest, throwing them away like dead flowers.

Sir Charles Horner, who had been in town, arrived at the Abbey on the Tuesday, and announced that he was going to spend Holy Week with the Community.

323

"We have no chaplain," Mark told him.

"No chaplain!" Sir Charles exclaimed. "But I understood that Andrew Hett had undertaken the job while Father Burrowes was away."

Mark did not think that it was his duty to enlighten Sir Charles upon the dispute between Brother George and the chaplain. However, it was not long before he found out what had occurred from the Prior's own lips and came fuming back to the Guest-chamber.

"I consider the whole state of affairs most unsatisfactory," he said. "I really thought that when Brother George took charge here the Abbey would be better managed."

"Please, Sir Charles," Mark begged, "you make it very uncomfortable for me when you talk like that about the Reverend Brother before me."

"Yes, but I must give my opinion. I have a right to criticize when I am the person who is responsible for the Abbey's existence here. It's all very fine for Brother George to ask me to notify Bazely at Wivelrod that the brethren wish to go to their Easter duties in his church. Bazely is a very timid man. I've already driven him into doing more than he really likes, and my presence in his church doesn't alarm the parishioners. In fact, they rather like it. But they won't like to see the church full of monks on Easter morning. They'll be more suspicious than ever of what they call poor Bazely's innovations. It's not fair to administer such a shock to a remote country parish like Wivelrod, especially when they're just beginning to get used to the vestments I gave them. It seems to me that you've deliberately driven Andrew Hett away from the Abbey, and I don't see why poor Bazely should be made to suffer. How many monks are you now? Fifteen? Why, fifteen bulls in Wivelrod church would create less dismay!"

Sir Charles's protest on behalf of the Vicar of Wivelrod was effective, for the Prior announced that after all he had decided that it was the duty of the Community to observe Easter within the Abbey gates. The Reverend Father would return on Easter Tuesday, and their Easter duties would be accomplished within the Octave. Withal, it was a gloomy Easter for the brethren, and when they began the first Vespers with the quadruple Alleluia, it seemed as if they were still chanting the sorrowful antiphons of Good Friday.

> *My spirit is vexed within Me: and My heart within Me is desolate.*
>
> *Is it nothing to you, all ye that pass by: behold and see if there be any sorrow like unto My sorrow, which is done unto Me.*
>
> *What are these wounds in Thy Hands: Those with which I was wounded in the house of My friends.*

Nor was there rejoicing in the Community when at Lauds of Easter Day they chanted:

V. In Thy Resurrection, O Christ.
R. Let Heaven and earth rejoice, Alleluia.

Nor when at Prime and Terce and Sext and None they chanted:

> *This is the day which the Lord hath made; we will rejoice and be glad in it.*

And when at the second Vespers the Brethren declared:

V. Christ our Passover is sacrificed for us, therefore let us keep the Feast.
R. Not with the old leaven, nor with the leaven of malice and wickedness; but with the unleavened Bread of sincerity and truth. Alleluia.

scarcely could they who chanted the versicle challenge with their eyes those who hung down their heads when they gave the response.

* * * * *

The hour of recreation before Compline, which upon great Feasts was wont to be so glad, lay heavily upon the brethren that night, so that Mark could not bear to sit in the Cloister; there being no guests in the Abbey for his attention, he sat in the library and wrote to the Rector.

The Abbey,
Malford, Surrey.
Easter Sunday.

My dear Rector,

I should have written before to wish you all a happy Easter, but I've been making up my mind during the last fortnight to leave the Order, and I did not want to write until my mind was made up. That feat is now achieved. I shall stay here until St. George's Day, and then the next day, which will be St. Mark's Eve, I shall come home to spend my birthday with you. I do not regret the year and six months that I have spent at Malford and Aldershot, because during that time, if I have decided not to be a monk, I am none the less determined to be a priest. I shall be 23 this birthday, and I hope that I shall find a Bishop to ordain me next year and a Theological College to accept responsibility for my training and a beneficed priest to give me a title. I will give you a full account of myself when we meet at the end of the month; but in this letter, written in sad circumstances, I want to tell you that I have learnt with the soul what I have long spoken with the lips—the need of God. I expect you will tell me that I ought to have learnt that lesson long ago upon that Whit-Sunday morning in Meade Cantorum church. But I think I was granted then by God to desire Him with my heart. I was scarcely old enough to realize that I needed Him with my soul. "You're not so old now," I hear you say with a smile. But in a place like this one learns almost more than one would learn in the world in the time. One beholds human nature very intimately. I know more about my fellow-men from association with two or three dozen people here than I learnt at St. Agnes' from association with two or three hundred. This much at least my pseudo-monasticism has taught me.

We have passed through a sad time lately at the Abbey, and I feel that for the Community sorrows are in store. You know from my letters that there have been divisions, and you know how hard I have found it to decide which party I ought to follow. But of course the truth is that from the moment one feels the inclination to side with a party in a community it is time to leave that community. Owing to an unfortunate disagreement between Brother George and the Reverend Andrew Hett, who came down to act as chaplain during the absence of the Reverend Father, Andrew Hett felt obliged to leave us. The consequence is we have had no Mass this Easter, and thus I have learned with my soul to need God. I cannot describe to you the torment of deprivation which I personally feel, a torment that is made worse by the consciousness that all my brethren will go to their cells tonight needing God and not finding Him, because they like myself are involved in an earthly quarrel, so that we are incapable of opening our hearts to God this night. You may say that if we were in such a state we should have had no right to make our Easter Communion. But that surely is what Our Blessed Lord can do for us with His Body and Blood. I have been realizing that all this Holy Week. I have felt as I have never felt before the consciousness of sinning against Him. There has not been an antiphon, not a versicle nor a response, that has not stabbed me with a consciousness of my sin against His Divine Love.

"What are these wounds in Thy Hands: Those with which I was wounded in the house of My friends."

But if on Easter eve we could have confessed our sins against His Love, and if this morning we could have partaken of Him, He would have been with us, and our hearts would have been fit for the presence of God. We should have been freed from this spirit of strife, we should have come together in Jesus Christ. We should have seen how to live "with the unleavened Bread of sincerity and truth." God would have revealed His Will, and we, submitting our Order to His Will, should have ceased to think for ourselves, to judge our brethren, to criticize our seniors, to suspect that brother of personal ambition, this brother of toadyism. The Community is being devoured by the Dragon and, unless St. George comes to the rescue of his Order on Thursday week, it will perish. Perhaps I have not much faith in St. George. He has always seemed to me an unreal, fairy-tale sort of a saint. I have more faith in St. Benedict and his Holy Rule. But I have no vocation for the contemplative life. I don't feel that my prayers are good enough to save my own soul, let alone the souls of others. I *must* give Jesus Christ to my fellow-men in the Blessed Sacrament. I long to be a priest for that service. I don't feel that I want by my own efforts to make people better, or to relieve poverty, or to thunder against sin, or to preach them up to and through Heaven's gates. I want to give them the Blessed Sacrament, because I know that nothing else will be the slightest use to them. I know it more positively tonight than I have ever known it, because as I sit here writing to you I am starved. God has given me the grace to understand why I am starved. It is my duty to bring Our Lord to souls who do not know why they are starved. And if after nearly two years of Malford this passion to bring the Sacraments to human beings consumes me like a fire, then I have not wasted my time, and I can look you in the face and ask for your blessing upon my determination to be a priest.

Your ever affectionate

Mark.

When Mark had written this letter, and thus put into words what had hitherto been a more or less nebulous intention, and when in addition to that he had affixed a date to the carrying out of his intention, he felt comparatively at ease. He wasted no time in letting the Father Superior know that he was going to leave; in fact he told him after he had confessed to him before making his Communion on Easter Thursday.

"I'm sorry to lose you, my dear boy," said Father Burrowes. "Very sorry. We are just going to open a priory in London, though that is a secret for the moment, please. I shall make the announcement at the Easter Chapter. Yes, some kind friends have given us a house in Soho. Splendidly central, which is important for our work. I had planned that you would be one of the brethren chosen to go there."

"It's very kind of you, Reverend Father," said Mark. "But I'm sure that you understand my anxiety not to lose any time, now that I feel perfectly convinced that I want to be a priest."

"I had my doubts about you when you first came to us. Let me see, it was nearly two years ago, wasn't it? How time flies! Yes, I had my doubts about you. But I was wrong. You seem to possess a real fixity of purpose. I remember that you told me then that you were not sure you wanted to be a monk. Rare candour! I could have professed a hundred monks, had I been willing to profess them within ten minutes of their first coming to see me."

The Father Superior gave Mark his blessing and dismissed him. Nothing had been said about the dispute between the Prior and the Chaplain, and Mark began to wonder if Father Burrowes thought the results of it would tell more surely in favour of his own influence if he did not allude to it nor make any attempt to adjudicate upon the point at issue. Now that he was leaving Malford in little more than a week, Mark felt that he was completely relieved of the necessity of assisting at any conventual legislation, and he would gladly have absented himself from the Easter Chapter, which was held on the Saturday within the Octave, had not Father Burrowes told him that so long as he wore the habit of a novice of the Order he was expected to share in every side of the Community's life.

"Brethren," said the Father Superior, "I have brought you back news that will gladden your hearts, news that will show I you how by the Grace of God your confidence in my judgment was not misplaced. Some kind friends have taken for us the long lease of a splendid house in Soho Square, so that we may have our priory in London, and resume the active work that was abandoned temporarily last Christmas. Not only have these kind friends taken for us this splendid house, but other kind friends have come forward to guarantee the working expenses up to £20 a week. God is indeed good to us, brethren, and when I remember that next Thursday is the Feast of our great Patron Saint, my heart is too full for words. During the last three or four months there have been unhappy differences of opinion in our beloved Order. Do let me entreat you to forget all these in gratitude for God's bountiful mercies. Do let us, with the arrival once more of our patronal festival, resolve to forget our doubts and our hesitations, our timidity and our rashness, our suspicions and our jealousies. I blame myself for much that has happened, because I have been far away from you, dear brethren, in moments of great spiritual distress. But this year I hope by God's mercy to be with you more. I hope that you will never again spend such an Easter as this. I have only one more announcement to make, which is that I have appointed Brother Dominic to be Prior of St. George's Priory, Soho Square, and Brother Chad and Brother Dunstan to work with him for God and our soldiers."

In the morning, Brother Simon, whose duty it was nowadays to knock with the hammer upon the doors of the cells and rouse the brethren from sleep with the customary salutation, went running from the dormitory to the Prior's cell, his hair standing even more on end than it usually did at such an hour.

"Reverend Brother, Reverend Brother," he cried. "I've knocked and knocked on Brother Anselm's door, and I've said 'The Lord be with you' nine times and shouted 'The Lord be with you' twice, but there's no answer, and at last I opened the door, though I know it's against the Rule to open the door of a brother's cell, but I thought he might be dead, and he isn't dead, but he isn't there. He isn't there, Reverend Brother, and he isn't anywhere. He's nowhere, Reverend Brother, and shall I go and ring the fire-alarm?"

Brother George sternly bade Brother Simon be quiet; but when the Brethren sat in choir to sing Lauds and Prime, they saw that Brother Anselm's stall was empty, and those who had heard Brother Simon's clamour feared that something terrible had happened.

After Mass the Community was summoned to the Chapter room to learn from the lips of the Father Superior that Brother Anselm had broken his vows and left the Order. Brother Dunstan, who wore round his neck the nib with which Brother Anselm signed his profession, burst into tears. Brother Dominic looked down his big nose to avoid the glances of his brethren. If Easter Sunday had been gloomy, Low Sunday was gloomier still, and as for the Feast of St. George nobody had the courage to think what that would be like with such a cloud hanging over the Community.

Mark felt that he could not stay even until the patronal festival. If Brother George or Brother Birinus had broken his vows, he could have borne it more easily, for he had not witnessed their profession; fond he might be of the Prior, but he had worked for human souls under the orders of Brother Anselm. He went to Father Burrowes and begged to leave on Monday.

"Brother Athanasius and Brother Chad are leaving tomorrow," said the Father Superior, "Yes, you may go."

Brother Simon drove them to the station. Strange figures they seemed to each other in their lay clothes.

"I've been meaning to go for a long time," said Brother Athanasius, who was now Percy Wade. "And it's my belief that Brother George and Brother Birinus won't stay long."

"I hoped never to go," said Brother Chad, who was now Cecil Masters.

"Then why are you going?" asked the late Brother Athanasius. "I never do anything I don't want to do."

"I think I shall be more help to Brother Anselm than to soldiers in London," said the late Brother Chad.

Mark beamed at him.

"That's just like you, Brother. I am so glad you're going to do that."

The train came in, and they all shook hands with Brother Simon, who had been cheerful throughout the drive, and even now found great difficulty in looking serious.

"You seem very happy, Brother Simon," said Mark.

"Oh, I am very happy, Brother Mark. I should say Mr. Mark. The Reverend Father has told me that I'm to be clothed as a novice on Wednesday. All last week when we sung, '*The Lord is risen indeed, and hath appeared unto Simon*,' I knew something wonderful was going to happen. That's what made me so anxious when Brother Anselm didn't answer my knock."

The train left the station, and the three ex-novices settled themselves to face the world. They were all glad that Brother Simon at least was happy amid so much unhappiness.

CHAPTER XXX

THE NEW BISHOP OF SILCHESTER

The Rector of Wych thought that Mark's wisest plan if he wished to be ordained was to write and ask the Bishop of Silchester for an interview.

"The Bishop of Silchester?" Mark exclaimed. "But he's the last bishop I should expect to help me."

"On the contrary," said the Rector, "you have lived in his diocese for more than five years, and if you repair to another bishop, he will certainly wonder why you didn't go first to the Bishop of Silchester."

"But I don't suppose that the Bishop of Silchester is likely to help me," Mark objected. "He wasn't so much enamoured of Rowley as all that, and I don't gather that he has much affection or admiration for Burrowes."

"That's not the point; the point is that you have devoted yourself to the religious life, both informally and formally, in his diocese. You have shown that you possess some capacity for sticking to it, and I fancy that you will find the Bishop less unsympathetic than you expect."

However, Mark was not given an opportunity to put the Bishop of Silchester's good-will to the test, for no sooner had he made up his mind to write to him than the news came that he was seriously ill, so seriously ill that he was not expected to live, which in fact turned out a true prognostication, for on the Feast of St. Philip and St. James the prelate died in his Castle of High Thorpe. He was succeeded by the Bishop of Warwick, much to Mark's pleasure and surprise, for the new Bishop was an old friend of Father Rowley and a High Churchman, one who might lend a kindly ear to Mark's ambition. Father Rowley had been in the United States for nearly two years, where he had been treated with much sympathy and where he had collected enough money to pay off the debt upon the new St. Agnes'. He had arrived home about a week before Mark left Malford, and in answer to Mark he wrote immediately to Dr. Oliphant, the new Bishop of Silchester, to enlist his interest. Early in June Mark received a cordial letter inviting him to visit the Bishop at High Thorpe.

The promotion of Dr. Aylmer Oliphant to the see of Silchester was considered at the time to be an indication that the political party then in power was going mad in preparation for its destruction by the gods. The Press in commenting upon the appointment did not attempt to cast a slur upon the sanctity and spiritual fervour of the new Bishop, but it felt bound to observe that the presence of such a man on the episcopal bench was an indication that the party in power was oblivious of the existence of an enraged electorate already eager to hurl them out of office. At a time when thinking men and women were beginning to turn to the leaders of the National Church for a social policy, a government worn out by eight years of office that included a costly war was so little alive to the signs of the times as to select for promotion a prelate conspicuously identified with the obscurantist tactics of that small but noisy group in the Church of England which arrogated to itself the presumptuous claim to be the Catholic party. Dr. Oliphant's learning was indisputable; his liturgical knowledge was profound; his eloquence in the pulpit was not to be gainsaid; his life, granted his sacerdotal eccentricities, was a noble example to his fellow clergy. But had he shown those qualities of statesmanship, that capacity for moderation, which were so marked a feature of his predecessor's reign? Was he not identified with what might almost be called an unchristian agitation to prosecute the holy, wise, and scholarly Dean of Leicester for appearing to countenance an opinion that the Virgin Birth was not vital to the belief of a Christian? Had he not denounced the Reverend Albert Blundell for heresy, and thereby exhibited himself in active opposition to his late diocesan, the sagacious Bishop of Kidderminster, who had been compelled to express disapproval of his Suffragan's bigotry by appointing the Reverend Albert Blundell to be one of his examining chaplains?

"We view with the gravest apprehension the appointment of Dr. Aylmer Oliphant to the historic see of Silchester," said one great journal. "Such reckless disregard, such contempt we might almost say, for the feelings of the English people demonstrates that the present government has ceased to enjoy the confidence of the electorate. We have for Dr. Oliphant personally nothing but the warmest admiration. We do not venture for one moment to impugn his sincerity. We do not hesitate to affirm most solemnly our disbelief that he is actuated by any but the highest motives in lending his name to persecutions that recall the spirit of the Star Chamber. But in these days when the rapid and relentless march of Scientific Knowledge is devastating the plain of Theological Speculation we owe it to our readers to observe that the appointment of Dr. Aylmer Oliphant to the Bishopric of Silchester must be regarded as an act of intellectual cowardice. Not merely is Dr. Oliphant a notorious extremist in religious matters, one who for the sake of outworn forms and ceremonies is inclined to keep alive the unhappy dissensions that tear asunder our National Church, but he is also what is called a Christian Socialist of the most advanced type, one who by his misreading of the Gospel spreads the unwholesome and perilous doctrine that all men are equal. This is not the time nor the place to break a controversial lance with Dr. Oliphant. We shall content ourselves with registering a solemn protest against the unparagoned cynicism of a Conservative government which thus gambles not merely with its own security, but what is far more unpardonable with the security of the Nation and the welfare of the State."

The subject of this ponderous censure received Mark in the same room where two and a half years ago the late Bishop had decided that the Third Altar in St. Agnes' Church was an intolerable excrescence. Nowadays the room was less imposing, not more imposing indeed than the room of a scholarly priest who had been able to collect a few books and buy such pieces of ancient furniture as consorted with his severe taste. Dr. Oliphant himself, a tall spare man, seeming the taller and more spare in his worn purple cassock, with clean-shaven hawk's face and black bushy eyebrows most conspicuous on account of his grey hair, stood before the empty summer grate, his long lean neck out-thrust, his arms crossed behind his back, like a gigantic and emaciated shadow of Napoleon. Mark felt no embarrassment in genuflecting to salute him; the action was spontaneous and was not dictated by any ritualistic indulgence. Dr. Oliphant, as he might have guessed from the anger with which his appointment had been received, was in outward semblance all that a prelate should be.

"Why do you want to be a priest?" the Bishop asked him abruptly.

"To administer the Sacraments," Mark replied without hesitation.

The Bishop's head and neck wagged up and down in grave approbation.

"Mr. Rowley, as no doubt he has told you, wrote to me about you. And so you've been with the Order of St. George lately? Is it any good?"

Mark was at a loss what to reply to this. His impulse was to say firmly and frankly that it was no good; but after not far short of two years at Malford it would be ungrateful and disloyal to criticize the Order, particularly to the Bishop of the diocese.

"I don't think it is much good yet," Mark said. He felt that he simply could not praise the Order without qualification. "But I expect that when they've learnt how to combine the contemplative with the active side of their religious life they will be splendid. At least, I hope they will."

"What's wrong at present?"

"I don't know that anything's exactly wrong."

Mark paused; but the Bishop was evidently waiting for him to continue, and feeling that this was perhaps the best way to present his own point of view about the life he had chosen for himself he plunged into an account of life at Malford.

"Capital," said the Bishop when the narrative was done. "You have given me a very clear picture of the present state of the Order and incidentally a fairly clear picture of yourself. Well, I'm going to recommend you to Canon Havelock, the Principal of the Theological College here, and if he reports well of you and you can pass the Cambridge Preliminary Theological Examination, I will ordain you at Advent next year, or at any rate, if not in Advent, at Whitsuntide."

"But isn't Silchester Theological College only for graduates?" Mark asked.

"Yes, but I'm going to suggest that Canon Havelock stretches a point in your favour. I can, if you like, write to the Glastonbury people, but in that case you would be out of my diocese where you have spent so much of your time and where I have no doubt you will easily find a beneficed priest to give you a title. Moreover, in the case of a young man like yourself who has been brought up from infancy upon Catholic teaching, I think it is advisable to give you an opportunity of mixing with the moderate man who wishes to take Holy Orders. You can lose nothing by such an association, and it may well happen that you will gain a great deal. Silchester Theological College is eminently moderate. The lecturers are men of real learning, and the Principal is a man whom it would be impertinent for me to praise for his devout and Christian life."

"I hardly know how to thank you, my lord," said Mark.

"Do you not, my son?" said the Bishop with a smile. Then his head and neck wagged up and down. "Thank me by the life you lead as a priest."

"I will try, my lord," Mark promised.

"Of that I am sure. By the way, didn't you come across a priest at St. Agnes' Mission House called Mousley?"

"Oh rather, I remember him well."

"You'll be glad to hear that he has never relapsed since I sent him to Rowley. In fact only last week I had the satisfaction of recommending him to a friend of mine who had a living in his gift."

Mark spent the three months before he went to Silchester at the Rectory where he worked hard at Latin and Greek and the history of the Church. At the end of August he entered Silchester Theological College.

CHAPTER XXXI

SILCHESTER THEOLOGICAL COLLEGE

The theological students of Silchester were housed in a red-brick alley of detached Georgian houses, both ends of which were closed to traffic by double gates of beautifully wrought iron. This alley known as Vicar's Walk had formerly been inhabited by the lay vicars of the Cathedral, whose music was now performed by minor canons.

There were four little houses on either side of the broad pavement, the crevices in which were gay with small rock plants, so infrequent were the footsteps that passed over them. Each house consisted of four rooms and each room held one student. Vicar's Walk led directly into the Close, a large green space surrounded by the houses of dignitaries, from a quiet road lined with elms, which skirted the wall of the Deanery garden and after several twists and turns among the shadows of great Gothic walls found its way downhill into the narrow streets of the small city. One of the houses in the Close had been handed over to the Theological College, the Principal of which usually occupied a Canon's stall in the Cathedral. Here were the lecture-rooms, and here lived Canon Havelock the Principal, Mr. Drakeford the Vice-Principal, Mr. Brewis the Chaplain, and Mr. Moore and Mr. Waters the Lecturers.

There did not seem to be many arduous rules. Probably the most ascetic was one that forbade gentlemen to smoke in the streets of Silchester. There was no early Mass except on Saints' days at eight; but gentlemen were expected, unless prevented by reasonable cause, to attend Matins in the Cathedral before breakfast and Evensong in the College Oratory at seven. A mutilated Compline was delivered at ten, after which gentlemen were requested to retire immediately to their rooms. Academic Dress was to be worn at lectures, and Mark wondered what costume would be designed for him. The lectures took place every morning between nine and one, and every afternoon between five and seven. The Principal lectured on Dogmatic Theology and Old Testament history; the Vice-Principal on the Old and New Testament set books; the Chaplain on Christian worship and Church history; Mr. Moore on Pastoralia and Old Testament Theology; and Mr. Waters on Latin, Greek, and Hebrew.

As against the prevailing Gothic of the mighty Cathedral Vicar's Walk stood out with a simple and fragrant charm of its own, so against the prevailing Gothic of Mark's religious experience life at the Theological College remained in his memory as an unvexed interlude during which flesh and spirit never sought to trouble each other. Perhaps if Mark had not been educated at Haverton House, had not experienced conversion, had not spent those years at Chatsea and Malford, but like his fellow students had gone decorously from public school to University and still more decorously from University to Theological College, he might with his temperament have wondered if this red-brick alley closed to traffic at either end by beautifully wrought iron gates was the best place to prepare a man for the professional service of Jesus Christ.

Sin appeared very remote in that sunny lecture-room where to the sound of cawing rooks the Principal held forth upon the strife between Pelagius and Augustine, when prevenient Grace, operating Grace, co-operating Grace and the *donum perseverantiae* all seemed to depend for their importance so much more upon a good memory than upon the inscrutable favours of Almighty God. Even the Confessions of St. Augustine, which might have shed their own fierce light of Africa upon the dark problem of sin, were scarcely touched upon. Here in this tranquil room St. Augustine lived in quotations from his controversial works, or in discussions whether he had not wrongly translated ἐφ' ᾧ πάντες ἥμαρτου in the Epistle to the Romans by *in quo omnes peccaverunt* instead of like the Pelagians by *propter quod omnes peccaverunt*. The dim echoes of the strife between Semipelagian Marseilles and Augustinian Carthage resounded faintly in Mark's brain; but they only resounded at all, because he knew that without being able to display some ability to convey the impression that he understood the Thirty-Nine

Articles he should never be ordained. Mark wondered what Canon Havelock would have done or said if a woman taken in adultery had been brought into the lecture-room by the beadle. Yet such a supposition was really beside the point, he thought penitently. After all, human beings would soon be degraded to wax-works if they could be lectured upon individually in this tranquil and sunny room to the sound of rooks cawing in the elms beyond the Deanery garden.

Mark made no intimate friendships among his fellows. Perhaps the moderation of their views chilled him into an exceptional reserve, or perhaps they were an unusually dull company that year. Of the thirty-one students, eighteen were from Oxford, twelve from Cambridge, and the thirty-first from Durham. Even he was looked at with a good deal of suspicion. As for Mark, nothing less than God's prevenient grace could explain his presence at Silchester. Naturally, inasmuch as they were going to be clergymen, the greatest charity, the sweetest toleration was shown to Mark's unfortunate lack of advantages; but he was never unaware that intercourse with him involved his companions in an effort, a distinct, a would-be Christlike effort to make the best of him. It was the same kind of effort they would soon be making when as Deacons they sought for the sick, poor, and impotent people of the Parish. Mark might have expected to find among them one or two of whom it might be prophesied that they would go far. But he was unlucky. All the brilliant young candidates for Ordination must have betaken themselves to Cuddesdon or Wells or Lichfield that year.

Of the eighteen graduates from Oxford, half took their religion as a hot bath, the other half as a cold one. Nine resembled the pale young curates of domestic legend, nine the muscular Christian that is for some reason attributed to the example of Charles Kingsley. Of the twelve graduates from Cambridge, six treated religion as a cricket match played before the man in the street with God as umpire, six regarded it as a respectable livelihood for young men with normal brains, social connexions, and weak digestions. The young man from Durham looked upon religion as a more than respectable livelihood for one who had plenty of brains, an excellent digestion, and no social connexions whatever.

Mark wondered if the Bishop of Silchester's design in placing him amid such surroundings was to cure him for ever of moderation. As was his custom when he was puzzled, he wrote to the Rector.

> The Theological College,
> Silchester.
> All Souls, '03.
>
> My dear Rector,
>
> My first impressions have not undergone much change. The young men are as good as gold, but oh dear, the gold is the gold of Mediocritas. The only thing that kindles a mild phosphorescence, a dim luminousness as of a bedside match-tray in the dark, in their eyes is when they hear of somebody's what they call conspicuous moderation. I suppose every deacon carries a bishop's apron in his sponge-bag or an archbishop's crosier among his golf-clubs. But in this lot I simply cannot perceive even an embryonic archdeacon. I rather expected when I came here that I should be up against men of brains and culture. I was looking forward to being trampled on by ruthless logicians. I hoped that latitudinarian opinions were going to make my flesh creep and my hair stand on end. But nothing of the kind. I've always got rather angry when I've read caricatures of curates in books with jokes about goloshes and bath-buns. Yet honestly, half my fellows might easily serve as models to any literary cheapjack of the moment. I'm willing to admit that probably most of them will develop under the pressure of life, but a few are bound to remain what they are. I know we get some eccentrics and hotheads and a few sensual knaves among the Catholic clergy, but we do not get these anæmic creatures. I feel that before I came here I knew nothing about the Church of England. I've been thrown all my life with people who had rich ideas and violent beliefs and passionate sympathies and deplorable hatreds, so that when I come into contact with what I am bound to accept as the typical English parson in the making I am really appalled.
>
> I've been wondering why the Bishop of Silchester told me to come here. Did he really think that the spectacle

of moderation in the moulding was good for me? Did he fancy that I was a young zealot who required putting in his place? Or did he more subtly realize from the account I gave him of Malford that I was in danger of becoming moderate, even luke-warm, even tepid, perhaps even stone-cold? Did he grasp that I must owe something to party as well as mankind, if I was to give up anything worth giving to mankind? But perhaps in my egoism I am attributing much more to his lordship's paternal interest, a keener glance to his episcopal eye, than I have any right to attribute. Perhaps, after all, he merely saw in me a young man who had missed the advantages of Oxford, etc., and wished out of regard for my future to provide me with the best substitute.

Anyway, please don't think that I live in a constant state of criticism with a correspondingly dangerous increase of self-esteem. I really am working hard. I sometimes wonder if the preparation of a "good" theological college is the best preparation for the priesthood. But so long as bishops demand the knowledge they do, it is obvious that this form of preparation will continue. There again though, I daresay if I imagined myself an inspired pianist I should grumble at the amount of scales I was set to practice. I'm not, once I've written down or talked out some of my folly, so very foolish at bottom.

Beyond a slight inclination to flirt with the opinions of most of the great heresiarchs in turn, but only with each one until the next comes along, I'm not having any intellectual adventures. One of the excitements I had imagined beforehand was wrestling with Doubt. But I have no wrestles. Shall I always be spared?

Your ever affectionate,

Mark.

Gradually, as the months went by, either because the students became more mellow in such surroundings or because he himself was achieving a wider tolerance, Mark lost much of his capacity for criticism and learned to recognize in his fellows a simple goodness and sincerity of purpose that almost frightened him when he thought of that great world outside, in the confusion and complexity of which they had pledged themselves to lead souls up to God. He felt how much they missed by not relying rather upon the Sacraments than upon personal holiness and the upright conduct of the individual. They were obsessed with the need of setting a good example and of being able from the pulpit to direct the wandering lamb to the Good Shepherd. Mark scarcely ever argued about his point of view, because he was sure that perception of what the Sacraments could do for human nature must be given by the grace of God, and that the most exhaustive process of inductive logic would not avail in the least to convince somebody on whom the fact had not dawned in a swift and comprehensive inspiration of his inner life. Sometimes indeed Mark would defend himself from attack, as when it was suggested that his reliance upon the Sacraments was only another aspect of Justification by Faith Alone, in which the effect of a momentary conversion was prolonged by mechanical aids to worship.

"But I should prefer my idolatry of the outward form to your idolatry of the outward form," he would maintain.

"What possible idolatry can come from the effect upon a congregation of a good sermon?" they protested.

"I don't claim that a preacher might not bring the whole of his congregation to the feet of God," Mark allowed. "But I must have less faith in human nature than you have, for I cannot believe that any preacher could exercise a permanent effect without the Sacraments. You all know the person who says that the sound of an organ gives him holy thoughts, makes him feel good, as the cant phrase goes? I've no doubt that people who sit under famous preachers get the same kind of sensation Sunday after Sunday. But sooner or later they will be worshipping the outward form—that is to say the words that issue from the preacher's mouth and produce those internal moral rumblings in the pit of the soul which other listeners get from the diapason. Have your organs, have your sermons, have your matins and evensong; but don't put them on the same level as the Blessed Sacrament. The value of that is absolute, and I refuse to consider It from the point of view of pragmatic philosophy."

All would protest that Mark was putting a wrong interpretation upon their argument; what they desired to avoid was the substitution of the Blessed Sacrament for the Person of the Divine Saviour.

"But I believe," Mark argued, "I believe profoundly with the whole of my intellectual, moral, and emotional self that the Blessed Sacrament *is* our Divine Saviour. I maintain that only through the Blessed Sacrament can we hope to form within our own minds the slightest idea of the Person of the Divine Saviour. In the pulpit I would undertake to present fifty human characters as moving as our Lord; but when I am at the Altar I shall actually give Him to those who will take Him. I shall know that I am doing as much for the lowest savage as for the finest product of civilization. All are equal on the altar steps. Elsewhere man remains divided into classes. You may rent the best pew from which to see and hear the preacher; but you cannot rent a stone on which to kneel at your Communion."

Mark rarely indulged in these outbursts. On him too Silchester exerted a mellowing influence, and he gained from his sojourn there much of what he might have carried away from Oxford; he recaptured the charm of that June day when in the shade of the oak-tree he had watched a College cricket match, and conversed with Hathorne the Siltonian who wished to be a priest, but who was killed in the Alps soon after Mark met him.

The bells chimed from early morning until sombre eve; ancient clocks sounded the hour with strikes rusty from long service of time; rooks and white fantail-pigeons spoke with the slow voice of creatures that are lazily content with the slumbrous present and undismayed by the sleepy morrow. In Summer the black-robed dignitaries and white choristers, themselves not more than larger rooks and fantails, passed slowly across the green Close to their dutiful worship. In Winter they battled with the wind like the birds in the sky. In Autumn there was a sound of leaves along the alleys and in the Gothic entries. In Spring there were daisies in the Close, and daffodils nodding among the tombs, and on the grey wall of the Archdeacon's garden a flaming peacock's tail of Japanese quince.

Sometimes Mark was overwhelmed by the tyranny of the past in Silchester; sometimes it seemed that nothing was worth while except at the end of living to have one's effigy in stone upon the walls of the Cathedral, and to rest there for ever with viewless eyes and cold prayerful hands, oneself in harmony at last with all that had gone before.

"Yet this peace is the peace of God," he told himself. "And I who am privileged for a little time to share in it must carry away with me enough to make a treasure of peace in my own heart, so that I can give from that treasure to those who have never known peace."

> *The peace of God, which passeth all understanding, keep your hearts and minds in the knowledge and love of God, and of his Son Jesus Christ our Lord; and the blessing of God Almighty, the Father, the Son, and the Holy Ghost, be amongst you and remain with you always.*

When Mark heard these words sound from the altar far away in the golden glooms of the Cathedral, it seemed to him that the building bowed like a mighty couchant beast and fell asleep in the security of God's presence.

After Mark had been a year at the Theological College he received a letter from the Bishop:

High Thorpe Castle.
Sept. 21, '04.

Dear Lidderdale,

I have heard from Canon Havelock that he considers you are ready to be ordained at Advent, having satisfactorily passed the Cambridge Preliminary Theological Examination. If therefore you succeed in passing my examination early in November, I am willing to ordain you on December 18. It will be necessary of course for you to obtain a title, and I have just heard from Mr. Shuter, the Vicar of St. Luke's, Galton, that he is anxious to make arrangements for a curate. You had better make an appointment, and if I hear favourably from him I will licence you for his church. It has always been the rule in this diocese that non-graduate candidates for Holy Orders should spend at least two years over their theological studies, but I am not disposed to enforce this rule in your case.

Yours very truly,

Aylmer Silton.

This expression of fatherly interest made Mark anxious to show his appreciation of it, and whatever he had thought of St. Luke's, Galton, or of its incumbent he would have done his best to secure the title merely to please the Bishop. Moreover, his money was coming to an end, and another year at the Theological College would have compelled him to borrow from Mr. Ogilvie, a step which he was most anxious to avoid. He found that Galton, which he remembered from the days when he had sent Cyril Pomeroy there to be met by Dorward, was a small county town of some eight or nine thousand inhabitants and that St. Luke's was a new church which had originally been a chapel of ease to the parish church, but which had acquired with the growth of a poor population on the outskirts of the town an independent parochial status of its own. The Reverend Arnold Shuter, who was the first vicar, was at first glance just a nervous bearded man, though Mark soon discovered that he possessed a great deal of spiritual force. He was a widower and lived in the care of a housekeeper who regarded religion as the curse of good cooking. Latterly he had suffered from acute neurasthenia, and three or four of his wealthier parishioners—they were only relatively wealthy—had clubbed together to guarantee the stipend of a curate. Mark was to live at the Vicarage, a detached villa, with pointed windows and a front door like a lychgate, which gave the impression of having been built with what material was left over from building the church.

"You may think that there is not much to do in Galton," said Mr. Shuter when he and Mark were sitting in his study after a round of the parish.

"I hope I didn't suggest that," Mark said quickly.

The Vicar tugged nervously at his beard and blinked at his prospective curate from pale blue eyes.

"You seem so full of life and energy," he went on, half to himself, as though he were wondering if the company of this tall, bright-eyed, hatchet-faced young man might not prove too bracing for his worn-out nerves.

"Indeed I'm glad I do strike you that way," Mark laughed. "After dreaming at Silchester I'd begun to wonder if I hadn't grown rather too much into a type of that sedate and sleepy city."

"But there is plenty of work," Mr. Shuter insisted. "We have the hop-pickers at the end of the summer, and I've tried to run a mission for them. Out in the hop-gardens, you know. And then there's Oaktown."

"Oaktown?" Mark echoed.

"Yes. A queer collection of people who have settled on a derelict farm that was bought up and sold in small plots by a land-speculator. They'll give plenty of scope for your activity. By the way, I hope you're not too extreme. We have to go very slowly here. I manage an early Eucharist every Sunday and Thursday, and of course on Saints' days; but the attendance is not good. We have vestments during the week, but not at the mid-day Celebration."

Mark had not intended to attach himself to what he considered a too indefinite Catholicism; but inasmuch as the Bishop had found him this job he made up his mind to give to it at any rate his deacon's year and his first year as a priest.

"I've been brought up in the vanguard of the Movement," he admitted. "But you can rely on me, sir, to be loyal to your point of view, even if I disagreed with it. I can't pretend to believe much in moderation; but I should always be your curate before anything else, and I hope very much indeed that you will offer me the title."

"You'll find me dull company," Mr. Shuter sighed. "My health has gone all to pieces this last year."

"I shall have a good deal of reading to do for my priest's examination," Mark reminded him. "I shall try not to bother you."

The result of Mark's visit to Galton was that amongst the various testimonials and papers he forwarded two months later to the Bishop's Registrar was the following:

To the Right Reverend Aylmer, Lord Bishop of Silchester.

I, Arnold Shuter, Vicar of St. Luke's, Galton, in the County of Southampton, and your Lordship's Diocese of Silchester, do hereby nominate Mark Lidderdale, to perform the office of Assistant Curate in my Church of St. Luke aforesaid; and do promise to allow him the yearly stipend of £120 to be paid by equal quarterly instalments; And I do hereby state to your Lordship that the said Mark Lidderdale intends to reside in the said Parish in my Vicarage; and that the said Mark Lidderdale does not intend to serve any other Parish as Incumbent or Curate.

Witness my hand this fourteenth day of November; in the year of our Lord, 1904.

Arnold Shuter,

St. Luke's Vicarage,

Galton,

Hants.

I, Arnold Shuter, Incumbent of St. Luke's, Galton, in the County of Southampton, bonâ fide undertake to pay Mark Lidderdale, of the Rectory, Wych-on-the-Wold, in the County of Oxford, the annual sum of one hundred and twenty pounds as a stipend for his services as Curate, and I, Mark Lidderdale, bonâ fide intend to receive the whole of the said stipend. And each of us, Arnold Shuter and Mark Lidderdale, declare that no abatement is to be made out of the said stipend in respect of rent or consideration for the use of the Glebe House; and that I, Arnold Shuter, undertake to pay the same, and I, Mark Lidderdale, intend to receive the same, without any deduction or abatement whatsoever.

Arnold Shuter,

Mark Lidderdale.

CHAPTER XXXII

EMBER DAYS

Mark, having been notified that he had been successful in passing the Bishop's examination for Deacons, was summoned to High Thorpe on Thursday. He travelled down with the other candidates from Silchester on an iron-grey afternoon that threatened snow from the louring North, and in the atmosphere of High Thorpe under the rule of Dr. Oliphant he found more of the spirit of preparation than he would have been likely to find in any other diocese at this date. So many of the preliminaries to Ordination had consisted of filling up forms, signing documents, and answering the questions of the Examining Chaplain that Mark, when he was now verily on the threshold of his new life, reproached himself with having allowed incidental details and petty arrangements to make him for a while oblivious of the overwhelming fact of his having been accepted for the service of God. Luckily at High Thorpe he was granted a day to confront his soul before being harassed again on Ember Saturday with further legal formalities and signing of documents. He was able to spend the whole of Ember Friday in prayer and meditation, in beseeching God to grant him grace to serve Him worthily, strength to fulfil his vows, and that great *donum perseverantiæ* to endure faithful unto death.

"Not everyone that saith unto me, Lord, Lord," Mark remembered in the damasked twilight of the Bishop's Chapel, where he was kneeling. "Let me keep those words in my heart. Not everyone," he repeated aloud. Then perversely as always come volatile and impertinent thoughts when the mind is concentrated on lofty aspirations Mark began to wonder if he had quoted the text correctly. He began to be almost sure that he had not, and on that to torment his brain in trying to recall what was the exact wording of the text he desired to impress upon his heart. "Not everyone that saith unto me, Lord, Lord," he repeated once more aloud.

At that moment the tall figure of the Bishop passed by.

"Do you want me, my son?" he asked kindly.

"I should like to make my confession, reverend father in God," said Mark.

The Bishop beckoned him into the little sacristy, and putting on rochet and purple stole he sat down to hear his penitent.

Mark had few sins of which to accuse himself since he last went to his duties a month ago. However, he did have upon his conscience what he felt was a breach of the Third Commandment in that he had allowed himself to obscure the mighty fact of his approaching ordination by attaching too much importance to and fussing too much about the preliminary formalities.

The Bishop did not seem to think that Mark's soul was in grave peril on that account, and he took the opportunity to warn Mark against an over-scrupulousness that might lead him in his confidence to allow sin to enter into his soul by some unguarded portal which he supposed firmly and for ever secure.

"That is always the danger of a temperament like yours?" he mused. "By all means keep your eyes on the high ground ahead of you; but do not forget that the more intently you look up, the more liable you are to slip on some unnoticed slippery stone in your path. If you abandoned yourself to the formalities that are a necessary preliminary to Ordination, you did wisely. Our Blessed Lord usually gave practical advice, and some of His miracles like the turning of water into wine at Cana were reproofs to carelessness in matters of detail. It was only when people worshipped utility unduly that He went to the other extreme as in His rebuke to Judas over the cruse of ointment."

The Bishop raised his head and gave Mark absolution. When they came out of the sacristy he invited him to come up to his library and have a talk.

"I'm glad that you are going to Galton," he said, wagging his long neck over a crumpet. "I think you'll find your experience in such a parish extraordinarily useful at the beginning of your career. So many young men have an idea that the only way to serve God is to go immediately to a slum. You'll be much more discouraged at Galton than you can imagine. You'll learn there more of the difficulties of a clergyman's life in a year than you could learn in London in a lifetime. Rowley, as no doubt you've heard, has just accepted a slum parish in Shoreditch. Well, he wrote to me the other day and suggested that you should go to him. But I dissented. You'll have an opportunity at Galton to rely upon yourself. You'll begin in the ruck. You'll be one of many who struggle year in year out with an ordinary parish. There won't be any paragraphs about St. Luke's in the Church papers. There won't be any enthusiastic pilgrims. There'll be nothing but the thought of our Blessed Lord to keep you struggling on, only that, only our Blessed Lord Jesus Christ."

The Bishop's head wagged slowly to and fro in the silence that succeeded his words, and Mark pondering them in that silence felt no longer that he was saying "Lord, Lord," but that he had been called to follow and that he was ready without hesitation to follow Him whithersoever He should lead.

The quiet Ember Friday came to an end, and on the Saturday there were more formalities, of which Mark dreaded most the taking of the oath before the Registrar. He had managed with the help of subtle High Church divines to persuade himself that he could swear he assented to the Thirty-nine Articles without perjury. Nevertheless he wished that he was not bound to take that oath, and he was glad that the sense in which the Thirty-nine Articles were to be accepted was left to the discretion of him who took the oath. Of one thing Mark was positive. He was assuredly not assenting to those Thirty-nine Articles that their compilers intended when they framed them. However, when it came to it, Mark affirmed:

"I, Mark Lidderdale, about to be admitted to the Holy Order of Deacons, do solemnly make the following declaration:—I assent to the Thirty-nine Articles of Religion, and to the Book of Common Prayer, and the ordering of Bishops, Priests, and Deacons. I believe the doctrine of the Church of England, as therein set forth, to be agreeable to the Word of God; and in Public Prayer and Administration of the Sacraments I will use the Form in the said Book prescribed, and none other, except so far as shall be ordered by lawful authority.

"I, Mark Lidderdale, about to be admitted to the Holy Order of Deacons, do swear that I will be faithful and bear true Allegiance to His Majesty King Edward, his heirs and successors according to law.

"So help me God."

"But the strange thing is," Mark said to one of his fellow candidates, "nobody asks us to take the oath of allegiance to God."

"We do that when we're baptized," said the other, a serious young man who feared that Mark was being flippant.

"Personally," Mark concluded, "I think the solemn profession of a monk speaks more directly to the soul."

And this was the feeling that Mark had throughout the Ordination of the Deacons notwithstanding that the Bishop of Silchester in cope and mitre was an awe-inspiring figure in his own Chapel. But when Mark heard him say:

Receive the Holy Ghost for the office and work of a Priest in the Church of God,

he was caught up to the Seventh Heaven and prayed that, when a year hence he should be kneeling thus to hear those words uttered to him and to feel upon his head those hands imposed, he should receive the Holy Ghost more worthily than lately he had received authority to execute the office of a Deacon in the Church of God.

Suddenly at the back of the chapel Mark caught sight of Miriam, who must have travelled down from Oxfordshire last night to be present at his Ordination. His mind went back to that Whit-Sunday in Meade Cantorum nearly ten years ago. Miriam's plume of grey hair was no longer visible, for all her hair was grey nowadays; but her face had scarcely altered, and she sat there at this moment with that same expression of austere sweetness which had been shed like a benison upon Mark's dreary boyhood. How dear of Miriam to grace his Ordination, and if only Esther too could have been with him! He knelt down to thank God humbly for His mercies, and of those mercies not least for the Ogilvies' influence upon his life.

Mark could not find Miriam when they came out from the chapel. She must have hurried away to catch some slow Sunday train that would get her back to Wych-on-the-Wold tonight. She could not have known that he had seen her, and when he arrived at the Rectory tomorrow as glossy as a beetle in his new clerical attire, Miriam would listen to his account of the Ordination, and only when he had finished would she murmur how she had been present all the time.

And now there was still the oath of canonical obedience to take before lunch; but luckily that was short. Mark was hungry, since unlike most of the candidates he had not eaten an enormous breakfast that morning.

Snow was falling outside when the young priests and deacons in their new frock coats sat down to lunch; and when they put on their sleek silk hats and hurried away to catch the afternoon train back to Silchester, it was still falling.

"Even nature is putting on a surplice in our honour," Mark laughed to one of his companions, who not feeling quite sure whether Mark was being poetical or profane, decided that he was being flippant, and looked suitably grieved.

It was dusk of that short winter day when Mark reached Silchester, and wandered back in a dream toward Vicar's Walk. Usually on Sunday evenings the streets of the city pattered with numerous footsteps; but tonight the snow deadened every sound, and the peace of God had gone out from the Cathedral to shed itself upon the city.

"It will be Christmas Day in a week," Mark thought, listening to the Sabbath bells muffled by the soft snow-laden air. For the first time it occurred to him that he should probably have to preach next Sunday evening.

And the Word was made flesh, and dwelt among us.

That should be his text, Mark decided; and, passing from the snowy streets, he sat thinking in the golden glooms of the Cathedral about his sermon.

EXPLICIT PRÆLUDIUM

BIBLIOBAZAAR

The essential book market!

Did you know that you can get any of our titles in large print?

Did you know that we have an ever-growing collection of books in many languages?

Order online:
www.bibliobazaar.com

Find all of your favorite classic books!

Stay up to date with the latest government reports!

At BiblioBazaar, we aim to make knowledge more accessible by making thousands of titles available to you- *quickly and affordably*.

Contact us:
BiblioBazaar
PO Box 21206
Charleston, SC 29413

Made in the USA
Charleston, SC
28 October 2012